QUARRY OF GOR

QUARRY OF GOR

GOREAN SAGA * BOOK 35

John Norman

OPEN ROAD

INTEGRATED MEDIA

NEW YORK

978-1-5040-5831-5

Distributed in 2019 by Open Road Distribution
180 Maiden Lane
New York, NY 10038
www.openroadmedia.com

QUARRY OF GOR

CHAPTER ONE

I am Zia

I am Zia.

There is a light metal collar on my neck.

It encircles my neck closely.

It is locked there.

I cannot remove it.

Masters will have it so.

Too, my thigh is marked with the cursive *kef*.

Masters will have it so.

I am a slave girl, one of many, on the planet Gor.

We are not important. We are commodities, goods, properties. We are owned.

This planet, as I understand it, is in the same system of worlds as my former world, one called "Terra," or "Earth." Accordingly, this world, and my former world, share a common star. We spoke of it as the sun, or Sol; they speak of it as Tor-tu-Gor, Light-upon-the-Home-Stone. My former world is commonly referred to by Gorean men, those apprised of the Second Knowledge, as "the slave world," presumably because women such as I are frequently brought here for their markets. Those limited to the First Knowledge think of "Earth" as a distant, barbarous land. We are commonly brought to the towns and cities in naked, scorned, marched coffles, subject to the impatient whips and straps of masters, or naked in slave wagons, our ankles shacked to a central bar, parallel to the sides of the wagon bed. In this way the ships by means of which we are brought here are not in evidence. Indeed, I have never seen such a ship myself, nor I suspect, have most others. We are commonly rendered unconscious on Earth, as I was, and then awaken on Gor. It is soon clear, of course, that we have been brought to a different world. The slight difference in gravity is noticeable when we first awaken, though it is common for us to deny the difference, sometimes hysterically. Yet, soon, no one notices it, no more than the gravity of our former world. Too, of course, there are three moons here, the White Moon, the Yellow Moon, and a smaller moon called, for some reason, the Prison Moon. The air is unbelievably fresh, and bracing. On Earth I had not realized the foulness, and the pollution, of the air I had no choice but to breathe. Food here, too, is fresh, nourishing, and often delicious, even when we must eat it from bowls placed on the floor, denied the use of our hands. Such things help to remind us that we are slaves, though, I assure you, we are in little danger of forgetting that. It is as clear to us as the collars on our necks, the marks on our thighs, the tiny, revealing garments permitted us, when we are permitted garments. Gor is an incredibly beautiful, natural world, much as Earth might once have been. Indeed, Goreans love beauty, light, and color. Their buildings, inside and out, are bright with color. Even slaves, when clothed, as we need not be, as we are animals, are commonly clothed in bright, attractive tunics, or less. These tunics, of course, are tunics fit for slaves, and designed to conceal little of the charms the suggestion of which doubtless first brought us to the attention of our acquirers. The plant life of Gor is much like that of my former world, but there are many differences, as well, different trees, flowers, vegetables, and so on. There are many differences in animals, as well, and in birds and insects. Culturally, too, of course, one soon comes to realize one is on a different world. Perhaps the first thing one learns is that one is not free, but a slave, only a slave. We are quickly marked, and fitted with collars. No longer then can we bargain with our bodies and sell ourselves to advance our own prospects and fortunes. Now, owned by others, we are marketed to advance the prospects and fortunes of others, our masters. No longer are we without identity; our identity is now clear; we are slaves; we now know how to behave, act, and speak; we are to behave, act, and speak, as what we now are, slaves, when we are permitted to speak. No longer are we useless; the slave has her uses. No longer are we without purpose; we now have a purpose; it is to serve and please our masters.

Garmenture, in locales with which I am most familiar, is reminiscent of Earth's Greco-Roman civilization. I have seen no firearms and very little technology, though I know such things, or similar things, must exist somewhere. Surely one does not traverse the lonely seas between worlds with ships of wood. The principal language on this world, as far as I have been able to determine, is Gorean, spoken of commonly, simply, as "the language," as though there might be no other. Needless to say, we must learn it quickly, and as well as possible. The free are not easy or patient with us. We are slaves. We quickly learn to fear the switch and whip. One who does not speak Gorean natively is commonly accounted a barbarian. The distinction between barbarian and nonbarbarian, thusly, is commonly drawn in terms of language. To be sure, Goreans apprised of the Second Knowledge, those better informed, aware, for example, that Earth and Gor are planets orbiting a common star, tend to regard Earth as a barbarous planet. Who but barbarians would taint their food, poison their atmosphere, foul their rivers, lakes, and seas, and crowd, despoil, and disfigure a lovely, innocent world, their own? Have they no understanding, no love? Have they no guilt, no shame? Have they no Home Stone? What is such a world good for, save the extraction of slaves, to serve their betters? Many, mostly free women, feel that such as we should not be brought to Gor, that we should be left on Earth, to reside in our own squalor. But others, say, merchants, disagree. We are attractive, abundant, easily obtained, and sell well. So we are trapped, caged, and brought to market. I personally suspect that the motivations of the Gorean free women who object to our importings as cargo and merchandise, as domestic animals, are not so much a matter of fittingness or propriety as of personal animosity, even jealousy. Gorean men find us attractive. Is it so strange that a lightly-clad, collared, owned animal, sexual and beautiful, exciting and needful, her slave fires kindled by the will and doings of men, might be found, however undeservedly, of interest to men? What man would wish, save for social or economic advantage, to indefinitely pursue, with exasperation and misery, a coy free woman when, with a snapping of his fingers, a slave will hurry to his feet, to cover them with kisses and beg to please him, and in the ways of the female slave? What man does not wish, at least upon occasion, that one of his lofty, disdainful, arrogant free women, opaquely veiled and encumbered in her voluminous robes, were stripped before him, marked, collared, and thrown to his feet, a slave? How momentous and catastrophic must be that transition for a Gorean free woman, given her lofty status and the awe in which she is commonly held, when, as in the fortunes of

war, she might fall into bondage! As harrowing and dramatic as it
may seem to us at first, the transition from freedom to slavery is
less hard, I suspect, for us, imports from Earth, than for a Gorean
free woman, for on Earth almost all are free and when all are free,
freedom is of little interest or consequence. Indeed, in a sense,
no one is really free or not free. Perhaps better, where there is no
slavery, freedom is neither special nor important, and certainly is
not momentous.

I am attractive; otherwise I would not have been brought here;
otherwise I would not have been collared and marked. But, like
most girls, I am not expensive. Many of us are cheap. Most men,
even poor men, can afford a female slave. I would suppose that you
could buy me, if you wished. There are, of course, many to choose
from. It is interesting, that even a beautiful girl from my former
world, one whose beauty might have led to wealth and position,
may, on this world, be owned by a poor man. Let her then, in
her collar, barefoot, in her rag, at her labors, think on that. There
are many beautiful women on this world. Accordingly, they are
cheap. Indeed, many are natively Gorean, stolen, seized in raids,
taken as prizes in war, and such. The female of the enemy is commonly regarded as a slave not yet in one's collar. She is a familiar
form of loot. Indeed, many male Goreans think of all women as
slaves, only that some, the legally free, have not yet been put in
the collars in which they belong.

It does not take us long to learn that we are animals, and properties. We are, as noted, marked and collared. Is that not fit for
beasts? We are herded, caged, and chained. We are stripped and
exhibited. We are bought and sold.

On my world, interestingly, I had long suspected that I was
a natural slave. Why should it not be admitted, at least now? As
a slave I am not permitted to lie. A free woman may lie, but a
slave may not. That is one of the many differences between a free
woman and a slave. A slave can be severely punished for lying.
Yes, I had often suspected that I was a natural slave. In my dreams,
and reveries, I had worn many collars and served many masters. I
do not know, of course, if this sort of thing is the case with other
women. I can speak only for myself. How I had fought this suspicion, the dreams and reveries, this whispering, pressing convic-
tion that I was a slave, a natural slave! Was I such that I should be
a rightless possession? Did I long to be owned, to have a master?
Did I long to love and serve, surrendered and vulnerable, help-

less, owned, and choiceless, to serve rightlessly, helplessly, self-lessly? How fearful, how terrible! What tumult, what misery! It was antithetical to all that I had been taught, against all the rules and prescriptions I was not to question, opposed to all the lies and artificialities in which one must pretend to believe, so uncritically and unquestioningly. One is torn between convention, armed and aggressive, and socially coercive, and truth, between formulas and words and one's heart and blood.

So it seemed with me.

Let it be with you, as you might wish.

I do not legislate for you; do not legislate for me.

Oh, I resolved to fight the thoughts, the dreams, and reveries, the collar! I did what I could, what I thought I should. I tried to be true to the conditioning program to which I had been subjected, ever since the innocence of childhood, only later recognizing what it was, what it had tried to do to me, what it had tried to make me. The pins and nails of lies try to pin us to the boards of others. One trembles, one struggles, one tears one's flesh and wings, but one can escape.

One tries to find oneself, not a picture or image of oneself imposed by others, not the self you are told to be, but one's true self, the authentic self.

And then I was brought to Gor, and found myself a slave, then in all legality no more than an object, an animal, a property.

Think of yourself as a property, if you can. It is what I am, and what you, too, could come to be. I was doubtless scouted, assessed, considered, and decided upon without my knowledge, and then my acquisition was arranged. Perhaps you, too, have been noticed; perhaps you are, even now, without your knowledge, being scouted, assessed, considered. Should you then not be more careful of your posture, the tilt of your head, the line of your body, the grace of your movements? Should you not present yourself fittingly? Should you not endeavor to be more beautiful and pleasing, as befits one being considered for the collar? Surely you wish to appear worthy. Surely you wish to create a favorable impression on the acquirers, the masters. Do they regard you and think, "That is a pretty one; she might do well on a block; I think we could make some money on her"? Perhaps you have already been given a number, and a place on a shipping list. Perhaps there is already a collar on Gor, one of hundreds, waiting in a slaver's house, which will be put on your neck. If not, one of the caste of metal workers can easily supply this lovely, light, identificatory device, nicely measured to your throat. Many slavers think of a woman as a slave as soon as she has been decided on, as soon as she has been added to their list. In this sense, as you go about your day, aware of nothing, thinking of nothing, shopping, chatting, dining, dating, and such, you may already, without your knowledge, be a slave. How do you think your date, your male friends, would view you, if they understood you were a slave? How would they think of you, how would they treat you? Would they pity you and commiserate with you, or would they do with you what they would feel like doing, would want to do, would have a right to do, and should do, remove the lying presumption of clothing from your body, and force your lips down to their boots?

I had known, of course, in a superficial sense, verbally and intellectually, of the radical sexual dimorphism of the human species. How could I have ignored it or dismissed it, for years? Had it no consequences? Did it mean nothing? Supposedly not. The most fundamental dichotomy in human biology was not to be noticed.

The men who processed me, and the others, of course, had no interest in my ruminations, my tumults, questions, alarms, and fears. Do the stockmen in stockyards concern themselves with the inner life, the thoughts and dreams, the wants and needs, of the goods they deal with, with the beasts they handle? We were naked, as the animals we are. We were denied speech. When one or two of us protested or tried to speak, she was whipped, and was then, as the rest of us, silent. We were lined up, our hands braceleted behind us. Our left thighs were locked in a rack, and, one after the other, we were routinely marked. I wept as I was marked, but was not whipped. We were then fitted with house collars. The mark was small and graceful. I later learned that it was the cursive *kef*, a common brand. '*Kef*' is the first letter of the word '*kajira*', which is the most common Gorean expression for a female slave. The house collar, I later learned, had the house name and a number. The first Gorean words I was made to say were '*La kajira*'. I found out later what they meant. 'I am a slave girl'. Freshly branded and collared, we were unbraceleted and placed in a long line, before a long, waist-high chain to which our wrists, crossed, were bound. This chain then, by a windlass, was drawn upward, before us, and our bound wrists were drawn high over our heads, so that we stood beneath the chain, our bodies stretched. Our heels could not touch the floor. Then only the tips of our toes could touch the floor. Our arms so positioned, held high over our heads, our breasts were lifted. We were well exhibited. We were aware of the metal on our neck. One does not forget the snapping shut of the lock. It is a small, sharp, decisive sound. Our bodies were extended, strained, stretched. We were helpless.

Two men, tunicked, stepped to the side, and a third man, sturdy, with cropped hair, approached, robed in blue and yellow, carrying a whip. He walked up and down our line, regarding us, and then assumed a position near the center of the line, a few feet before us.

He glared at us.

I feared he found us displeasing.

We were helpless, and naked.

He snapped the whip once, in seeming annoyance, unexpectedly, fiercely, abruptly.

I, and several of the others, cried out with fear. Misery coursed down the line. The chain shook above us. Surely he must not strike us. He must not do that! We would have not a strand of silk between our bodies and the fiery hiss of that supple, dark, glistening, dread implement!

He recoiled the whip.

Our agitation subsided.

He seemed impatient, and angry. He scowled, and grimaced.

How could this be?

Surely he must be pleased, a man, to have beauty such as ours, stretched and exhibited, helpless and naked, before him.

What true man would not wish to have us so?

But we, astoundingly, despite our obvious health, youth, and beauty, were disparaged.

"What a miserable lot," he said, in English. "I have never seen so pathetic a display of strung, dangling, worthless meat. Have our suppliers gone blind? Were they all drunk? I have seen better slabs of meat hung in a butcher shop. We ask for beauty. They give us pigs and garbage." We looked wildly, uncomprehendingly, at one another. Never had I seen so much beauty in so small an area. Was he mad? Surely these women were amongst the most beautiful I had ever seen! Each, in her own way, was outstandingly lovely. They were the sort of women of whom men dream, the sort of women who are avidly sought, whose beauty could open doors and smooth ways, women who were accustomed to having their way with men, the sort whom men hastened to please. Could this sort of beauty, so rare on Earth, be common, be familiar, be scarcely noteworthy, on this world? Surely not! "You should all be ground up for sleen feed," snarled the man. "It is all you are good for." I had no idea what a sleen, or sleen, might be. "Is this the best that your sorry world, with its teeming millions, can do?" continued the man. "To be sure," he said, "how could so sorry a world as your Terra produce even one female whom one might glance at twice? Surely this is the ugliest lot I have ever seen. Cast them to eels, feed them to urts, throw them to leech plants!" He then handed his whip to one of the other men, and stormed away, leaving the chamber.

The fellow to whom the whip had been surrendered, tunicked, perhaps in his early twenties, then took his place before our line. He said something to his fellow, which I did not understand, and then faced us. "As you may suspect, my homely, naked, two-legged beasts," he said, speaking English, as had his predecessor, "your lives have changed. Yes, they have changed, completely, and for the better. On your world you were worthless, but now, for the first time in life, you have some worth. You will now, for the first time in your life, be good for something. You have been branded, as the animals you are. The brand is permanent. You are marked. It shows what you are. The collar also shows what you are, but it bears a legend. Collars can be changed, but do not expect to be without one. Merchant law requires that such as you be collared."

"What are we?" I wondered, but feared I knew.

What else, stripped, collared, and branded, and strung up like meat, could we be?

"This is a whip," he said, lifting the supple implement in his hand. "You will learn to respect it, and fear it."

I knew I already did so.

But we were women!

Surely it could not be used on us!

At this point several other men, tunicked attendants, entered the chamber from behind us. Twisting in my bonds, looking back, I saw, trembling, that each of these men carried such a whip. There was then one behind each of us.

I did not believe, for a minute, the disparaging remarks which had been uttered by the robed fellow, nor those of the tunicked fellow to whom he had handed the whip. We were clearly attractive, and many of us were beautiful. Were we so shabby and worthless as they suggested, we would not have been brought here, and would not now, naked, utterly helpless, our bodies stretched, be fastened to the high, overhead chain. Perhaps we were of less quality than some shipments. But surely we were not homely, nor "pigs and garbage." When the acquirers had populations of millions to choose from, and could choose as they wished, it was highly likely that the average shipment would be of high quality. And surely then, ours was of high quality, as well. What was startling to me, and somewhat unsettling, was the comprehension that our beauty, rare as it was on Earth, might, given the selections of the acquirers, be unremarkable on this world, at least amongst importations such as we. How then might women native to this world, for there must be such, view us? Not pleasantly, I supposed. But, still, given our attractions, our beauty, why should we have been so unaccountably slighted, so demeaned and ridiculed? I think it was intended to shock us, informing us that our beauty here was not special, and it was not enough on this world to be beautiful. On Earth, a beautiful woman need be little but beautiful. Society is at her feet; men vie to serve and please her. Here, on this world, on the other hand, where beauty is common, at least amongst slaves, and she is not special, she must obey, work, and perform, must now strive herself, fearfully and zealously, to please and be found pleasing.

"Some of you," said the man, continuing in English, "may not understand what has been done to you, what you now are. That is interesting. Does the fact that you have been stripped, as the animals you are, mean nothing to you? You have been branded and your necks are collared. Can you not suspect the meaning of that? You are fastened in place, at the pleasure of others, helplessly. Is that so hard to understand? We have, hitherto, refrained from making explicit what you now are. To be sure, in the language, you have already, each of you, pronounced what you are, but, of course, you may not speak the language, and thus did not know what you openly and publicly proclaimed yourself to be. Perhaps some of you are still in doubt. Perhaps some of you, the more stupid, do not know what you are. I shall then allow you to draw an inference."

We looked at one other, apprehensively.

"In this world," he said, "the only women who may be whipped are slave girls—"

And here, at the bare mention of the word 'slave girls', there were cries of dismay and protest, and whimpers of fear.

The chain shook with much agitation.

"In this world," he said, continuing, "the only women, the only women, who may be whipped are slave girls, who may be whipped if and when, and as, the masters and mistresses may please."

We looked wildly at one another.

We were then whipped.

If any of us had been in doubt, we now well knew what we were.

We were then released from the chain, our wrists were unbound, and we were put to all fours.

"It has happened to me," I thought. "I am a slave."

We were herded into another room where there was a long, trough-like opening in the floor. We were aligned, on all fours, facing this opening. Swills of gruel, from a bucket, were splashed into this opening. "Feed," we were told. "Do not use your hands." We put down our heads, and fed.

Our training had begun.

On the first night, clutching a thin, ragged blanket about me, lying on the stone floor of a cell, my left ankle chained to a ring, I tried to marshal the tumult in my mind, sort through a thousand perceptions, try to comprehend what had occurred, what had been done to me, what I now was. I thought, as earlier on my former world, that I should fight the collar, but I knew that it was a fight I could never win. I had not even been able to win that fight on my former world. The thoughts, the dreams and reveries, returned to me, persistently, irresistibly, again and again. I tried to be horrified, but failed. I tried to denounce myself, but was instead content. If I was so terrible a person, I did not care. It was what I was. On the other hand, it did not seem terrible to me. It seemed lovely to me, as it was what I was. Had I not yearned to belong, completely and absolutely, wholly and perfectly? Had I not longed to be owned; had I not longed for a master, one before whom I could kneel, his belonging, his naked collared slave? I wanted to serve selflessly. For one who is fittingly a slave, surely slavery is fitting. To me, bondage seemed reassuring, rewarding, appropriate, precious. I wanted to submit to a man, I wanted to have no choice but to do so. How fortunate then that I had been taken in hand, and now, helplessly, unable to alter my condition in any way, was a slave. I would be sold, as the goods I was. I hoped I would have a kind master. Does not every animal hope that? But, too, I wanted a master who would own me uncompromisingly, a master to whom I could never be other than his slave. I did not wish to be whipped, but I wanted to be subject to his whip, and know that if I were not pleasing it would be used on me.

I lay there, on the stones, clutching the tiny blanket about me, in pain, miserable, my body aching, the chain heavy on my ankle, but I was not discontent. I was at last marked and collared. The searing brand had muchly stung, burning as it was applied and lifted, so routinely, so unmistakably and efficiently, but, in my weeping, there were mixed tears of joy. Any on this world, male or female, could now recognize me as what I was. I was no longer nothing. I was now something. I had an identity. No longer was I worthless. I now had value, as goods, as a property, however minimal that value might be. The collar, too, reassured me. How appropriate it was that it should be on me, not only displaying my bondage so clearly, and indisputably, but, as I had been given to understand, given the number and legend, proclaiming, or making public, to whom or what I belonged! How right a collar seemed on my neck! How pleased I was! I loved the collar! How I would strive to be a pleasing slave!

I shall not enter into the details of my training. Understand, of course, that it was the training of a female slave, having to do with the serving and pleasing of masters. We learned the kisses, and caresses, the kneelings, the rollings, and beggings, the obeisances, the floor movements of a property girl, and so much more. We learned to bathe and clothe men, to fetch on all fours, objects held in our teeth, sandals, a switch, a whip, a leash, or such. We were taught, even, something of slave dance, dances by means of which a slave hopes to please her master. For Ahn a day we were drilled in Gorean, taught by switch-bearing female slaves who cared little for barbarians. Mistakes were punished promptly by strokes and humiliations. We strove zealously to learn the language. We must. It was the language of our masters. We were highly intelligent, and did well. I was surprised to learn that the acquirers value intelligence in a woman highly, more so, I fear, than the men of Earth. Indeed, they would often sacrifice beauty for intelligence. An intelligent woman of course, makes a better slave. She is, for example, more aware of her own feelings and needs, and more alert to, and aware of, others, and so on, than a simpler woman. Also, having a far more sensitive body, she is much more responsive to punishment, which she will feel much more keenly than a more phlegmatic, duller woman, and will, accordingly, strive zealously, with all her intelligence, wit, beauty, and charm, to avoid it, by striving, to the best of her ability, to be fully pleasing to her master.

I suppose it must be pleasant for a man to own a beautiful woman, to have her in his collar and have absolute power over her, to be her absolute master, to have her at his feet, perhaps naked, perhaps in chains, desperate to please him, in all ways. In any event, Gorean men, the uncompromising, masterful brutes, acculturated so differently from the men of Earth, do not seem to object to this arrangement. I wonder if they understand, or care, for the feelings of their properties, their goods, if they are aware of, or care about, the interior life of the merchandise they have purchased, the joy a woman can find in bondage.

When the mistresses were satisfied, however grudgingly, we would be thrown food. We were taught personal hygiene, and cleanliness, perfumes and cosmetics, the stringing of jewelries, the affixing of bangles, bracelets, and beads, the draping of tunics, the binding on of a camisk, the subtleties of the ta-teera, or slave rag, seemingly so artless, and yet so cunning. We learned how to move attractively, how to walk, kneel, lie, and rise attractively, how to clothe ourselves attractively, even given the tiny garments we might be permitted, and how to strip ourselves attractively. The free woman may be stiff and clumsy; the slave, in movement, posture, and attitude, must be beautiful.

We must, too, become more aware of our surroundings, and their ambiences, of sunlight and shadow, of warmth and coolness, of air and moisture, of textures and surfaces, the feel of tiles or rugs to our knees, the feel of cloth on our bodies, however light or diaphanous, the sense of our body where it was bare, vulnerable, waiting to be touched or felt, the pinioning of shackles, the weight of chains, the different sense of encircling ropes or straps on our bodies, each rendering us helpless. Our senses, our skin, our bodies became alive, open to the richness and diversity of impinging sensation, so frequently unnoticed and neglected on our former world. The life of the female slave is a life of vitality and awareness, an awakened life, a sentient life, a sensuous life, a so-much-alive life! To be sure, clad as we were, when clad, it is easier to be aware of such things. In more than one way, one is more exposed to the world, to nature, and the reality in which one exists.

Imagine the contrast between us, in the streets, clad as we might be, in our brief tunics and collars, and the scorning free women, resplendent in their robes and veils. How we, slaves, dread and fear them! How they hate us, how cruel they are to us! Who is to protect us from them, save our masters?

Please, Masters, protect us! Oh, Masters, please protect us!

We learned, too, personal deportment, deference, and suitable diction. All free men are addressed as "Master," of course, and all free women as "Mistress."

The slave is to be lovely, graceful, unobtrusive, and obedient.

Perhaps surprisingly we were also taught domestic tasks. Most masters have at most one slave, and she must keep the domicile for him. Accordingly we were taught a number of homely tasks, shopping, cooking, cleaning, laundering, ironing, sewing, the care of leather, and such, tasks fit for us, slaves, the least of women. Yet these tasks can be precious for us, as they are necessary and give us ways of pleasing our masters. We take great pride in giving our masters a clean, well-kept, attractive home. Indeed, if we do not, we will hear from his switch or whip!

There are many things which keep us as we are, slaves. We are branded and collared, and suitably clad, if clad. Such things keep us as we are. There is no mistaking us. Many other things, of course, keep us as we are, for example, markets and economics, law and custom. The slave is subject to many bonds, legal and personal, bonds both internal and external. Certainly she is no stranger to the obduracies of rope, chain, and leather. She is well held in her place, as a master may wish, say, at the foot of his couch, to a public chaining ring, and so on. What comfort and reassurance she finds on a chain! On the other hand, the bond which holds her most securely is her own need, aroused and enflamed. Nothing puts her more at a man's feet than her own need. Men, in their cruelty, in their lack of concern for a slave, do things to her which make her ever more helplessly a slave. Ignoring her own feelings, even pleas, they do what they wish with her. They make her the victim of her own needs. They do not consult her or spare her. They do this to her, because they wish her so. In her vulnerable, helpless belly they enkindle incandescences, heats, and flames, which will then periodically, irresistibly, torment her, and make her ever more dependent on men.

When a woman is owned and collared she is no longer permitted to deny her emotions, her body, her blood, her appetites, her needs, her sex. She comes to realize that she is not really a social artifact, but something real, a woman, and, as a woman, a profoundly sexual creature.

And the most sexual of all women is the female slave. What other choice has she? What other choice does she want?

How helpless we are in a world in which we can be only what we are!

How this frees us to be what we are, needful slaves.

I am such, a needful slave.

I know I am in a collar.

I have learned my collar.

I love my collar.

But what fears and terrors it may hold!

Let me now begin my story.

It begins some months ago, in the coastal city of Brundisium.

CHAPTER TWO

I am to be Sold

I was kneeling, naked, before him, the slaver's man, outside the cage, my wrists thonged behind my back.

I could hear, as though from far off, the calls of the auctioneer, bids called down from the tiers, responses from the crowd.

"Kiss the whip," he said.

"Yes, Master," I said, lifting my lips to the whip, kissing it.

As he did not remove the whip from before me, I moved my head to the side of the coil, and, eyes closed, pressed my check against it, lovingly. Then it was again at my lips, and I, again and again, tenderly, gratefully, kissed it. Then, looking up at him, into his eyes, I licked the coil, softly, again and again, beseechingly. Then he removed the implement, and looked to the side, to the ramp.

I was naked at his feet, bound.

He paid me no attention.

"May I speak, Master?" I said.

He was not looking at me.

"Yes," he said.

"May I not be soon used?"

I had been denied the touch of a master for five days.

Some of the other slaves, none of them barbarians, for I was the only barbarian in this lot, who had been longer in their collars, had writhed in their cages, thrashing, whimpering, and begging. "They know well how to prepare us for our sale," I thought. Had I been longer in the collar, I supposed I might have been as helpless as they.

"Perform well on the block," he said.

"I shall try, Master," I said.

How pleased I was to address men as "Master." It seemed so right. I was so slight, and soft, compared to them. I was so much at their mercy! Too, of course, as a slave, I must address them as "Master," and to me, in all legality, as well as in the order of nature, they were "Master."

It was my first sale.

I hoped I would do well. Certainly I did not want to be whipped.

"Take your place in the line, on the ramp," he said.

"Yes, Master," I said, rising, head down. The lowered head betokens submission.

Some girls, I knew, do not do well on the block, particularly in a first sale.

I hoped I would do well.

Perhaps they had not been sufficiently trained. Perhaps they had been brought to the market too soon, before they were ready. Sometimes a girl is brought to the block before she has fully learned her collar. Sometimes they are stiff, and wooden. Perhaps they think they are still free women. Sometimes they are half paralyzed, and cannot move, and can hardly stand. I hoped I would not be too terrified. There is deep sawdust on the block. It can come to one's ankles. It is sometimes damp, and yellow. Bits of it can cling to one's ankles and calves. Those who faint are dashed with cold water and prodded to their feet. Those who would fight, or struggle, or cry out, are hurled to the surface of the block and whipped. They are then, trembling, weeping, eager to obey, the auctioneer's hand in their hair, yanked to their feet and exhibited.

A slaver's man on the ramp unbound my hands.

"Thank you, Master," I said.

I was unsteady. I was frightened. I hoped I would not fall.

I put my hand to my neck. The collar was there.

I knew the market was not a fine one, and it was night, and late in the season. At such a time, I did not think the crowd would be large. There are many such small markets, held at various times, almost casually, in Brundisium, a great sea port. Some women sold here were imported from what was called The World's End, which was lands, or islands, across green, turbulent, mighty Thassa, the Sea. Others would doubtless be purchased for export to the Farther Islands, or, even beyond them, to the World's End itself. I knew little of Gor. I knew only it would be done with me as masters might please.

I began to feel even more frightened.

I felt an impulse to turn about and run.

But to where might one run? I was naked, and collared, and branded. The society accepted, and wanted, slaves. I did not think I could have made it to the foot of the ramp without being seized by a slaver's man. On the street, if I could reach it, I would be conspicuous, not even tunicked. My collar proclaimed the house which owned me. I would be noted, and apprehended, almost immediately. There is no escape for what I was, a Gorean slave girl.

"To the ramp, Adraste," I heard, from behind me.

"Now there is a beauty," said the slaver's man on the ramp, he who had unbound my wrists.

I looked back, and gasped. Behind me, standing proudly, insolently, her hands still fastened behind her back, was one of the most beautiful women I had ever seen, dark-haired, green-eyed, olive-skinned, of medium height, excitingly figured. Her carriage bespoke not so much the supple, lithe beauty of the slave, so deliciously submissive, so aware of her collar, so hoping to please, as the arrogance of a free woman.

Why do not men make all women slaves, I wondered.

A slaver's man, a bit lower on the ramp, freed her hands, and she rubbed her wrists, disdainfully.

"You may thank me for freeing you," he said.

She tossed her head, looking away, and then she cried out, sharply, in pain. The massive hand of the slaver's man was twisted in her hair, cruelly. Her head was pulled far back, her body bent backwards, almost in the "slave bow," which so dramatically accentuates the excitements of a woman's figure. "Thank you, Master!" she gasped. His hand tightened even more in her hair. She winced. "Thank you, Master," she said, again. "Who thanks Master?" he asked. "What mere, worthless slave thanks Master?" "Adraste, the mere, worthless slave, thanks Master!" she whispered, tears bursting from her eyes, running down her cheeks. He then released her hair, and she straightened her body. "Keep your head down," said the man, "and cross your wrists behind your body, and hold them there. You are bound by the master's will."

"Yes, Master," she said.

"And you will remain so, head down, bound by the master's will until you ascend the block."

"Yes, Master," she said.

I heard the ringing of a gong, from somewhere above, and to the left. I wondered what the merchandise had gone for.

I did not think that the patrons of such a market, many of them mariners, artisans, and dock workers, would be burdened with heavy purses.

The line moved up, a little, toward the top of the ramp.

There were four girls ahead of me now, and some six behind me, including the head-lowered, bound-by-a-man's-will, green-eyed, dark-haired beauty, Adraste.

The fellow who had removed the straps from the dark-haired slave's wrists ascended the ramp to stand beside the fellow who had freed my wrists.

"That one," said he who had discomfited the dark-haired beauty, gesturing toward her with a nod of his head, "does not yet know there is a collar on her neck."

"She will learn soon enough," said the fellow who had freed my wrists.

"I do not understand why she is being sold in this market," said the first man. "Our clientele is a copper-tarsk clientele, most often come here after work. Why was she not sold to a more expensive house?"

"There is doubtless a reason," said the second. "Clearly she has recently been free. You can see it in her carriage and attitudes. She has not yet learned she is a slave. She has not yet learned to grovel in terror on her belly, a master's foot on her back. She has not learned to squirm gratefully toward a bowl of gruel on the floor. She is not yet the victim of slave fires, hoping for, and begging for, the least caress of even a hated master."

"Keep your head down, Adraste," said the first man, sharply.

"Yes, Master," she said, lowering her head.

I heard the gong ring once more.

"I think," said the second man, "she was a woman of position and power, perhaps well known, say, the daughter of an administrator, high merchant, or judge, stolen by a disgruntled petitioner, a dissatisfied customer, an unsuccessful litigant, to be disposed of discreetly, as an act of vengeance, or for personal amusement, in a slave market, a lesser market, an obscure market, in which she would be unlikely to be recognized."

"No," said the first man. "She was an import, with others, from the World's End."

"Her accent suggests Ar," said the second man.

"That means nothing," said the first man. "Following the defeat of Ar by Cos, Tyros, and their allies, mercenaries and others,
and before the restoration of Marlenus, thousands of women of
Ar were taken as spoils and distributed throughout hundreds of
markets."

"Why does the house not postpone her sale, and sell her to a
great house, such as that of Tenalion of Ar?" said the second man.
"Such a woman is worthy the central block in the Curulean."

I saw the slave, Adraste, look up, briefly, before hastily lowering her head again. In her eyes I saw, for a moment, stark terror.
The men did not notice this tiny breach of discipline. Why, I wondered, should she fear being sold in Ar, and from such a famous
block as the central block in the Curulean? Might not thousands
of slaves dream of such a sale? Too, I had gathered that the wealth
of Ar, hub of trade in the northern hemisphere of this world, was
being recouped. Merchants came from as far away as remote Turia
in the south to buy and sell in Ar.

"Arrangements were doubtless made," said the first man,
"probably as a condition of her sale."

"Who sold her?" asked the second man.

"It seems," said the first, "the agent of a warrior."

"Why would he not keep her?" asked the second. "She would
look well, stripped, collared, at his feet."

"Perhaps she is a cold *tasta*," said the first. "You observe her
mien. She seems less a slave than a free woman in a collar."

"Any woman can be taught the collar," said the second.

"If I owned her," said the first, "she would soon beg to press
her lips to my boots."

The gong rang again.

I trembled.

"Steady, slut," said he who had unbound my wrists.

There were now two girls before me.

"What is wrong with her?" asked his fellow.

"It is her first sale," said the other.

I suddenly realized, viscerally, in my belly, in every cell in my
body, waiting on the ramp, that I was going to be sold, actually
sold, really sold, as an object, as much so as a mirror or scrap of
cloth! I had known, of course, that such a moment would come.
I had long had an intellectual understanding of this eventuality.
Did I not know I was a slave? Was it not clear enough, when I
was released from the cage, and knelt, my head to the floor, my

crossed wrists lifted high behind me for binding? Could there be any doubt about the matter when I knelt, bound, before the master, and, my head lifted, the whip was put to my lips? Did I not understand these things well enough when my hands were freed, and I took my place in the line on the ramp? Surely! But now, suddenly, I was on the brink of being sold, literally sold, like a shoe or belt, a dog or pig! It was impossible! It could not be! I could not be sold! I was free, free! It was a nightmare! I must awaken, I must awaken! I was overcome with terror. The room began to swirl about me.

"What name has been put on you, slut?" asked he who had unbound me. His hand on my left, upper arm kept me standing. When addressed by a free person, it is common for a slave, recognized, to kneel. It is appropriate. It shows respect for the free, and that one is a slave.

"'Zia', Master," I said, held upright. I was frightened to be on my feet, even held so, before a free person.

I shook my head, to retain consciousness.

"Let me go," I said, suddenly, blurting it out. "This is all a terrible mistake! Clothe me! Take this collar off my neck! I should not be here! This is not my world! I do not belong here! I cannot be sold! I am a woman of Earth! Of Earth! I cannot be sold! I am free, free!"

He looked at me, puzzled.

I suddenly realized, I had foolishly blurted out my words in English. My Gorean, in which I was moderately adept, given my time on this world, vanished. I could think of nothing in Gorean.

The gong then sounded again.

There was then one girl ahead of me.

"I am afraid," I said, finally, in Gorean. "I think I am going to be sick."

"Do not vomit," said the other man. "Or, if you must, wait for the sawdust on the block. If you soil the ramp, or the stairs, you will lick up and feed on your own discharge, and the residue you will mop with your hair. You will then, your stomach empty, be washed, whipped, and brought again to the ramp. With this understanding in place, you will not vomit, not now, will you?"

"No, Master," I said.

I knew I would not vomit, not now, or later.

"Good," he said. "Too, you do not want the other slaves to hold you in contempt, do you?"

"No, Master," I said.

Interestingly, I feared not only the views of the free, but those of my sister slaves.

"Similarly," he said, "you will hold your urine, at least until you are on the block."

"Yes, Master," I said.

"The female slave," said the other man, "is not a free woman. She is to be clean, neat, attractive, presentable, lovely."

"Yes, Master," I said.

"Masters want them that way," said the first man.

"Sales are to be well-staged, and attractive, not sordid, or disgusting," said the second.

"Yes, Master," I said.

I heard the gong ring again.

I shuddered.

I was at the head of the ramp.

"This may be hard on you, particularly the first time," said he, kindly, he who had unbound my wrists, "but try to do well. If you present yourself well, you are unlikely to be beaten by the auctioneer, and you would be likely to obtain a better-placed master, one with more coin to waste on a worthless slave."

"Yes, Master," I said.

"You are very pretty and you have pleasant slave curves," said the other man. "Further, you are clearly a natural-born slave, that is clear, and such as you can find fulfillment only in the collar."

I was silent, but suspected he was right.

"It was clever of the house master to put this one, a plainer girl, and a barbarian, before Adraste," said the fellow who had relieved Adraste of her bonds. "In that way, by contrast one accentuates the beauty of Adraste."

I was not pleased to hear this.

I did know that much thought, however, even in a lesser house, goes into the display of slaves. What merchant is not aware of such things? It is not unusual to display a plainer woman first, in order to dramatize the greater value of the subsequent merchandise. I did not regard myself as plain, of course, and I doubted that many masters would have done so.

In any event, angrily, I resolved to do better than well, and show the tiers goods for which bids would be fierce, goods which could be removed from the block only dearly.

I heard Adraste laugh behind me.

Perhaps she had sensed my resolve.

I was angry.

I was thrust forward, up the ramp, and, stumbling, saw the stairs leading up to the block. A slaver's man was at the foot of the stairs. He carried a whip. The auditorium was largely in shadows. The block was lit by torches. I heard the murmur of the crowd, but I did not think it was large. It was night. There were many empty places in the tiers. I did not know how many bidders were in such a place. Some men come merely to watch the sales. Some of the men sitting on the tiers had slaves with them, kneeling at their feet.

CHAPTER THREE

I am Sold

"Do not dally," said the slaver's man, gesturing upward, toward the surface of the block, with the whip. "Ascend the stairs. Up, pretty beast. They are waiting to buy you."

There were six steps leading to the surface of the block, as there are six letters in the Gorean expression '*Kajira*', the most common word in Gorean for a female slave. There was no railing or bannister. The steps were broad, but I was afraid to stand on them. My legs seemed weak. I crawled upward, to the surface of the block, and then, on all fours, my hands and knees were in the large, concave depression in the block. The sawdust was clean, or, perhaps, had been changed or replenished.

I heard the slaver's scribe, at his desk before the block, reading, droning, describing the next offering, my hair and eye color, my height and weight, my current name, my collar size, wrist-and-ankle-ring sizes, my training, of some weeks, which was largely restricted to what were regarded as essentials, an estimate of my fluency in Gorean, and such. I was, of course, illiterate. Too, naturally, it was made clear that I was a barbarian. A house can be burned if it misrepresents its merchandise. Goreans dislike deceit. If a girl's hair color is not natural, that must be made clear. Often a girl is whipped, and her head is shaved, that the hair may grow back in its natural color.

"Here, noble masters, at my feet," said the auctioneer, standing to my left, his whip in his right hand, "we have, as noted, a medium-heighted barbarian, imported recently from the slave world, for there is such a world, as many of you know, picked like fruit for your delectation. You can see that she is fresh and luscious. She has also been administered, as is done routinely, the stabilization serums, which preclude the onslaught of the drying, withering disease, age, so prevalent on her barbarous world. Accordingly she will remain indefinitely as you see her now, vital and soft, shapely and lovely, vulnerable and helpless, a dream of pleasure in her collar! Would you not like to have her at your feet?"

I had heard of the stabilization serums, but did not fully understand them. Supposedly they prevented ageing. I found this hard to believe, but I had never seen a Gorean who seemed to me old. If what I had heard was true, age, understood as a disease, had been conquered on Gor. These stabilization serums were not limited to free persons, but were administered to slaves, as well, that they might retain their value. I supposed there must be Earth women who would prefer to be free and gradually grow weak, decrepit, haggard, miserable, and die, but I supposed that there might be some who would not mind retaining their youth and beauty indefinitely, even at the cost of a collar on their neck. I did not personally have to deal with this decision, as I had had no choice in the matter. I had been simply, without my consent, acquired, branded, and collared, and then given the serums, that I might not cease to be pleasing to masters. Had I been given the choice, however, I would have chosen the retention of youth and beauty. I would have been vain enough to make that decision. Too, as I knew myself to be a natural slave, it being what I wanted to be, the decision would have been appropriate. Would I not then be more pleasing to a master? Let each person decide as they wish. The stabilization serums, of course, do not guarantee invulnerability or confer immortality. In a thousand ways one may bleed and die. Such serums provide no protection from the thrust of a knife or spear, from a strangling bowstring, from the subtleties of poison, from the claws and fangs of beasts.

"Too," continued the auctioneer, "this lovely toy, which for a few tarsk-bits could be your possession, has been administered, as is our practice, slave wine. Accordingly, she will not conceive unless administered a releaser, that in case you wish to hood her and cross her with a male slave in the breeding stalls."

I shuddered, remembering the slave wine. My hands had been tied behind me, and I had been knelt down, my head held far back by the hair. My nostrils had been pinched shut and my mouth forced open, and the spout of a metal container was thrust in my mouth, and the foul brew, like a hideous, polluted lake, flooded my oral cavity. I could not believe the horror of this. I could not close my mouth for the spout between my teeth. I tried to shake my head negatively. My eyes begged mercy. I would be shown none. I tried not to breathe. The spout was removed from my mouth. I looked up at him. I struggled not to breathe. He smiled. Then I must breathe! But I could not breathe until I swallowed the dreadful concoction. "Good *Kajira*," said the man, soothingly. "Every bit of it now, do not lose a drop." I then gasped for breath. "Good, pretty beast," he said. I was thrust to the side, and fell on my left shoulder. "Next," said the man. My hands were left tied behind me for a time so I could not disgorge the noxious fluid. I am told the releaser is delicious. Our breeding, like other aspects of our being, as we are slaves, is at the discretion of our masters.

"As you were informed, noble masters," said the auctioneer, "this item is a barbarian, extracted from the polluted world, a world where few slaves are in their collars."

There was laughter from the tiers.

"As they should be," said the auctioneer.

There was more laughter.

"But this one," he said, "is now in her collar."

"Where she belongs," called a man from somewhere in the tiers.

"Yes!" called more than one man from the tiers.

"That world from which she has been removed," said the auctioneer, "is a world without a Home Stone."

Several in the audience reacted in surprise.

"It is a world which is not loved," said the auctioneer. "It is a world which is soiled, and neglected. Selfishness and greed abound. Men sacrifice the air and sky, the land and sea, as it were, for tarsk-bits. Coin is supreme; honor is scorned. Rulers do not rule, but enrich themselves while pandering to mobs. Each man would subvert and outdo his fellow. Treason is rewarded and praised, whilst loyalty is scorned and mocked. And these betrayers and despoilers of a world commend rapacity as growth, and ruination as achievement. And their shameless women, their faces as naked as those of slaves, abet these crimes, and, fearing only that they might not profit in their turn, barter, as the shallow mercenaries they are, their smiles and favors for gain."

There were cries of rage from several in the tiers.

"And here, at my feet now," said the auctioneer, "is such a woman, guilty of such crimes! What should be her fate?"

"Feed her to sleen!" cried a man.

Sleen, I had learned, are large, sinuous, vicious, six-legged carnivores. In the wild, they are commonly burrowing animals and nocturnal. Domesticated and trained, they commonly serve as guard beasts and hunting beasts. They are Gor's keenest and most tenacious trackers.

"Throw her to leech plants!" cried another.

No animals graze on leech plants. Leech plants grow in thick, matted patches and bristle with hollow, fanglike thorns. These plants, triggered, can strike like a snake, and suck blood into distendable pods. In a matter of Ehn even a large animal can be drained of blood.

"No," cried a man. "For such a slut, the collar, the collar!"

"Yes, the collar!" cried more than one man.

"And it seems to be on her neck," said the auctioneer.

There was laughter, and cries of approval.

"On her world she was worthless," said the auctioneer, "but here, on this world, for the first time in her life, she will be worth something, if only a handful of tarsk-bits."

"Yes," cried a fellow. "Yes!"

"Behold then," said the auctioneer, "here, at my feet, a comely barbarian slave, naked, on all fours before you, new to her collar, ready to be trained to your tastes. Yes, *ela*, she is a barbarian, only that, forgive the House of Anesidemus, for daring to offer such inferior, shabby goods to such discerning discriminating buyers, but perhaps some of you have heard rumors of the nature of these barbarians, of how they crawl to the whip, of how they beg, perhaps have heard rumors of their needs, their helplessness, and their responsiveness. Why should that be? There is a simple explanation. Great numbers of the men on their world have been taught to betray their blood, to repudiate it, and fear it. Many of the men of her dismal world have been crippled, tamed, reduced, subdued, and conquered, taught to prize themselves in direct proportion to the extent they do treason to their manhood. They are taught to ignore their might, judgment, strength, and agility, taught to be ashamed of the promptings of their blood. Would not their sick society collapse and their miserable world perish if even a hint of manhood were suspected? And so we have an unnatural, artificial world, a shallow, petty world in which men are to be punished for being men and women are mocked and scorned for being women. But one wonders. Could it be that under all the pretenses and lies, under all the conventions and cloaks, there might lurk the hereditary coils of a form of being which, in an honest world, need not be denied and suppressed, but might thrive and flourish, might lift its head, look about, and find itself once more in the kind of world for which, in a thousand generations, it was bred, a world of men and a world of women?"

There was silence in the tiers.

"But do not the pathetic sluts of that sorry world have something, after all, to commend them, their exquisite features, their smooth, cascading, glossy hair, their pretty necks, waiting for the collar, their soft shoulders, their bellies and breasts, their thighs and ankles, their luscious bodies so fit for ropes and straps, their limbs for manacles and shackles? See the miserable creature at my feet. Despise her, if you will, and appropriately, but note that she has the curves of a slave. She is obviously a natural-born slave. On her sorry world such natural-born slaves are often permitted to run free, even to their misery, and the misery of men, for there are few masters to take them in hand. But, on this world, we repair such an oversight. We do with them what should be done with them. We mark them, fit them with collars, and sell them!"

"Good!" called several men from the tiers.

"Put her up for auction!" called a man.

I shuddered, my head down, my neck in its collar, on all fours, in the sawdust.

"In a moment," called the auctioneer. "But first let me call to your attention a hitherto unnoted fact, one perhaps implicit, to be sure, but not yet made explicit. For millions of women on the sorry world from which this stripped slave was extracted, their world is a sexual wasteland, a sexual desert. They are miserable with unsatisfied need. Where men may not be men, how can women be women? They would kneel and offer food and drink to a master, and there is no master. They would kneel and clasp the knees of a master, and there is no master. They would kneel and lick the thigh of a master, and there is no master. They would kneel and press their lips to the feet of a master, and there is no master. And then some, like this shapely beast at my feet, are brought to Gor, for your interest and pleasure. No longer are they in a sexual wasteland or desert. They are now helpless, rightless slaves, vendible beasts who must now serve and please their masters, immediately, unquestioningly, and wholly, in the thousand delicious ways of the abject slave. So, noble masters, consider buying a bar-

barian. They are cheap. I do not think you will be disappointed!"
The auctioneer then turned to me and touched my left shoulder
with his whip. "Get up," he whispered, "and be a slave."

"I cannot get up, Master," I said. "My legs will not hold me."

"Must a command be repeated?" he asked.

"No, Master," I said. The repetition of a command can be a
cause for discipline.

I struggled to my feet, and stood unsteadily. I looked out, and
up, into the darkened tiers. I could see some faces clearly, in the
lower rows. And I knew there were others here and there in the
tiers, some even with their own slave, kneeling beside them.

"Stand straight, softly, be graceful," said the auctioneer.

"What am I bid?" he called to the crowd.

I was being sold!

My head began to swim, and the chamber seemed to turn
about me, and I had the brief sense that I was losing consciousness, and then I must have fallen.

I do not know how long I was unconscious, but I suspect that
it was only a short time.

I cried out in misery, shocked, chilled, rudely jarred awake by
a drenching of chilled water. I gasped, and raised my head a little.
I was in a puddle of water, lying in the concavity of the block, and
much damp sawdust clung to my body.

Looking up, I saw that he had hooked the whip on his belt.

His right hand was then free.

"Get up," I was told.

Then I screamed with pain as I was jerked by the hair, up to a
kneeling position. The kneeling position is very stable.

I cried out, again.

"Please do not hurt a poor slave, Master," I begged.

"This is your first sale, is it not?" he asked.

"Yes, Master," I whimpered, wincing.

"Do you think that that is an acceptable excuse for doing
poorly on the block?" he asked.

"No, Master," I said.

"Do you wish to be whipped," he asked.

"Please do not whip me," I begged.

He was clearly annoyed, but I did not think he would whip
me. Such men are alert to a variety of cues, verbal and behavioral,
and I am sure he realized I had no intent to be recalcitrant or un-
cooperative. Few Gorean masters will gratuitously strike a slave,

or punish one who honestly cannot help herself, and would, if she could, obey and be pleasing. Had I attempted to deceive him, however, or if I had tried to present a response which was not genuine, I am sure I would have felt the leather, and well. Body language, or something subtle, a tone of voice, or such, I am sure, would have given me away. Still I knew he was not pleased, and this frightened me. Too, my scalp burned, and his hand was still fixed tightly in my hair.

"Noble masters," called the auctioneer, turning to the crowd. "This is, I gather, this item's first sale. Perhaps she is reluctant to be sold. Perhaps she does not truly understand that she is being sold. Surely we shall think little of her fainting before you. It is unlikely she would do so again. Have we not seen even more deplorable behavior, upon occasion, in the first, or even the second, sale of a former Gorean free woman, taken, say, in a slave raid, or acquired as a part of the loot of a fallen city? If a first sale can be surprising, or trying, even for a mere barbarian, one clearly born for, and destined for, the collar, what must it be for a former Gorean free woman, deprived of her Home Stone, deprived of her robes, deprived of her privileges, honors, and dignities, finding herself stripped, branded, and collared, exhibited as the slave she would be, before strangers, and enemies? Might they not faint, lose their water, disgorge their gruel, and such? I fear so. Have we not seen it happen, amusing to the tiers but, I assure you, unpleasant on the block." He then, to my relief, removed his hand from my hair. I went to all fours, my head down. How small I felt, at his feet.

"Andar," he said, and his man, the one who had been at the right side of the block, to my left, as I had climbed the stairs, ascended to the surface of the block, and hooked his own whip to his belt. The auctioneer, to my apprehension, now removed the whip from his own belt. The whip, coiled, of course, may be used to call attention to one feature or another of the displayed merchandise.

The fellow called Andar lifted me to my feet, and, standing behind me, holding me by the upper arms, held me before the crowd.

"Master," I said to the auctioneer, "I am stronger now. I can stand."

"Can you follow my verbal commands?" asked the auctioneer.

"Yes, Master," I said.

"Stand straight, softly, gracefully, as a slave," he said.

"Yes, Master," I said.

There was a murmur of interest from the tiers.

I suddenly realized that I was desirable. It was not as on Earth, when I knew I was pretty, or when I caught a young man furtively looking at me. This was different. I now realized that I was truly desirable, as an object, a commodity, as a slave. How real that was! I suddenly realized that I had worth, as a domestic beast, and that men might pay for me, as one might, for a dog or horse.

"You are Zia, are you not?" asked the auctioneer. My name had been mentioned by the slaver's scribe before the sale, with my measurements, my collar size, my ankle-ring size, and such.

"If it pleases Master," I said.

Slaves, as other animals, may be named, if named, as the masters might wish.

"You are a slave, are you not?" he asked.

"Yes, Master," I said, "I am a slave."

"Are you ready to be sold?" he asked.

"Yes, Master," I said.

"Do you beg to be sold?" he asked.

"Yes, Master," I whispered, "I beg to be sold."

"What am I offered for this lithe, sleek, nicely curved, lovely barbarian beast, new to her collar, fresh from the barbarian world?" called the auctioneer. "Is she not a splendid catch? Consider her! Regard the beauty of her face, the fineness of her features, her sweet throat, encircled closely with locked metal, the dark, brown hair, too short now, but it will grow, the loveliness of her shoulders, the softness of her bosom, the narrowness of her waist, the width of her love cradle!"

"Twenty tarsk-bits, tarsk-bits of Brundisium!" called a voice from the tiers.

I had been bid upon, or at least I supposed so.

I did not understand the nature of the bid. Our instructresses had not informed us of such things.

There was laughter.

"A pleasant joke, Master," said the auctioneer.

"She is only a barbarian!" called another fellow from the tiers.

"Even so, Master," responded the auctioneer, "one would offer more for a she-tarsk."

"She is a she-tarsk!" called a voice from the tiers.

"Scarcely," said the auctioneer.

"All barbarians are she-tarsks," called a woman's voice from the tiers.

"Yes!" called more than one woman from the tiers.

I did not know what a tarsk was.

"Twenty-one tarsk-bits of Brundisium!" called another voice.

"Let us be realistic, noble masters," said the auctioneer.

"Twenty-two Brundisium tarsk-bits," called a fellow, laughing.

Some of the women in the tiers laughed. These were free women, thoroughly robed, most veiled. There were few women in the tiers, perhaps fifteen or sixteen free women, and perhaps four or five slaves, who were silent, who knelt at the knees of their masters. I wondered if it were safe for free women to attend a night auction in the vicinity of the wharves. Presumably they were accompanied, even perhaps, waiting outside, by armed men.

"The House of Anesidemus," said the auctioneer, "as you are doubtless aware, places no reserves on its merchandise, but, if it is not satisfied with any bid, it reserves the right to bid in its own name."

This announcement was met with hisses and the angry stamping of feet.

"So," said the auctioneer, "let us return to the sale."

"Ninety copper tarsk-bits, coinage of Brundisium," called a man.

"I have a bid of ninety tarsk-bits, of Brundisium," said the auctioneer. "Do I hear a copper tarsk, a copper tarsk?"

"A copper tarsk!" called a man.

"A copper tarsk, fifty," called another fellow.

In Brundisium, a great mercantile port, there were a hundred tarsk-bits to the copper tarsk. This allowed a subtlety, a delicacy and precision, of bidding, particularly for smaller articles. The values of Gorean currency, particularly to the annoyance of the caste of merchants, varies considerably from city to city, with respect to weight, to purity of metal, and even denomination. In many cities for example, there were only four or eight tarsk-bits to a copper tarsk. This is apparently indexed to the ease of dividing a round coin into equal parts. The tarsk-bits of Brundisium, however, were individual tiny copper coins, either small disks or tiny droplets of copper. Given such vagaries, and the shaving of coins, particularly those of more precious metals, scales are often used in transactions, certainly in a polity's "Streets of Coins." Fortunes, I have been told, have been made in speculating on the shifting, comparable values of these diverse coinages. The double tarn, of gold, minted in the city of Ar, is usually accepted as the single, most valuable coin on Gor. Many cities in the northern hemisphere, even cities hostile to Ar, supposedly, privately, use Ar's "Gold Tarn," the single Tarn, to rank, standardize, and value their own currency. Unfortunately this coin, bearing only, by proud tradition, the simple sign of Ar, is easy to imitate. So one understands the importance of scales, and, as one might expect, the occasional charges and countercharges having to do with the accuracy of the weights used to balance the scales. Weights are standardized against official weights, so to speak, housed in a merchant fortress in the vicinity of the Sardar Mountains. Merchants may have access to this fortress four times a year, during the great Sardar fairs. Similar provisions are made for standardizing liquid and linear measures. Another important, well-known coin, is the golden stater of Brundisium. In the southern hemisphere, the coinage of Turia plays a similar role to that of Ar in the north.

"I have a copper tarsk, fifty," called the auctioneer.

"Is that not enough, in Brundisium, for a red-silk barbarian?" asked a fellow.

That I was "red-silk" had been made clear when my hair and eye color, my measurements, my lineaments, and such, prior to my exhibition, had been made clear to the crowd by the slaver's scribe at his desk below the block. On my former world, Earth, my sexual experiences, few as they had been, and they had been very few, had been disappointing. I had searched for a master, and I had found none. No one would see my slave and command it. I dared not reveal it, lest I be ridiculed and scorned. How miserable it is to be a slave in a world without masters. Once I even refused to remove my gown to see if one fellow, such a weakling, would not slap me for my insolence and tear it from me. But he did not. Once I pretended to slip before a fellow of Earth, and, for a moment, I was on my knees before him, looking up, into his eyes, but he did not hold me in place, but hastened, red-faced and embarrassed, to lift me to my feet, as though I had actually fallen. He did not hold my hair and press my lips to his feet; he did not put me to my belly and place his foot on my back, so that I could not rise. Another fellow I had intrigued with the prospect of sex and then, when we were alone, I demurred, seemingly unaccountably, in amusement, and told him to leave. I was standing imperiously before the bed, on which, unmistakably, lay a white, silk scarf and some coils of light rope. He did not strip and gag me, and fasten me across the bed for his pleasure. Sometimes, in the gentle, diffident arms of one man or another, I would pretend, secretly, to be a slave, but I knew they were not the arms of a master. When we had concluded our little encounter, so empty and meaningless, we would go our separate ways. I would not be chained to the foot of his bed, a bowl to the side. If I were not satisfactory, I would not be whipped. I tried to chastise myself for my needs, and tried to deny my heart. What more could I have done to try to conform to the rules others would, against my will, attempt to impose on me? There is little joy in denying and belittling oneself, in trying to lie to oneself. I do not think one garment, one pair of shoes, one thought, one life, fits all. Lonely, and then angry, frustrated, arrant, and contemptuous, I had come to despise the males of Earth as weaklings, as little more than docile, pliant sources of gifts, books, flowers, candy, jewelry, free dinners, free entertainment, and such. I knew I was attractive, and that pleased me. Surely a woman is not without power, unless, perhaps, there is a collar on her neck. And then, soon, in my continuing contempt for the men of Earth, their softness and timidity, their fear of being men, their treason to their very nature, I began to enjoy arousing hopes I had no intention of satisfying, taunting the weaklings and fools with prospects of gratification which would inevitably fail to materialize. I enjoyed making them miserable. But then, of course, there was no collar on my neck. Now I was a slave on Gor! These brutes, the masters, whether I willed it or not, had put the beginnings of slave fires in my belly, and I sensed they would rage, and grow, inevitably, continuously. We, as slaves, become the pathetic, helpless prisoners of our needs. They make us so. They would have us so. Already I was ready to crawl on my belly to a master, begging for his touch. I recalled the other slaves, thrashing and weeping in their cells and kennels. No longer did I have dignity, prestige, respect, or independence. I was now only a needful, collared slave.

"Behold the object now for sale," called the auctioneer, "a comely red-silk barbarian! Note the sweetness of her thighs, the curvature of her calves, and the slimness of her ankles, ready for the clasping of your shackles. Imagine her heeling you in the street, hurrying behind you, barefoot, in her tiny tunic, your collar on her neck, kneeling at your side, on her leash, lying beside you when you read!"

"A copper tarsk, seventy!" called a fellow.

"Why not a tiny yellow tunic?" said the auctioneer. "Yellow would go nicely with her dark hair."

"A copper tarsk, eighty!" called a man.

"This little beast," said the auctioneer, "has not yet had a private master. Which of you would you like to be her first master? Which of you would like to be the first to teach this barbarian what it is to be a slave?"

"One, ninety," called a man.

"Own her, train her to your personal tastes!" called the auctioneer. "What foods do you prefer, what drinks? How will your *kal-da* be spiced? At what Ahn will you be awakened? What temperature shall be your bath? What oils will you use? How will your robes be laid out? Let her on all fours bring your sandals to you, in her teeth. Let her bring the whip to you similarly, and drop it at your feet and beg to be lashed, if she is not fully pleasing!"

"Two copper tarsks!" called a fellow.

"Of Brundisium?" inquired the auctioneer.

"Of Brundisium," said the man.

"I have two copper tarsks, of Brundisium," said the auctioneer. "Who will bid more?"

There was silence in the tiers.

"Turn, face away from the noble masters," he said.

"Please, no, Master!" I wept.

"Now," he said.

"Yes, Master," I said.

"Two copper tarsks, twenty!" called a fellow.

"Two copper tarsks, forty!" called another.

"Noble masters," called the auctioneer, "this female was brought to Gor for your pleasure! Think on that!"

"They all are," called a fellow from the high tiers.

There was laughter.

"Turn, again," said the auctioneer. "Face the noble masters."

I complied.

It can be frightening to face bidders, as the livestock one is, waiting to be owned. It is hard not to be aware, as a purchasable object, of the desire and lust in the tiers, against which one will be helpless to defend oneself. But facing away is no particular refuge or remedy. The desire and lust is still there. Too, facing away, in a first, or even a second sale, can be humiliating, as one is then exhibited as little more than a form of possible interest. How better can one reduce and degrade a woman? Later, however, one does not object, *per se*, to this display of merchandise, oneself. Indeed, a slave soon takes pleasure in her richness and wholeness, in its manifest aspects. She hopes to be found pleasing, in all ways. In an early sale, however, aside from humiliation, as a new slave may be more sensitive to such things, it can be frightening to be facing away, unable to see the tiers. Is there not an uneasiness, knowing that something, perhaps dangerous or predatory, might be behind you, and you may not look about? Does one not feel more at risk, more vulnerable, when one may not look about?

"Zia," said the auctioneer.

"Master?" I said, startled.

"Are you trained?" he asked.

"A little," I said. Certainly I did not want much to be expected of me. I would much rather a master be pleasantly surprised than disappointed. Too, why should he ask me this? Had not the slaver's scribe, below the block, earlier, in his description, alluded to my level of training? It was rudimentary at best, but, in it, I had learned I was where I should be, in a collar.

"Speak up," he said.

"A little," I said, more loudly. I now realized I was supposed to be heard in the tiers.

"Petition to be bought," he said.

I had been instructed as to how to respond to this command.

"Buy me, Masters!" I called. "I beg to be bought!"

It is said that only slaves beg to be bought. If a captured free woman should beg to be purchased, for example, to be freed, she has thereby pronounced herself a slave.

And then, desperately, suddenly, I added something on my own. "And be kind to me, Masters!" I begged.

There was laughter from the tiers. I reddened. I had not realized that this request would be taken to be as naive or ridiculous as it had been. Was such a request truly so preposterous? I suddenly realized, even more deeply than before, what it might be to be a slave girl.

"You spoke without permission," said the auctioneer.

I had not thought. I paled. "Please do not whip me, Master," I begged.

"Do you now beg to please a man, any man?" he asked.

"Yes, Master," I said, hastily.

"Louder," he said.

"I beg to please a man, any man!" I said.

"Nothing is owed to a slave girl," he said.

"I understand," I said.

"Do you deserve to be treated with kindness?" he asked.

"I do not understand," I said.

"Noble masters," called the auctioneer to the crowd, "let me tell you something of the males, I do not say "men," of the slave world. They are taught to rejoice in their reduction, weakening, stunting, and crippling. They are instructed to collaborate in their own oppression and subjection. The true male is he who is least a man. A pallid, mechanistic, unnatural, and artificial society fears manhood and what it might mean. The larl must pretend to be a verr, lest it be devoured by swarms of urts. He who does the greatest treason to his own blood is accounted most a hero, or should one say, "heroine"? In a machine constructed of interchangeable parts there is no place for men or women. Biology is an embarrassment, an obstacle to be overcome. Men are thus to become less like men, and more like women, and women are to become less like women, and more like men. The machine, with its own needs, and its own best interests in mind, will have it so. But the transformation of men and women into pliable, pitiable, sexless neuters proceeds imperfectly. The pursuit of perfection, which by definition is unobtainable, leads to pathology. Theory succumbs to fact. Reality is recalcitrant. It is repudiated only at one's risk. Poison does not nourish, but sickens or kills. Consider then a world in which politics is given priority over nature. That is the slave world! Values and conventions become not roads, mountains, horizons, and wings, but fences and shackles. And so one has a world of men at war with themselves and women at war with themselves, a war in which victory is identified with one's own loss and defeat. And much of this is sensed by its victims, even when denied. And how do males and females in this world, meeting in its crevices, at permitted times, relate to one another? The hapless, pathetic males sue for smiles, and offer gifts, which they can often ill afford and the women, scorning such males, accept those gifts and solicit more. The supposed free women of the slave world, such as this now-stripped barbarian before you, are exploitative, mercenary creatures bartering their beauty for gain!"

There were cries of anger from the tiers.

I was frightened.

"Is it not so, slut?" he snarled.

"Yes, Master," I said.

"And were you not such a woman?" he asked.

"Yes, Master," I said. I knew it was true. How often I had played such games with men!

"You did such things deliberately, and were petty, cruel, and worthless," he said.

"Yes, Master," I said.

"Doubtless you well used the promise of your body to arouse, taunt, provoke, tease, and lure males, to win gain from them, to obtain largesse, to turn their frustrated desire to your own profit."

"Yes, Master," I wept.

"And you were doubtless fully clothed, for the most part," he said.

"Yes, Master," I said.

"And see her now," he said, turning to the tiers, "owned, a property, exhibited as we wish, on sale!"

"Good!" called more than one fellow.

"She is now as she deserved to be, even then!" said the auctioneer.

"Yes, yes," called men.

"And will she now reap gain from her beauty?" said the auctioneer.

"No!" cried men.

"Others will now reap gain from her beauty," said the auctioneer, "those who sell it!"

"Yes!" cried men. "Yes!"

"From the feckless men of Earth," said the auctioneer, "we take which of their women we please and bring them to Gor."

"Good," called a fellow.

"As meaningless and worthless as they are," said the auctioneer.

There was laughter.

"Now, for the first time in their lives," he said, "they will be worth something, as abject slaves."

"Excellent," said a fellow.

"You see," said the auctioneer, turning to me. "You do not deserve kindness."

I was silent.

"Do you deserve kindness?" he asked.

"No, Master," I said.

"Shall we not see that she, this petty, greedy, exploitative, spoiled woman of the slave world, the gray, polluted world, is punished, for what she was on the polluted world?" asked the auctioneer.

"Yes, yes!" called men.

The auctioneer then replaced his whip on his belt. I was pleased at this. He apparently had no intention then, despite his remark, of punishing me, at least immediately. The typical punishment of a slave is to be switched or whipped. That is, mercifully, quickly over. We do understand the switch and whip. What slave does not? That action, replacing the whip on his belt, did free his right hand.

"Oh!" I cried, for the auctioneer had seized me by the hair, turned my right side to the tiers, and bent me backward, holding me cruelly in the "slave bow." I dared not speak, so held, so displayed.

"I have, I recall," said the auctioneer, "a bid in hand of two copper tarsks, forty."

"Three copper tarsks!" cried a man.

"Three, twenty!" called another.

The auctioneer pulled me upright by the hair and lifted his hand, tangled in my hair, and I was on my tip toes, my hands futilely on the auctioneer's wrist. I am sure now that he had realized that I would try to reach up, to ease the pain on my hair, and, in attempting this, would lift my breasts, further displaying the merchandise which I was.

"I have three twenty, three twenty," called the auctioneer. "Who will make it three, fifty?"

"Three, twenty-five!" called a fellow.

"I want three fifty, three fifty, at least!" said the auctioneer.

"Too much!" called a man.

The auctioneer released my hair and I stood, bent over. I feared I might fall.

"Examination position," he said.

I straightened my body, spread my legs, I could feel the sawdust about my ankles, put my hands, clasped, behind the back of my neck, and looked upwards. I could see the roof of the hall. Sometimes the hands are clasped behind the head.

"Spread your legs more," said the auctioneer.

"Yes, Master," I said.

The spreading of the legs makes it more difficult to move. In a sense, it holds one in place. The hands behind the neck or head removes the hands from a position where they might obstruct an assessor's view. Also, clasped, they are held in place. This posture also, besides rendering the slave helpless and vulnerable, lifts her breasts nicely. The lifting of the head, looking upward, makes it difficult to anticipate the touch of an assessor. What I did not understand was why I had been commanded to such a position on the block. The block is high, and I was several feet from the tiers. And surely it was seldom that a bidder would be permitted to ascend the block. There might be several interested men in the tiers, making this impractical, and the merchants are eager to keep the sales moving, one item after another. The examination position is more commonly required on a slave shelf or in a sales camp, where a given buyer, perhaps shopping, may be interested in a particular slave, one which he may wish to inspect more closely. My puzzlement was short lived. I could not see behind me. I did not realize, for example, that the auctioneer had now, again, removed the whip from his belt.

"I have a bid of three, twenty-five," said the auctioneer. "Surely that is not enough for this comely dark-haired slave. Is her hair too short? It will grow. Is she too spare and lithe? You can fatten her up. She may not have the sturdy limbs, and strength of some slaves, but not all slaves need carry weighty sacks of suls or pit their strength against the straps of plows. Surely you can think of other things to do with such a slave. Imagine her naked and perfumed, chained by the neck at the foot of your couch. And when you wish to work her, the whip will see to her efficiency and zeal. Who will bid three fifty, and higher?"

But the tiers were silent.

"Aii!" I cried, startled, reacting involuntarily, violently, spasmodically, and fell to my knees, shaken and miserable. How I had been exposed, displayed, and revealed! I wept. My body, I fear, was a scarlet sheet of flame.

I had been administered the "slaver's caress."

"Do not dare to cover your breasts with your hands," snapped the auctioneer. "You are a slave."

"Master!" I protested, beggingly.

"*Nadu*, slave!" he snapped.

I then knelt at the auctioneer's feet, facing the tiers. I knelt back on my heels, my back straight, my belly sucked in, my shoulders back, the palms of my hands down on my thighs, my head lifted.

"Widen your knees more," he said.

"Yes, Master," I said.

"You see, noble masters," said the auctioneer, "our suppliers select not only for comeliness and high intelligence, as is well known, but for uncontrollable slave reflexes."

There was laughter.

"And this pretty slut," said the auctioneer, "has been on Gor for only several days, and already she will leap, writhe, squeak, moan, and whimper like a tarsk in heat."

"They all do!" called a man.

There was more laughter.

I, kneeling in *nadu*, felt devastated, humiliated.

My feelings had not been respected. I was nothing. I did not count. No one had consulted me, or warned me. It had been done to me without my consent, without my permission. I had been revealed as a helplessly sexual creature, one for sale, a slave!

Tears sprang from my eyes, and ran down my cheeks.

I could not wipe them away, held in *nadu*.

Was I, as a slave, I thought, permitted to retain no shred of dignity? No, I thought, I was not. I was a slave. Everything about me, even my needs and responses, were public. How exposed and displayed I felt! More about me had been exhibited than unveiled features and a bared form. I had had no choice but to betray my-self as a slave, a woman who would be helpless in the hands of a master. On Gor I had hoped to find a master who would love me and whom I might love. Now I realized I would be the helplessly responsive, writhing, begging toy of any man who might own me. I was a slave, only a slave!

"Three copper tarsks, forty tarsk-bits, of Brundisium!" called a fellow from the tiers. I did not even see who uttered the bid.

"I want three, fifty," called the auctioneer, "at least three fifty. Who will bid more? Who will bid more?"

The tiers were silent.

"Three, fifty!" said the auctioneer.

The auctioneer was standing a bit to my left, a little before me. I could see the whip in his right hand.

There was no response from the tiers.

"You may break position," said the auctioneer.

I broke position. I remained kneeling, at his feet, but I closed my knees, and put my head down.

"Surely more!" called the auctioneer.

But the tiers were still silent.

"Very well," said the auctioneer. "Three copper tarsks, forty. Done!"

He replaced the whip on his belt.

I heard the sound of a gong.

I had been sold!

"Forgive me, Master," I begged, putting my cheek, head down, to his leg, "for not having been sufficiently pleasing."

But he paid me no attention.

Why should he pay attention to a slave?

He seemed to be examining the tiers. I did not know why he was doing this. Then, apparently satisfied, perhaps he had seen something, or someone, he looked down at me. I was kneeling beside him. I then lifted my head, and looked up at him, and then, tears in my eyes, I began, softly, to lick and kiss the coils of the whip he carried in his hand. It seemed appropriate to me to do so. Some women can understand this. If they found themselves at the feet of a Gorean male, I suspect all women could understand it.

"Forgive me, Master," I said.

He put his hand in my hair, and shook my head, good-naturedly. The caress was much as one might have bestowed on a dog on my former world. Gratefully, I realized I was not likely to be beaten.

"You may have difficulty standing," he said. "Crawl from the block on all fours. We do want you to stumble on the stairs. You will be caged and picked up in the morning. Off with you."

"The next slave is Adraste," said the slaver's scribe, calling up from his position before and below the center of the block, "one of those brought in from the World's End."

"I know," said the auctioneer, looking out again, toward the tiers.

I then left the block as the auctioneer had specified, on all fours, and descended the stairs similarly. In this way I was less likely to fall, possibly being injured or bruised. I, as goods, was to be delivered to a purchaser undamaged. At the foot of the block, on its right side, as one would face it from the tiers, a slaver's man pulled me to my feet. I stood unsteadily. "Leading position," he said. I then bent down, and put my head to his left hip. He then took my hair in his hand, and conducted me through certain passages, and then, arresting his journey, he put me to all fours before a small cage, one of several, some already occupied, and opened the gate. I crawled within, and then turned to look up at him. He locked the gate. I grasped the bars. My cage, and each of the others, as well, had a sign, each the same sign. "Master," I said, "may I speak?" "Surely," he said. "What do the signs say?" I asked. I could not read Gorean. "'Sold'," he said. "I am sorry I did not sell for more," I said. "There is a glut of slaves on the market," he said. "I have never seen so many. One can scarcely give them away. It is impossible to keep track of them all. We process them like herds of tarsks. It has to do with the season, the influx from the World's End, and the fall campaigns. If I had my way, we would hold them off the market until spring, but they eat. To be sure, what one loses on single sale, one may, with luck, make up in volume."

"This is not an important market, is it?" I asked.

"Lesser known, and more obscure than I would like," he said. "We do not even keep papers on our girls."

I supposed then it would be hard to trace slaves marketed through the House of Anesidemus.

"Still," I said, "I am sorry I did not sell for more."

"You sold for three copper tarsks, and forty tarsk-bits, Brundisium," he said.

"Yes, Master," I said.

"We only expected to get two copper tarsks for you," he said.

"Oh," I said.

"Someone must have wanted you," he said.

"For what?" I asked.

"Do not be naive," he said.

"Forgive me, Master," I said.

"Still," he said, "over three copper tarsks, in this market. That is interesting."

"'Interesting'?" I asked.

"Yes," he said. "Perhaps you are in some way special to someone."

"Perhaps," I said, "to some man I am the most beautiful woman he has ever seen."

"Perhaps," he said.

"Then," I said, "I will have an easy life. He will be eager to please me. I can control him. He will do whatever I ask."

"And you will be well lashed," he said.

"Oh," I said. I gathered that the men of Gor were different from those of Earth.

He smiled.

"In what other way could I be special?" I asked.

"I do not know," he said, "unless it is because you are new to this world, and know little of it."

"Master?" I asked.

"I must get back to the block," he said. He then turned and left.

Why should that matter, I wondered, that I might be new to this world and knew little of it?

I was pleased to see that there was a small blanket in my cage.

CHAPTER FOUR

Adraste

I lay down in the cage. It was a small cage, a typical slave cage, sturdy and closely barred. One can kneel or sit in it, but little more. One may not fully stretch out in such a cage. Aside from the obvious custodial aspects of such a device, it has its aesthetic and psychological aspects, as well. Aesthetically, men apparently find us attractive in cages. And, psychologically, they enjoy seeing us as the slaves we are, helplessly caged, confined within the limits they have seen fit to impose on us, and, of course, from the slave's point of view, psychologically, we well understand ourselves to be the slaves we are. And, of course, as slaves, we are animals, and is it not appropriate that animals be caged?

In the distance, through the passages, I heard the gong sound. Adraste, then, she supposedly brought in from the World's End, who had been the slave behind me in line, must have been sold. She, exquisitely featured, excitingly figured, dark-haired, green-eyed, and olive-skinned, was surely one of most beautiful women I had ever seen. I recalled that two of the slaver's men, before I had ascended the block, had been bemused that such an item, supposedly worthy of the central block of the Curulean, whatever that was or wherever it might be, should be offered in this market, near the wharves, in an evening sale.

Shortly after the sounding of the gong, Adraste, bent over, in leading position, at the side of the slaver's man, her hair in his grasp, appeared. She was put to all fours and ensconced in a cage two cages from mine. The intermediate cage was empty, and we could see one another, though not easily, through the bars. "Did you see the tarsk?" she said. "He put me, me, in leading position, as though I might be a slave!"

"I do not understand," I said. And then I was frightened. I had never seen a Gorean free woman closely. I had seen some tonight, in the tiers, with escorts. They were at a distance, and the light was poor, except in the vicinity of the block. I recalled clearly, however, the terror of my instructresses in my training, in the house, at the bare mention of free women. One of the slaver's men once threatened to sell them to a free woman, and the two instructresses, so frightening to us, with their strictness and switches, and contempt of us, new, naked, collared slaves, had suddenly themselves become piteous, terrified, groveling slaves at the fellow's feet, begging to be spared such a fate. How they had wept, and licked and kissed, his feet. I had then realized more about free women than I had hitherto understood. And my alarm was all the more increased when I came to better realize the chasm which, on this world, divides the free and the slave. The slave to the free woman is less than the dirt beneath her dainty slippers. We are clothed, when clothed, in such a way as, in the opinion of the free women, to shame, humiliate, and degrade us, but, perhaps to the chagrin of free women, we soon grow fond of our tunics and collars. Perhaps the free women begrudge us that. Perhaps they wish that they, too, were so clad, and under the eyes of proud, free, greedy, lustful masters, who well know how to look upon helpless, vulnerable slaves. In any event, surely there is no mistaking us for free women. Robes and veils are one thing; tunics and collars are another. We yield them position, withdraw from their path, efface ourselves before them, dare not meet their eyes, and kneel, if addressed, or looked upon, commonly with our head to the ground. We dare not raise our voice in their presence, and, if we are permitted the honor of speaking to them, will commonly do so softly, head down, with extreme deference. The least suggestion, even imagined, of hesitation, impatience, unwillingness, presumption, recalcitrance, pertness, or sarcasm on our part is likely to bring a beating. We are much at the mercy of free women. They hate us and they can switch or lash us with impunity, which it seems they enjoy doing. The interest taken in us by free men outrages them. Too, most slaves are attractive. If they were not so, they would not, for the most part, have been put in the collar. Men would not have wanted them. Thus, in their way, the mark and the collar, are badges of approval. The woman who is marked and has a collar on her neck knows that she has been found desirable, worth marking and collaring. What strong, fine male does not want a beautiful woman at his slave ring?

"May I speak, Mistress?" I asked.

This mode of address seemed to mollify the beauty.

"Yes," she said.

"Is Mistress not a slave?" I asked.

"She-tarsk!" she hissed.

"Forgive me, Mistress," I said.

"I am marked and collared," she said, angrily. "I have been put to use by various masters, who did with me what they pleased. I have just been sold, to whom I know not!"

"Surely Mistress then is a slave," I said.

"Yes!" she said angrily. "I am a slave. I, I, of all women, of all women, have been made a slave!"

"'Of all women'?" I asked.

"I was once free," she said, carefully.

"So, too, was I," I said.

"I was of high caste, noble, important!" she said.

"I had no caste," I said.

"You were nothing before," she said. "Now you are less than nothing!"

"You are a slave," I said.

"Yes," she snapped.

"As much so as I?" I said.

"As much so as you, she-tarsk," she said.

"If you are a slave," I said, "why should you object to being put in leading position?"

"I am not a common slave," she said.

"You are very beautiful," I said.

"That tarsk who dared to insult me by putting me in leading position should have been boiled in oil," she said.

"Oh?" I said.

"Once," she said, "I could have had it done."

"He also put you to all fours, and caged you," I said.

"So a thousand tortures," she said, "and then boiling in oil."

"I am Zia," I said.

"A meaningless slave name," she said, "like Lita, or Lana."

"What sort of name is Adraste?" I asked.

"Do you dare use my name?" she asked.

"Why should I call you 'Mistress'," I asked, "as you are a slave, as I am, and you are not "First Girl" to me?"

"Impudent barbarian," she said.

"I saw your mark," I said. "I have not seen one like it."

"It is the mark of the city of Treve," she said.

"You are from Treve then?" I said.

"No," she said.

"Where are you from?" I asked.

"Do you know accents," she asked, "that of Cos and Tyros, of Ti, of Torcadino, of Thentis, of Port Kar, of remote Turia?"

"No," I said.

"Your mark," she said, "is the common *kef*. Almost all slave girls wear it, common girls, particularly in the northern hemisphere, even as far east as the barrens."

"It is a lovely mark," I said.

"It looks attractive, burned into the hide of a common girl," she said.

"I have not heard the name 'Adraste' before," I said.

"It is not an unknown name in the nearer islands, Cos and Tyros," she said.

"Then you are from Cos or Tyros," I said.

"No," she said.

"From where?" I asked.

"From far away," she said.

"I understand you were brought here from what they call the World's End," I said.

"Yes," she said.

"Then," I said, "you are from the World's End."

"Yes," she said, cautiously, "I am from the World's End."

I heard the sales gong sound in the distance. Doubtless Adraste heard it, too. Another girl had been sold.

"We are named, of course, as masters wish," I said.

"Of course," she said.

"We are animals," I said.

How true that was!

I now understood myself, profoundly, as an animal, only an animal.

"You are a pretty animal," she sneered.

"And you," I said, "are a beautiful animal."

She grasped the bars of her cage, and shook them, angrily, futilely.

"You cannot escape," I said. "You are caged."

"She-tarsk!" she said.

"Surely you understand that you are an animal," I said.

"Yes," she said, bitterly, holding to the bars. "I am an animal."

"Accept yourself as such," I said, "and be fulfilled."

I had, long ago, in the joy of my collaring and marking, welcomed that I was now an animal, which, helpless and rightless,
could be owned. I found freedom, liberation, and fulfillment in
the collar of a slave.

What had I been before?

Only an uncollared slave.

"I named my slaves as I wished," she said.

"You once had slaves?" I said.

"I told you," she snapped, "that I was of high caste, that I was
noble, and important!"

"Yes," I said.

"I was rich," she said, "and powerful!"

"Very powerful?" I asked.

"We have spoken enough," she said, warily.

"How many slaves did you have?" I asked.

"As many as I wished," she said.

"Several?" I said.

"Of course," she said. "One needs several slaves, some for the
care of one's hair, some for the bath, for lotions and creams, some
for the care of one's robes and veils, some for dressing one, and
so on."

"I see," I said.

"Slaves are useful," she said. "They can carry messages; they
can be distributed about, in the streets and markets, to listen and
gather information; the slave girl, unsuspected, can follow men
and women unobtrusively. I can place them in houses and taverns.
They can serve wine and paga; they can wheedle secrets from
boastful, naive males. They can apprise themselves of facts which
I find valuable, economically and politically, allowing me to later
control and manipulate others, sometimes others of standing and
power. They can learn even the moods of cities, the existence of
disgruntlement and discontent, discover even the threads of plots
and conspiracies."

"You use them as spies," I said.

"Informants," she said.

"I see," I said.

"I direct them whom to cultivate, whose favor to win, whose
confidence and trust to secure, whom to bed with, whom to inter-
rogate."

"'Whom to bed with'?" I said.

"Of course," she said, "and learn from."

"You employ their charms and bodies for your own purposes," I said.

"Surely," she said. "They are slaves."

"Yes," I said, "they are slaves."

"And if they are in the least bit hesitant, inefficient, or displeasing, I have them well lashed," she said.

"I see," I said.

"It is amusing to see them weep and writhe under the whip."

"I do not think I would care to belong to you," I said.

"You need not fear," she said. "I would not stoop to owning a barbarian. They are ignorant and stupid."

"I am ignorant," I said. "I am not stupid."

"Do you think you are intelligent?" she asked.

"Yes," I said, angrily. "I am quite intelligent."

"I suppose you have been taught to kneel and belly, to roll and squirm, to lick and kiss," she said.

"Yes!" I said.

"Slave!" she said.

"Have you not been taught such things," I asked, "if only by the rod, switch, and lash?"

"She-tarsk!" she hissed.

"I see you have," I said.

"Worthless, barbarian slave," she said.

"I imagine you would dance quickly enough," I said, "to the snap of a whip."

"Doubtless you applied your high intelligence to well learn such lessons," she said.

"I tried to master them," I said, "I paid attention, I applied myself, but I do not think intelligence was much involved. I found such things congenial, natural, a matter of innate dispositions, of instinct. Certainly I wanted to learn how to please a master. I wanted to learn how to be a desirable slave. What slave does not wish to please her master? And she had better please him, or she will feel the lash! But I think intelligence is important. Surely if one is highly intelligent, one will be more adept at pleasing a master."

"Yes," she said. "The brutes enjoy having a highly intelligent woman naked at their feet."

"I long to be at a man's feet," I said. "It is where I want to be, where I belong."

"I once knew a man from your world," she said. "He was a weakling, grateful for a smile."

"Perhaps he has changed," I said.

"I despise him," she said.

"I think you have not yet met your master," I said.

"I conquer men with my beauty," she said.

"Perhaps when you were free," I said.

She was silent.

"I expect it would be difficult to conquer men when one is on one's knees, stripped and collared," I said.

"I hold men in contempt," she said.

"They are beasts, of course," I said, "but we belong to them."

"Like sandals and tarsks!" she said.

"Have you no desire to kneel gratefully at the feet of a master?" I asked.

"Were I free," she said, "I would have the skin lashed from your bones!"

"You are a woman," I said. "You need a master."

"Be silent," she said. "Someone approaches."

"It is the slaver's man," I said, "and he has a newly vended girl with him. She is in leading position." This was easier for me to see, than for Adraste, given the location of our cages.

"Do not speak," whispered Adraste. "We could be beaten."

Slave girls are commonly at liberty to speak to one another, but it is quite a different thing if a free person is present. In such a situation, the free person may not wish to hear the discourse of slaves.

The new girl was placed in the cage next to that of Adraste, to my right. She was a blonde, short and sweetly figured.

She had scarcely been ensconced in her cage and the slaver's man departed than she turned to me, speaking through the cage that separated us. "I went for six copper tarsks. What did you go for?"

"I went for three copper tarsks, forty tarsk-bits," I said, adding, "of Brundisium."

"You are only a barbarian," she said.

"Yes," I said.

"But that is a good price for a barbarian, in this market," she said.

"Thank you," I said.

"I am Fina," said the new girl.

"I am Zia," I said.

"I do not know why they hold sales this time of night," she said, "here, near the wharves. Who will attend them?"

"Some, I suppose," I said.

"It is almost as though they did not want the best prices," she said.

I did not fully understand what she was saying.

"I understand it was a regularly scheduled sale," I said.

"The venue is obscure," she said.

"Perhaps the time and place are convenient for a certain clientele," I said, "dock workers, mariners, warehouse men, and such."

"True," she said.

"I take it you are natively Gorean," I said.

"Of course," she said.

"It is kind of you to speak to me," I said. Many Gorean slaves would not deign to converse with a barbarian.

"Who else is there to speak with?" she asked.

"She to your right," I said, puzzled.

"The great *Tatrix*?" she scoffed.

"What is a *Tatrix*?" I asked.

"A female administrator, commonly of a city," she said.

"Was she a *Tatrix*?" I asked.

"Of course not," she laughed. "We call her that because her bearing is so haughty, so superior, and offensive. She, no more than a slave, puts on airs, carries herself as though she were free, and of high caste, too, and will hardly speak with us."

I was surprised that Adraste had not spoken up, that she had not retorted in some way. She had certainly spoken with me, a mere barbarian. I wondered if she feared this new girl for some reason, but had had no fear of me, a barbarian.

"She is very beautiful," I said.

"She is no different from us," she said. "She, too, is in a collar."

"I gather she was once important, even rich," I said.

"She is a liar, from the World's End," she said.

Adraste was lying in her cage, curled up, facing away from us. I could sense a stiffening in her body, and anger, but she remained silent.

"Still she is very beautiful," I said.

"She went for a silver tarsk, fifty, fifty copper tarsks," said Fina. "I was behind her. I heard. That is far more than she was worth."

"She-tarsk!" said Adraste, not turning about.

"She-tarsk!" responded Fina.

"I would tear out your hair, and scratch out your eyes," hissed Adraste, not turning about.

"And the masters would cut off your ears and nose!" said Fina.

"Where are you from?" I asked Fina.

"From Venna," she said, "not far from Glorious Ar."

We heard the gong sound, again, seemingly far off.

"I wonder what she went for," said Fina.

I lay down, again.

Fina, too, in her cage, lay down.

Adraste was silent.

I had asked Fina from where she was. I had had a reason for doing so. Apparently she was from a place called Venna, somewhere in the vicinity of a place called Ar, even "Glorious Ar." I certainly did not know where Venna was, or "Glorious Ar," but I had asked because the accents of Adraste and Fina had seemed strikingly similar.

Many people are unaware they have an accent, though it is clear enough to others, those who do not share the accent.

I lay quietly.

I did not know who owned me, only that I must no longer be the property of the house of Anesidemus, near the wharves, in the coastal metropolis of Brundisium.

I fell asleep.

CHAPTER FIVE

We Are Taken from the House of Anesidemus

I do not think I had been asleep very long when I became aware of the ringing of an alarm bar in the distance. I heard, too, the shouts of men, far off. I rose to my knees, and grasped the bars of my cage, frightened. I did not know what was going on. Fina was on all fours, in her cage. "Masters! Masters!" cried Adraste, from her cage, to the right of Fina's cage. There was terror in her voice. I was startled, because Adraste had seemed, earlier, so cool, so self-assured, so superior and precise. "So," I thought, "she is a woman, too, only a woman, and a slave, too, no different from us!" But her fear was communicated to me. I clutched the bars more tightly. Adraste knew more of this world than I, a barbarian imported for its markets. Then Fina, too, now kneeling, her cage to the left of that of Adraste, cried out, piteously, "Masters!" Similar cries emanated from other cages in the chamber as well. The only light in the chamber now, this late, was from a single lamp, suspended from the ceiling.

"What is wrong?" I called out, hoping someone would answer.

"Release us!" cried a slave.

I heard weeping.

No one paid me any attention.

I pressed my face against the bars and tried to look to my left, down the passage through which I and the other girls had been brought to this chamber.

It was dark.

"What is it?" cried a slave.

"An attack!" cried one.

"Slavers, a raid!" cried another.

"Cos!" I heard.

"Tyros!" cried another.

"Port Kar!" wept another.

"Do not be foolish!" cried Adraste. "Brundisium hosted and abetted the fleets of Cos and Tyros in the great invasion."

I did not understand this.

"I smell smoke!" cried a girl.

"It is an attack by Ar!" cried another girl. "Her tarnsmen are aflight, high in the night, in their hundreds, hurling vessels of fire on Brundisium."

"No," cried Adraste. "Marlenus would own Brundisium, not destroy her!"

I did not know who Marlenus might be.

"Marlenus is a madman who would destroy what he cannot own!" said Fina.

"It cannot be Ar," said another girl. "If Ar wished to punish Brundisium, she would have done so long ago."

"Ar needs Brundisium," said another girl. "How else could she outfit and supply a fleet for the invasion of Cos and Tyros?"

"I, too, smell smoke," cried another slave.

A slave screamed.

I was not sure there was a smell of smoke. Imagination can be easily enflamed. In the house of fear, perception and invention are much akin. Then I, too, suddenly, unmistakably, smelled smoke.

"Raiders!" cried a slave.

"We are women, and slaves," wept a girl, "nothing, only prizes, only loot, only booty."

"It may not be raiders," said a slave. "It is an attack in force!"

"You do not know that," said another.

We knew little on this lower level, in our cages.

"It is Ar!" cried another slave. "It is rumored that Talena, she who betrayed the Home Stone of Ar, Talena, the puppet Ubara, the false Ubara, the traitress, the fugitive, is hiding in Brundisium."

"And in a hundred other cities, as well," said a slave.

"They would not destroy the city for her," said another. "She might die in the flames. That would be too easy. It would cheapen the vengeance of Ar. They want her alive for months of torture, followed by slow impalement."

"It is well known," said another, "that Talena was given sanctuary in Cos."

"Yes," said another slave.

"Then it is Port Kar, her raiders, outside, in the streets, the scourge of Thassa!" cried a slave.

There was a shriek of fear.

"You do not know that," said she who had spoken before.

How little we knew!

"No, no, not Port Kar!" wept another slave.

"To any city but Port Kar!" cried another.

There was terror in the voices.

"It is said the chains of a slave girl are heaviest in Port Kar," wept a slave.

"We will be carried there, and, stripped, shackled, and lashed, sold in her markets!" wailed another.

"To pirates and cutthroats!" cried another.

A slave on the other side of the room, in her cage, was hysterically trying to tear the light, obdurate circlet of steel from her neck.

"Struggle in vain, fool," said another. "It is on you, and will remain there."

The slave then collapsed, weeping, huddled in her tiny cage, her fingers still clutching the attractive, close-fitting, locked, identificatory device.

I knew nothing of Port Kar, but I gathered that it would be a terrifying fate to be a female slave in Port Kar.

I touched my own collar.

I could not remove it, no more than the others could remove theirs.

We were helpless and rightless. We were properties. It would be done with us as masters might please.

I was very much afraid.

I now better realized what it might mean to be a slave, and a slave on Gor.

"Fools," said a girl, she who had cautioned patience and skepticism, "cease your screaming and weeping, your babbling and whimpering. There are no raiders, from Port Kar or elsewhere."

"The alarm bar!" protested a slave.

"I hear no axes on gates, no clash of swords, no screams of slaughtered men," said the first slave.

"The smell of smoke is stronger!" cried a slave.

"Masters! Masters!" cried another.

"There is no sign of fire here," said the first slave.

This observation was met with silence.

"Masters will not allow us, their goods, to be destroyed," she said.

I recalled then something I had heard when I was in training. In many situations, as in war, it was far safer to be a slave than a free person, as the slave, as a domestic animal, had value, as an acquisition. The slave was viewed not as an enemy or combatant, but, as other goods, silks, vessels, coins, and such, as booty.

I looked again to my left, as I could, my face against the bars, to the passageway through which I and the others had been introduced into the holding chamber, with its tiny, sturdy cages.

"A lantern approaches," I called out.

I could see the light, down the passageway.

"Another, another lantern!" I said.

Three or four, perhaps five, men were in the passageway.

"Masters! Masters!" cried several of the slaves.

"Silence!" snapped the first fellow into the chamber. Instantly the slaves were silent, as a free man had spoken. "You are in no danger, no immediate danger," he said. He then suspended his lantern from a dangling hook, its chain fixed in the ceiling. "There is a fire on the wharf," he said, "a warehouse fire. It will surely be contained, and extinguished. Yet we will not risk it. It might spread. As a precaution, the building will be evacuated. You will be taken into the streets." One of the men, of which there were five, had several coils of rope over his shoulder. Another, with a single key, now moved rapidly from cage to cage, opening the gates. "Out," called the fellow who had been first in the chamber. "On all fours, tandem, in a line, facing the passageway!" The second lantern was held high by another of the men. The passageway itself was not illuminated.

I crawled from the cage, and took my place in the line being formed by the released slaves. On all fours, the slave is well reminded of her slavery.

"Here, this place, here," said one of the men, he aligning us.

The first slave crawled to the place indicated, I, and the other slaves, following her.

"What of our new masters?" asked a slave.

"You will be picked up in the morning," she was told.

Adraste was before Fina, and Fina was before me. There were some fifteen or twenty slaves, several before us, and some behind us.

The fellow with the rope, beginning with the last girl, moved forward, adding us, one by one, to the coffle. I felt the rope looped about my neck, knotted, and then passed on, to the next girl. This is commonly done, from rear to front, presumably so that the girl cannot see the approach of the rope or chain, and then she is added to the coffle. This lessens the likelihood that a slave, presumably a new slave, terrified, may bolt before being secured.

"Where are our tunics?" begged a slave. "Surely we will not be taken into the streets as we are."

"No, not as we are!" said another slave.

"Clothe us!" begged another slave.

"You are already clothed," said he who was adding us to the coffle. "You have your clothing, your collars. How could those such as you be more appropriately clothed?"

"Please, Master!" begged a slave.

"Be silent," he said.

"Yes, Master," she whispered, her head then lowered humbly, as befits a slave.

"Have no fear, pretty beasts," said another man. "You will not be cold. We will see to that. Each of you will have a nice warm slave sheet."

The slave moaned, and another man, nearby, laughed. This was, I gathered, a joke. A slave sheet is light. It provides little, or no, warmth. Its purpose is to conceal the slave. The masters, I gathered, outside in the darkness and confusion, did not wish to tempt ruffians, or predators, by the display of attractive slaves, poorly secured and perhaps ill-guarded. Had we been in a chain coffle, as is common in moving slaves, the risk of assault or theft would have been considerably reduced. A blow can render a girl unconscious. A knife can quickly cut a rope. And who is likely, in the darkness, men rushing about, to challenge a fellow bearing away a slave which might well be his own?

We were properties, and properties can be stolen.

"Move, soft, pretty animals," said a man.

The coffle began to move up the passageway. I wondered how the proud, scornful, Adraste, brought in from the "World's End," enjoyed being herded along, in her place, on all fours. She had yet to learn, I feared, that she was truly a slave. She had yet, I suspected, to meet her master. She had cried out, of course, in misery and terror, when the alarm bell had sounded. Clearly she was a slave, for all her airs, no different from the rest of us. Are we not all women, no more? Conquered and subdued, I suspected she would lie contentedly, gratefully at the feet of a master.

I saw no sheets.

In a few minutes we had ascended the passageway and, turning to our right, had crawled down a long corridor, leading to a minor exit from the house of Anesidemus. The exit was open, and I could see the street outside, and men going to and fro. I could feel the fresh air from the exit. I could also, now, even more clearly than before, smell smoke.

There were several men near the door. I was surprised to see the auctioneer amongst them. He must then, I supposed, be an employee of the house. I had not thought him so. I had not seen him about the house, not before tonight. Most auctioneers are hired independently. Some, as I understand it, command high wages. Some exact a set fee; others demand a fee, abetted with a commission. The incentive of a commission is often granted by a house, particularly by a cheaper house, which is likely to be parsimonious with respect to a guaranteed fee. Most such matters seem subject to negotiation. On Gor there seem to be few fixed prices, for vegetables, for boots, for slaves.

Shortly we were in the vicinity of the door. The first slave in our coffle was half across the threshold.

It was cool.

I shivered.

The men at the door were joined by another fellow, who carried an armload of slave sheets.

The typical slave sheet is light, small, square, and cheap. Its usual intent, as suggested earlier, is to conceal a slave. It is not intended for comfort, for who is concerned with the comfort of a slave, nor is it concerned with the slave's modesty, as slaves are not permitted modesty. It is often thrown over the slave's head and fastened in place with a cord or thong about her neck. Whereas its common purpose is concealment, it may also be used to provoke interest or curiosity. In such a case, a greater or lesser extent of the slave's legs will be visible, surely at least the calves, and the rest is left to the imagination of passing masters. This appertains to the slave particularly when she is upright, sitting, or lying. We, of course, were on all fours, and thus the sheet would be likely to do little more than hide the slave from sight. As it was night, and late, and there was confusion in the streets, the masters, I am sure, were more than content with this limited objective. Lastly, it might be noted that the slave sheet, when fastened about the head, not only conceals the slave's features, but, in its way, to some extent, hoods the slave, thus making her less aware of her surroundings and more manageable.

A sheet was put about the first slave in the coffle. I was uneasy when I noted it was put over her head and fastened in place. Below the fastening it was parted, dangling to each side of the coffle rope. For the rest, it was draped over her back. It hung to the sides, and would not impede her movement. Then the second slave was similarly treated. One fellow carried the sheets and a second fellow affixed them on the slave. The auctioneer stood by, watching. The fellow affixing the sheets then came to Adraste. He then moved on to the next girl, Fina. The auctioneer had seemed suddenly alert. I had noted nothing, however, to have had him stir so, ever so slightly. Then the next sheet was thrown over me, put over my head, fastened about my neck, and then draped back over my body. I was effectively hooded and concealed. He then continued on his way. Shortly thereafter he seemed to have finished his work and taken his departure.

"Are the docks aflame?" I heard a man ask.

"No," he was told, "only a warehouse."

"What warehouse?" he was asked.

"That of Flavius Minor," he was told.

"One of the largest houses," said a fellow.

"The flames may spread," said another.

"I do not think so," said a fellow.

"They are moving the stock anyway," said a man.

"Of course," said another.

To my surprise, as I waited, I felt someone unknotting the cord from about my throat, that which held the sheet on me. The sheet was then drawn away. I saw it in the hands of one whom I took to be a slaver's man. The auctioneer was no longer in the vicinity. I did not wish to risk asking for permission to speak. I feared I might be beaten. I saw the sheet had been removed from Adraste, as well. It lay beside her. The fellow then fastened my sheet on Adraste, picked up the sheet which had been on her, and fastened it on me. I saw no difference between the sheets.

I did not understand this.

Why should the sheets have been exchanged? Were they not all the same?

"Is the house cleared?" called a man.

"It is cleared," he was told, from somewhere back in the passageway.

"Move the coffle," I heard.

"Move," we were told.

The coffle then moved, over the threshold, out into the night, into the cool air.

Even within the sheet, the smell of smoke was strong.

CHAPTER SIX

What Occurred in the Street; What Occurred Later, in an Alcove

I followed the gentle movement of the rope on my neck, which rope, over the sheet, by my left side, went back to the throat of the girl behind me.

I could feel the stones of the street with my knees and the palms of my hands. Then the coffle was halted. We were not, I was sure, more than some yards from the house, no more I supposed than would be deemed sufficient for our safety.

I wondered if there were sparks drifting in the air.

The alarm bar was still sounding.

Given the sheet covering my head and fastened about my neck, I could see very little. I could see the light of torches as they passed me, and, blocking the light, often, moving darknesses, which must be men. Most were moving down the street, presumably toward the wharves. Twice I was buffeted. "Make way for the pump wagons!" I heard. Two heavy carts trundled by. I heard the scratching of what might be heavy claws on the stones, and heard shouts, and what might be the pounding of sticks on massive bodies, and angry, protestive, snorting, hissing reptilian noises. I shuddered. I knew little of the world to which I had been brought to serve my masters.

"How goes the blaze?" I heard.

"It rages, it will consume the docks," I heard.

"No," said a fellow. "It will be contained. Hundreds are at the wharves. Containers, on their ropes, are cast into gleaming Thassa, and make their way, passed from hand to hand, to be cast upon the fire."

"What of the ships?" asked a man, anxiously.

"Safe," said a man. "Some depart their moorings. Others are guarded, masts lowered, decks and sails soaked."

"What of the house of Flavius Minor?" inquired a man.

"It can scarcely be approached," said a man. "It is in flames, fiercely so. I doubt the fire can be extinguished before morning."

"We will lose more houses," said a man.

"Think of the goods lost," said another.

"The house of Flavius Minor is done," said a man. "Little, if anything, can be saved."

"How did the fire start?" asked a man.

"I do not think that is known," said another.

"The other houses?" inquired a man.

"Much is being brought forth, set on the wharves," said a man.

"And there is theft, fighting, killing, looting, all well-lit by the flames," said a fellow, bitterly.

"Surely there are guardsmen," said a man.

"Not enough," said another.

"They dare not interfere," said a man.

"And some help themselves," said another.

"Let us hurry to the wharves," said another, "quickly, before order is restored, where loot, strewn about, invites seizure."

"Assist, rather, in fighting the flames," said a man.

"Why should others profit, and not we?" asked a man.

"Let us hurry, before the street is sealed off," said a fellow.

Some men, I gathered, then took their leave.

"Lawlessness abounds," said a man, angrily.

"It is strange," said a man. "Some risk their lives to protect the goods of men they do not even know; others, in the same situation, think nothing of seizing goods not their own."

"Dismiss such men from your thoughts," said a fellow. "They are the dregs of the lower districts, aliens, migrants, drifters. They are surely not of Brundisium. Clearly they do not share our Home Stone."

"Perhaps they have no Home Stone," said another.

"Can such a thing be?" said another.

"Yes," said a man. "I have heard that there is a far world, an entire world, without Home Stones."

"How then," asked a man, "could there be honor, order, civility, trust, respect, law, harmony, courage, and fellowship?"

"I do not know," said another.

"It must then be a sorry world," said a man.

"True," said another.

"How could it then be respected, treasured, loved, or cared for?" asked a man.

"I only report what I have heard," said the first man.

I waited on all fours. I had not been given permission to sit, kneel, or lie down. How helpless I felt, my head down, the sheet tied about my neck, hooding me, on the neck rope, one of several slaves so secured. So positioned and hooded, I did not dare to speak, even to ask permission to do so. I did not wish to be whipped. I had recently been sold. I now had a master, whom I did not even know. I remained in my place, as I had been placed. I was bewildered, and frightened. I trembled on the rope, head down, tethered. So much had occurred, so suddenly, so seemingly incomprehensibly! How inexplicably, how radically, my life had changed! Could this have happened to me, I wondered. Could it be? Surely it was not real! But it was real. It must be a dream. But it was not a dream! I had suspected nothing. How naive I had been, no more, for all my supposed intelligence, than a pretty simpleton and fool! I had anticipated nothing! Then it had happened. I had been noted and acquired. I had not realized such things could exist. I felt the harsh stones of the street on my knees and under the palms of my hands. Beneath the sheet I was naked, as a beast and slave is naked, slave naked. There was a collar on my neck, which I could not remove. On my left thigh, high, below the hip, I was marked. I had anticipated nothing, and now I was on Gor, a slave. I recalled the men I had led on, and then rebuffed. How I had despised them! How I had delighted in raising hopes, which I then, to my delight, dashed. How easy it was to lure and then reject a male, to provoke interest and then, pretending innocence, to feign astonishment and dismay when interest was aroused. How I had gloried in the exercise of such vain, petty powers, attracting and then dismissing and humiliating the weaklings of Earth, so little of the man in them, so little of the master! And now I was a slave on Gor! I had little doubt but what the men of Gor would know what to do with me, whatever they wished. And I must strive to please them, wholly, desperately, and as the most female of all females, the female slave. How I longed, a woman of Earth, to lick and kiss the whips of such men!

I think that I was perhaps some two-thirds of the length of the coffle from its front. As we were hooded, we did not have too clear an idea of what was going on, but we knew, surely, about the fire, and were aware of the speech and movements of men about us, some milling, mostly coming and going. Another pump wagon, I gathered, rolled by. The alarm bar was still sounding. Sometimes, as far as we could tell, from shouts and conversations, it seemed the fire was on the verge of being managed, if not extinguished, and then, later, it seemed it raged even more fiercely. This may have had to do with a shift in the wind, easily marked at the docks, but not evident where we were, on the street between buildings, or, perhaps, it was occasioned when the fire reached different materials in the affected building or buildings. We remained as we were. We had not been moved. There was much smoke in the air. Sometimes we were passed by men, some of them coughing, moving up the street, away from the docks, toward the market district. It was not particularly cold, but, as it grew later, I was grateful for the sheet. Through it one could see the light of lanterns. Twice I heard slaves cry out, startled, presumably having been unexpectedly fondled. Little is thought of such attentions when bestowed on a slave. Slaves must expect such things. Resistance is not accepted, for it might displease a master. One is a slave. I heard some drunken men nearby. There must be, I supposed, a tavern in the vicinity. I suspected we had been something like twenty or thirty Ehn in the street, placed to one side of the street that we might not obstruct traffic, and opposite the house of Anesidemus, presumably that we be on the side of the street farthest from the fire. When we had been brought into the street the coffle had soon been turned, that it might, later, be conducted more expeditiously back into the building. As mentioned, I was something like two-thirds of the way back from the head of the coffle.

"I have come from the wharves," said a man. "The fire lessens!"

"Again?" asked a fellow.

"No," said another. "It subsides."

"Good," said another.

I was sure then that we would soon be returned to our cages. This was none too soon for me, as the weather had freshened, and the sheet hooding me and draped over my back, afforded me small comfort. The cage chamber was warm, and each cage was furnished with a small blanket. One, as a slave, an animal, a belonging, is grateful for such things.

There was suddenly an angry shout from somewhere near the head of the coffle. "Ho!" was the cry. "look, lout, where you

are going!" "Move to the side!" "I am here!" "Go about!" "I will
not!" "Do so!" "Impede my way, will you?" "Watch your purse!"
"Sheath your dagger!" "Beware!" "He has a club!" "They are
drunk!" "Peace, peace in the streets!" "Call guardsmen!" "Guardsmen, guardsmen!" I heard a slave scream, from somewhere near
the front of the coffle; then another cried out, perhaps buffeted.
There was clearly something transpiring, something in the nature
of an altercation, some yards ahead, near the beginning of the
coffle. I heard harsh words. Then there must have been a scuffle.
"Fight!" called out more than one man, eagerly. I heard booted
feet racing past me, climbing the street. Brundisium is a major
port, her mighty harbor berthing vessels from a thousand ports,
vessels large and small, square-rigged and lateen-rigged, clinker
built and carvel built, ships mercantile and naval, round ships
and long ships, come from as far as Schendi in the south, and
Torvaldsland to the north, vessels hailing from Tabor, Asperiche,
and Anango, vessels from the mouths of the Cartius and Vosk,
from Port Kar, on the shallow Tamber Gulf, whose waters mingle
with those of Thassa, from the Ubarates of Cos and Tyros, and
the Farther Islands, from as far away, even, as the World's End.
Sometimes these cities are at war with one another, and the "truce
of the port," rather like the "truce of the Sardar fairs," is occasionally sorely stressed. Even putting aside municipal rivalries, wars,
vendettas, blood feuds, and such, it is not difficult to understand,
given that quarters are close on a ship, and discipline unquestioning and severe, sometimes for weeks or months at sea, that strong
men, brawny, vital oarsmen, and such, come ashore, freed of such
restraints, impatient and quick-tempered, copper and silver in
their purses, seeking the taverns, brothels, and gambling houses,
and thence spilling into the streets, drunk on paga, might enliven
civil life, particularly in the wharf districts. "Fight, fight!" called
more than one man hurrying past me. Then my part of the coffle
was suddenly much alone. Through the sheet I was aware of a
lantern nearby. There were also some four or five men, together.
But they were not rushing past me, hastening to witness, if not
participate in, the ruckus toward the head of the coffle.

"Which is she?" I heard.

The lantern was closer now, no longer lifted, but held lower,
at waist level.

"The sheet," I heard, "consider the sheet."

"Here!" said a man's voice.

At the same time a hand was pressed closely over the sheet, over my mouth. I could make not the least sound. My head was pulled up and back, forcibly. Then I felt a knife blade thrusting into, and cutting through the sheet, by my throat. "Be silent, absolutely silent, *kajira*," said a voice, "or you die, instantly." I could not see, for I was still muchly hooded. I felt the blade of the knife, edged like a razor, tight against my throat. I feared if I moved I would cut my own throat. Terrified, I remained absolutely still.

I sensed someone cutting the coffle rope, before me, and then behind me.

"I am going to remove my hand from your mouth, *kajira*," I heard. "As soon as I do, you will open your mouth as widely as possible." I could still feel the knife against my throat. The hand was suddenly jerked from my mouth, upward, and it thrust the sheet up, though not enough that I could see. At the same time, the knife at my throat, I opened my mouth as widely as possible. No sooner had I opened my mouth than a folded leather wadding was thrust into it, deeply, which expanded, as it was secured with cords, tightly, behind the back of my neck, over the sheet. An opaque, lined canvas hood was then pulled over my head and buckled under my chin.

"Get rid of the sheet, as you can," said a voice softly. "This is to be a common slave, one off the streets, one out of the taverns."

"Ho," whispered one of the men. "This is a pretty one."

The sheet, its neck cord cut, was muchly pulled away. Little remained of it now but part of that which had had hooded me, now enclosed within the canvas hood, and, I suspect, a shred or two caught under the gag's fastening.

"*Bara*," I was told.

Instantly I went to *bara*. The stones of the street were damp, and cold. My head was turned to the left. My wrists, as I had crossed them behind me, were quickly, expertly, snugly, thonged. Then my ankles, which I had crossed behind me, were similarly served. The fellow was clearly familiar with the handling and binding of slaves. More than once in my training, I had been similarly tied. Once I had been left for Ahn, encouraged to free myself. I could not, of course, begin to do so. Gorean capture knots are not meant to be escaped. The slender thongs might have been burst with a man's strength, but they were more than adequate to hold a woman. I was helpless, woman helpless, slave helpless.

I do not think that Fina, before me, and the girl behind me, both hooded, were aware of what was transpiring. The men spoke softly, and there was still much shouting and tumult at the head of the coffle. Too, men were passing, in the darkness, to and fro, sometimes conversing, or calling out. I even heard a woman's voice, as well. The slaver's men, if aware of what was transpiring, would doubtless have intervened, taking one action or another, but it seems they were at the head of the coffle, trying to soothe disputants. Passers-by might be aware of little but a slave's being cut out of the coffle, for one reason or another.

When the knife had been at my throat, I had, of course, dared not disobey. Yet, interestingly, I knew that even if the knife had not been poised at my throat, I would have obeyed, instantly and unquestioningly. I was no longer a free woman of Earth. I was now a Gorean slave girl. I had learned my sex, and that I must obey men.

I was lifted to the right shoulder of one of the men, my head to the rear.

I squirmed a little, futilely.

I realized that I was being carried downward toward the wharves.

We had gone only a few steps when one of the men whispered, "A guardsman."

"Hold," I heard, a new voice.

We stopped.

"Where are you going with that slave?" asked the guardsman.

"She is a stray," said he who carried me. "We are returning her to the chains of an alcove."

"The Sea Sleen?" asked the guardsman.

"Yes," he was told.

I began to struggle violently, trying to communicate my distress to the guardsman.

"No wonder she is agitated," said the guardsman. "Is she to be mutilated and hamstrung or merely beaten?"

"That must be decided," said he who carried me.

I instantly lay quietly.

"Good girl," I heard.

I would be still.

I did not want to be mutilated or hamstrung. I feared even the whip, as a slave girl fears the whip. I had felt it on the day when I was branded, when my wrists, as those of the other slaves, bound together, had been high over my head, fastened to the overhead chain. I had felt it, too, twice, in my training. Those who do not fear the whip have not felt it. The whip, even hanging inertly on its peg, keeps a girl well in her place. The slave girl attempts to please; she well knows that she is subject to the whip, and that it will be used on her if she is not pleasing. That is fully appropriate. She is a slave.

"How goes the fire?" asked one of the men in our party.

"Well," he was told. "It is contained."

"Good," said a man.

I supposed the reduction of the fire had something to do with the guardsman's present location, presumably leaving the vicinity of the fire. Also, I realized that the alarm bar was no longer sounding.

"I wish you well," said the guardsman.

"I wish you well," said he who carried me.

We then continued on our way, down the street, toward the wharves.

Slaves, as other properties, may be stolen. The common procedure is to take the girl to another city, preferably far off, and sell her there. Many slave girls are chained at night to the foot of the master's couch, usually naked. Few things better convince a girl that she is a slave. On the other hand, aside from its monitory, custodial, and instructive aspects, and its convenience for the master, this arrangement also reduces the likelihood of slave theft.

What I could not understand was why I should have been stolen and not another. Surely several of my sister slaves were more attractive than I, though, to be sure, much depends on the interests and tastes of a given master. I was even a barbarian.

Surely anyone would have done as well as I. I hoped they would not object to my being a barbarian. On the other hand, some Gorean masters are fond of barbarians, taking them in hand and teaching them the collar.

How startling it is for a woman of Earth to learn that she is no longer free, and is now to be taught a collar.

The intelligent girl learns it quickly.

I knew, even from Earth, that it belonged on my neck.

But I did not want to be stolen.

I wanted a kind, but firm, master, one who would fulfill my slave, that yearning, hoping, needful slave which was I.

The ambiance of our journey suddenly changed, as he who carried me turned to the left. I heard the swinging of the leaves of a door, and then conversation, and the clink of goblets. A flute was playing somewhere inside. I and my party, sometimes stopped, apparently passed through some men and, perhaps, tables. The chamber was crowded. When we were stopped, I was touched more than once, and pinched sharply, twice. I knew such things were done to slaves but I was not accustomed to being subjected to such attentions. Such things, in their way, of course, are compliments. They indicate that the slave has been found of interest. It would be unthinkable of course, to do such things to a free woman. The free woman is not a slave. I heard a stout leather curtain being swept aside. I was then deposited on a bedding of thick furs, and a manacle was snapped about my left ankle. I was then, as far as I knew, left alone. I heard the leather curtain drawn shut. I did not know how many men had been involved in my theft, but I thought at least four. I tried the bonds a little, uselessly, and then lay quietly. Out in the street, there had been mention of the Sea Sleen, which must be a tavern. I was sure then that I lay in an alcove, presumably in the Sea Sleen, a tavern, an alcove to which such as a paga girl, whose use goes with the price of a drink, might be brought.

How horrifying, I thought, to be a paga girl.

Yet I thought, as I had heard, how zealously they compete to please the masters! They were desperate to have about them the arms of masters, and those who might be less zealous would be whipped, until they, too, later, their slave fires kindled, and raging, would compete as well, and desperately, to draw themselves, as the others, to the attention of free men, hoping and begging to be chained at their mercy.

Perhaps some might so interest a man that he might buy them.

What slave does not wish to kneel at the feet of a private master?

It is permissible for a slave to beg to be purchased.

What slave is not familiar with the "Buy me, Master" call?

I lay in the furs, seemingly neglected.

I thought it must be in an Ahn or so before dawn.

I could feel the weight of the shackle on my left ankle. I moved my leg, pulling on it a little, and gauged that its chain was fastened to the wall to the left of the alcove as it would be entered. I did not know who bore the key to that shackle. I was in no danger, on such a chain, of being again stolen. The thieves who had taken me had assured themselves that I would remain in the alcove, secure from being carried away, hooded and bound, as I might be, by another.

"The guardsman did not return?" asked a male voice, softly, on the other side of the leather curtain.

"No," he was told, "nor are there others about."

"There is no sign of suspicion, or pursuit?" asked the first voice.

"None," said the second voice. "We can move her, safely."

"Best before light," said another.

"I would be done with this," said a voice. "Let us proceed. I am anxious to collect the balance of our fee."

"Why should anyone pay so much to reclaim a single slave, particularly one sold only in the house of Anesidemus?"

"Do not inquire," said another. "The world is filled with mad men. Fill your purse, and be content."

I heard someone at the curtain, apparently preparing to draw it aside.

"Your mask," he was told.

There was a moment's pause, and then the curtain was pushed back.

Someone entered the alcove. Then a key was thrust into the shackle, and it was parted, and put aside.

At this point, from outside, presumably from within another alcove, I heard a woman cry out with misery, and then I heard, again and again, the fall of a lash.

Some slave, I gathered, had failed to be fully pleasing. Perhaps she had spoken without permission; perhaps she had uttered a tart word; perhaps she had seemed the least bit cross, impatient, or critical; perhaps she had been hesitant to obey or, demurring, had questioned a command. Perhaps her manner had suggested something of the haughtiness of the free woman. Perhaps her fault lay in her diction or in some subtle lapse of deference.

I heard the lash fall, six times more.

Perhaps she had dared to put on airs.

I supposed that she was now well reminded that she was a slave, not a free woman.

I lay very quietly.

I felt the hands of a man unbuckle the lined, canvas hood I wore, and then it was thrust up, and pulled from my head. He who had removed the hood was masked. He brushed away the bit of the sheet which had been trapped within the hood. I blinked my eyes against the feeble light, from the small lamp in the alcove. I dared not meet the eyes of a free man. Then to my relief he undid the gag's binding from behind my neck and drew the detestable gag, with its wadding, away. I had a foul taste in my mouth.

He stood up, standing over me, and put the gag and the hood in his pouch.

I had some sense of the alcove, the depth of the furs, the leather curtain, the tiny lamp in its niche, to the left as one would enter, chains, manacles and shackles, strands of leather, a coil of rope, a whip, a switch, such things.

Paga girls, I knew, could be ordered to such an alcove.

How much they were at the mercy of free men, but are not all slaves at the mercy of the free?

The curtain was open. I could see men and tables outside.

I saw a flash of silk and a lithe, collared beauty, bearing a goblet, moved past the opening of the alcove, and, having approached one of the tables, knelt before it, and, her head down between her extended arms, proffered the goblet to a fellow sitting cross-legged at the table, who took the cup, scarcely noticing her, and continued his conversation with two other fellows, similarly seated. She then withdrew, gracefully, rising and backing away.

The flute was still playing.

The fellow in the alcove had not moved.

I lay on my right side before him, naked, bound hand and foot.

I had been an arrogant, proud woman of Earth, selfish and vain, inpatient and demanding, one fond of exploiting and taunting men. I now lay at the feet of a Gorean male. I rolled to my stomach and pressed my cheek softly against his boot. I then, my head down, pressed my lips to his boots, and kissed and licked them.

He drew me to a sitting position, and, kneeling a bit behind me, drew a vial and a soft cloth from his pouch. From the contents of the vial he dampened the cloth.

"You are going to take a little nap, *kajira*," he said.

He then held the cloth over my nose and mouth, and shortly thereafter I lost consciousness.

CHAPTER SEVEN

What Occurred on Board a Moored Ship; The One-Legged Man; A Case of Mistaken Identity

I awakened.

I had again been hooded.

My right shoulder was sore and my right hip, from how I had been placed, on my right side, on the boards.

I was still naked. One thinks little of such things with a slave. Masters are often fond of keeping their girls naked. Too, naked, the slave, in her collar, contrasts nicely with those who are fully clothed. But, too, of course, the tunic, the camisk, the ta-teera, or slave rag, and such, serve much the same purpose. Such things, such habiliments, mark the slave, as well as her collar and brand. Many things distinguish the slave from the free.

On Gor that distinction is momentous.

My hands and feet were still bound.

I was no longer gagged.

I felt a slight movement of the floor, a subtle rocking motion, and realized I must be on some ship. The ship was, I conjectured, from the movement, not at sea, but moored, presumably one of a great many ships berthed at the wharves of Brundisium.

"He will be here shortly," said a voice. I recognized it. It was that of one of the men who had removed me from the coffle of Anesidemus.

"Is he on board?" asked one of the men who had abducted me.

"I think so," said another.

I suspected that I, while unconscious, and being transported to this point, had not been hooded. If there were alarms, monitions, or notices about, pertaining to a stolen slave, surely a hooded girl might arouse suspicion. On the other hand, one carried openly, boldly, about, would be likely to attract little attention. By not hiding her she might be best hidden, so to speak. But here, it seemed, on this moored craft or barge, the hood had been replaced. I suspected this was because the men were not now masked, and did not wish me to see their faces. I recalled that the fellow in the alcove had masked himself before entering the alcove. On the other hand, the explanation might be simpler.

We are slaves. They like to keep us helpless.

How better to remind a girl that she is a slave?

"I wish he would hurry," said a man. "I want our second silver stater before the tide turns."

"What a fool he is," said another, "to give two silver staters for the recovery of a single slave. One might buy six for such a price, even in Brundisium."

"Perhaps he misses her, and is fond of her," said a man.

"Fond," asked another, "of a slave?"

"Some men are such," said another.

"Fools," said the first.

I sensed there were more men in the chamber, or cabin, than the four I had conjectured earlier.

"I think vengeance is involved," said a man. "She must have strayed, or run away, and then been picked up and subsequently sold to the house of Anesidemus. I would guess he wants to cut off her nose and ears, and feet, and then cast her into a public garbage pit, where she may then compete with urts for the peels of larmas and suls."

"He is late," said a man.

"His pace is measured," said a man, "and I think he does not care to be noted."

"Hold," said a fellow. "I think he is coming.'

I tried to listen.

Someone, or something, was approaching, perhaps through a nearby corridor or companionway.

There would be a silence, and then, a moment later, a sound, as of wood striking wood, coming ever closer.

"Masks," said a man.

The masks, I suspected, were for my benefit.

"How shall we address him?" asked a man.

"As he wishes," said he whom I conjectured was first amongst my abductors, "as Bruno of Torcadino."

"He is no more of Torcadino than I am," said a man.

"No," said another. "Suspicious, I referred to the drought-threatened reservoir of Torcadino, and he did not respond or gainsay me."

"Not everyone knows," said another "that the fountains of Torcadino are fed from an aqueduct, its waters drained from the heights of the Voltai."

"He comes from the World's End," said one of the men.

"Yet his accent suggests Ar," said another.

I heard a door open. I sensed the men had risen to their feet. There must have been at least ten in the room.

"Tal, noble Bruno of Torcadino," said he whom I took to be chief amongst my abductors."

"Tal," said a harsh voice, enflamed with eagerness.

"I report the successful completion of our charge," said he whom I took to be the leader of my abductors. "Indeed, we did not even need to fire a building last night as planned, that the slaves of the house of Anesidemus be brought into the street. Chance bestowed upon us a signal advantage, as, delightfully, an independent fire broke out on the wharves, originating in the house of Flavius Minor. It was easy to take advantage of this felicitous coincidence. Our confederates in the house of Anesidemus, suborned employees of the house, as directed, put your slave, Luta, toward the back of the coffle and put the marked sheet over her, that she be easily recognized. Six of us staged the diversion you prescribed at the head of the coffle and while the attention of the men of Anesidemus was thus engaged, the rest of us obtained your Luta, who now lies before you, returned to you, helpless, hooded, and bound."

"Excellent, excellent!" cried the newcomer, and I heard wood strike wood, sharply, thrice, as, I gathered, he approached more closely.

"We now claim the balance of our fee," said he whom I took to be chief amongst my abductors.

"Another silver stater," said another of the men.

"Haste is important, time is short, the tide," said another.

"Yes, yes!" said the newcomer. "You shall have it!"

I heard two more strokes of wood on wood. I conjectured that the newcomer carried a staff, which he, for some reason, saw fit to strike on the floor before him, as he moved. Sometimes it scraped on the boards.

"The stater," said a man.

"Something is awry," said the newcomer, suddenly, wildly.

"Bring her more into the light," said he whom I took to be the leader of my abductors.

I was dragged, by a bound arm, some feet across the floor, close now, I thought, to the newcomer.

"Fools, fools!" cried the newcomer.

"Unhood her!" said he whom I took to be chief amongst my abductors.

The hood was hastily unbuckled and drawn away.

"There is your Luta," said he whom I took to be first amongst my abductors.

I gasped, helpless, trembling.

The men were masked, with the exception of the newcomer, whose visage, as he glared down at me, was terrible with rage. He was bearded, fierce- eyed, wolf-eyed, and mighty of mien. Seldom had I looked upon features more forbidding; seldom had I sensed greater menace in a countenance. Too, this looming figure, so fierce in aspect, had but one leg. What I had heard striking on the floor was the base of a heavy, rounded crutch, whose height was fitted into a stout, rounded crosspiece. That aid to balance, that support, in itself, might have constituted a formidable weapon. I sensed that this large figure, terrifying even now, must, before the loss of its limb, have been an unusually quick, intelligent, active, dangerous man, and surely the remnants of such features yet lingered in the frame before me.

"That is not she!" he cried. "The hair is brown, not black, not like the sheen of sable tarn; the complexion is wrong; the eyes are wrong! That is not she!"

"It was she who was covered in the marked sheet," said a man.

"Impossible," said the one-legged man. "What game is this? Do you think me a fool?"

"Do you think we are fools?" asked a man.

"Here are the remains of the marked sheet," said he whom I took to be first amongst my abductors, at the same time drawing a goodly portion of the sheet from his pouch. "I brought it to confirm our catch."

"And to guard against your reneging or betrayal," said another man.

"This is she whom the sheet bedecked," said another man. "Give us our money."

"This is not the slave," said the one-legged man.

"I do not understand," said he whom I took to be first amongst my abductors. "What happened?"

"You have been tricked! We have all been tricked!" said the one-legged man.

He then lifted his head and howled with rage and disappointment.

"He is mad," said a fellow, uneasily.

"We have done our work," said another. "Give us now our stater, a silver stater, one of Brundisium."

"Would I had my leg, and a sword!" cried the one-legged man. "You would pay me ten gold staters, to be permitted to live!"

"Take this slave, instead," said he whom I took to be the leader of my abductors, brushing me with his boot. "She is comely, a likely slut, a pleasant item, an attractive piece of collar meat. Surely she will squirm and kick, as well as another."

So, I thought, this is the light in which men think of slaves. But is it not one of the things that slaves are for? I had little doubt but what, in time, in the arms of a master, I, once of Earth, now a Gorean slave, would squirm and kick, uncontrollably, helplessly. Slave fires had begun to burn in my belly. I would be unable to help myself, nor would I wish to do so. How free a slave is, to be a woman! How could one be more a woman, than a slave?

"My Luta," screamed the one-legged man, "was sold last night! By now she has doubtless been picked up and might be anywhere."

"No slave, Luta, was sold last night," said a man.

"Fool," cried the one-legged man. "She was not sold under that name, but another!"

"What name?" asked he whom I took to be the leader of my abductors.

"Adraste!" cried the one-legged man.

"Ah," said a fellow, "I remember that one, a beauty, but not yet broken to her collar."

"That can be done with any woman," said a man.

"Who bought my Luta?" snarled the one-legged man. "I want his name, his caste, his city!"

"The House of Anesidemus does not keep such records," said the man. I took it that he had not only been present at the sales last night, but was familiar with the practices of the house. In-

deed, I wondered if he might not be an employee of the house,
though I had not seen him amongst the slaver's men. I surmised
that he, at least, must be in contact with someone in the house. I
was not surprised, given what I knew of the House of Anesidemus, that they kept no records. It was a dingy, poorly located
house. I would not have been surprised if they handled stolen and
contraband slaves. It would be difficult, I gathered, to trace a slave
marketed through such a house.

"Show me the sheet," said the one-legged man.

This was done.

"See the mark?" said he whom I took to be the leader of my
abductors.

"It is the mark, it is the right sheet," said the one-legged man.
"The sheet was changed."

"Why would that be?" asked he whom I took to be first
amongst my abductors.

The one-legged man looked down, angrily.

"There is more here, I suspect," said he whom I took to be
chief amongst my abductors, "than you have made clear to us."

"It is a private matter," said the one-legged man, looking from
face to face. I sensed that, if he had been whole, and armed, he
might have moved with a terrible swiftness, and that none of my
abductors, though they were ten in number, would have left the
chamber, which I now saw to be a cabin, alive.

"I would know the substance of this private matter," said he
whom I took to be the leader of my abductors.

The one-legged man, scowling, was silent.

"Why would you risk two staters of silver, weighty staters,
staters of Brundisium, worth several silver tarsks of most cities,
to recover a single slave?" asked he whom I took to be the leader
of my abductors.

"Return to me my silver stater," said the one-legged man. "You
have failed, abjectly, miserably. You have not earned it."

"We discharged our commission, in good faith," said he whom
I took to be the leader of my abductors. "We took risks. The streets
were troubled. Men of the House of Anesidemus might have noted
us. Guardsmen were about. We could have been set upon by citizens. We did our part. The error was not ours."

"Return to me my stater," said the one-legged man.

"We brought you the girl under the marked sheet," said a
man. "That was our task. It was done. Give us the second stater!"

"Get out," snarled the one-legged man. "Get out!"

"He was prepared to pay," said one of my abductors. "Thus he has the stater with him, and perhaps more. We are ten. He is only part of a man. Let us collect our fee, and more, given our trouble."

"Yes," said more than one man, eagerly.

The one-legged man crouched down on his one leg, and both hands gripped the crutch. It was as though he, steadying himself, had grasped a small tree. I sensed how it might lash out. I would not have cared to be the first to approach him. The eyes of the one-legged man moved from one of the men to another. "Who will be first?" he asked.

The men looked from one to the other.

"I will tell you," said the one-legged man. "He will be first who is most eager to die."

"Time is short," said a man. "The tide."

"Let us be content," said another. "We have a stater, a silver stater, of Brundisium. That is not a bad fee for a night's work."

"But he has more," said another man.

"Then go, and take the more from him," said another.

But the man did not move.

"I wish you well, noble Bruno of Torcadino," said he whom I took to be the leader of my abductors.

"Leave the slave," said he so addressed. "I can sell her."

"I think not," said he whom I took to be first amongst my abductors. He then crouched down, beside me, and, with strong fingers, undid the thongs on my ankles. He then seized me by the left arm and drew me to my feet. He steadied me, holding me, as I might, having had my ankles bound for so long, have fallen.

"You cannot sell her," said the one-legged man, "not here, not safely, so soon, in Brundisium. She is doubtless in the collar of the House of Anesidemus. Guardsmen may have her description. The wharves may be watched."

"We will sell her to you for a silver stater, of Brundisium," said he whom I took to be the leader of my abductors.

There was much laughter.

"Get out," snarled the one-legged man.

"What is your true name?" asked one of my abductors.

"Bruno, of Torcadino," said the one-legged man.

"And mine," said a fellow, "is Marlenus, of Ar."

There was laughter.

I had heard the name 'Marlenus' before. I gathered that he, for some reason, was well known.

"Get out!" hissed the one-legged man.

"Can you stand?" asked he whom I took to be the leader of my abductors.

"Yes, Master," I said, "now."

He then, still steadying me, conducted me into the corridor or companionway, outside the cabin. His men followed him. The one-legged man did not follow us, but remained in the cabin. I heard him cry out in frustration and anger, and strike his crutch savagely on the floor behind us. I sensed he was capable of terrible violence. I feared such a temper.

"May we hood you, pretty kajira?" inquired he whom I took to be chief amongst my abductors.

I was terrified that he had addressed this question to me, as though my permission might have been required. "Please, Master," I begged, "do not whip me!"

The slave girl is always vulnerable to the whip.

He smiled, and shook out the hood, preparing to draw it over my head.

"I do not understand the so-called Bruno of Torcadino," said one of my abductors. "Why would he not have bid upon this Luta, or Adraste, openly, at the auction?"

"He seems concerned to conceal his identity," said he whom I took to be the leader of my abductors.

"Why?" asked another.

I did not regard it as wise to be standing amidst free men speaking. Accordingly, I knelt. In such a situation it is common for a slave to be on her knees. In such a situation, is not that where she belongs?

"I do not know," said he whom I took to be first amongst my abductors.

"What is her interest or importance?" asked another. "Why would he offer so much to have her stolen?"

"He claims to be her former master, desiring to recover her," said another.

"Perhaps eager to have her again at his slave ring," said another.

"Or angry, to enact a vengeance upon her," said yet another.

I knelt among the men, naked, my head down, my hands thonged behind my back. I was not noticed, as slaves are often not noticed. How strange it seemed. How helpless I was! How different things were! How faraway was Earth!

"I doubt he ever owned her," said he whom I took to be the leader of my abductors.

"Then he is acting for another," said a man.

"Consider him," said he whom I took to be the leader of my abductors. "He does not seem to be one likely to act for another."

"Then her value goes beyond her slave price," said a man.

"I think so," said another. "If he was willing to expend two silver staters to obtain her, she is probably worth more to him than two silver staters."

"I think, somehow, much more," said he whom I took to be the leader of my abductors.

"How could that be?" asked a man.

"I do not know," said he whom I took to be the leader of my abductors.

It seemed to me that the masters were overlooking a most obvious possibility. I lifted my head to he whom I took to be the leader of my abductors. "May I speak, Master?" I asked.

The men seemed startled that I had spoken. This made me uneasy. One does not care to be kicked or cuffed. Even a master's frown can be frightening.

I feared I should not have called attention to myself. Commonly a slave is to be at hand, ready to serve at so little as a glance or a snapping of fingers, but is not to be obtrusive.

"Yes," he said.

"I have gathered that masters are puzzled, as to aspects of the night's business," I said.

"Very much so," he said.

"I think, Master," I said, "that I understand the mystery of Adraste, the motivation of Master Bruno, and why, apparently, such a large sum of money, surprisingly, was involved."

"I attend," he said. "What is your conjecture?"

"I know Adraste slightly," I said. "We were caged in proximity to one another. She was, I gather, if she was not lying, of high caste, and of some prominence. The matter then is simple. Suppose her family is wealthy and of high station. Perhaps Bruno of Torcadino is a relative, and wishes to recover her, to restore her to the glories of her freedom, but, to avoid shame and scandal, wishes to do so surreptitiously. Better that it not be known that she was ever in a collar. Thus he would not wish to be identified, and would be willing to pay a ransom, so to speak, far beyond what I take would be the value of a mere slave." I was pleased with this conjecture, and puzzled that something so plausible had not figured in the conversation of the masters.

My words were greeted with amusement. I was chagrined. I saw no cause for merriment in what I had said. I thought it plausible, insightful.

"You are a barbarian, are you not?" he asked.

"Yes, Master," I said. "Doubtless my accent has given me away."

"Rather, your ignorance," he said.

"Master?" I said.

"You have not been long on Gor, have you?" he asked.

"No, Master," I said.

"Do you realize that you are a slave?" he asked.

"Yes, Master," I said.

"Fully?" he asked.

"Yes, Master," I said. I had no doubt about that. I realized that every inch of me was a slave.

"Perhaps you realize, and fully, that you are a slave," he said, "but perhaps you do not realize, and fully, what it is to be a slave—on Gor," he said.

"Master?" I said.

"Perhaps you do not yet realize the degradation, the debasement, the wholeness of the collar," he said.

"I do not understand," I said.

"Consider the stain to a family's honor," he said. "Suppose a daughter is enslaved, that she is marked and collared. Who could support such things? She is then no longer of the family. She is then repudiated, and denied. She is ignored and forgotten. She is then only a beast, a slave. What family could endure such shame? What a reproach is there, what a humiliation! She will commonly be kept in her collar. She may be retained as a house slave, no different from the other house slaves, save that she, a former mistress, will now be the least amongst her fellow slaves. Most often she will be sold to a far city, and all records of her past destroyed. At best, she will be hidden away, a humiliation, an embarrassment, kept from view, kept sequestered in her shame."

"I did not know," I said.

"Perhaps now you better understand what it is to be a slave on Gor," he said.

"Yes, Master," I whispered. I now better understood the meaning of my collar, how, as a slave, I was viewed. I was nothing, an
object to be bought and sold. My bondage was abject. How abased
I was! And yet I relished my abasement. I wanted to be a slave. I
had always wanted it. I rejoiced in the collar I wore, which I could
not remove.

"Up, *kajira*," he said.

I rose to my feet.

The lined canvas hood was then drawn over my head, and
buckled under my chin. My hands were still thonged together,
behind my back.

Before my head was enclosed in the hood I lifted my eyes,
briefly, to those of he whom I took to be first amongst my abductors. His mask, black, covered most of his face. I noted a small,
triangular scar on the right side of his face, low, to the right of
his mouth. Then I lowered my eyes, fearing that I might be found
presumptuous, and the hood was drawn over my head, and fastened in place.

"Masks," said he.

And I gathered then that the masks worn by the men were
removed.

We moved to the open, to the deck. I could feel the change in
the air.

"Is the way clear?" he asked.

"Yes," he was told.

I was steadied on the gangplank, a hand on my arm, as we left
the ship.

CHAPTER EIGHT

What Occurred at Sea

The hatch was thrown back.

I could see the sky, a bright blue, with white, scudding clouds.

I had been freed of my ankle chain, fastening me to a ring below.

I was to be permitted on deck.

Gratefully, I climbed the ladder.

I was no longer ill. We had been some days at sea. We were moving north.

I paused near the top of the ladder. The sun, Tor-tu-Gor, was high, and hot. The deck would be warm. There was a gentle wind from astern. I saw the long, large, low-rigged sail, so beautiful, sweet with wind. The vessel, gently rolling, was moving well. I could see the shore to our right. Most Gorean vessels remain, when possible, in sight of land. Indeed, many beach at the end of the day, and return to the water in the morning. The oarsmen were idle, resting, or amusing themselves, some with cards, or the game of stones. Two were playing a board game. It is called 'kaissa'. The pieces had a tiny spike on the bottom, which would be inserted into corresponding holes in the squares of the board. In this way, the movement of the ship, rolling, breasting swells, and such, will not dislodge the pieces. Yesterday, one of oarsmen, in camp, had strummed a stringed instrument, a kalika. The hortator was sleeping next to his mallets and drum. The two helmsmen were in their places, as the ship was double ruddered. The mast was fixed, which is common in round ships. In a ram ship, the mast can be raised and lowered. This makes the ship, when the mast is lowered, more difficult to detect, and, in battle, the mast and sail down, the ship is less vulnerable and more maneuverable.

A lookout was currently atop its height. Another was at the stern. He seemed vigilant. I crawled from the ladder, onto the gently rolling deck, and, on all fours, approached the keeper. It would not be my first time on deck. I was, of course, naked. Slaves are commonly transported that way.

When I reached the keeper I put my head down, and licked and kissed his feet. Such forms of deference are suitable for a slave. The slave is slave. The master is master. I felt happy, and fulfilled, to do this. I had never, on Earth, known men such as those of Gor. Perhaps they existed, possibly in secret, but I never knew them. How privileged I felt, a barbarian, a woman of Earth, in her collar, to be permitted to lick and kiss the feet of a Gorean male. He had permitted it. Not all slaves are permitted to touch the body of a master. "May I speak, Master?" I whispered. "Yes," he said. "Zia is grateful," I said, "to be permitted to come on deck, to feel the air, the freshness, the sun, and wind."

"It will not be necessary to chain you to a deck ring, will it?" he asked.

I was startled. I looked up at him, from all fours. "No, Master," I said.

"Good," he said, and turned away. "Is all clear?" he called to the lookout at the stern. "Yes," he was told. "Is all clear?" he called to the lookout within his ring, near the summit of the mast. "Yes," he was told. He then went to converse with one of the helmsmen.

The keeper was commonly generous in permitting the slaves time on deck. I certainly looked forward to such interludes, freed from my chain in the hold. I touched the new collar at my throat. It had never been read to me. I did not think the keeper was my master. I did not know to whom I belonged. Not in the vicinity of a free person I rose to my feet, and went to the rail, to look out, and saw the shore in the distance.

"She is a pretty one," said an oarsman.

I was pleased, pretending not to hear. The air was bracing. I loved the sound of the timbers of the ship, creaking, the sound of the long yard, responding to the wind, the occasional snap of the canvas.

"She will do," said his fellow.

It was not my fault if many slaves were more beautiful than I, or, in any event, would sell for more than I. I had been found acceptable by slavers, had been brought to this world, had been branded, collared, and sold. Surely some men had found me of interest. Otherwise I would not now be in a collar. To be sure, I supposed that notions of female beauty might vary from one time, and one culture, to another. Interestingly, the figures of most of the slaves I had seen were very much those of the typical, natural woman, a bit short, and well-curved, as opposed to those often favored in commercial advertising on my former world.

"She is a barbarian," said the first oarsman.

"Barbarians juice helplessly," said the second.

I blushed. I did not think that this was detected. I trusted not. But why should I have blushed? Surely there was nothing wrong with being vital, and needful. Certainly masters would not object to having a hot, needful, begging slave at their feet. What man, truly, does not want a woman so?

"Perhaps you can buy her," said the first oarsman.

"I do not think she is for sale," said the second.

I did not understand that. I thought that I would be for sale.

I looked to one side.

She was there, the girl who, allowed on deck, had sprung overboard. I had heard the splash, and the shouts, earlier in the afternoon. At the foot of the ladder, below the closed hatch, I, and the two other girls, on our ankle chains, fastened to the ring fixed in the floor of the hold, had strained to hear. "I wish you well, Fools!" she had cried. "Now I escape!" "Let her go," we heard.

I supposed she hoped to swim to the shore, perhaps a pasang or so off to the right.

Why, I wondered, were the masters willing to view her departure with such equanimity?

How she had abused the privilege of being allowed on deck!

Happily, it seemed, her action had not resulted in the suspension of such a privilege for myself and the other two. The four of us had been purchased in Brundisium, from different houses. I was the only one who had been purchased from the House of Anesidemus. Our ship was a merchant vessel, called a "round ship," though its beam was not that much broader than that of a long ship, as I now know, with its ram and shearing blades. Our cargo, other than ourselves, was largely carvings and vessels of jade, a green gemstone, purchased in Brundisium, and apparently brought in as trade goods from afar, from, as it was said, "the World's End."

"She swims well," had said one of oarsmen, presumably at the rail, watching.

"She was a bath girl, at the Capacian, in Ar," had said another oarsman, presumably watching, as well.

I had been angry at the fugitive. Perhaps now, I had thought, the privileges of the deck might be denied to the rest of us, privileges we coveted and for which, occasionally, we had long waited.

"Take in some sail," I heard.

Were they not going to lower the longboat, and pursue the fugitive? The swiftly rowed longboat could overtake her in a short time, long before she could reach the shore. And should she manage to reach the shore, I had little doubt but what her pursuers, young, long-striding men, would easily outrun her and bring her back to the beach on a rope. If not, a sleen might be rented from a village. This beast, of which I had heard, given the scent of her blanket, might then lead her pursuers to her, or, depending on the command, herd her back to the shore, where her pursuers, perhaps encamped, would be waiting.

But the men, interestingly, did not seem interested in pursuing her. I did not realize why this might be.

Surely she was of some value. Are we not all of some value?

"What a fool she is," said one of my sister slaves.

I did not think her a fool, but I thought her act horribly ill-judged, and foolish. Surely it could only have been motivated by some terror or desperation. Surely she could not think seriously of escape. She, as we, was naked, collared, and branded. There is nowhere to escape to. The world sees us as slaves, and will keep us as slaves. The most that might be achieved, if one were not, to one's dread and terror, returned to a displeased master, would be to fall into a new slavery and, as one would be recognized as a fugitive or stray, a far sterner slavery. There is no escape for the Gorean slave girl.

I was terrified even to think of escape. I did not want to be whipped. I did not want to be hamstrung, or have my feet cut off. I did not wish to lose my ears and nose. I did not wish to be run for sleen. I did not wish to be cast to blood-hungry plants. I did not wish to be tied in the woods and left for the feeding of wild sleen or the nibblings of urts.

So, I wondered, what could have motivated the slave's effort to escape? What did she fear so terribly that she was willing to try to escape?

Still the men did not lower the longboat. "Let her go," one of them had said. I did not understand this. Were they really "letting her go"?

"They are turning," said a man. "They are closing in."

I did not understand this.

"She will see them in a moment," said one of the oarsmen.

"The fins," said another.

There was, at that point, a scream of misery, a woman's voice, a cry of unmitigated terror, from several yards to the right of the ship.

"Do you think she will have time to return to the ship?" asked an oarsman.

"I do not know," said another. "She is a good swimmer."

"She has turned about. She is returning to the ship," said an oarsman.

"She swims well," said another.

"She should," said another. "She is swimming for her life."

"Will we take her aboard again?" asked an oarsman.

"The captain will decide," said another.

"Masters!" shrieked the girl. "Oh!" she cried.

"One of them investigates her," said an oarsman.

"Oh!" cried the girl.

"And now another," said an oarsman.

"I advise you not to thrash about," said an oarsman, presumably to the girl in the water.

I gathered several of the oarsmen had gathered at the rail, watching.

I supposed that a thrashing in the water might, as it suggested injury or distress, lure in marine predators. Fish thrashing at the end of a line, might be half eaten before they could be brought into a boat.

"Oh!" cried the girl again.

"At least she is not bleeding," said an oarsman.

I had heard of marine predators who could detect blood in the water at a distance of half a pasang.

"She has been displeasing," said a fellow. "Let us bring her aboard, cut her, and then throw her back in the water."

"Masters! Masters!" I heard.

I recalled something I had heard, from long ago, that sharks, even far from shore, may follow a ship for days, to feed on garbage thrown overboard. To be sure, such creatures are most likely to be found in the vicinity of shallower waters, where the sunlight encourages the marine growth which lures in smaller fish to feed. Such creatures, too, given their biological rhythms, are suppos-

edly most active and dangerous early in the morning and toward
dusk, in the morning after a night of hunger, one supposes, and,
prior to the falling of darkness, to obtain enough nourishment to
carry them through a foodless night.

"Please, Masters! Save me!" cried the girl.

"That big one is going to make its strike," said an oarsman.
"He is clearly satisfied."

"He is going to roll," said another.

The same extended, tapering snout which facilitates a smooth
knifelike movement in the water militates against a direct seizing
of prey. Accordingly, the creature rolls to its side to bring its wide,
fang-lined, traplike mouth into play.

"Masters, mercy!" screamed the girl.

"Captain?" asked a man.

"Put down an oar," said a voice.

We gathered then, from the foot of the ladder, under the closed
hatch, in the hold, that an oar had been lowered, which had been
seized by the slave, who had then been brought, cold, terrified,
shuddering, and soaked, to the deck.

"Shall we whip her?" asked a man.

"No," said a voice, presumably that of the captain. "Chain her
to a deck ring. If we put her in the hold now I fear the other slaves
would show her little mercy."

"Gruel?" asked a voice.

"None for her until tomorrow," said a voice, presumably that
of the captain.

"Free the sail," I heard.

"Yes, Captain," said a voice.

There was a snap of canvas, and the ship surged ahead.

It was shortly after that that the hatch was opened, and I was
allowed to come on deck.

The slave who had been recovered from the sea lay on the deck.
She was on her right side, her knees drawn up. She was chained
by the neck to a stout deck ring. She was still shuddering. She did
not meet my eyes. Both her hands were on the chain that fastened
her to the deck ring.

I looked away from her.

I could see the shore in the distance.

There were rocky beaches, and behind them, in places, trees.
There were fields occasionally and, I think, orchards. We were too
far north for vineyards. I saw more than one small village. Each, I

supposed, had its Home Stone, probably as much cherished there, in such a remote, humble place, as were those elsewhere, even those of mighty cities, such as Ar, Turia, or Brundisium. And each dwelling, too, I supposed, even a shack or hut, would have its own Home Stone. In his own hut, with its own Home Stone, even the least of men, it is said, is a Ubar.

I heard a small sound of chain, and I turned about, again. The slave was now on her belly, on the boards of the deck, and she still held the chain in her hands. Then she wept and, putting down her head, kissed the chain.

I wondered, again, what could have tempted her to leap from the ship.

I was hooded and naked, my hands thonged behind my back, some days ago when I was assisted by him whom I took to be the leader of my abductors, his hand on my arm, down the gangplank of the ship in the harbor at Brundisium.

"Thank you, Master," I had said, steadied.

I could sense the other men behind us on the gangplank.

One was close behind.

"The least cry, or untoward sound, from you, *kajira*," said he who held my left arm, he whom I took to be leader of my abductors, "and you will have a knife in your back."

"Yes, Master," I said.

"Oh," I said, softly, wincing. I felt the point below my left shoulder blade.

Then I felt the boards of the wharf, thick, rough, and warm, beneath my feet. I could still smell smoke from the night before.

We went to the right for perhaps better than a quarter of a pasang. We must have passed more than a hundred moored vessels. It was early, but there was already business on the wharves, calls and cries, men coming and going. I heard the sound of a chain and sensed the passing of a coffle. Girls are commonly coffled by the neck, or wrist. In this fashion, freed of shackles, they can move more easily, more gracefully. The female slave is expected to move gracefully. Neck coffling is generally preferred. It is commonly deemed more aesthetically pleasing. Too, it is more secure. One might occasionally slip a wrist ring, but no girl slips a neck ring or, for that matter, an ankle ring. When a girl is chained at a master's slave ring, it is usual to chain her by the left ankle. I became aware, gradually, uneasily, that most of the men who had left the ship with us had now slipped away. Two only were with me now, he whom I took to be the leader of my abductors and the other fellow, at my back, he with the knife. I did not know how many streets we might have passed, streets leading up, away from the wharves. The smell of smoke was stronger here.

The hand on my arm stopped me. I was then turned to the left.

"Ahead, climbing," said he whom I took to be the leader of my abductors, "is the House of Anesidemus."

"Yes, Master," I said.

"On your neck," he said, "is the collar of the house. It would be risky for us to have it removed at a metal worker's shop, and madness for us to sell you with it on your neck. Too, we must be soon away."

"Yes, Master," I said.

I had seen little of my abductors for I had been muchly hooded, and when I was freed of the hood, they had been masked, muchly masked.

I had gathered, from accents, remarks, and such, that they had come from different cities, and different walks of life. I did not doubt but what had brought them together, in one place or another, in one city or another, in one tavern or another, in one brothel, or another, was a sense of what they had in common, ambition, a lack of scruples, opportunism, and greed.

I did not know what I should do.

I was uncertain.

I stood still.

Then suddenly, there was an unexpected, abrupt, loud report. I cried out, shocked, startled, in pain, and stumbled forward, almost losing my balance. I knew that sound, and the associated feeling, like fire, both from my original house of training, whose name and location I did not know, and from the House of Anesidemus, from which I had been sold. Had I not felt it before? Is it not an experience sufficiently familiar to an attractive, negligible female slave? I had been stung sharply below the small of my back, with a sudden, forcible blow, delivered with the fierce, swift flat of a man's hand.

We are not free women.

Such things may be done to us. We must expect such things.

I caught my balance, and hurried forward.

I had been sped on my way.

Within the hood, tears of helpless humiliation burst from my eyes. I heard a man's laugh, from behind me.

What brutes are men!

How they do with us what they please!

I moved on for a time. I was then sure that he whom I took to be the leader of my abductors and his fellow, he with the knife, how sharp and cruel it had felt, had now slipped away, doubtless now lost amongst the workers and passers-by on the docks. I stopped. Where was I? Where was the house of Anesidemus? I was suddenly miserable, and helpless, now no more than a slave on a far, exotic world. Where was Earth? Where was my familiar world? I had been brought here, in effect, as an animal, to be collared and trained for the pleasure of masters. I was naked, bound, and hooded. I could feel warm boards beneath my bared feet. Suddenly, how helpless and frightened I was! Hooded and bound, collared, marked, and naked, what is one to do, where is one to turn? Yet, was it not fitting, I thought, that I should be here, and as I was? Certainly I had learned on Gor how I, a natural slave, should be, and what I, a natural slave, was for. Surely I had well suspected such things, even on Earth. I knew I would train well. I had long known that I belonged in a collar. I pulled at the thongs fastening my wrists behind my back. How well they were pinioned! How easily, and well, did the men of Gor secure slaves! How vulnerable I was! I could not see within the hood. A soft breeze arose. It ruffled the hood, and I felt the air on my body. How sensitive, and alive, is an unclothed body! I stood still. There was conversation to my right. As far as I knew, no one remarked me. Perhaps a hooded, bound, naked slave was not that unusual in Brundisium, particularly in the dock district. I feared I should be moving or kneeling. Why should a slave be standing? Surely she should be occupied. Had she no fetching to accomplish, no message to deliver, no errand to do? I was suddenly alert. I heard the movement of robes passing me. Had that movement stopped, or had I been accosted, I would have instantly thrown myself to my knees, my head down to the boards of the dock. How different all this was from my former world! Somewhere ahead of me, I gathered, surely, was the House of Anesidemus, in which, yesterday, I had been sold. I, how incredible it now seemed, sold! Sold as the object, property, and animal I now was! I had no more to say about this than any other vended beast. Yet how natural, and right, that seemed to me. That I was a slave was now clear to me. I acknowledged it, and gratefully. It was what I was. Collared, I was a thousand times more free than I had ever been on Earth. I must try to reach the house, from which I would doubtless be turned over to someone I did not even know, who was now my master. I would try to serve him well.

Only a few Ehn before, I had been struck below the small of my back, a swift, sharp slap.

My fundament still stung.

I smiled.

Why should I be humiliated? Why, rather, should I not be grateful, be proud?

Let the free woman be humiliated, surely not the slave!

Commonly, I knew, it is only attractive slaves who are struck so.

The slave wishes to be attractive to men. Much in her life can depend on that, and, too, it is natural for her, for she is a slave.

How free one is as a slave!

I moved forward, afresh.

I must hasten to the House of Anesidemus.

It would not do for a slave to dally.

I must soon call out. Surely I required assistance. Surely I could beseech a master. Surely a man could see me to the House of Anesidemus. One might conduct me there, or turn me over to a guardsman, who would shortly thereafter deliver me to its cages. It must be near. I hoped I had not inadvertently passed it. I did not think so. Still, paving stones were now beneath my feet. Even a slave might help me, if she were not loath to do so, as my accent might betray me as a barbarian. Indeed, perhaps I might encounter another barbarian, as collared and marked as I. Barbarians might be rare in their collars, but they surely existed. I had been brought to this world as one in such a shipment, as one in such a catch, flock, or herd.

"Oh!" I cried, in dismay, for my right shoulder had struck against voluminous robes, these enveloping a figure as slight and soft, and not much larger, if at all, than my own.

"Stupid, filthy, clumsy beast!" cried a shocked, outraged voice.

"Forgive me, Mistress!" I cried, throwing myself to my knees, my head to the paving stones. "I am hooded. I could not see you!"

"Your accent!" she cried. "You are a barbarian!"

"Forgive me, Mistress," I begged.

"Barbarians are sometimes in need of discipline," she said. "They soon learn that they are abject slaves!"

"Forgive me, Mistress," I begged. "I know well that I am worthless, and the least of slaves."

Was it not so, I, as a barbarian? Yet I had heard that men often wanted us in their collars. How one understands oneself, when one is collared! Everything is then clear, perfectly clear.

Why, I wondered, as the other was presumably not hooded, had she not been able to avoid me, or warn me? Within the hood, I could not see, save for the sense of light or darkness. Surely such an unfortunate jostling, or contretemps, could not be blamed on a hooded slave!

"You struck against me," she said, "you, not even Gorean, but a barbarian!"

"It was not my fault, beautiful, noble Mistress," I said.

"Ah!" cried the woman. "I thought so! You deliberately discomfited me, a free woman!"

"No, Mistress!" I said, trembling. I had heard much of free women in my training, both in the first house and in that of Anesidemus.

"Lying slave!" she screamed. "Do you think me a fool!"

"No, Mistress!" I said.

"You convict yourself of deliberate insolence," she said, "for which you might be cut to pieces!"

"No, Mistress," I said, puzzled, terrified.

"You must be able to see in the hood," she said, "or you would not know that I am beautiful!"

I sensed a crowd was gathering.

"You are free," I said. "It is well known to worthless slaves that all free women are beautiful, and noble, as well."

"Even of low caste?" she inquired, archly.

"In their freedom," I said.

"I am of high caste," she said, "as you can see through the hood."

"I cannot see through the hood," I said.

Why, I wondered, if she were free and on the streets, was she not veiled? Surely a veil, suitably draped and adjusted, might easily conceal beauty, as well as arouse speculation. To be sure, some free women, the taunting and more brazen, were careless of their veiling. How easy it was for a fold or two to slacken or part.

"I am of the Merchants," she said, "as you can see."

"I cannot see, Mistress," I wept. "I am hooded!"

It was my understanding that the Merchants was not considered, at least generally, as a high caste on Gor. To be sure, they were generally accounted the richest of castes.

"So you compound your insolence," she said, "by calling me a liar!"

"No, noble Mistress," I said. "Perhaps noble Mistress is mistaken."

"Hear the slave," said the woman, presumably to those gathered about. "She dares to criticize a free person!"

"No, Mistress!" I protested.

My forehead was down, to the stones.

"Who is your master?" demanded the woman.

"*Ela*," I wept, "I do not know!"

"Liar!" cried the woman. "Do you think to escape punishment so easily?"

"No, Mistress," I said.

"Who is your master?" she demanded, again.

"I do not know," I said. "I truly do not know!"

"She is in flight," said another woman's voice. "Yes!" said another. "She is a runaway slave!" said yet another. "Let the tendons behind her knees be severed," said another. "Let her feet be cut off," said another. "She will not run away again," said another.

"I am not a runaway slave," I said. "I am a helpless slave, naked, hooded, and bound!"

"Who is your master," inquired the first woman, yet again.

"I do not know," I said. "I was sold last night from the House of Anesidemus. I do not know to whom I was sold. It will be on the records of the House of Anesidemus. Even now I seek the House of Anesidemus."

"Insolent slave," said the first woman.

"No, Mistress," I said.

"How dared you buffet me, how dared you strike against a free woman?" asked the first woman.

"I could not see," I said. "It was an accident. I could not avoid Mistress. I beg Mistress' forgiveness."

"Perhaps you think the fault was mine?" said the woman.

"Surely not, Mistress!" I said.

"Perhaps you think that I was unobservant," she said, "careless, my attention directed elsewhere, that I might have been distracted, or such?"

"No, Mistress!" I said.

"Then you acknowledge that the fault was entirely your own?" she said.

"Yes, Mistress," I said.

"You should then be punished," she said.

"Mercy, Mistress!" I begged. "I beg mercy, sweet, compassion-
ate, beautiful, noble Mistress!"

"We shall see," she said.

I waited, head down, helpless, frightened.

Some Ihn passed.

I gathered that she had relented, that I would not be punished.
How kind she was!

"Thank you, Mistress," I whispered, gratefully.

"Oh!" I cried in misery, stung by the lash of a switch. Many
free women carry such an implement with them. It comports with
their authority, their dignity, and status. Slave girls look upon
that device with well-justified apprehension. They well know
its meaning. Have they not felt it, often enough? Free women,
who resent and hate, even loathe, female slaves, scantily clad and
collared, often use it on them with little or no provocation. Presumably this has much to do with the pleasure males derive from
female slaves. Could the free women be actually jealous of slaves,
such meaningless, worthless beasts? Do they envy them their
brands and collars? Do they themselves wish to feel the kiss of the
searing iron and the clasp of the degrading metal collar?

I screamed in misery and writhed on the wood for the first
stroke of the switch was soon followed by a rain of strokes.

I twisted, and wept, struck again and again.

Then I lay on my belly, shuddering, trembling, submitted.

My legs and back were afire.

"There, insolent slave!" cried the woman, gasping for breath.
"Perhaps, in the future, you will be more careful of where and
how you walk."

"Yes, Mistress," I said. "Forgive me, Mistress."

She then kicked me in the left thigh.

"Slave," she hissed.

"Yes, Mistress," I said.

"You are tired," said a woman's voice. "Let me beat her now."

"Do so," said the first woman.

"No," said a man's voice. "She has had enough."

"Who are you?" asked a woman.

"Agent," said he, "of the House of Anesidemus."

I recognized the voice. It was that of one of the men of the
House of Anesidemus. He had been one of the men in the hall,
while the slaves were on all fours, waiting to be herded into the

street outside the house, to protect them from the possible spread of a fire which had begun on the docks. He, and perhaps others, may have been in the streets looking for me.

"Guardsman!" called a woman.

"What is going on here?" asked a male voice.

The fellow who had intervened, I was sure it was he, it must have been he, drew me by an arm up to my knees, and, his hand on the hood, pulled my head back, far back.

"The collar of the House of Anesidemus," said the other male voice, presumably that of a guardsman.

"A mistake was made last night," said he who had intervened. "In the confusion of the fire, and the alarms, this slave was separated from the coffle. I have been making inquiries, and looking about for her. Now I have located her."

"You are fortunate she is not now on her way to the Farther Islands, in chains," said the other male voice.

"Officers of the port authorize departing vessels, after an examination of cargo," said he who had intervened.

"The collar?" asked he whom I took to be a guardsman.

"Papers would be requested," said he who had intervened.

"You think some sort of mistake was involved?" said he whom I took to be a guardsman.

"Clearly," said he who had intervened.

"You have doings with the House of Anesidemus?" asked he whom I took to be a guardsman.

"My credentials," said he who had intervened.

"Proceed," said he whom I took to be a guardsman, and, apparently, he stepped away.

Similarly, I gathered the crowd had now dissipated.

"Can you stand?" asked he who had intervened.

"Yes," I said, struggling to my feet.

"Master," I said.

"Yes," he said.

"I did not mean to obstruct the way of the free woman," I said.

"You did not do so," he said. "I saw her watch you. She smiled, removed, the switch from her belt, and placed herself in your path. You could not help yourself."

"It was deliberate?" I said.

"Certainly," he said.

"Why would she do that?" I asked.

"Free women," he said, "do not care for *kajirae*."

"I might have been beaten even further, by the other women," I said.

"Undoubtedly," he said. "Two, without switches, had removed a slipper, with which to strike you."

"If you saw what happened," I said, "why did you not speak out, why did you not denounce the free woman, and protect me?"

"You know little of Gor," he said. "One does not criticize free women. They are free. Would you have had her gainsaid? Would you proclaim her to be in error, or, worse, lying? Would that not be unthinkable, insupportable? Would it not be grievously insulting? Would you dare to hint, even privately, that she, in her status and freedom, might be flawed, might be less than righteously perfect?"

"I see," I said, bitterly.

"And you, on the other hand," he said, "are a slave."

"I see," I said.

"What does it matter," he asked, "if a slave is switched?"

"She is only a slave," I said.

"Precisely," he said. "Too," he said, "I thought a switching for you might prove beneficial. I thought it would be instructive. It will help you to better understand that you are a slave and, in particular, it will help you to better understand that you are not a free woman. The free woman, as you will learn, hates the slave. Moreover, the free woman is mistress. She is mighty and powerful, and the slave is vulnerable, defenseless, helpless, and at her mercy. You will learn to tremble in the presence of free women."

"Yes, Master," I whispered.

"Let us now return to the House of Anesidemus," he said.

"May I be unhooded?" I asked.

"Later, in the house," he said. "Let us keep your features concealed, for the present."

"Why?" I asked.

"Curiosity is not becoming in a *kajira*," he said.

"Does Master know to whom I have been sold?" I asked.

"Certainly," he said.

"To whom?" I asked.

"Curiosity is not becoming in a *kajira*," he said.

"Yes, Master," I said. "Forgive me, Master."

I had heard a small sound of chain, and I had turned about, again. The slave was now on her belly, on the boards of the deck, and she still held the chain in her hands. Then she wept and, putting down her head, kissed the chain.

I wondered, again, what could have tempted her to leap from the ship.

Surely there was some mystery here.

I knelt beside her, curious.

"The masters are not watching," I said.

She shuddered, and pressed her lips again to the chain.

"You are safe now," I said.

"The sharks," she whispered.

"You are safe now, on the deck, on the chain," I said.

She was silent.

"Euphrosyne," I said.

"Yes," she said.

"We were angry with you below," I said. "You might have cost us our deck privileges." Surely it was not pleasant to be chained in the hold of a round ship. "The masters were kind enough to allow you on deck. You abused their forbearance and trust."

"You are ignorant," she said, bitterly, "only a barbarian."

"Why did you leave the ship?" I asked.

"How little you know," she said.

"Teach me," I said. "Inform me."

"I overheard the masters," she said.

"I do not understand," I said, apprehensively. "What did you hear?"

"Nothing," she said, bitterly.

"Something so fearful that you would leave the ship?" I said.

"I knew the risks," she said. "They follow vessels at sea, the sharks, to seize garbage, anything cast into the sea."

"And yet you leapt overboard?"

"In the water I lost my nerve," she said. "I turned back to the ship. I was frightened. I was weak, a coward. I should have continued on."

"You could never have reached the shore," I said.

"I was afraid to die," she said. "I clung to life."

"You are now safe on board," I said. "You are safe on your chain."

"I kiss it," she wept, "I am such a slave!"

"You could have been killed," I said, "eaten alive, only yards from the ship."

"I should have permitted the sharks to seize me, and feast on me."

"Surely not," I said.

"Surely it would have been better," she said.

"Surely not," I said.

"I should, when possible, seize up a sword or knife," she said.

"No," I said, frightened. "A slave can be slain for daring to touch a weapon."

"To throw myself upon it," she said.

"Do not do so," I said.

"I could dash my head against the ring," she said.

"Banish such thoughts," I said.

"But I am afraid," she said. I am weak. I am a coward. "I cling to life—despite what I know."

"What do you know?" I asked.

She wept, and put her head down, beside the chain.

"Better to perish in the water, torn by the fangs of sharks," she said.

"What fate could be so horrible," I asked, "that to it you would prefer so frightening, so terrible, a fate?"

"I hoped to reach the shore," she said.

"And escape?" I said.

"Yes," she said.

"Do you not know that you are unclothed, that you are marked, that you are in a collar?"

She was silent.

"We are slaves," I said. "We are helpless in our collars. We will be kept in them. Even to think of escape is absurd."

"I know," she said. "But I was frightened. Everything reeled. Things began to go black. Then I saw the shore."

"Why did you leave the ship?" I asked. "What did you over-hear?"

She shook her head, shuddered, and did not speak.

"Tell me," I said.

"No," she said.

"You could not have escaped," I said. "The men, if they wished, could overtake you. They could hire hunting sleen. Peasants could apprehend you. You can see the villages on the shore. Then you would have a miserable slavery, a rural slavery, worked from dawn to dark, often whipped, chained at night, in the open, in the cold and rain, to a stake in the yard, penned with tarsks, housed in a cramped, damp, log kennel."

"You do not understand," she said.

"No," I said, "I do not."

"Surely you rage against the collar on your neck, the mark on your thigh," she said.

"Seldom," I said, "though I understand their meaning and my helplessness."

"You do not understand," she said. "What I heard! What I heard!"

"I love my collar," I said. "I would not change it for a necklace of diamonds. I am a slave, a natural slave. I have known this even from girlhood. I want to be owned, to belong, to be a possession. I want to be dominated, mastered. I want to be rightless. I want to surrender to a man, wholly, to be his, wholly, his animal, his property. I want to kneel, kiss, caress, obey, love, and serve."

"I, too," she said.

"I want a kind, strong master," I said, "who will own me completely, and fulfill me, as the slave I am."

"I hope for that, too," she said.

"Would," I said, "that we could choose our masters."

"But we cannot," she said.

"Why then did you flee?" I asked. "Why did you leap overboard? Of what were you so terrified, that you would risk sharks, recapture, peasants, hamstringing, or being fed to sleen?"

She turned, and looked up at me, tears in her eyes.

"Tell me," I said.

"I will," she said.

At that point there was a cry, from the height of the mast. "Ho!" I heard. "Ship, ship!" And almost at the same moment, from the lookout at the stern, I heard, "Ship aft, to the right!" The hortator awakened, shook his head, and reached for his mallets. The *kaissa* board and pieces were set aside. Cards and game stones were put in small sacks. The oarsmen took their places on the benches.

Euphrosyne knelt up, beside me.

"Get up, look," she said to me. "It is hard for me to see." She could not rise for the length of chain which held her to the ring would not permit her to stand erect.

I rose to my feet.

Behind us, to my left, as I stood, looking back, as though appearing from nowhere, doubtless just departed from some concealed or inconspicuous inlet, for its presence had just been noted, was a lovely ship, low in the water.

"Speak, speak," said Euphrosyne.

"It is a ship," I said. How beautiful, I thought, were the galleys of Gor. To be sure, there seemed a subtle menace to that form.

"Is its sail set?" asked Euphrosyne.

"I see no sail," I said.

"The mast is down," she said.

"I see no mast," I said.

"The ship is hard to see, is it not?" she said.

"It is low, close to the water," I said.

"It is green, like the green of Thassa," she said.

"It is such a color," I said. I supposed such a color would blend in well with a common mood of Thassa, the sea.

"It is long, and narrow, like a knife in the water," said Euphrosyne.

"We have seen other ships, from time to time," I said.

"Its prow wears a snout of iron," she said.

"I see nothing like that," I said.

"Then it is below the water, just below the water," she said.

"On each side of the bow," I said, "as on some ships moored at Brundisium, there is a large, flat hemisphere of metal, an armor, a shield, to protect the ship from injury."

"Naive barbarian," she said.

I did not know, at that time, the function of those mighty blades.

"How so?" I asked, not pleased.

"What do you think its business is?" she asked.

"How should I know?" I asked.

"It is a cargo ship, you suppose, a round ship, casually, surprisingly encountered," she said.

"One supposes so," I said.

"That is no cargo vessel, no round ship," she said.

"How can you tell?" I asked.

"It is a long ship," she said, "no sail set, the mast down, thus less detectible at a distance, painted green, not easily noticed in the swells of Thassa."

"You sense danger?" I asked.

"An honest ship, by day, would be at sea," she said, "not just emerged, between us and the shore."

"You do sense danger," I said.

"What I do not understand," she said, "is why the men are so calm. The alarm has been given. Are they obtuse? Does the tabuk note the presence of the larl with equanimity? Does the verr choose to ignore the prowling sleen?"

"If there were truly danger," I said, "the men would evince agitation; they would behave differently."

"At least we are slaves," said Euphrosyne, joyously, "animals of value. We have nothing to fear. We will be spared. We need only wait to be put on our bellies and tied, as the animals we are. We will be rescued."

"'Rescued'?" I said.

"For different chains," she said happily, "to be vended in a different market."

I understood better then what it might be to be a female slave on this world.

"And to think," said Euphrosyne, laughing, "I put myself into the sea, and might have been eaten by sharks! What a fool I was! I did not know! Who could have known! How glorious, how fortunate, that I managed to return to the ship! There is now nothing to fear!"

I myself was not sure of that.

"Builder's glass," called the captain, and an officer handed him that object. The captain stood at the stern rail, and trained the glass on the approaching ship. "A corsair," he said, "flying the colors of Cos."

The keeper had recently returned from the vicinity of the helmsmen, and was standing near me. As soon as I realized this, I knelt, now almost at his thigh.

"If you wish to stand," he said, "you may do so."

I rose to my feet. He was kind. He must have sensed that I would wish to have a better view of what was to ensue. I placed myself on his left and a bit behind him. I was a female slave and he was a free man. That is a common heeling position. I did not wish to be beaten.

"Oars ready!" called the captain.

Oars were grasped.

"Oars out!" called the captain.

I heard these mighty levers, with a rattle of wood, thrust through the thole ports. There were two oarsmen to each oar.

"May I speak?" I asked.

"Yes," he said.

"The other ship approaches," I said.

"Yes," he said.

"The captain," I said, "spoke of a corsair."

"It is a corsair," said the keeper, "undoubtedly."

"It is following us," I said.

"Yes," he said.

"We do not have warriors aboard," I said, "neither bowmen nor spearmen."

"No," he said.

"Surely we must then attempt to outrun the other ship," I said. "We have oarsmen, and a sail. The other ship, if it has a mast and sail, it has not yet raised them. We can thus gain time. I do not understand why the captain has not yet committed the oarsmen. Too, I do not understand why there is so little fear on board. Surely pirates, corsairs, are dangerous."

"Other things may be more dangerous than they," he said.

"Lacking defenses," I said, "we must flee."

"It seems so," he said.

"Surely, with oars and sail, we can outdistance the stranger," I said. I noted, with apprehension, that the other ship was closer now, indeed, perhaps no more than a half pasang away. Our oars were not yet in the water, but only poised.

"We could never outdistance the corsair," he said. "We do not have the lines. It is a long ship. A crippled vulo could more easily escape a striking tarn."

"Then we must put into shore, while we can," I said, "and attempt to escape inland."

"Surely you note that the corsair has positioned itself between us and the shore," said the keeper. "And, even if we were willing to risk villages of rapacious peasants, armed with the great bow, we could not reach the shore."

"And," I said, "if we turn out to sea, the corsair could overtake us?"

"Within the Ahn," he said.

"Why then is there so little concern on board?" I asked.

"Do not fear," he said. He then looked about, and then, shading his eyes with his hand, looked back, at the corsair. "I think it is time," he said. "We shall now exhibit fear, consternation, and desperation."

"Master?" I asked.

At a gesture from the captain, the hortator struck his drum with a resounding blow from one of his two mallets. The oars then entered the water. At a second stroke on the drum, with the other mallet, the oars moved.

Almost at the same time we heard, from across the water, a similar sound from the approaching ship. They had not used the drum until now, perhaps hoping that their presence had not yet been discovered. Sometimes the stroke, by the hortator or an officer, is called from amidships, even softly.

"We will now," said the keeper, "seem to flee."

"The stranger gains upon us," I said.

The ship moved beneath my feet, oddly.

"Note," said the keeper, "the helmsmen have turned us toward the shore, but briefly. Now the ship turns again, this time toward the open sea. We have realized we could not beat the corsair to the shore, so we have no choice but to risk all on flight."

"An effort doomed to futility?" I asked.

"Precisely," he said.

"I am afraid," I said.

"But note," said the keeper, "as we turn to the open sea, we draw the corsair behind us."

"Yes?" I said.

"And he, too, then, is farther from the shore."

"I do not understand," I said.

At this point, perhaps in response to signals conveyed by the captain, or one of his officers, the hortator's strokes changed, some too closely together to be matched by the heavy oars, others widely spaced, and then occurring almost unexpectedly. The oars lifted and fell, and drew, not in unison, but sporadically, disjointedly, out of rhythm. I was reminded of an injured fish thrashing in the water. Does not such distress call itself to the attention of various marine predators, such as sharks? How avidly such then would hasten to inquire!

"Now," said the keeper, "at last, you see the signs of confusion, and terror."

I did not understand what was occurring.

"Now," he said, "we will recover, and begin our flight in desperate earnest."

"One impossible of success?" I asked.

"Our fellows must row well," he said. "It would not be well to be overtaken within the Ahn."

"The Ahn is important?" I asked.

"That, or a little more," he said.

"Yes, Master," I said, puzzled.

"Pull, lads," called an officer. "Hear the drum! Sweat! Be strong! Be patient! If they will have us, they must work for it!"

The long, inclined yard, creaking, swung about.

"The wind shifts!" cried a mariner.

"To our advantage!" cried another.

"We shall escape!" I said.

Ropes were secured. The sail billowed anew.

Euphrosyne wept with misery.

"Be silent!" I warned her. "The stranger falls back!" I said to the keeper, pleased. The same word in Gorean is used for "stranger" and "enemy."

"For now," he said grimly. "Listen."

The sound of the far drum carried well across the water.

"The beat increases," I said.

"Of course," said the keeper.

"The wind is with us," I said.

"Not enough," said the keeper.

Euphrosyne moaned.

An officer walked between the benches. "Be strong, lads," he said. "The rhythm, the rhythm. Stay with the drum."

I think that half an Ahn must have passed.

Twice in that time our beat had been increased.

I did not think our fellows could long maintain that pace. The round ship, larger and heavier, wider of beam, deeper in the water, higher bulwarked, laden with cargo, depends far more than a long ship on its sail.

"The stranger gains," I said.

Then two thirds of an Ahn, surely, had passed.

An officer, departing the side of the captain, who held his position aft, came between the benches, and looked up, to the fellow at the height of the mast, the lookout, he on his wooden platform, standing within the waist-high metal ring, who had first seen the stranger, who had first sounded the alarm. The officer then returned to the side of the captain.

The stranger then was no more than a hundred yards astern, like a snake in the water.

The captain put aside his Builder's glass and spoke to his officer.

The officer turned about. He cupped his hands. To the helmsmen he called, "Come about!" To the mariners he called, "In sail, down yard." To the benches he called, "Oars in!" The hortator put down his mallets. The oars were drawn inboard with their rattle of wood.

"Master?" I said to the keeper.

We were then, it seemed, turned about, adrift, loose in the water. Our port side, as it was now swung about, was exposed to the bow of the stranger. His drum stopped, and his oars, lifted, dripping water, were poised. The stranger then rocked, quietly, surveying us. He was no more than forty or fifty yards from us.

"As we are now overtaken, helpless, and unable to run," said the keeper, "it is now time, I conjecture, to show our desperation."

"I do not understand," I said.

"Is it not time to repel boarders?" asked the keeper.

"I fear we would meet with little success," I said. Surely the foe was a well-manned ship, a ship of war, so to speak, doubtless staffed and armed, prepared for such a contingency.

"Let us intimidate them," said the keeper, "displaying the formidable odds they would face, should they dare such a venture, a reckless boarding. Have we not secret forces aboard, representatives of the scarlet caste itself, warriors in fee?"

"No," I said.

"Behold," he said.

To my amazement my two sister slaves were freed of their chains in the hold and brought to the deck. Too, Euphrosyne's chain was adjusted, so that she might stand. Scarlet cloths were brought and cast about us. I clutched the cloth about me. I was pleased to be covered, even so strangely. Slaves, we need not be clothed. How grateful we are to be permitted clothing! How we prize even the tiny bits of cloth permitted us, the tunic, the camisk, the ta-teera! And we, in our vanity, are pleased, too, I admit, once we understand our collar, with how well such garments reveal us, and set us off! What woman does not wish to be revealed as excitingly desirable, so much so that men will be eager to buy and own her? Such garments, so shameful and degrading, so scanty and revealing, excite us, and the masters, as well. It is not surprising. They are designed to do so. How can we help our feelings, not that we desire to do so. Staves were placed in our hands.

"There," said the keeper. "See how easy it is to recruit defenders, and of the scarlet caste itself."

"This is a doomed ruse," I said. "Surely they have glasses of the Builders, and might detect this business easily, and at a goodly distance. And now, they are close enough to do so with the naked eye."

"So here, now," he said, "we have four stalwart warriors, for-
midably armed."

"Master jests cruelly," I said.

"Let them take heed," he said.

"Even were they deceived," I said, "we would be only four."

"The Gorean warrior," he said, "is trained to kill, swiftly, and
efficiently. Would you clamber over bulwarks to meet a blade
whose motion you might not even detect?"

"We are not warriors," I said. "We are only slaves, females,
weak and collared."

"Understanding that," he said, "they will surely be heart-
ened."

"More likely amused," I said.

"Even now," he said, "they are conjecturing your lineaments,
now muchly concealed, and speculating as to how you might appear, chained naked at their feet."

"We are slaves," I said. "We belong to the free. But do you not
fear for your lives?"

"Not now," he said.

"I do not understand," I said. "Your ruse is pathetic. It is
doomed. It fools no one. No one, at this distance, will mistake
slaves bedecked in scarlet, clutching staves, for those of the scarlet
caste. You do no more than suggest futility and desperation."

"So it seems," said he.

I noted that Euphrosyne had pulled the red cloth tight about
herself, accentuating her figure, and, as though by some careless
inadvertence, had arranged matters so that a bare shoulder might
be glimpsed, and the narrow, flat circlet of metal enclosing her
fair throat. Doubtless the men would beat her for that, if it should
later prove convenient to do so. But, fortunately for Euphrosyne,
this inadvertence, or betrayal, was not noticed by the men. Their
attention was on the corsair, now paused, oars at rest, a few yards
away. It seemed harmless at the moment, like a carnivore, now at
ease, resting, waiting, content that the chase was now done, eye-
ing spent prey.

"Will they strike our ship?" I asked.

"You know of rams?" he said.

"Very little," I said.

I had understood something of this sort from Euphrosyne. Surely,
if, at the sturdy, narrow bow of the corsair, invisible, just below
the surface of the water, fixed in place, there was a beak or snout

of metal, it would have some purpose. It seemed clear that such an object, moving with its ship, sped swiftly against the planking of another vessel, might inflict damage, perhaps considerable damage.

"No," he said, "they will want our ship, and its cargo."

I realized that I was a portion of the cargo.

I looked back to Euphrosyne. She had now covered herself up, discreetly, modestly. She looked content, demure, in the red cloth now held about her. She smiled at me. She, at least, was not alarmed. "Different chains," I thought. What was it, I wondered, that had so frightened her before? How could it be that she could bear our current peril with such equanimity?

I turned back to look at the corsair, gentle in the water.

"We have been caught," I said.

"It seems so," he said.

"I fear for masters," I said.

I understood that in Gorean warfare the free were commonly slain, whereas animals, amongst them slaves, would commonly be spared, as loot.

"Do not do so," he said.

"Are you not afraid?" I asked.

"Not now," he said.

"The hunter has been successful," I said.

"The hunter," he said, "pretty Zia, does not understand that it is he who is hunted."

"I do not understand," I said.

"The fools," he said, "they are distracted, they gloat, they suspect nothing. I see no lookouts. I see none with the glass of the Builders. None survey the sea about them. They do not realize this is the moment of their greatest danger."

"Master?" I asked.

"We have drawn them far from shore," he said.

"Master?" I asked, again.

The keeper then left my side.

"Soon," whispered Euphrosyne, "we will be in better chains!"

"I do not understand the keeper," I said to her.

"When we are boarded," she said, "go to *bara*."

There are several Gorean slave positions, of which *bara* was one. I had, of course, been trained in these positions, which must be assumed instantly and unquestioningly upon the command of any free person. They are designed with various purposes in mind; instantly placing oneself in positions in which one is helpless and vulnerable; positions of abject submission in which one's bondage is made clear to all; positions of display; positions facilitating appraisal, and such. In *bara*, one goes to one's belly, one's head facing to the left, one's wrists crossed behind one, and one's ankles crossed, as well. In such a position a slave may be quickly and conveniently bound, helplessly bound, hand and foot. All of these positions, both symbolic and practical, have certain things in common; for example, in all of them, the slave is presented as, and is understood as, both by herself and by others, a slave, and only a slave.

"The corsair," I said, "is putting down a long boat."

I saw it being lowered, in a rope harness, into the water.

I then heard a cry from the lookout platform, high on the mast. "She is closing," he called down. "The *Dorna*! The *Dorna*!"

I ran to the rail.

"What is it?" cried Euphrosyne. "What is it?"

"I do not know," I said. "I see nothing!"

Suddenly I did see that the long boat which was being lowered into the water, tilted wildly, and splashed down.

I heard shouts from the corsair, cries of alarm. A horn blared out, frantically, again and again. Men rushed to and fro. Consternation reigned on its deck. Some oars struck into the water. I heard its drum sound twice, only twice.

"There!" cried one of our men, pointing outward, past the corsair. "I see her!"

"Yes!" cried another.

Standing at the rail, holding it, my hands on it, near my shoulders, I saw nothing.

The corsair began to turn toward the shore. The longboat at its side was now righted. Some men, frantic, lowering themselves with ropes, clambered into it. Others were crowded at the rail of the corsair. Two men leaped from its deck into the water, swimming to the longboat.

Then I saw that of which the men must have spoken.

It was low in the water, painted a mottled green, scarcely visible at first, almost lost in the swells, moving swiftly, so swiftly that, propelled by the mighty levers of its oars, rising and falling, in unison, shedding water, it was like a living spear.

"The *Dorna*!" cried our men.

Almost at the same moment, amidst cries of terror and distress from across the water, there was a sudden, vast sound of buckling, broken, ruptured, splintering, shattering planking.

Our men cheered and flung their mariner's caps into the air.

"The *Dorna*, the *Dorna*!" they cried.

I gathered that the ship was well known.

The bow and stern of the corsair seemed to fold toward one another. The assailant back oared, dragging pieces of planking with it which then fell into the water. There must have been a gaping hole in the side of the corsair. I could hear water rushing into the vessel. In moments, its deck was awash.

The assailant ship, the *Dorna*, then turned slowly away.

"It is leaving," said a man, waving his cap in farewell.

There were cries of misery from men in the water, hands lifted.

There must have been a hundred men or more on the corsair.

The long boat was swarming with men, in the craft and clinging to it. I saw more than one fellow in the boat slash with a knife at those trying to climb into it.

"There will be blood in the water," I thought.

The long boat was low in the water, the waves lapping at its gunwales. Men began to fight in the boat and cast one another from the boat.

"Sharks," I heard cry, a wailing sound, and a man disappeared, dragged under the water.

The corsair then settled under the waves.

I saw the long boat turn, tip, and capsize, twenty or more men then clinging to the inverted hull, another twenty or so about it.

I heard another scream, and another man disappeared beneath the water.

Men in the water, some cursing, struggled to right the boat.

"The *Dorna* does not linger, to pick up survivors," said a man.

"No," said another. "The lesson taught must be terrible and unmistakable."

"Shall we pick up survivors, Captain?" asked a mariner, an oarsman.

"I do not think there will be any," laughed a fellow.

I heard more screams from the water.

"There are too many," said the captain. "It would be dangerous to do so."

I saw the ship, that called the *Dorna*, depart, its mast now raised and its lateen-rigged sail billowing.

At the summit of the mast, on its line, I saw a broad flag unfurl itself. On it, shaking and fluttering, snapping in the wind, was figured the head of a massive, fearsome, horned beast.

An officer put down a glass of the Builders. "The sign of the bosk," he said.

I heard Euphrosyne cry out in fear.

The long boat had now been righted, and some twelve or so men, perhaps as many as fourteen or fifteen, had climbed aboard. Of these, some with cupped hands or caps were bailing water while others, in water to their knees, stood at the gunwales and, with knives and clubs, were preventing others from boarding. Here and there a dorsal fin cleft the waves. Two men, with an oar, were striking, or thrusting at, fellows in the water. I heard another cry, and saw another man pulled under the water.

The keeper was standing near me.

"Surely we could save some, Master," I said.

"Which ones?" asked he.

"Any," I said, "surely any."

"Those men are corsairs," he said, "killers."

"Still," I said.

"Do not fear," he said. "There will be survivors."

"I heard speak," I said, "of a lesson, terrible and unmistakable."

"That is why there will be survivors," he said. "There is no point in a lesson's being given, if none survive to report the lesson."

I was silent.

I looked out at the horror some yards away, at the rocking, awash, beleaguered long boat, the struggles, the knives and clubs, the bloodied waters, the screaming men, the stirrings about of inquiring sharks.

"And who will be the survivors?" I asked.

"Presumably," he said, "the strongest and most ruthless amongst them, those most willing, expediently and without compunction, to kill their fellows."

"I see," I said.

"You are standing," he observed.

"Forgive me, Master," I said, and quickly knelt by Euphrosyne, who, now kneeling, her arms about herself, was shaking with distress, and the two others, also now kneeling. The scarlet cloths we had worn were drawn from us.

"Now Cos and Tyros will have to pay for their jade," said a man.

"What is wrong, Euphrosyne?" I asked.

"Now we are lost," said Euphrosyne.

"We are saved," I said.

"Ignorant barbarian," she wept.

"Oars out," called the Captain. "Slow stroke. Bring her about!"

Oars slid through the thole ports and entered the water.

Shortly thereafter the drum of the hortator sounded.

We felt the ship slowly come about.

The thunder of the hortator's drum again sounded.

"Raise the yard, free the sail!" called the captain.

The long, slanting yard turned on the mast, and the open, dropped sail, with a snapping of canvas, responded, swelling and tautening, curving, and was filled to the "brim," as the mariners sometimes put it, with the "wine of the wind."

The cries of drowning and dying men behind us became more faint.

The prow, with its painted eyes on either side, was pointed northeast. Within an Ahn or two I supposed we should have the shore again in sight, a situation wont to be favored by Gorean mariners, and then we would return to our original course.

"Into the hold, lovely *kajirae*," said the keeper. "You have had enough of deck privileges. You must not be spoiled. It is a foolish master who spoils a *kajira*. They are best when the bonds are tight and the switch is at hand."

Euphrosyne was freed of her chain and then she and the rest of us climbed down the ladder into the hold. The keeper followed us and our left ankles were soon shackled to the common ring. The keeper then ascended the ladder and the hatch was closed and battened down. We could look upward, through its grating. The shadow of the grating was on our bodies.

"Why are you crying, Euphrosyne?" I asked.

"You do not know whither we are bound," she said.

"No," I said.

"We are *kajirae*, animals," said another girl. "We are kept in ignorance. We are told nothing."

"Curiosity is not becoming to us," said the other girl.

Euphrosyne looked at me, tears in her eyes, the shadows of the high overhead grating on her body. "What do you think is our destination?" she asked.

"I do not know," I said.

"I heard the men speak earlier," she sobbed. "That is when I leapt from the ship, in a desperate and forlorn hope of attaining the shore."

"What is our destination?" asked one of the two other girls.

"—Port Kar," she whispered.

The two other girls cried out in dismay.

Euphrosyne broke out again in sobs.

I was puzzled. I did not understand their trepidation, their fear.

But I suddenly felt very naked on my chain.

CHAPTER NINE

Port Kar

I was tired and miserable.

I was sweating and hot.

My body ached.

I bent over the double basin, one of several in the large, low-ceilinged kitchen of the Golden Chain, one of the five or so prominent taverns in the city. I had no idea how many smaller such establishments might be in the city. There were presumably few who did not know the Golden Chain. It may be the largest tavern in Port Kar, or, surely, at least, one of the largest. There were ten of us in the kitchen. We were naked, and our ankles were shackled a few inches apart, presumably less for security than to help us keep in mind that we were slaves, as though, on this world, that might somehow slip our mind. My hands were immersed in the suds of the oven-heated water in the right-hand basin, its water, frequently replenished, heated on the long stove at the back of the kitchen. I held the metal plate in my left hand, under the water, wiping it with the cloth in my right hand. I lifted it, dripping, and rinsed it in the left-hand basin and then inserted it in the vertical rack, that it should drain dry. To my right was a basket of goblets. I could smell the residue of paga. When washed and rinsed, they would be inverted and placed on the horizontal rack. Some brushes were large and flat, for trays and flatware; others were narrower and rounded, for vessels. Scrapers were at hand; these were of wood and were widely bladed. The horrors that I had heard of Port Kar, either in Brundisium or on the voyage northward, largely from Euphrosyne, had turned out, happily, to my relief, and doubtless Euphrosyne's, to have been muchly exaggerated. We were, of course, Gorean slaves, and were

held under the perfection of Gorean discipline. But that would
be much the same in any Gorean city. Gor is Gor, and a slave is
a slave. The Gorean master is strict, and often demanding and
severe, but is seldom cruel. We know we will be whipped if we
are not pleasing, but we strive to be pleasing, and, accordingly,
are seldom, if ever, whipped. Sometimes we beg to be whipped,
if only to remind us that we are slaves. To us our bondage is precious, and we beg to be reassured of its reality. The Gorean master keeps us well on our knees, and we love him for it. To be sure,
it was not pleasant in the kitchen. Euphrosyne, almost as soon as
we arrived, coffled, at the Golden Chain, was thrown a paga tunic
and put on the floor. Was she that much more beautiful than the
rest of us? There is commonly something of a "turnover" in paga
girls, as it is not unusual for one to be purchased "off the floor."
We all yearn for a private master, and the boldest of us for a "love
master." Who knows? When a girl is ordered from the floor to
an alcove she may find herself in the arms of one who may later
prove to be her master. To be sure, she is to please, and wholly
in all ways, any patron who alcoves her. If she should in any way
fall short of the customer's expectations, and he expresses his
dissatisfaction to the proprietor of the tavern, she may be close-
chained and beaten, and may be sold to the laundries or fields,
or even given to a free woman. Paga girls often vie, as far as they
can, to put themselves before handsome masters. Sometimes this
results in unpleasant interactions off the floor. It is not uncommon for a girl to begin in the kitchen, and, as time goes by, and
girls are sold, to reach the floor. One "moves up," so to speak. I
looked to the side, apprehensively, at one of the large flat brushes.
I had dallied at the double basin one day and the kitchen master,
holding me by the hair, had flung me down on the wet floor and
used it on me. It had been quite unpleasant, and instructive, but
not really painful, nor did it harm me in any way. Gorean masters are careful not to mark or scar their girls. Such blemishes
commonly lower a girl's value. Even binding fiber tends to be
flat and soft, as well as strong. Similarly, the soft, wide blades
of the five-stranded Gorean slave whip commonly used on *kajirae*, so different from the "snake" used on men, are designed to
prevent any sign of permanent damage. On the other hand, less
happily, they are also designed to punish, and with terrible effectiveness. Only she who has never felt the attentions of such a
device could think little of it, or surmise that her responses to

its lavish caress would differ in any way from those of others. She who scorns the whip has never felt it. Let the slave strive to be pleasing. How better to see to it, that it remains on its peg? The sting of the switch is more likely to be felt. I had felt it often enough, particularly in my first days in the kitchen. Once I had not knelt quickly enough, twice I had forgotten to request permission to speak, and once, the worst time, I had dropped one of the metal plates and it had fallen, ringing and clattering, to the floor. I think that I had now been some fourteen or fifteen days in the kitchen. In this time, I had seen three new girls brought in from one market or another, and had seen two girls taken away, either to the floor or, perhaps, to be sold. I had also seen two girls brought to the kitchen from the floor, who had, I suppose, in one way or another, displeased one or more of the taverner's men. The kitchen, thus, can serve as a venue of reprimand as well as a simple kitchen. The taverner, he who owned the tavern, was a man named "Ho-Tosk," who had come from Ar to Port Kar years ago, supposedly under some cloud of obloquy. He was my master, and, I supposed, that of the others, as well. Interestingly the slave, Adraste, the arrogant, pretentious piece of collar meat whom I remembered from Brundisium, was also in the tavern, though amongst the floor girls. I had been told that she, on the side, was being trained as a tavern dancer. That amused me, that the proud Adraste, with all her airs, would be put on the dancing floor. I hoped that they would dance her naked, with a whip-bearing keeper at the edge of the floor, to assure that she would please the patrons, to see that she would well "dance her collar," so to speak. I did not know how Adraste had come to Port Kar. I presumed she had come north, as I had, on a ship, but I was sure she had not been on our ship. She was here when Euphrosyne, I, and the other two girls, coffled and back-braceleted, had been brought to the Golden Chain. I gathered that we had all been purchased in Brundisium by an agent for the Golden Chain. She must have come on a faster vessel. Whereas most of the kitchen work, and the scullery work, in particular, was done by slaves, the cooking was done by free men.

"Beware," whispered the girl to my right, she at another of the four double basins, "I hear steps!"

I tensed, waiting.

A moment later a voice called out, sharply, from outside the portal to the kitchen, "*Kajirae*, about, *nadu!*"

It was the voice of the kitchen master.

We all turned to face the voice, and knelt, back on our heels, our backs straight, our shoulders back, our heads lifted, the palms of our hands down, flat, on our thighs, our knees well spread.

The kitchen master then entered the kitchen.

"You are naked, are you not?" he asked.

"Yes, Master," we said.

"That is appropriate for kitchen slaves, is it not?" he asked.

"Yes, Master," we said.

"And you are kitchen slaves, are you not?" he asked.

"Yes, Master," we said.

"Then it is appropriate for you, is it not?' he asked.

"Yes, Master," we said.

"And you are nicely shackled, are you not?" he asked.

"Yes, Master," we said.

"And that is appropriate for kitchen slaves, is it not?" he asked.

"Yes, Master," we said.

"Good," he said, and he then turned away from us, to the cooks, inquiring about a number of dishes in preparation.

When he turned back to us, he said, "you may rise and return to your work."

We rose to our feet.

"Not you, Zia," he said.

Frightened, I turned back to face him, kneeling again, in *nadu*. I trembled. Tears came to my eyes. What had I done? Had one of the others lied about me? Was something amiss, for which I might be punished?

He came and stood near to me, before me.

"Look up," he said.

I looked up, frightened, into his eyes.

"Ho-Tosk wishes to see you," he said.

"May I speak?" I asked.

"Yes," he said.

"May I ask for what reason my master wishes to see me?"

"Lie on your belly," he said, crouching down, "bend your knees, put your feet up, behind you."

I complied, with a rustle of chain, and I felt, he beside me, through the clasping metal, a key inserted in the shackle locks. Then the shackles were removed. He rose to his feet and placed the shackles on the sill behind the double basin. In the kitchen the shackle locks all respond to a single key.

"May I ask for what reason my master wishes to see me?" I asked, again.

"Curiosity is not becoming in a *kajira*," he said.

"Forgive me, Master," I said.

I did not know what to do. A girl learns not to break position without permission.

"Rise up," he said, "and report to Ho-Tosk."

"Yes, Master," I said.

CHAPTER TEN

I Serve Paga

"Paga, Master?" I asked, kneeling beside the low, square table, at which two men had just been joined by another.

"Yes," said the new guest, not regarding me.

One grows accustomed to being looked at and not seen. There is a time for slaves and a time not for slaves.

At other times we find ourselves looked upon with avidity, as might be savory dishes by a hungry man.

And Gorean males, I had discovered, were often hungry, so to speak. But I suspect they were seldom less hungry than their putative prey. Indeed, the mass of sexual tissue distributed so abundantly throughout the female body, once ignited, often flames in need. How often one hopefully ties the bondage knot in one's hair! How often one kneels, frustrated and whimpering, at a male's feet, fearing to speak, hoping to be caressed! Once one's slave fires are kindled what can one be from then on but a begging slave? And do the beasts not know this, when they, to their amusement, put such fires unilaterally, whether we will it or not, in our vulnerable, helpless, owned bellies? I did not think that female passion, as I was coming to know it, was less than, or inferior to, male passion. Rather I suspected that it, in its unique and different way, in its biological complexity and breadth, in its preciousness of emotion, in its time and ramifications, far exceeded the soon-satisfied passion of men. Are not we, once our slave fires are lit, the most helpless and needful of the sexes? And yet the men are men. They decide, and we wait. They are the masters; we are the slaves.

Sometimes our bodies scream for satisfaction and we are ignored. Sometimes we go to our bellies and beg, and the men have no time for us.

Our needs make us theirs.

We are slaves.

I rose to my feet, and made my way to the paga vat, where a taverner's man would fill a goblet that I might then bear to the table. According to the ringing of the bars, it was somewhere after the eighteenth Ahn. I passed a fellow who lowered his head, that it not strike against a hanging tharlarion-oil lamp. Many taverns, particularly in the north, are low-ceilinged, I suppose to conserve heat in the winter. On the other hand, this architectural feature, accompanied by darkness, shadows, warm colors, and dim lighting, also tends to produce a sense of comfort, intimacy, and security. I saw Euphrosyne pass, carrying a tray to another table. She smiled. Doubtless she hoped to please one of the men. I had no doubt he would be a handsome fellow. As I waited in line, for the filling of the goblet, I looked about. The Golden Chain was a very large tavern, but it did not really seem so, as it contained many sections away from the large central area, to the side of which was the dancing floor, each of which constituted a relatively enclosed, private area, an enclave, so to speak, with its own intimacy and ambiance. The alcoves, ubiquitous in such a tavern, were ranged at the back of the wider, general area. These were low-ceilinged, low-portaled, and leather-curtained. They can be buckled shut from the inside. Each was furnished with a number of custodial devices, bracelets, chains, shackles, and such, as well as various instruments of pleasure and discipline. The girls were tunicked. The Golden Chain was not one of those shabbier taverns where the paga slaves serve naked, and sometimes chained. To be sure, the paga tunic, like most other Gorean slave tunics, and as would be expected in a garment designed to display a woman as a slave, leaves little to speculation. She is, after all, a slave. I watched the girls moving about, serving. I noticed a man or two coming and going. A taverner's man was collecting coins at a table, and putting them in the small, black coin box, slung from his belt, at his left hip. A goblet of paga is commonly a tarsk-bit, and the girl, if wished, comes with the price of the drink. Not all men, of course, come to a paga tavern for paga and the girls. Suppers may also be ordered, the prices of which vary with the nature and quantity of the provender. Too, some come and, for the price of a drink, linger, to talk with friends or hear the news; some come and play *kaissa*, or stones, cards, or dice. In some of the relatively removed, more private sections there are tables in whose surface, inlaid. are found the hundred squares of the *kaissa* board. In the tavern merchants may conduct business over a drink; mariners may regale rapt auditors with accounts of fabulous voyages; slavers may confer on sales and projected raids; at another table, a scribe may sit, ready to write or read letters. The Golden Chain, like most such establishments, opened at noon, the tenth Ahn, and remained open until the early morning. Commonly between the tenth and the twelfth Ahn restraint, quiet, leisure, and socialization characterized the Golden Chain. After the twelfth Ahn, or so, the tavern starts, gradually, to become quite different. It is roughly at that time that many markets and shops close, that work crews are dismissed, that passes are issued, that shifts change, and that many men, their day's work finished, look forward to refreshment and diversion. By the eighteenth Ahn, the Golden Chain is crowded. It is easily accessed by means of several streets and canals. It is on Palace Street, on which street the Palace of the Council of Captains is located, from which, I suppose, the name is derived. The Palace of the Council of Captains is the usual meeting place of the Council of Captains, which body is sovereign in Port Kar. I listened to the music, supplied by a *czehar* player, which, now, was soft, slow, and sensuous. No dancer was now performing. Later the *czehar* player would be joined by his fellows, two with *kalikas*, two with flutes, and one on the *tabor*. The *czehar* player was the leader of the group. That seems to be common. Most paga taverns will have their dancing floor, most commonly oval or square, the Golden Chain's was square, but not all can afford musicians, at least on a regular basis. A paga girl may be ordered, of course, to pose, roll, or writhe on the floor. It can cost a proprietor a goodly bit of coin to buy a fine dancer. They are not easily afforded. Many men will frequent a tavern for its dancer, or dancers. To alcove a dancer commonly costs more than to alcove a common paga girl. I am speaking, of course, of a trained, or fine, dancer. Any paga girl can be thrust on the floor. If the crowd is pleased, tarsk-bits may be cast to rattle on the floor, usually to be retrieved by a taverner's man. If the crowd is not pleased, the girl may be whipped. The tarsk-bits are sometimes retrieved by the dancer herself. If she is silked, she deposits the coins in a loop, basketlike, of her silk. If she is not silked, she utilizes a shallow copper pan at the side of the floor. In both cases, she will deliver the coins to a taverner's man, usually waiting on the other side of the beaded curtain. Some taverns do not have a dancing floor, but an area of sand,

again, commonly, oval or square. Occasionally a taverner's man
will rake the sand, by means of which action the sand is smoothed
and stray tarsk-bits may be detected and collected. I saw seven
men enter. From their smocks and caps, I took them to be employees of the great arsenal, with its inner harbor, its docks, warehouses, and shipyard. Free women are not allowed in a paga
tavern, which, I suppose, is just as well. Sometimes a free woman,
perhaps curious, or adventurously bold, or resentful, rankling
under the prohibition of such premises to her sex, will disguise
herself as a slave girl, even daring to affect the degrading habiliments of the *kajira*, and enter. These, commonly, are soon detected, given their tone, bearing, carriage, or mien. It is difficult
for the Gorean free woman, with her pride, assumptions, background, behaviors, and attitudes, to pass herself off as a slave.
There are too many differences, too many difficulties. The free
woman is not yet a slave; she has not yet been broken to the collar.
The discovered imposters are politely back-bound and escorted
from the premises. Then, their hands bound behind them, they
must make their way home. How then can they return to their
cached garments and dress themselves? Being so treated, of course,
openly and publicly, is scandalous to the free woman, and may be
ruinous to her reputation. Certainly her peers, afterwards, are
likely to shun her, and look upon her as little more than the female
slave she endeavored to counterfeit. If the free woman wishes to
make a scene, she may be back-bound and ejected naked, with
her tunic tied about her left, bound wrist. Sometimes she may be
remanded to guardsmen and held for a public trial, on charges of
conduct unbecoming to, and offensive to, free women. In such
cases, at the mercy of a presiding female judge, she stands naked
in the dock, waiting to learn her fate. Commonly her sentence is
the collar. Why should some free women behave so? I suppose
there might be many reasons. On the other hand, a common surmise is that they are "courting the collar." Why else should free
women risk lonely, ill-guarded districts after dark? Why else
should they undertake distant journeys without a suitable escort?
Why else should they, when alone, take lodgings in small inns on
dangerous roads? Why else should they embark on perilous voyages? In the high cities of Gor, the "Tower cities," why should
they frequent high bridges, alone, at night? Do they wish, suddenly, to note the shadow of the silent, soaring tarn on the moonlit bridge, feel the quickly closing loop of the tarnsman's capture

rope? In some cities, it is said that, in some taverns, there is a particular alcove into which, detected and gagged, a free woman is thrust, which alcove, by a concealed panel, and corridor, communicates with a secluded street or alley. The free woman then, bound and gagged in a slave sack, is removed from the tavern, and transported out of the city, to some distant venue where she will be suitably marked, collared, and sold.

"Wake up, slut," said the vat tender.

"Forgive me, Master," I said, and extended the goblet.

I then turned about, to look again at the tables.

I heard a ripping of cloth and heard a startled cry from a paga girl. There was laughter. She rushed away from the table escaping through the beaded curtain. A fellow at a table lifted the shreds of the tunic in his fist, like some won guerdon. Perhaps she had sought to move past him, pretending to ignore him. Perhaps an expression of hers had been less than pleasing, say, insolent, pert, or insufficiently deferential.

The *czehar* player had stopped briefly, looking up when the girl had cried out, but now resumed his playing.

I suspected he would soon be joined by his fellows, and that one or another of the tavern dancers would, with a flash of silk and a jangle of bells, rush to the floor.

The crowd was active and convivial, but not rowdy. There was the sound of utensils, and the hum of conversation.

Euphrosyne passed me, on her way to the kitchen, with an empty tray. She smiled at me. Clearly she expected to be alcoved. She was popular. She was frequently alcoved.

I looked out across the floor at the men sitting, cross-legged, at the low tables, and the girls serving, barefoot and tunicked, in the soft light of the dangling lamps. I saw one fellow, with a string, tie the hands of a girl behind her, and gesture her to the alcove in which she was to await him while he finished his conversation, and his meal and drink.

Watching, I wondered how several of the males I had known on Earth might have reacted to what I beheld. Some, I supposed, could not even have comprehended it. They would look upon it blankly, dully, understanding nothing. It would have been too unfamiliar, too different from the privations and sterilities to which they were accustomed, which they had been taught to unquestioningly accept, celebrate, and acclaim, which they took to constitute the single face of possibility. Others might have looked upon it aghast, scandalized, shaken, sweating, disbelieving, and trembling. Would they not be the ones who hastily, in terror of recognizing even the suspicion of their own possible manhood, lift a hoping, kneeling woman to her feet and shame her, lecturing her on what she should do and be, as though they knew more than she what it was to be a woman, lecturing her on how she should celebrate self-denial and sacrifice herself to imposed, alien conventions? If she is not a woman, they need not be men, which, suitably conditioned, they fear to be. But might not others clap their hands in gladness, spring to their feet, and cry out with joy? Might this not be a world long ago lost, now refound, a world surrendered on one world but never surrendered on another? And what if one of these males from my old world, one who knew me there, should encounter me here, as I am? One, I supposed, would understand nothing, would not even recognize me. Another, I supposed, anxious and disturbed, might fling his jacket about me and, red-faced, looking down and away, lest he see me as I am, hasten me from the tavern. But, I supposed, another might say, "This is the way I saw you, even on Earth, the way I wanted you to be," and would then put me to my knees where I belong.

"Must I have your neck marked?" inquired the vat tender, the "Vat Master."

"No, Master," I said, startled. "Forgive me, Master!"

The taverner's deputy, or acting deputy, carries a small marking stick. This is commonly used for changes, additions or deletions, to advertisements and notices. These advertisements and notices may be posted outside or inside the tavern. Outside the tavern such items are large, that they may be read at a distance, and are posted on either side of the gate. Within the tavern they are smaller, and usually appear on the wall to the right, as one would enter. These items are not to be confused with the posters which may be placed on walls throughout the city or on the public boards. The allusion of the Vat Master was to a small penalty mark occasionally placed on the left side of a girl's neck, if she has been found wanting or displeasing in some way. The mark may not be washed off until the girl, after leaving the floor, has been punished, usually with a switching.

I then rushed to carry the goblet to the table.

"Rise up," had said the kitchen master, "and report to Ho-Tosk."

"Yes, Master," I had said.

I had lost no time in leaving the kitchen, climbing the stairs, and making my way to the office of the taverner, the tavern master, my master, Ho-Tosk, whose office is on the second basement level of the tavern, one level above the kitchen level, one level below the level of the main floor. Food is conveyed from the kitchen to the main floor by means of a dumb-waiter arrangement, platforms in a shaft, raised and lowered on pulleys. The two leaves of the office door were back, and so I could see into the office. Ho-Tosk, burly and bearded, was sitting behind a small work table, on which were papers. He looked up, and I knelt outside the door, my head down, my knees together.

"Enter," he said.

I rose, advanced a few feet, and knelt again.

He returned to his work.

I had not been addressed, so I remained silent.

A few moments later, he looked up again.

"You are Zia," he said.

"Yes, Master," I said.

"A barbarian," he said.

"Yes, Master," I said.

"You are nicely curved," he said, "an attractive female animal."

"A slave is pleased, if she is found pleasing," I said.

"You know," he said, "that you are now, despite your origins, earlier pretentions, and background, a female animal, an owned female animal, that and only that?"

"Yes, Master," I said. "I am a slave."

"You have been in the kitchen for several days," he said.

"Yes, Master," I said.

"You have been simmering?" he inquired.

"Master?" I said.

"I trust your slave fires have been ignited," he said.

"They burn," I whispered.

Men had done it to me. I had had no choice. But I rejoiced, that it had been done to me. I had become so helpless and vulnerable, so needful and alive.

"You are a sleek, lithe, pretty beast," he said.

"I am pleased, if Masters are pleased," I said.

He rose up from behind the small table. He was a large, formidable man. I saw him turn and gaze at the slave whip, hanging on its peg to the side.

I remained very still.

I could think of nothing I had done for which I might be beaten.

Still, one does not know.

To my relief, he looked away from the whip.

To my consternation, he came about the table and stood before me.

"Do you think you could be attractive to men?" he asked.

"On my former world," I said, "I was found extremely attractive—to males."

"Do you think you could be attractive to *men*?" he asked.

"A slave hopes," I said, "that she might be found acceptable by masters."

"Would you like to beg clothing?" he asked.

My heart leaped!

"If it is acceptable to masters," I said, carefully.

"You may beg clothing," he said.

"I beg clothing, Master," I whispered, putting my head down and pressing my lips, softly, reverently, to his heavy, bootlike sandals.

"Are you entitled to clothing?" he inquired.

"No, Master," I said.

"Why not?" he asked.

"Because I am a slave, Master," I said.

"Do you deserve clothing?" he asked.

"No, Master," I said, "for I am a slave."

He then went to the side, to a cabinet, which he opened, and, from a shelf, one of several containing what appeared to be assorted, small, folded, pressed, layered cloths, withdrew one of these objects, from the middle pile, and cast it to me, against my body.

I seized it, gratefully, and held it to my bosom, shedding tears of joy. "Thank you, thank you, Master," I breathed.

"Put it on, get up, and turn before me," he said.

I did so.

I was grateful for this bit of cloth, but I was apprehensive, too. How men might see a girl so clad! There is little to a paga tunic.

"May I speak?" I asked.

"Yes," he said.

"Forgive me, Master," I said, "but is it not too short?"

"No," he said.

"Yes, Master," I said.

"I expect to make some tarsk-bits on you," he said.

"Yes, Master," I said.

I was much struck by that. I recalled how, on my world, I had bartered my beauty for attention, favors, advantages, opportunities, gifts, and such. Here, on Gor, its profits, if any, would accrue not to me, but to my owner.

How well aware I was then that I was on the planet, Gor.

Here women may be women, and a slave is given no choice.

"Tonight," he said, "you will go to the floor."

"Yes, Master," I said.

Sensing that I was dismissed, I then rose, backed gracefully away, and, head down, turned, and went out, onto the landing.

On the landing, out of sight of the taverner's office, there was a full-length mirror. I paused to regard myself. Part of me was shocked, terrified, and dismayed, and another part was excited, proud, and brazenly thrilled.

I saw myself.

I was collared!

I was a slave!

I was what I wanted to be.

I could now, in a collar, be what I had longed to be!

How furious would be free women, to see how a woman could be, beautiful, sexual, needful, and owned!

"I am a sleek, lithe, pretty beast, am I not?" I thought.

How faraway was my former world!

I climbed the stairs to the main level, and, looking down the corridor, past the area to the side, where most of the girls were caged, I could see the beaded curtain that led to the central area of the tavern.

That night I knew that I, with others, would part that curtain, and serve.

I hurried to the table.

I had escaped having the punishment mark put on my neck.

I knelt at the low table, at which were three men, the two who had been previously served, and the new arrival.

I knelt, my knees together, and held the goblet against my tunic. "Paga," I said, announcing my arrival. Beyond that, I did not wish to disturb the masters. One does not place the goblet on the table, and then leave. Rather, one offers the goblet to the master, and usually in a prescribed fashion. For this to take place properly, one waits for the master to turn to one, thus signifying that he is ready to accept the goblet. Accordingly, unless told to leave the goblet, I would wait for the third man, the newcomer, to turn to me.

These three men made me uneasy.

From their nondescript garb I was not clear as to their caste. They might have belonged to any caste, or no caste. In this way they could have been anyone, or no one. Did they wish not to be identified by, or remembered by, caste? Did they seek, without apparent caste, to achieve a certain invisibility or anonymity? Then I castigated myself for my foolishness. Many Goreans, now and then, in one milieu or another, omitted caste colors, or insignia. Indeed, some Goreans wore their caste colors primarily on holidays. I could make out little from the accents of the men. There is a medley of accents in Port Kar, as was also the case in Brundisium. This sort of thing is more common in port cities than inland cities. There are, I had been told, a great many accents in Gorean. These can differ from north to south, and east to west. Along the course of a single river, such as the Vosk, Cartius, and Ua, there may be many accents. Peasantry north and south of the Vosk, I have been told, their villages divided only by the river, may have accents almost unintelligible to one another. I had learned to distinguish some major accents, such as those of Cos and Ar. Euphrosyne's accent was Cosian. Adraste's accent, like that of many others, despite her name, which was Cosian, was that of Ar. The conversation of the two original men at the table had, when it had taken place at all, been casual and inconsequential. They had been waiting, I supposed, for the arrival of the newcomer, the third man. I did not think these fellows had come to the tavern for paga or girls. I did not think it likely that my hands would be tied behind my back and I would be ordered to an alcove. I thought that the meeting must have been prearranged, to discuss some matter of interest or moment, doubtless business of some sort. I suspected that the two original fellows might not have previously met the third. Might the meeting have been arranged by a fourth party?

I remained as I was, patient, not moving, quiet, the goblet pressed against my tunic. I had announced my arrival. Were I to be so unwary, or naive, as to repeat myself, it might well irritate a master, suggesting I was impatient, or that he might have failed to note my presence. For such an error a girl might be fortunate, were she only cuffed.

I became apprehensive.

I sensed the men were ready to speak with one another.

Sometimes the less a girl hears, or knows, or learns, the safer she is.

"You have come from a great distance," said one of the original two men to the newcomer.

"Gold is a beacon visible from afar," said the newcomer.

"You have your men?" asked the first man of the original two.

"Of course," said the newcomer. "And you have yours?"

"Of course," was the reply.

The newcomer then turned toward me and I instantly lowered my head, hair falling about my face, pressed the goblet back, low, firmly, against my body, feeling the metal pressing into my belly, and then I lifted it to my lips and kissed it, deferentially, and then, my head down between my extended arms, holding the goblet with both hands, proffered it to the newcomer.

He took the goblet and turned back to the other two men.

As he turned away, not seeing me, I had glanced upward, preparing to rise. He had paid me little attention, and had scarcely looked at me. Too, my head had been lowered, and my hair had been about my face. Too, the light was dim. I rose to my feet and backed away, and then looked back, for only a moment, and then hurried back to the girl wall, where we wait to be picked out by a customer, or sent to a given table by the Vat Master or the taverner's deputy. In that way we are not free to choose whom we wish to serve.

We attempt to be very pleasing to the Vat Master and the deputy, that we might be sent to one table, rather than another.

I stood against the wall, leaning back, my back against the wall.

I was sure, given the light, the serving, and such, that he had not recognized me.

Before, in Brundisium, when I had been unhooded, my captors had been masked. His mask, that of the leader of my captors, had covered most of his face, but not all.

The tavern light had been low and poor, to be sure, and I had had only a fleeting glance at him, looking up through my hair, as he had turned his head away, but I was sure I knew him.

I recognized the scar on his face, as I had seen it before, in Brundisium, that scar on the right side of his face, low, to the right of his mouth, that small, triangular scar.

CHAPTER ELEVEN

Euphrosyne;
I Encounter a Former Acquaintance,
One I Had Known on Earth,
Who Now Sees Me as I Am

Within the sprawling seawalls of Port Kar there are many canals, perhaps hundreds, fed with the waters of the Tamber Gulf. In many places, a portal can be reached only by means of a vessel, commonly one of the small single-oared skiffs which ply the canals. The sides of buildings often seem to rise from the very waters of the canal itself. In this way, many of the buildings, worn and stained, often touched with lichen, dampened by the lapping waters, swelling and ebbing with the tides of the gulf, are, in effect, island fortresses. In many places, windows, several feet above the level of the canal, may serve as coigns of vantage, and ports for the discharge of missiles. The roofs are commonly flat, and equipped with stones, debris, and covered vessels of pitch which, uncovered and ignited, might be cast down toward the water, and, in places, leaders are found through which, suitably adjusted, burning oil might be directed with what, from the point of view of those below, would doubtless seem to be a most alarming precision. The northern and eastern seawalls of Port Kar abut on the vast marshes of the Vosk delta, the western and southern on the Tamber. And beyond the Tamber, less than an Ahn's rowing, lies Thassa, the sea. In the marshes of the delta may be found the scattered, floating villages of the Rencers. These villages are formed from the interwoven stalks of the rence plant, from which a common form of cheap paper is made. Fresh rence is added to the surface of the villages, as older, submerged layers deteriorate, break apart, and rot. The delta is rich in fish and birds. Also, as would be expected, given the abundance of game, it is home, as well, to various predators, in particular, the marsh shark and various forms of tharlarion, some, like the Ul, winged. One gathers that relationships between the Rencers and those of Port Kar, relationships which are now warily cordial, were once strained. It seems that the Rencers adopted the peasant bow, a weapon used in peasant villages on the continent to maintain and defend the freedom and sovereignty of the villages. This bow is particularly effective in the delta, given the stands of rence. It is hard not to respect a foe who, unseen, can kill from a distance. Also, it is difficult to attack or retaliate against such villages, as they can be easily moved, being towed to new locations. Furthermore, these villages are now loosely confederated, a political development traced to a man named Ho-Hak, sometimes referred to as the Ubar of the Marshes. The Rencers, it seems, once predominantly hunters and gatherers, have now added transport and trade to their economic repertoire. In transport, Rencers guide and maintain barges, poled, sailed, and drawn by large, swimming tharlarion, this linking, through the trackless marshes of the delta, the Vosk towns with Port Kar and the coast, and Port Kar and the coast with the Vosk towns. Trade has primarily to do with rence, but some attention is devoted elsewhere, for example, to salted fish, mostly parsit and grunt, to tharlarion oil and leather, and to feathers, in particular those of the Vosk gull, which are commonly preferred in the fletching of arrows. It is speculated that these economic interdependencies may have done as much to assure peace in the delta as the peasant bow. As coin abets commerce, so trade abets peace. Whereas slave girls are not allowed on the walls unaccompanied, some will seek escape by scrambling to deserted segments of the walls and diving into the marsh waters below. Those who do not fall prey to the predators of the marshes are picked up by Rencers. The Rencers will then brand their foreheads and keep them as rence slaves, which, as I understand it, is a most laborious and unpleasant slavery, or, swathing them with ropes, return them to Port Kar for punishment, a tarsk-bit for returning a less beautiful slave, and two tarsk-bits for returning a more beautiful slave.

It must be understood, of course, that there are many dry, expansive, level areas in Port Kar, for example, plazas, markets, and

exercise yards. Too, several of the canals are bordered by walkways, often on both sides. Indeed, I myself was now on one such
walkway, called the Thieves' Way. Port Kar, I have been told, is the
only Gorean city in which there is an officially recognized Caste of
Thieves. To be sure, most of the thieving, I gather, is done outside
the city, in other cities, Port Kar then affording a refuge to which
successful members of that unusual caste may repair to enjoy the
profits of their labors. One may pass over the canals to the other
side by means of bridges. These are usually arched, small, and easily burned. I have never been in a Gorean high city, a tower city,
but I understand that the towers of such cities are often joined
by graceful, narrow, arching bridges, often high above the street
level, bridges which may be easily defended or destroyed in the
case of an attack, this rendering each tower an independent, defensible keep, each supplied with food, water, and weaponry.
One conjectures, similarly, that the vulnerability of many of the
bridges in Port Kar, like ornamented, lanterned, lovely, painted
tinder, is unlikely to be mere coincidence. A collapsed, charred
bridge is not only an inconvenience to the progress of a foe, but an
impediment should he wish to make an expeditious withdrawal.

The walkway on the Thieves' Way was some ten feet in width,
on both sides of the canal. To my left was the canal; to my right
were buildings, some portaled with stout, carved doorways, their
associated barred gates now open, to be closed at dark, and several housing open-sided stores and shops, furnished with folding,
wooden screens, to be shut after the time of business, which, as
with most Gorean businesses, opened at daylight, and closed either in the early afternoon or at dusk.

I was well within a pasang of the great arsenal of Port Kar, with
its warehouses, shops, vast shipyard, and inner harbor. By means
of four large, deep canals, in which even two round ships could
pass one another, one could, passing through the arsenal sea gates
and the western and southern sea gates, communicate with the
Tamber, and thence, shortly, with Thassa, the sea.

The reputation of Port Kar, I fear, is a dark one. I recalled the
terror and misery in Euphrosyne's eyes and voice at the very mention of its name. Port Kar is sometimes referred to as the "Scourge
of Thassa." I think this epithet was generated in an earlier time
when Port Kar had no Home Stone, when it may have been, indeed, little more than a "a den of pirates, thieves, and cutthroats,"
as dangerous to its own citizens as to its enemies, in particular,

the great maritime Ubarates of Cos and Tyros. Indeed, many of the buildings abutting directly on the canals, those fortresslike dwellings earlier alluded to, may have been designed originally to provide a defense not so much against foreign aggressors as local, domestic predation. It is interesting that men who might rob and slay one another without thought or compunction when ashore will when at sea, and "of the ship," as it is said, constitute a reliable, loyal, efficient, disciplined crew. Port Kar is protected not only by its walls, but by the vastness of, and the dangers of, the delta on her east and north, and by the sea on her south and west. There are few who have met the long, low, swift, knifelike ram ships of Port Kar, often painted green, which color blends in with many of the moods of Thassa, either as corsairs or attack vessels, who do not respect, even dread and fear them. As the story goes, Cos and Tyros, some years ago, built, equipped, manned, and launched a mighty fleet, to destroy Port Kar, to be done at last with "the Scourge of Thassa." This fleet was not only massive and formidable, but was generally seen as invincible. Panic, like wind and darkness, swept the streets. Goods were hastily gathered together, crated, and bundled. Ships were frenziedly readied for escape. As scavengers flee from the killing beast come to reclaim his prize, as urts speed from the path of the stalking larl, as bandits hasten to elude nearing, searching, avenging guardsmen, so the thieves, brigands, rowdies, miscreants, cheats, liars, cowards, and criminals of Port Kar, men without a Home Stone, prepared to burn and abandon their city. In the midst of this confusion, fear, and chaos, an amazing, startling rumor was suddenly abroad, first whispered, from ear to ear, and then shouted out, ringing from wall to wall. Men who had betrayed Home Stones, men who had abandoned them, men who had, by deeds or words, dishonored Home Stones, men who had lived for years, lost and separate, alone and miserable, without Home Stones, looked suddenly at one another, wildly. Port Kar had a Home Stone! Men then, resolute and joyous, no longer fled, but, weeping, embraced one another as fellows and brothers, and rushed to the great arsenal to seize oars and take their places on the rowing benches of waiting ships. Later a great sea battle took place. This battle is recalled, and celebrated, each Twenty-Fifth of Se'Kara. Port Kar had a Home Stone.

Those of Port Kar do not, of course, speak of their city as the "Scourge of Thassa," though, as I understand it, they find it convenient that others should do so. Many are the weapons of war, and a suitable reputation, one which might inspire caution, or trepidation, in a foe, is not negligible amongst them. Amongst her citizens, Port Kar is often spoken of as the "Jewel of Gleaming Thassa."

But what do slave girls know of such things, of Home Stones, and such? They are the business of the free. It is our role, as negligible beasts and vendible properties, mocked and scorned, bought and sold, derided and despised, to serve and please our masters.

There is a saying that in Port Kar the chains of a slave girl are heaviest. I doubt, however, that that is true. I suspect that our "chains," so to speak, are neither heavier nor lighter here than elsewhere. Much depends on the individual master. Such things are up to our masters. They are master. I assure you, however, that our "chains," wherever we are on Gor, are heavy enough. We are slaves, and, on the whole, we wish to be slaves, rightless, owned, and mastered. It is our meaning, our fulfillment, our happiness, and joy. Were it not for our terror of free women, who so despise us and who, for some reason, are so unconscionably cruel to us, we might pity them, for they do not know the warmth, the reassurance, and joy of the collar. How wonderful to belong, to be literally owned! And yet, sometimes, too, the collar has its miseries and terrors, for in it we are so vulnerable and helpless!

To my left there was a sudden stir, and splash, in the water, and I spun about on the walkway in time to see a large urt submerge, it ears back, its wet, glistening fur slipping beneath the water. I then moved, uneasily, more toward the center of the walkway. I had been to the left, as Goreans keep to the left side of paths, walkways, roads, stairs, and such. In this way, as most Goreans, as most humans, are right-handed, one's weapon hand faces oncoming traffic. The canal urts, some of which are quite large, are scavengers, and live, for the most part, off garbage in the canals. That is, in effect, their function. They clean the canals. On the other hand, many urts, particularly the larger ones, are aggressive and will attack anything in the water. It is not wise to swim in the canals. Indeed, as the sea gates must be frequently opened and closed, to facilitate ships moving to and from the Arsenal, and inner harbors, to the Tamber, an occasional shark finds its way into the city. The number of urts in the canals are reduced by licensed urt hunters. The usual arrangement is a hunter, in a small boat, accompanied by a slave girl. The hunter is armed with an urt spear, which is essentially a light harpoon with its attached rope, the coils of which are layered in a wooden bucket near the bow of the craft. The slave girl has a rope tied about her waist. This rope is several yards long and is fastened to a stout ring in the boat. The urt then is essentially fished for. The girl, serving as bait, swims near the boat. The hunter, in the bow, his spear ready, watches for urts. When an urt is sighted, the girl moves closer to the boat. Should the urt turn in the water and orient itself toward the bait, the hunter rises to his feet, the spear ready. Much may then happen very quickly, as the urt, in the water, over short distances, can move with great swiftness. Ideally it approaches, low in the water, like a furred streak, little but eyes and snout visible. More dangerously it approaches more slowly, but wholly submerged, either rising in the water below the prey or from the side. In any event, as the urt rushes to make its strike, to seize its prey, the hunter launches his harpoon. The slave girls of urt hunters are often called urt girls. For such slaves that designation is not derogatory, but merely descriptive. It may, however, when applied to other women, be used as an epithet, as though it were comparing the girl, or woman, to an urt. The slavery of the urt girl is not regarded as a desirable slavery. As the girl is attached to the boat by the rope, she is seldom in great danger. She may even be dragged to the boat, the urt still clinging to her body. The urt, in such a case, is an exposed, easy target. Even an ax might strike it. Urt girls are often recognized by means of the scarring on legs and arms. In some cities, free women found guilty of criminal offenses are remanded to Port Kar, with the understanding that they will be branded and collared, and used as urt girls.

"Move aside, *kajira*," said a male voice.

"Yes, Master," I said. "Forgive me, Master."

I had no time to kneel, as he was already past me.

I moved more to my left.

I had stayed rather near the center of the walkway, as I had been frightened by the nearness of the urt that had suddenly appeared, so near to me in the water below. Surely one would not wish to trip or stumble, or be jostled, into the canal.

Now on the other hand, I would certainly not wish, either, to impede the passage of a free person.

So I kept a yard or so of the walkway between me and the edge of the canal. I deemed that satisfactory.

Earlier in the afternoon, just past the Tenth Ahn, kneeling, head down, I had delivered a message from Boris, deputy to the tavern master, Ho-Tosk, of the Golden Chain, to his friend, Henrak, of the Parsit Market. It had to do with a projected rendezvous, from whence, I gathered, would ensue a convivial evening of taverning and wenching. Upon my return to the Golden Chain, I had been released until the Twelfth Ahn, and left to my own devices. I was not even shackled. To be sure, I was branded, collared, and tunicked. There is little about the scanty Gorean slave tunic to leave one in doubt that one is a slave. A slave, unless commanded by her master, would not dare to touch, let alone assume, the garmenture of a free woman.

I enjoyed my occasional walks alone, on one walkway or another. My favorite was the "Thieves' Way," whose walkways bordered the "Thieves' Canal." I would usually walk east on one side, the "Thieves' Way South," and then cross the "Thieves' Bridge," and return to the Golden Chain, walking west on the "Thieves' Way North."

One of the pleasures of this particular walk was the number and variety of shops and offices one passed, particularly on the Thieves' Way South. There were shops for clothing and footwear for the free; the robings and veilings for free women were particularly rich, abundant, luxurious, and colorful; I suspect that there are fewer free women in Port Kar than in most cities; this doubtless has something to do with the history of the city; I am told, incidentally, that there is one city on Gor, Tharna, noted for its silver mines, in which there is but one free woman, Lara, its Tatrix; doubtless this also has something to do with the history of that city; men of Tharna are commonly recognized by the two yellow cords, each some eighteen inches long, that they wear at their belt; such cords are convenient for the binding of a woman, hand and foot; visiting free women in Tharna must be in the custody of a male, and must be licensed and tagged; the custodial male must see that his charge spends no more than four days in the city or she will be seized and collared; some men bring unsuspecting free women to the city, sometimes arrogant free women interested in seeing such a city, to scorn it and its customs, willing even to endure the humiliation of tagging and licensing for such a pleasure, but somehow, doubtless inadvertently, fail to inform them of the law; the woman then, on the fifth day, is seized and reduced to bondage; she finds herself then become no more than another Tharnan slave; there were also shops for manufactured or crafted goods such as cups, goblets, vessels, pans, pitchers, dishes, and utensils; care and art commonly characterize even such simple objects on this world; there was a leather worker's shop and a cloth worker's shop, some weavers in view, at their looms, and two metal worker's shops. Outside the cloth worker's shop was a bin for irregular cloths, discarded patches, strips, shreds, and such; some masters, doubtless of a thrifty sort, avail themselves of such a trove to outfit their slaves; patches, even small patches, may be sewn together, to repair, or even form, a garment, say, a tunic; to the girls, of course, any clothing is precious, even a motley, scanty rag; do not we beg for even so little, and hope that it will be granted to us by the masters; in any event, for the most part, little money is wasted on slaves; we are kept nude as the animals we are, or are inexpensively clad, muchly bared, as with tunics, camisks, ta-teeras, and such. Outside one of these metal worker's shops, on racks and poles, hung a number of slave collars, slave bracelets, manacles, shackles, siriks, mixed chains, and various slave-holding devices, such as racks and spreaders. Toward the rear some slave cages were strewn about, in one of which, perhaps for purposes of display, there was, curled within its tiny confines, a nude slave. Sometimes stairs led up to a second floor where coins might be weighed and changed, or loans made; there is no designated "Street of Coins" in Port Kar; one could ascend stairs, too, to visit one or more physicians, or, if one wished, to solicit the services of a scribe, perhaps to have a letter read or written; many Goreans, particularly outside the cities, are illiterate; these stairwells, or some alleyways, leading from the walkway, bore signs; such things are helpful for those who cannot read; a green auscultation tube commonly signifies a physician; a set of wooden coins, painted white and gold, or white and yellow, hanging from a rod, usually signifies a handler of money, one who might furnish loans, accept pawnings, effect exchanges, and such; and a dangling blue scroll, or a dangling tablet with a stylus or pen, commonly stands for a scribe, and so on. Vegetables, cereals, fish, meat, and such are most often found in the open markets, some roofed, not in the stores or shops. One shop dealt with weapons of various sorts, swords, daggers, balanced throwing knives, spears, darts, javelins, and such. There were crossbows, as well, with cases of quarrels. I did not see any examples of the peasant bow, or quivers of long shafts. Perhaps such might be purchased near one of the smaller sea gates leading to the marshes. One could also have edges ground or honed at that shop; sometimes I could see sparks flying from the spinning sharpening stone. Some such stones are pedaled, others are turned with a handle or crank. Another shop specialized in grades of tharlarion oil, and another in perfumes, and another in flowers. I hurried quickly past a shop featuring binding straps, switches, and whips, many of the latter items colorfully beaded. A free woman was bargaining with the shopkeeper. There are few fixed prices on this world. Free women often carry a switch. Slaves note such things. One dealer had set up a stall on the walkway, to sell brightly plumaged birds. Happily, on my route, there were no slave shelves or slave cells. I do not think I would have liked to walk past such premises, for I am sure I would have been idly assessed by the chained slaves on the shelves or those incarcerated in the cells, just as I might assess them, each wondering what price we might bring, what men would pay for us. I now passed a small pottery shop. I also passed two stalls, in one of which a fellow was exhibiting drawings, paintings, carvings, and small pieces of metal artwork, while in the other a man was offering *kaissa* sets, cards, and dice for sale, displayed on a table, while, behind him, arranged on hooks and shelves, oddly enough, were flutes, *tabors*, and *kalikas*.

I would tend to move well to the side, my head lowered, if passing a free woman, while, if passing a free male, I would tend to keep my eyes straight ahead.

One is wary about meeting the eyes of a free person.

One is a slave.

Sometimes it struck me, given my former life, how strange it was to be a slave, to be now owned, as any other domestic beast is owned, to have a master. And yet I knew I had always longed for it, to be a man's animal, his possession, his vulnerable, helpless slave. There is an incredible, precious freedom in the collar. In it one has no choice but to be what one is, and wants to be. How glad one is to put aside artifices, disguises, pretenses, conventions, disguises, and lies, and be oneself!

What greater freedom is there, but to be oneself?

My tunic was tiny, thin, clinging, and short. It had no nether closure. It was all I wore, save my collar.

I would walk well when I passed a free male. What slave, or what woman, would not? I could sense his eyes upon me. I was vain, doubtless, but I enjoyed his appraisal.

I was, was I not, a commodity, and, hopefully, one of some value?

Surely slaves are entitled to their vanity. A woman does not cease being a woman when she is collared. It is then she most becomes a woman.

Sometimes the men made a small, sucking, clicking sound as they passed. That is a sound even a free woman could understand.

Might they not then faint in the street for dismay?

They, after all, are high, precious, priceless, exalted, and free.

I did not dare to turn, to see if the men had paused, to look after me.

I had seen them do that with other girls.

But I was pleased.

What woman does not wish to be attractive to men? And who can be more attractive than the slave? On Earth I had noted that even women who claimed to hate men wished, nonetheless, to be attractive to them. Such women lacked only being stripped, put to their knees, and collared.

I thought they would make excellent slaves. If necessary, the whip would see to it.

I glanced to the side, to my left, to the canal, and stopped, frightened.

I had seen, briefly, a coarse gray back and dorsal fin rise from the water, glide for a moment, and then sink from sight. Sharks are rare in the canals, but they occasionally slip through the sea gates, either from the marshes or from the Tamber itself. Usually, after a few days, they find their way back to the open waters from whence they came. I inadvertently put my fingers to the collar I wore.

I loved my collar.

Yet how vulnerable and helpless one is when collared!

Can you conceive of yourself, collared?

Try to do so, for moment. Can you sense it on your neck? What then are you?

One looks up, frightened and awed, at the high walls, reached by narrow, open, ascending stairs. One is under the scrutiny of the free, particularly that of hostile free women. One notes vigilant guardsmen. Who is courageous enough to swim the canals, or dive to the marshes, and perhaps into the jaws of tharlarion? We must be able to give an accounting of our actions and locations to any free person who might inquire. We require the permission of the free to leave the house, and must furnish the rationale for our departure, and the time of our expected return.

Indeed, the time of our return is often specified by the master. We are not allowed out alone after dark. And who, in any event, can escape the confines of a house, or the chains which fasten us to the foot of a master's couch? We are seldom allowed outside the walls of a city, if not in the company of our master, or in some comparable custody.

I looked down, to my left, into the canal. I recalled the movement in the waters, the brief appearance, softly gliding, that movement, so silent, and smooth, of the gray spine, and high fin.

I shuddered.

As a slave I was unable to alter my condition, no matter how much I might wish to do so; I was utterly helpless; my will was nothing. I well knew that my bondage, as that of others like myself, was perfect, and complete. There is no escape for the Gorean slave girl, as is well known, as is clear to all. We are distinctly garmented, if garmented; we are collared and branded. There is nowhere for us to run, nowhere to which we might escape. We are goods. The culture wants us as slaves, and will keep us as slaves. Who wishes to be returned to a former master for condign punishment, as is almost invariably the case; and who would wish to fall into the hands of a new, apprehending master, who, recognizing us as a fugitive, would doubtless plunge us into a slavery far more confining and cruel than that from which we fled? Woe to the woman who is kept, or clandestinely sold, as a runaway!

How far I was from my former life. How helpless I was!

"Ho, Zia!" I heard.

I smelled fresh bread. Almost all bread on Gor is fresh, as it is frequently baked. There is very little in the way of packaging, transportation, storage, shelving, and such. Indeed, it is frequently eaten shortly after emerging from the oven. On my former world I had never eaten fresh bread. Only on Gor had I learned how marvelous is the taste of fresh bread. The common Gorean loaf is flat and circular, and is divided, if divided, into either four or eight slices.

I turned. "Master!" I said, happily, instantly kneeling.

It was Leander, the Baker.

As I passed this way every day or two, or every two or three days, I knew some of the shopkeepers by appearance and name. I was sometimes called to their feet and questioned with respect to what was current in the city. The taverns, in their way, rather like the markets, provide a clearing house for reports and ru-

mors, for facts and lies, for information and misinformation, and
the paga girls, by default, so to speak, are likely to be amongst
the best informed sources of information and misinformation in
the city. They are curious and hear much; and they frequently
chat amongst themselves, and share what they have heard, and,
I suspect, often more than they have heard. Goreans, bond and
free, are eager for news, but the channels of its conveyance, for
the populace at large, it lacking post riders and hired informants,
tend to be unreliable and haphazard. It can take months for the
news of some event of importance in Schendi or remote Turia
to reach Kassau or Hunjer, or Port Kar, or even Cos, or Tyros.
And even then what reaches the taverns and markets is likely to
be only incomplete and garbled accounts, passed from to hand
to hand, so to speak, and often founded, ultimately, I fear, on
the ramblings of merchants and mariners, perhaps enunciated
through the fumes of paga. Access to local news, of course, is
likely to be more prompt, if not more accurate.

So I knelt before Leander, hoping for a roll or bit of bread, and
told him the latest gossip and rumors, the freshest scandals and
stories, which had circulated amongst the patrons of the Golden
Chain. As a slave, one grows extremely sensitive to the moods, the
expressions, the subtle attitudes, the little things, about the free,
and, accordingly, I paid close attention to items which I sensed
pleased Master Leander, and those in which, from my memory, I
suspected he might be especially interested, and then I elaborated
on them, and embellished them shamelessly.

I thought I did it quite nicely.

It would be nice to be rewarded.

"You prattle well," he said.

"Thank you, Master," I said, not wholly pleased.

He then asked me, as he always did, if there was news of Talena
of Ar.

"Very little that is definite, Master," I said. "I have heard that
she has been seen in Tabor and Anango, and in Bazi, and in the
valley of the Ua, and in far Skjern, and that she has been apprehended by a dozen bounty hunters who scheme to keep her
capture secret, lest she be stolen from them, before she can be
brought to Ar. And I have heard that four bounty hunters have
already brought women to Ar, claiming them to be Talena. But I
have heard, too, that she is protected, and safe, in Cos, received as
a refugee by the glorious Lurius of Jad."

"That is possible," said Leander. "She much abetted the policies of Cos and Tyros during the Woes of Ar."

I knew little of the politics of Gor, and less of the mysterious, notorious Talena of Ar. She had apparently betrayed her Home Stone, conspiring with others to bring about the downfall of Ar, a large city in the middle latitudes of Gor's northern hemisphere, far to the south and east of Port Kar. This took place during the absence of Marlenus, the city's Ubar. For a time she had ruled harshly and arrogantly, as a puppet Ubara, under the supervision of Cos and Tyros. It was a time of tyranny, exploitation, misery, uncertainty, fear, deprivation, treachery, and profiteering. Then, somehow, the figure of Marlenus had reappeared, and the city rose, violent and savage, eager and vengeful. The occupying forces, in days of terror and blood, overwhelmed by a massive revolt of a swarming populace, armed sometimes with no more than pointed sticks, staves, clubs, torches, and fragments of pavement, fled. Then began the seeking of blood, the publication of the proscription lists, and the search for profiteers, traitors, and collaborators. During the confusion and chaos of the restoration of Marlenus, Talena, and certain others high amongst the betrayers of the city, disappeared. It was said that the reward for her capture was ten thousand tarns of gold, tarn disks of double weight. With such a sum, I understood, one might buy cities. I knew little or nothing of Talena, and I suspected that most Goreans knew little more than I. She was allegedly the daughter of Marlenus, the Ubar, himself, which status had doubtless facilitated her ascent to the throne in his absence. She was also said to be the most beautiful woman on Gor, but I am sure this appellation is one shared by dozens of daughters of Ubars and Administrators in dozens of cities throughout Gor. Are not the daughters of Ubars and Administrators always the most beautiful women on Gor? How could it be otherwise, and who is bold enough, or stupid enough, to challenge such an asseveration, particularly in the presence of the Ubar or Administrator, or even within the walls of the polity in question? Might not such a surmise eventually reach the corridors of the palace? To be sure, I was quite willing to suppose that this Talena might be an extraordinarily beautiful woman. I had always thought myself extremely attractive on my former world, but, on Gor, I had discovered that my beauty was not unusual, particularly amongst slaves. Free women, in their unwonted arrogance, in their unwarranted, unconscionable, preposterous vanity, in their well-recognized stupidity, commonly take themselves to be far more beautiful than slaves, but it is difficult to assess this claim, even if one were to take it seriously, given the common impediments to vision supplied by the robes of concealment, the layers of veils, and such. It might be noted, too, that the great majority of slaves were once free women. How then could there be such a difference? Too, it is obvious that the collar much enhances the beauty of a woman. Even a plainer woman, collared, becomes exciting and attractive, probably, at least in part, because of what the collar says about her, and what may be done with her. Too, the more beautiful a woman is the more likely it is that she will be noticed, and seized for the brand and collar. In any event, it seemed clear that Talena of Ar, she in whom such interest was evinced, doubtless primarily because of the reward offered for her capture and return to Ar, was well hidden. She could be in a hundred cities, or remote villas or strongholds, incognito, well secure within the robes of concealment and multitudinous veils befitting her lofty station, as a free woman.

"Well, pretty Zia," said Master Leander, "you may now spring up, and hasten on your way."

He then turned away, back toward one of the shop's ovens.

"Master?" I said, plaintively.

But he was busied, his back toward me.

I rose to my feet, miserable, and turned back toward the Thieves' Way. I had gone only a step or two, when I heard him call, "Zia."

I turned back.

"Master?" I said.

I saw him cast a roll to the walkway.

It rolled several feet, toward me.

I was muchly elated.

I looked about, quickly, wildly, to the west and east. There was no other slave in sight. The prize was mine! I hurried to the object.

"As what you are, you nicely curved, worthless slut!" he said, smiling.

"Yes, Master," I said, dropping to all fours, head down.

On all fours, it is easy to remember that one is an animal, and, of course, on all fours, it is clear that one is not to use one's hands.

We are seldom permitted to forget we are a slave. Masters will have it so.

In a moment, I had reached the gift.

"Not yet," he said.

I remained still, anxious.

"Now," he called.

I then put my head down, quickly, and bit at it.

I heard him laugh.

In a moment, holding it in place, against the walkway, with my mouth, I had, in a few bites, managed to finish the roll. It was warm, and fresh.

I lifted my head, gratefully. "Thank you, Master," I called.

But his back was turned.

I was dismissed.

I rose to my feet.

Ahead on the walkway were more shops, amongst them something of an emporium for scrolls, some of which might be purchased, and others rented.

I could not read Gorean, of course. Most slaves are not taught to read. An exception seems to be the slaves of scribes. I do not know why that is. Perhaps they wish their slaves to be special, or of assistance to them, or such. Also, if they wish to discard her, literacy is likely to improve her market value. Or perhaps they merely regard a capacity to read as very precious and they wish to share it with others, even meaningless slaves. A slave who was once a free woman, of course, particularly if she was formerly of high caste, is likely to be literate.

I had relished the roll.

I supposed that Adraste could read.

She thought herself so beautiful, so superior! Perhaps she could even read. Suppose it was true, if it was true, that she had once been of high caste. What did that matter? She was no longer of high caste. There was a collar on her neck now, locked there, as mine on me. The proud Adraste was now no more than I, only another slave.

Then I put the haughty, pretentious Adraste from my mind.

As I continued on my way, a sudden rage welled up in me. I had knelt before Leander of Port Kar, the Baker. I had tried to delight and flatter him, hoping to be fed. I had feared that I would not be fed. As I had departed, he had called out to me, and cast a roll to the walkway. I had hurried to it, elated. Then I could not pounce upon it until permitted. Then I must eat it without the use of my hands, as a collared beast!

I went well to the side of the walkway and kept my head down, as a free woman passed. She carried a switch.

Do they not enjoy kneeling us, often not even knowing us, and lashing us about the neck, the arms, and calves?

How helpless we are in their presence, half naked, vulnerable, not permitted to resist, who must accept and endure, uncomplainingly, without the least demur or protest, their abuse, only slaves.

Next, two free men passed. I kept my eyes straight ahead, as I knew myself assessed, as what I was, a purchasable female animal.

Yet what woman, slave or free, does not thrill to the curious, admiring scrutiny of a handsome, powerful male who one day might prove to be her master?

Ambivalences warred within me, excitement, rage, joy, warmth, shame, humiliation, pride!

How dare these monsters take for granted, so easily and unassumingly, and assert and enact, so simply and unquestioningly, the powers of their nature? Why does their society not reduce, cripple, and enshackle them? Why does their society not forbid them to be themselves, or force upon them an alien, unnatural self, to serve its own ends?

But perhaps biology is not the foe of happiness.

I knew what I was supposed to feel and think on my former world. Had I not been taught it? Why then had I not felt it, and thought it?

How effective can it be, to lie to nature?

What can be the test of truth, if not its consequences?

I had retired one fall night on my former world, thinking of nothing, aware of nothing. Then I had awakened in a Gorean cell, naked and chained, hand and foot, and neck, soon to find myself at the total mercy of men such that I had not suspected could exist, save in my dreams.

I did not even know, at that time, what had been done to me.

I soon learned.

I had been selected to be a Gorean slave.

I put my head down, as I passed another free woman.

How was I so different from she?

Take away her abundant, colorful, glorious robes and veils, every last stitch and thread of her clothing, and brand and collar her, and own her! Would we not then be the same, nothing, only slaves?

Yet what a mighty social chasm now separated us, the oceans and continents, the skies and earths, that separate the slave from the free!

I continued on, tunicked, collared, and branded.

I felt the wind blow the tunic back, against my body.

I supposed that the men, the beasts, would like that.

But I did not object.

Rather it thrilled me.

Then I was angry again.

What right had men to enslave us, I asked, to strip and brand us, to collar us, to put us in tiny, revealing tunics, if that, tunics without nether closures, tunics exhibiting us as properties and goods? Then I answered my own question, the right of nature, the right of men, the right of masters.

Leander had cast me a roll, and I had eaten it, eagerly, as an animal. Part of me was then, when I had risen up, angry, and I had smarted with humiliation, but another part, I recalled, when I had been on all fours, was gratified, and grateful; how warm, right, and perfect, how reassuring and fulfilling, it had seemed for me, to be so fed, fed as what I was, a slave. Is a dog not grateful to be fed as a dog, a slave as a slave?

Then I became angry again.

A free man passed me.

I kept my eyes straight ahead.

My tunic concealed little, my collar proclaimed much.

Then suddenly I stopped, startled, gasped, caught my breath, and nearly swooned. I backed against the wall to my right, away from the canal, that I might not fall. I struggled to retain consciousness.

Surely it could not be!

A few yards ahead, standing before a street bin of cheap rence-paper scrolls, on the walkway, in front of the scroll shop, chatting, in street robes, were two men. One was holding, partly opened, a scroll, the spindles or rollers of which, knobless and unornamented, were of natural wood, neither stained nor varnished. A white ribbon was tied to one of the spindles or rollers which, I supposed, as there was writing on it, identified the scroll. Different-color ribbons are commonly indexed to one consideration or another, most commonly the asking price for a scroll, after which negotiations commonly begin. Scrolls with purple ribbons, as I had learned on former walks, were usually kept behind the counter, in the back, in pigeon holes or racks.

One of the men, he who had held the scroll, briskly rewound the scroll, smiled ruefully, and dropped it into the bin with the others. "It is not authentic," he said. "It is not the work of Tius, of Citium." "I did not think so," said the other. "Beware of bargains," said the first. "Most assuredly," said the second. The first fellow then, wishing the other well, took his leave, and the other watched him leave.

I was breathing hard, gasping for breath.

I did not want to faint.

I feared I would fall.

It was the fellow, he, who had lingered behind, by the bin of scrolls!

I had seen him.

I was sure of it!

And I had seen him not here, not on this world, I was sure, but on my former world, had seen him occasionally, at one party, or restaurant, or another. I had once been formally introduced to him, as I recalled, at a cocktail party. His name, as I recalled, was Steele, Addison Steele. The first name had seemed unusual, or odd, or pretentious, to me, 'Addison'. That is perhaps why I remembered him. Or I may have remembered him because he made me feel uneasy. I had found him disturbing. Annoying. Certainly I did not know him well. Who would want to know such a person well? I had taken him to be in his early thirties. He was tall and well-built, with dark hair and eyes. He had been dressed casually with a blue jacket and slacks, and a blue, open-necked shirt. How different he seemed here, easy, in a street robe, and sandals, on the walkway, against the so-different background, the walls, the canal, the sky. At the party, when I had first been introduced to him, I had decided to attract him, as was frequently my wont when introduced to a new male, for the sport of it. It is easy to do, to be charming, to smile, to turn in certain ways, to affect a rapt interest, and such. One can so gain attention, interest, dates, and gifts. If one were as attractive as I, it is easy to do. He had been polite, and smiled, but had seemed distant, and aloof, perhaps preoccupied. He seemed to look past me, to others. Did he find others more interesting or attractive? I found that difficult to believe. Surely I was not accustomed to being overlooked, ignored, or dismissed. That this was done with all politeness and cour-

tesy rankled me no small bit. I was not used to this sort of thing.
My invitations were abundant, and my dates were frequent, and
my escorts were invariably complaisant, attentive, and generous,
often to the point of a heedless, unjustified extravagance, the consequences of which would later, doubtless, be keenly felt. I had
found it irritating that this new acquaintance, if one were to call
him that, Mr. Addison Steele, had not only, at least seemingly,
failed to be moved by my charms, but was actually indifferent
to me. He had looked at me once, carefully, and then, apparently
having reached some opinion, had smiled, and turned away, to
engage others in conversation. I was concerned, and puzzled, and
annoyed. Surely my ensemble was tastefully and carefully thought
out, the basic short, black cocktail dress, set off with pearls. It
was chic, simple, tasteful, and severely elegant. Somewhat apprehensive and somewhat annoyed, I had withdrawn shortly thereafter to the apartment's bathroom, to examine my attire, hair, and
makeup. A few moments later, satisfied that nothing was obviously amiss, I returned to the party, and, from time to time, as one
might, found myself in the vicinity of Mr. Steele, who, though
acknowledging my presence with a smile or nod, seemed, on the
whole, not to notice me. His opinions on various matters, when
expressed, seemed unusual or unorthodox, if not actually incor-
rect. There are, in all groups, I suppose, various positions, values,
and views which are expected to be shared, uncritically, unquestioningly. Do not herds, and ilks, bond so, and thus reassure one
another? Truth, I suspect, is complex and obscure; ideology, on
the other hand, is simple and clear; it is thus not surprising, I
suppose, that it might be frequently preferred to truth. On the
whole, however, he seldom spoke but, rather, listened to others,
apparently carefully. Few listen, I suppose, because it is difficult
to listen when one is oneself speaking. I had the sense that he
thought about what he was saying when he spoke, despite the
trivial, hazy ambiance of the location, that of such a party, and
the accepted customs of such gatherings. Sometimes he would actually turn away from me, though politely. I had seen him later
once in a while, here or there, but we had never spoken save for
an exchange of routine pleasantries. He never asked me for the
date which I had planned to deny him. It was not so much that he
did not know that I existed, as that he recognized my existence
and did not find it much worth noticing. I decided to hate him. I
found him disturbing. Then, eventually, I had put him from my

mind. I had not seen him for months on my former world, before
I was brought to Gor.

Now, incredibly, here he was, on this fresh, green, simple,
strange, untainted, beautiful world!

Or was it he?

How could it be he?

Surely it could not be he.

How could he be here? It must be another who, in virtue of
some strange coincidence, resembled him.

I backed further, more against the wall.

No, it was he.

I was sure of it!

He adjusted the street robe, shifted the position of the wallet
which hung over his shoulder, and, clearly, was preparing to leave
the vicinity of the bin of scrolls, the venue of the scroll shop.

"Addison!" I cried, rushing forward. "Addison! Addison Steele!"

He turned about, startled.

I hurried wildly to him. "You know me!" I cried. "I know you!
From Earth! From Earth! I know you! You know me! From Earth!
From Earth!"

He was here, on Gor! He was in the garb of the free! He would
know me! He must have connections, relationships, power! He
would free me! He would rescue me! He would save me! I would
be released from the horrid degradation of slavery! He would deliver me from the miseries of helpless and total bondage! I would
be liberated and returned to Earth, a free woman, no longer a vulnerable, helpless, collared slave, at the complete mercy of whoever
might own me!

I stopped short, my hands extended piteously to him.

He was regarding me, disbelievingly.

"Addison, Addison Steele!" I cried. "Surely you recognize me,
surely you recognize me? Do you not recognize me, Mr. Steele?"

Then suddenly I felt cold, and terrified.

I trembled.

My knees felt weak.

I, a woman of Earth, now on Gor, on a walkway in Port Kar, a
slave, half naked in a tiny, over-the-head tunic and fastened collar,
was looking into the eyes of a Gorean master.

"You collared slut," he exclaimed, "on your knees! Head down!
Lips to my feet! You dare to speak the name of a free man? You, a
mere slave?"

I knew the voice! It was indeed he, Addison Steele, but very different from the Addison Steele I had thought I had known.

I flung myself to my knees before him, trembling, and, head down, pressed my lips to his sandaled feet.

As he said nothing, I began to lick and kiss his feet. I continued to do this, for some time.

Finally, after two or three minutes, keeping my head down, not daring to raise it, I whispered, "May I lift my eyes to yours?"

"Do so, slave," said he.

"Look upon me!" I begged. "You see me before you, kneeling, half naked, on an alien world, helpless, collared, a slave! Surely you view me with keen commiseration! Surely you view me with pity!"

"Not at all," he said. "You are now where you belong, and as you belong."

"No!" I wept.

"You were a taunting slut," he said. "Now you are as you should be, on your knees, the meaningless property of men."

"Pity me!" I begged.

"No," he said.

"The paving stones are hard on my knees," I said.

"You will remain as you are," he said.

I remained as I was.

How helpless one is, as a slave!

"You were Margaret Henderson," he said.

"Yes," I said, eagerly, "yes, yes!"

"No more," he said.

I wept before him, shuddering, a slave held in place, by a master's will.

"What name has been put on you?"

"'Zia', 'Zia'," I said.

"Then you are Zia, only Zia," he said, "until masters are pleased to put another name on you."

"Yes, Master," I said.

He then viewed me, as a master views one such as I, a slave.

"You blush," he said.

"Forgive me, Master," I said.

"On Earth," he said, "as I recall, you had painted fingernails, and, doubtless, I would suppose, painted toenails, as well."

"Yes, Master," I said.

"They are now plain," he said.

"Such things were scraped off, in my house of training," I said.

"And had your hair been dyed," he said, "your head would have been shaved. Goreans prefer natural women, the fully naked slave, so to speak. A slave dealer who falsifies his merchandise can be mobbed, and his emporium burned."

"I have seen slaves with lipstick and eye shadow," I said.

"They were not sold that way," he said.

I supposed that true.

"We saw one another on Earth," he said. "I wondered, idly, then, what it might be to have you. I shall now learn. A tavern is nearby. If I am not satisfied with you, you will be whipped."

"What are you going to do?" I asked, disbelievingly, uncertainly.

"What I want," he said.

"I do not understand," I said.

"This is not Earth," he said.

"I do not understand," I said.

"How stupid you are," he said.

"I do not understand," I said.

"We shall see how you squirm, squeak, cry out, beg, and moan," he said.

"No," I wept.

"What else, petty, shallow slut, are you and your sort good for?" he asked.

"Mercy!" I begged.

"Remove your clothing," he said, "the scrap that there is of it."

"Surely not here, not on the walkway!" I said.

"Now," he said.

I slipped the tunic away, over my head, clutched it, and looked up at him.

"I am exposed," I said. "I am bared, helplessly so, utterly so!"

"Do not concern yourself," he said. "You are an animal, a property."

"Can you think of me so?" I asked.

"Easily," he said.

"You regard me boldly," I said, angrily. "Appraisingly!"

"Your lineaments are much what I conjectured they would be," he said.

"We were both of Earth!" I said.

"On your feet," he said.

I rose to my feet.

"Your neck looks well in a collar," he said.

"Please!" I begged.

"I thought it would," he said.

"Please!" I said.

"We shall see how you writhe," he said, "in chains."

"No!" I said.

"All women writhe well in chains," he said. "And slaves, such as you, writhe the best of all, by far. If not, the whip will see to it."

"You knew me!" I cried.

"Not well," he said.

"Remember Earth!" I begged.

"This is Gor," he said.

I wept, humiliated, uncontrollably.

"You see the sign to the tavern," he said, "a hundred paces, that or more, ahead?"

"Yes, Master," I moaned.

"It is the *Whip and Chain*," he said. "Do you know it?"

"Yes," I said. "It is a low tavern. I have hurried past it, scarcely daring to look within, many times."

"I suspect you looked within," he said.

"I could see little or nothing," I said, "the gate."

"Perhaps you were curious as to what might occur within such a tavern," he said.

"No!" I said.

"Liar," he said.

I trembled, for a slave girl, unlike a free woman, may be punished for lying.

"Please be kind," I said.

"You are a slave," he said.

"Yes, Master," I said.

I well knew how slaves could be treated.

"You were curious," he said.

I was silent.

"Were you not?" he said.

"Perhaps," I said.

"'Perhaps'?" he said.

"Yes," I said, "Master," quickly, frightened. "I was curious." I feared to displease him. I was a slave, and he was free.

"Now," he said, "you are going to find out," he said.

"Please, no, Master," I said.

The wooden sign which jutted out, from over the door of the

tavern, was a placard on which, crudely, were represented, as one would expect, a whip and chain.

"When we reach the gate," he said, "you will drop to all fours, and crawl within. Then you will crawl to whatever alcove I designate."

I had known him from Earth!

"Yes, Master," I said—bitterly.

"Precede me," he said.

"Master!" I protested.

"I will enjoy walking behind you," he said, "and I would recommend that you walk well."

"You do not own me," I protested.

"I do not intend to own you, only to enjoy you," he said.

"Surely you cannot be serious," I said.

"I shall try you out," he said, "as a meaningless sex object, no more, the meaningless sex object you were before and now are, appropriately, in full legality, a worthless, branded, collared slave."

"No!" I wept.

"It is what you should have been on Earth," he said, "and, in many times, and in many places, would have been."

"Mercy," I begged.

"Let us not dally," he said, "I have other business to attend to."

"I am to be back at the Golden Chain, by the Twelfth Ahn," I said.

"You are a paga slut at the Golden Chain?" he said.

"I am a paga girl at the Golden Chain," I said.

"I find that hard to believe," he said. "The Golden Chain commonly has better girls."

"Some men," I said, "find me quite attractive."

"There must be another reason you are there," he said.

"Quite attractive," I said.

"You have not begun to be attractive," he said.

"I must be back by the Twelfth Ahn," I said.

"Do not be concerned," he said. "I will not keep you long. I will finish with you quickly. You are not worth spending time with."

I was furious.

"Are you displeased?" he asked.

"No!" I said, quickly.

"The least sign of displeasure, hesitation, reluctance, or disinclination on the part of a slave may bring the whip," he said.

"I know," I said.

"I told you to precede me," he said.

"Yes, Master," I said, trembling.

"Must a command be repeated?" he asked.

"No, Master," I said.

The repetition of a command is often cause for discipline.

I then preceded him to the tavern, my tunic clutched in my right hand.

He did not hurry with me, as it turned out, but mastered me, wholly, and repeatedly. I had thought I might, in the beginning, as subtly as I could, deny him pleasure, feigning inertness, but the collar of a slave was on my neck, and Gor had touched me too deeply. Shortly, to his amusement, I became no more than what he knew I would become, a helpless, sobbing, begging, yielding slave in his arms. Gorean men had well prepared me for him. When he was finished with me, he inserted a coin, a tarsk-bit, into my mouth. I felt the tiny coin in my mouth. "That is for your master," he said.

Shortly thereafter I rose, stiffly, drew on the tunic, and left the alcove.

The tarsk-bit belonged to my master. It belonged to him. It was a payment for my use.

I recalled my responses.

How helpless a slave is in the arms of a man of Gor. How easy it is to understand how one could beg for their caresses. How easy it would be to belong to such a man. How easy it would be, as a helpless slave, subdued and owned, to fall in love with such a man, one of a thousand masters. I recalled with bitterness, when I had lain at his feet, after he had used me for his pleasure yet another time, how I had lifted my hand to him, and, tears in my eyes, begged to be bought. "Only a slave begs to be bought," he had said, scornfully, standing over me. "Yes, Master," I had said. "Buy me, Master." "When I had seen you on Earth," he said, "you dining with, and exploiting, one weakling or another, I had thought you might make an acceptable slave, naked, crawling under the table, at a man's knees, in your collar, hoping to be fed." "Do you think so little of me?" I said. "Less," he said. "You thought of me so, even then?" "Of course," he said. "Then you knew of Gor, even then?" I said. "Of course," he said. "Who do you think submitted your worthlessness for consideration, who do you think called you to the attention of the acquirers, who do you think proposed you for only what you would be good for, meaningless block meat?"

I regarded him, aghast.

"Yes," he said.

"It was you, then," I said, "who so despised me, who held me in such contempt, that you would do such a thing to me, you, who, by your will, without my least consent or knowledge, at your pleasure, called me to the attention of masters and dealers, you who are responsible for this utter, radical transformation in my life, for my abject reduction to total bondage, for my branding and collaring, for my now being no more than a property, an object, a vendible animal!"

"You had to be found suitable by others, too, of course," he said.

"Undoubtedly," I said, angrily.

"You will be pleased to know," he said, "that you were assessed as acceptable."

"Merely acceptable?" I said.

"Superbly acceptable," he said. "Like many other selections, you had excellent slave reflexes, even prior to your collaring."

"Oh?" I said.

"All women have excellent slave reflexes," he said, "only some must first learn they are slaves. Others, in their heart, such as you, on one level or another, know that they are already slaves."

"How could you know of such a thing?" I asked.

"What thing?" he asked.

"Slave reflexes," I whispered.

"You were assessed," he said.

"I do not understand," I said.

"Perhaps you recall," he said, "a particularly vivid dream?"

"No!" I said.

"I see you do," he said.

How vulnerable are women!

"Perhaps you received a finder's fee?" I said, archly.

"No," he said, "it was a personal matter."

"I see," I said.

"Too," he said, "you were not that beautiful."

"I hate you!" I said.

"Of course," he said.

"Buy me!" I begged. "Own me! I beg to be your slave!"

It was then that he had knelt beside me and placed the tarsk-bit in my mouth. He then rose up, and, with his foot, scornfully thrust me to the side, and withdrew. I went to my stomach, and, head lifted, looked after him. Then I had struck the furs, angrily, futilely, in frustration, again and again, with my fists.

His laughter had rung behind him.

How well I knew then that I was no longer Miss Margaret Henderson, of Earth, but now only Zia, of Gor, an animal, a property, a slave.

"Ah, Zia," said Euphrosyne, "it seems you were raped in the street."

"In a tavern," I said.

"Were you any good?" she asked.

I dropped the tarsk-bit from my mouth into the palm of my hand. "Excellent," I said.

"You must have been," she said. "You were not whipped."

"No," I said.

"Your master was even paid for your use," she said.

"Of course," I said.

"It would not do to keep the tarsk-bit too long," she said. "I would hasten to the master, kneel, lower your head. and lift the coin to him, and hope not to be beaten."

"I will do so," I said.

"Then," she said, "hurry to the floor. There is a crowd. The tavern is busy. Paga flows, and many are the alcoves which will be strapped shut from the inside."

I stood for a moment, hesitant, bemused.

I was trying to understand my feelings. When I had hurried to Master Addison on the walkway, I had, as had seemed appropriate under the circumstances, he being of Earth, and such, and I being confused and startled, and emotionally in tumult, astounded at seeing him, mouthed expected, prescribed bromides about despair, misery, shame, deliverance, rescue, release, liberation, and such. Surely that seemed appropriate at the moment. Would not such things be expected of me? But, too, almost immediately, I had seen through the fraudulence of such an act. Almost immediately I had feared that I might have been taken from myself, denied to myself, and plunged into the loneliness, the estrangement, the alienation, the meaninglessness, the misery, the despair of freedom. Let the free be free, and the slaves be slaves. I had found the fulfillment of my deepest desires, urges, needs, and being on Gor. I was fearful of being imprisoned in a freedom imposed on me, one foreign to my own nature.

I remembered Addison Steele

I remembered I had begged to be his slave.

He had spurned me, but such things are not that unusual for a slave.

We are often spurned.

We are slaves.

I wiped a tear from my eye.

"Zia," said Euphrosyne.

"I am on my way," I said.

I could hear the sounds of the crowd in the tavern, and the music. I looked through the dangling beaded curtain. On the square of dancing sand, Adraste would dance, a keeper standing nearby, his whip ready to be used on her.

Clutching the tarsk-bit in my hand I then turned about and hurried down the stairs, to the office of the proprietor of the tavern, Ho-Tosk, my master.

I would kneel before him, lower my head, lift the coin to him, and hope not to be beaten.

CHAPTER TWELVE

I Cannot Forget Addison Steele;
I am Hooded;
I Discover that I have been Reserved

Seven days had passed since Addison Steele, a free man, a former acquaintance from Earth, unexpectedly, amazingly, encountered on Gor, in Port Kar, on the Thieves' Way South, had taken advantage of me, a helpless slave, putting me to his pleasure.

How unlike the men of Earth he had been! How helpless I had been in his arms, no more than a worthless, grateful, yielding slave!

I had been well ravished.

Let me now speak briefly on a matter, the elucidation of which bears on my story.

My experiences on Earth had not prepared me for the typical Gorean male, free of programmed conflicts, guilts, and weaknesses, the uncrippled, unreduced male, so open, simple, honest, and direct in his unassumed, unquestioned, natural animal manhood, in his assurance, confidence, strength, and appetites. I supposed he might be diffident or ill at ease in the presence of one of those exalted, lofty Gorean free women, secure in her status, haughty, mercenary, and demanding, protected by a shared Home Stone, but his relation to the female slave, a half-naked property, purchasable, collared, and marked, was quite different. He knows, and we know, that we are pleasure animals. It is a simple dyadic relationship, that of master and slave. We see ourselves and understand ourselves in terms of that relationship, just as we are so seen and so understood by free men. I think this must be the natural relationship of the male and the female, for the men seem so healthy and vital, and I, at least, have never felt so alive, so real, so meaningful, and vital as in a collar. How glorious it is to be in the arms of a Gorean male, and as a slave! How I pity the poor free women, lacking a collar. No wonder they so envy and hate us. And no wonder we so fear them!

Returning to my story, I had been so certain of my view of the men of Earth that I had assumed that Addison Steele was no different from so many others I had known on my former world; I had approached him on the Thieves' Way South as though he might be a typical man of Earth, concerned, weak, pathetic, and manipulable, and how terrified I had been when I found myself on my feet, before the fierce gaze of a Gorean master. How quickly, trembling, reprimanded, I had gone to my knees before him, my head down, my lips to his feet! What a fool I had been! I had even dared to address him not as 'Master' but by his name, the name of a free man, putting that name on a slave's lips, an effrontery bordering on insolence or explicit disobedience!

How stern he had been with me, yet so lenient, in a way, for I had not even been lashed. Perhaps he had thought that I, a new slave, might not yet be fully in my collar. But little did he know how perfectly I was in my collar! Surely that became clear enough in the alcove! How amused he had been to see that the proud, vain, pretentious Margaret Henderson he had so properly disdained, if not despised, on Earth was now no more than a groveling, needful Gorean slave. And was it not he who had called me to the attention of slavers, thereby releasing my hidden slave, and giving me to her, she who was myself! I had thought much of Addison Steele since that interlude. My attitudes and emotions concerning him swept from pole to pole, from horizon to horizon, in gamuts ranging from stinging humiliation at how he had treated me, I, a woman of Earth, educated and intelligent, a former acquaintance, now half-naked, collared, and marked, now an abject slave at his mercy on another world, to an overwhelming, submissive awe at his manhood, his rightful power over me, from rage at how he had scorned and commanded me, handling me as though I might be no more than a domestic animal, to a slave's desire to surrender herself, flaming and begging, in tears, to his least touch. I hated Addison Steele, and longed for his collar.

He had not lashed me, but I had little doubt he would have done so, had I been in the least bit displeasing.

How my slave's body and heart had responded to his dominance!

I hated him, and wanted him to own me. I hated him, and wanted to be his slave.

I had begged him to buy me, this making it clear to him, and to myself, what I was.

I had been on my belly to him, and had been scorned.

Well did I then understand I was a slave!

He had put a tarsk-bit in my mouth and returned me to my master.

How I hated him, and had never forgotten him!

Each night, in serving, I had scanned the customers, fearing to see him, dreading to see him, hoping to see him. I recalled he had been surprised that I served in the Golden Chain, apparently thinking me too plain for the quality and prestige of that establishment. How little he knew! Was he so blind to beauty? I was sure a master could get a good price for me on the block. I was proud of my bondage, and what it said for my attractiveness. Had not slavers, discriminating professionals in such matters, selected me, included me on their cargo manifests, and shipped me, with others, like the animals we were, to the markets of Gor?

Every bit of me was now a slave.

Had I not seen the eyes of masters often on me?

Was I not frequently alcoved?

"Be busy, idle girl," snapped the Vat Master, pointing to a table, "or I will put the punishment mark on your neck."

Before we were caged, our necks were examined by the Whip Slave.

"Forgive me, Master!" I cried, hurrying to the indicated table.

"Hold," said the taverner's deputy.

"Master?" I asked, paused at the beaded curtain, preparing to enter upon the floor.

Euphrosyne slipped past me, and the beading of the curtain, in its colorful strands, with its tiny clatter, fell again into place.

The taverner's deputy made a slight adjustment of my collar. When a master lifts, inspects, or adjusts the collar, one commonly lifts one's chin that the matter may be easily and conveniently attended to. Interestingly, one then becomes much more aware of one's collar. Commonly one does not even think of it, or notice it, but, of course, however unaware one may be of its presence, it is always there, locked nicely about one's neck. I was surprised that he adjusted the collar. Surely it could not have been much awry. Before we enter upon the floor we inspect ourselves in a full-length mirror. Certainly I had done so. It is well-known that the sight of a female in a collar is sexually stimulating to a man. I suspect this is because it suggests that the female is a desirable animal, a prize animal, and fittingly to be owned and enjoyed. And, in the case of the slave, of course, this is literally true. I felt his fingers touch my neck, and felt heated. How slave I was! Yet I, shamelessly, thrilled to my responsiveness. The slave is free to be uncritically, unquestioningly sexual, free to be her vital, natural, needful, uninhibited self. Indeed, should she be reluctant or hesitant in such matters, perhaps as a consequence of some oppressive upbringing or restrictive education, or as a result of having been subjected to some pathological, negativistic, societally inculcated conditioning program, she may feel the lash.

Well she then knows that her world has changed.

She is now choiceless.

She must be herself.

If necessary, the whip will see to it.

It was yellow-tunic night at the Golden Chain.

One of the indications of the quality of the Golden Chain, aside from the excellence of its paga and provender, apart from the richness of its music and the beauty of its slaves, was the varying of its décor and appointments, often indexed to holidays of one sort or another. Today was the fourth day of En'Var, or En'Var-Lar-Torvis, which month follows the last day of the Third Passage Hand, which is the summer solstice. On this day, in Year Eleven of the Council of Captains, the Palace of Captains, actually a rather fortresslike structure, had been completed by the men of the Builders, one of Gor's high castes, the caste color of which is yellow. Generally it is taken that there are five high castes, the Initiates, Scribes, Physicians, Builders, and Warriors, whose colors, respectively, are white, blue, green, yellow, and red. The Merchants often claims to be a high caste, which claim, if accepted, would bring one to six high castes. The colors of the Merchants are white and yellow, or white and gold. The Slavers is commonly accounted a subcaste of the Merchants, but some deem it an independent caste. The caste colors of the Slavers are blue and yellow. Much on Gor varies from city to city. Unfortunately, there is no common coinage, but two important coins, at least in the northern hemisphere, against which other coins are often measured, are the silver and gold tarn disks of Ar, and the silver and gold staters of Brundisium. Needless to say, many transactions are conducted by means of scales. The Council of Captains, which body is sovereign in Port Kar, meets in the Palace of Captains.

The taverner's deputy brushed back my hair. I pursed my lips and thrust my head a little toward him, my eyes closed. My left cheek suddenly stung, sharply slapped.

"Forgive me, Master," I said, opening my eyes and looking away. I felt a tear course down my stung cheek.

His hands then were at my yellow tunic, pressing against my hips, and then drawing it down, more tightly against my body.

I forced myself not to respond.

"You are well-curved and pretty, as many meaningless barbarians," he said.

"Thank you, Master," I said, careful not to meet his eyes.

"It is all you are good for," he said.

"We hope to please our masters," I said.

His hands had excited me. How well I would pour paga tonight, how mutely I would plead in a slave girl's thousand ways, to be alcoved!

The taverner's deputy now stood back and regarded me.

I, as were my chain sisters, was now in a brief, wrap-about yellow tunic. It had a light belt of yellow cloth, supported by four loops, which belt, fastened by a slip knot, might be easily undone, allowing the folds of the tunic to be delicately or rudely parted.

I spoke of my "chain sisters" but there was a mighty gap between us, between Gorean beauties in their collars and barbarians, perhaps beauties, in theirs. I thought of Adraste and others, so arrogant, so superior, in their contempt of barbarians, who were themselves, as slaves, no better than the barbarians they scorned. And, I knew, we sold as well, if not better, than they. Gorean masters did not share their scorn and were fond of having us, mere barbarians, lowly as we might be, needful and begging, chained at their feet.

I was not ashamed at being from Earth.

Do not some of the finest slaves come from Earth?

Surely slavery was nothing new to my former world.

I stood beautifully, as a property and slave.

I did not move, as I had not been dismissed.

Aglaia and Daphne pressed past me, making their way through the beaded curtain.

The taverner's deputy, to my uneasiness, stepped behind me.

I did not, of course, dare turn my head.

I heard a rustle of thick cloth and leather behind me.

"Hold, steady," said the taverner's deputy.

Then I could not see, for a slave hood had been pulled down, over my head. It was of layers of thick, opaque cloth, fitted with a ringed, threaded neck belt. I felt the leather encircle my neck closely at which point, at the back of my neck, adjusted, it was fastened shut by means of a padlock snapped through two rings. The hood was thus locked upon me. It is difficult to convey to one who has not worn a slave hood how disconcerted and helpless one is in such a device, how much at the mercy of others one is. It is particularly frightening to be switched or whipped in such a device.

"May I speak, Master?" I begged.

"Yes," he said.

"Have I not been pleasing?" I asked. "I have striven to be pleasing."

"Why then," said he, "should you be afraid?"

"Perhaps I fear I may have failed in some way, a way I do not even understand, to be pleasing, fully pleasing."

"Do not concern yourself," he said.

"I am afraid," I said.

"Why?" he asked.

"I am hooded," I said.

"Do not concern yourself," he said.

"I can see nothing, and am utterly helpless," I said.

"Do not concern yourself," he said.

"Am I not to be sent out upon the floor?" I asked.

"Perhaps later," he said. "Now, for a time, you are reserved."

"'Reserved'?" I said.

"Yes," he said.

"I do not understand," I said. "I am not special. No one knows me."

"I will conduct you momentarily to a designated alcove," he said.

"No one knows me," I said.

"Surely you have served many customers," he said.

"Most do not know my name," I said, "even when they bind and alcove me. I am only another slave to them."

"You are right," he said. "It is interesting."

"I do not understand," I said.

"Perhaps you are known to someone you do not know," he said.

Instantly I thought of Addison Steele, but why would he not simply avail himself of me, if interested or so inclined, like a pastry or a drought of paga? Too, he had seemed to enjoy observing my slightest nuances of expression, tone, or movement. I remembered the alcove in the cheap, low tavern, the sordid Whip and Chain, on the Thieves' Way South. Surely one could take only a despised woman, perhaps the daughter of an enemy, or a slave, to such a place. I had found I could hide nothing from him. How all of me had been revealed to him! How frightening it is to be truly seen by a man, and as a slave! I feared that my heart had been as displayed to him as fully as my collared body. What woman can be more truly seen, understood, and known than when she is in a collar?

I felt the firm grip of the taverner's deputy on my upper left arm.

"I will conduct you to the designated alcove," he said.

"Yes, Master," I said.

We then, I being guided, brushed through the beaded curtain, and turned left, toward the alcoves.

CHAPTER THIRTEEN

I am Interviewed

I knelt in the alcove, waiting.

I had not been told to remove my tunic, nor even to leave it parted. This perplexed me, and made me uneasy, for it suggested that, at least initially, I had not been reserved for slave use. What then might masters wish, in such a place and at such a time?

The leather curtains of the alcove had been drawn shut. I supposed that some sign or token had been placed on the curtains, on the outside, to indicate that the alcove was temporarily unavailable to the public. On the inside of the curtains there are fastenings by means of which the alcove, once entered, may be secured, the curtains tied shut, this protecting the privacy of its occupants.

The taverner's deputy had chained my left ankle to a wall ring in the alcove before taking his leave, closing the curtains.

Slaves are often bound or chained, sometimes blindfolded or hooded, sometimes gagged, and so on. I think one would be mistaken if one took this sort of thing, in most instances, to be simply, or even primarily, custodial in nature. Obviously I, even if not hooded, even if not chained, even were it not for the preciousness of my collar to me, could not, in any practical sense, flee. I, no more than others similarly tunicked, marked, and collared, had any realistic prospect of escape. Consider merely the slave's garmenture. She is clad, when clad, in a very distinctive fashion, one instantly and easily recognized, commonly in a brief, revealing tunic, a form of garmenture which would not only scandalize a free woman but plunge her into the throes of shame, consternation, and dismay. A former free woman, recently embonded, must often be whipped into the streets before she dares to show herself publicly so. In time, of course, as she learns the collar, she comes to find such garmenture not only appropriate for her, but thrillingly so. It arouses her, and those who look upon her. And should the slave, stressed and distraught, beside herself and foolish, be tempted to run, where shall she run? There is nowhere to run. The society accepts slavery as a valuable and important institution. Every hand would be against us. There is no escape for us. We are slaves and will remain slaves, unless the free should deem otherwise. And so, commonly, the slave is constrained primarily not to prevent her escape, but because she is a slave. It seems appropriate that she, being a slave, be bound or chained, or such. Beyond that, constraints can exercise a mnemonic function. She is reminded, in no uncertain terms, that she is a slave, and at the mercy of the free. Bonds also can be sexually stimulatory to the slave, reminding her of her helplessness and vulnerability, and to the master who looks upon her, defenseless, at his mercy. Bonds reassure the slave of her bondage. Chained, the slave is in no doubt that she is a slave.

I sensed a movement outside the alcove, and suddenly I heard the leather curtains parted, sharply, quickly, and, a moment later, I knew that I was no longer alone. Almost at the same time I heard the curtains being tied shut on the inside. As soon as I had heard the curtains parted I had gone to first obeisance position, kneeling, head to the floor, the palms of my hands on the floor, on either side of my head.

"Kneel up, slave," said a male voice. "*Nadu, nadu.*"

It had not been the voice of Addison Steele!

I instantly went to *nadu*, kneeling up, back on my heels, my back straight, my head up, my knees spread, the palms of my hands down on my thighs. The commands of a master are to be obeyed immediately and unquestioningly. Hesitation or reluctance can be a cause for discipline.

A tear ran down my cheek, inside the hood.

While I had been awaiting the pleasure of a master, I had rehearsed my responses to the possible arrival of Addison Steele. Might it not be he who, for some reason, perhaps fearing to face me after his unconscionable mistreatment of me, had arranged this odd charade, even my hooding? I would show him my rage, an icy fury. He would not escape my wrath. I would visit upon him my contempt and hatred, the fearful indignation of a proud woman of Earth, whose temper was to be feared, whose scorn was to be dreaded. Doubtless he had already suffered for days recalling his indiscretion, and was now desperate to beg my forgiveness. One might even feel a little sorry for such a fellow, so miserable, so stung with remorse, so self-castigating, and self-torturing. Perhaps, I thought, I might even hint, mercifully, that, in time, say, a long time, I might relent and forgive him, after which we might consider arranging a suitable, meaningful relationship, founded on respect and equality. After all, was he not a male of Earth, another pathetic, manipulable male fool, putty in the hands of a clever woman such as I? Surely I could arrange matters to my satisfaction. But these thoughts, so natural to the promptings of my terrestrial indoctrination, my Earth training, the dictates of a pathological conditioning regimen, had almost immediately been swept aside. I knew I did not want him to be another exploitable, weakling of Earth. I knew I wanted to lie chained at his feet. I knew I wanted his collar on my neck. I knew I wanted to be his slave.

But the voice had not been that of Addison Steele!

Within the hood tears streamed down my cheeks.

So I knelt in *nadu* before whom I knew not. In such a position a woman well knows she is a slave.

I wondered what my visitor might wish of me.

I did not sense that he had removed, or was removing, his garmenture.

The cloth belt of my tunic was not undone.

I was not seized, and thrown beneath him, or flung as an object to my belly.

I did not understand my hooding, my being reserved. These things were mysterious to me and, I suspected, had been mysterious to the taverner's deputy, as well.

It is unusual for a paga girl to be held for a given customer, to be reserved. Others may want her.

I remained silent.

"You are Zia," said the voice. "You are a barbarian. Your first public sale was in Brundisium, at the market of Anesidemus. You were sold for three copper tarsks, forty. You are currently a paga girl at the Golden Chain, and your current master is Ho-Tosk, Taverner of Port Kar."

"Yes, Master," I said.

"Do you know one who calls himself Rutilius of Ar or Bruno of Torcadino?"

"I encountered one spoken of as Bruno of Torcadino in Brundisium," I said, "a one-legged man."

"Do you know Decius, of Venna?" the voice asked.

"I do not think so," I said.

"I think you have met him," said the voice.

"I do not know the name," I said.

"Are you familiar with a *kajira* named 'Adraste'?" the voice asked.

"Yes, Master," I said. "Very much so. She may be on the floor now. She is a paga girl here, at the Golden Chain. I know her even from Brundisium."

"She was sold directly after you," he said.

"Yes, Master," I said, surprised.

"What do you know of her?" I was asked.

"Very little," I said. "She is very beautiful. Her accent reminds me somewhat of yours."

"It is an accent of Ar," he said.

"I think her name is Cosian," I said.

"It is," he said.

"She was imported from the World's End," I said.

"With many others," he said.

"Yes, Master," I said.

"In Port Kar, one hears many accents," he said.

"Yes, Master," I said.

"Tell me of Adraste," he said.

"I know little about her," I said. "She claims to have been of high caste."

"Perhaps she is lying," he said.

"Perhaps," I said.

"What do you think of her?"

"She is insufferable," I said. "She is cold, arrogant, and supercilious. She despises us. I do not think she knows she is in a collar. One would think she was free."

"You do not like her?"

"Who would like her?" I asked. "I do not know how Ho-Tosk puts up with her."

"Perhaps she does not belong to Ho-Tosk," he said.

"Master?" I asked.

"You know little of Gor," he said, "of its events, and history."

"I am a barbarian," I said.

"You do not recognize my voice," he said.

"No, Master," I said.

"Yet you have heard it," he said.

I was very uneasy. "Perhaps long ago, and far away," I said. "Or briefly. I do not recall."

"I suppose," said he, "in the light of torches, exhibited, it is hard for a slave to look into the darkness of the high, far tiers."

"You know me?" I said.

"It was I who purchased you and a confederate, one temporarily in fee to the house of Anesidemus itself, who purchased another, both of us acting on behalf of a principal who needs not be named," he said. "You, in particular, cost us more than we expected, three copper tarsks, forty, forty tarsk-bits."

"The house was surprised," I said.

"You are worth more now," he said. "If I had kept you, I might have turned a nice profit on you."

I wished Addison Steele had heard this remark.

"Thank you, Master," I said.

"Considerably more," he said. "You have blossomed in the collar."

"You have seen me on the floor," I said.

"And on the streets," he said, "near the arsenal, by the canals."

"You have observed me," I said.

"Even in your training," he said.

"I am flattered," I said.

"Adraste was sold after you," he said.

"I know," I said.

"Do you know what she went for?" he asked.

"I heard later, in the cages below," I said, "a silver tarsk fifty, fifty copper tarsks."

"It was a cheap market, catering to a less affluent clientele."

"I see," I said.

"A low market," he said, "one in which a particular slave might be discreetly vended."

"I do not understand," I said.

"Who did you think bought you?" he asked.

"I did not know who bought me," I said.

"What do you think you were purchased for?" he asked.

"I, and others, to be transported to Port Kar," I said, "for the taverns."

"In a sense, yes," he said.

"There is more?" I asked.

"Possibly," he said.

"I am owned by Ho-Tosk, Master of the Golden Chain," I said. "Surely Adraste, too, is his property."

"Perhaps, not," he said.

"I do not understand," I said.

"A slave, sometimes," said he, "for one reason or another, is not always kept in the house of her master, but is loaned out, so to speak, or rented."

"Their rental cost," I said, "being easily defrayed, that in virtue of the additional business their beauty might bring to an establishment."

"Precisely," he said.

"Thank you, Master," I said, rather pleased. "Need I be hooded?"

"Do you wish to be switched?" he asked.

"No, Master," I said.

"Perhaps you are curious as to the purpose of this interview," he said.

"Very much so, Master," I said.

"Slave girls, as other properties," he said, "are subject to theft. Even you, a barbarian, understand that."

"Yes, Master," I said.

"For example, as you are doubtless aware, an attempt was made in Brundisium to steal Adraste."

"Yes, Master," I said. "A one-legged man was trying to recover a slave, Luta, who had, as it turned out, been sold under the name 'Adraste'. During a dock fire, sheeted slaves were to be removed from the house of Anesidemus. Sheets were exchanged, mine with Adraste's, in such a way that abductors thought me Adraste."

"And thus was the attempt to steal Adraste foiled," he said.

"Clearly," I said.

"Let me tell you of Luta," said the voice.

"Please," I said.

"This is to be held in the strictest of confidences," he said. "You must not even mention this to Adraste, lest she collapse in dismay, fearing her discovery."

"I understand," I said.

"The slave, Adraste," he said, "was originally a free woman of Ar, the Lady Julia Leta, of a minor banking family, the Claudian Marcelliani. It is an unimportant house on Ar's Street of Coins. Indeed, few know of the establishment or would even recognize the name. I do not think it is any longer in business. Do not inquire into the matter further. The Lady Julia Leta, cunning and vain, and fond of expensive raiment and jewelry, turned to peculation

and the falsification of records. Bit by bit, over months, funds
were drained into an account which was her own, held under
an assumed name. But, *ela*, how unsatisfactory was this arrangement. How could one exhibit and enjoy the display of luxurious
goods beyond one's presumed capacity to own? Surely explana-
tions would be required. Too, there was always the danger that,
sooner or later, her embezzlements might be detected. Accordingly, under the pretense of conducting business at the Fair of
En'Kara, she determined to flee the city. Her intended destination
might have been either Harfax or Besnit, or even Market of Semris.
We do not know. In order that her disappearance might be successfully managed, she changed her name and changed caravans
at the caravanserai of Hogarth on the Viktel Aria. In certain ways
this was an intelligent choice as the new caravan was small, plain,
cheap, nondescript, and obscure. Neither it nor its goods or passengers would be likely to be much noted. It consisted of six wagons two of which were closed. In one of the latter, the Lady Julia
Leta, her passage arranged and its fare paid, concealed herself.
Unfortunately for the plans of our lovely thief what the caravan
offered in the way of obscurity it lacked in the way of security. It
was ill-guarded. No more than fifty pasangs from the caravanserai
of Hogarth it was set upon, in a desolate area, by a small pride of
rogue tarnsmen, or, possibly, licensed raiders from Treve. A state
of war, as you doubtless know, exists between Treve and Ar."

"I did not know," I said.

"Surely you are familiar with Treve," he said.

"No, Master," I said. "Forgive me, Master."

"The richest prize for the raiders," said the voice, "a welcome
and unanticipated bonus, was our curvaceous fugitive, our absconding beauty, the clever Lady Julia Leta, together with her
baggage, rife with notes and coins. Shortly thereafter she had
been stripped and tied, belly up, over a tarn's saddle apron, and
was well on her way to some camp or other, where she was marked
and collared. Soon after, she was disposed of to an itinerant slaver exhibiting goods at a roadside market. Thus, the proud, free
woman, the Lady Julia Leta, became a slave. The name 'Luta'
might have been suggested by 'Leta', or it might have been suggested by 'Lita'. As you know, 'Lita' is a common Gorean slave
name."

"Yes, Master," I said, "I know." I was pleased that I knew
this, at least, for I was acutely conscious of my ignorance of

thousands of things Gorean. I was often derided by my chain-sisters, if I may use the term, for my ignorance. But I was learning. I was learning, every day. I was not stupid, but ignorant. Gorean slavers prize intelligence in a woman. I found this gratifying. What powerful, intelligent man, say, an Addison Steele, would want a stupid slave?

"Some attribute the very downfall of the Claudian coin house in Ar, that of the Marcelliani, to the Lady Julia Leta, her thieveries and flight supposedly undermining confidence in the house," said the voice. "This charge is scarcely credible but it is taken seriously in some quarters. It became clear, in Brundisium, that some, presumably failed coin merchants and defrauded patrons, presumably through one or more agents, were seeking the former Lady Julia Leta, now the slave, Luta, to return her to Ar's Street of Coins, one supposes for use in restoring the name of the Claudian house and serving more generally as an example of what might be done with thieves, her punishment serving as a warning to any who might be tempted to abuse a house's trust."

"How would she be punished?" I asked, frightened.

"Presumably to be exposed, naked, on the Street of Coins itself, in a tiny, dangling cage, in heat and cold, in wind and rain."

"I would not wish such a thing, even on Adraste," I said.

"It is particularly unpleasant in the summer, when the body is smeared with honey," said the voice.

"I trust Adraste is now safe, here in Port Kar," I said.

"We think so," said the voice. "I think there is little to fear. We are far from Ar, and, in any event, very few, in any case, could recognize the former Lady Julia Leta, given the veiling common to the free woman."

"She is then safe," I said.

"Yet her master, for whom my confederate purchased her, remains apprehensive that another attempt might be made on his property."

"You are not her master," I said.

"No," he said, "nor is Ho-Tosk, your master. Her master is my principal, he on behalf of whom I act."

"May I inquire as to his name?" I asked.

"No," said the voice.

"Surely Adraste knows the name of her master," I said.

"She thinks her master is Ho-Tosk, proprietor of the Golden Chain," said the voice.

"Why should her master wish his identity to remain undisclosed?" I asked.

"Should her identity be discovered," said the voice, "that she was the former Lady Julia Leta, might that not prove embarrassing to her master?"

"Particularly," I said, "were her master of the Merchants, and most particularly if he should be a Merchant of Coins."

"You are extremely clever, Zia," he said.

"Thank you, Master," I said.

"Your inferences are uniformly shrewd," he said.

"Thank you, Master," I said.

"And invariably in error," he added.

"Oh?" I said.

"Do not be displeased," he said. "One expects little of a barbarian."

"I see," I said.

"Doubtless," said the voice, "as you kneel here before me, in *nadu*, chained and hooded, you wonder what all this might have to do with you?"

"I did not wish to press Master on the matter," I said.

"That was wise," he said.

One learns many things in a collar, amongst them that masters seldom like to be importuned.

"But you are curious, are you not?" he asked.

"Very much so," I said.

"Adraste is a valuable slave," said the voice.

"I suppose so," I said.

"It is obvious," he said.

"Perhaps," I said.

"Her master wishes to keep her, at least until he would give her away, sell her, lose her at dice, or such."

"If he fears her being stolen," I said, "why does he not keep her in his house?"

"And make nothing on his investment?" asked the voice.

"I see," I said, "he is then indeed of the Merchants."

"Perhaps," said the voice.

Hearing this, I was pleased. I suspected then that my inferences might be much sounder than my interlocutor would have me believe. I suspected that, for some reason, he wanted to confuse and mislead me.

"Your role in this is simple," said the voice. "You are to watch Adraste and, more especially, any who might seem to watch

Adraste or pay her any attentions other than those likely to be accorded to any other paga girl. You are to be aware of words, or looks, or movements, which might seem odd, surprising, uncommon, untoward, or suspicious. If you sense that theft is plotted, or portends, contact Ho-Tosk immediately, directly, or indirectly, through another."

"My master, Ho-Tosk," I asked, "is apprised of these matters?"

"Certainly," said the voice.

"I am afraid," I said.

"Do not be afraid," said the voice. "I think there is little, if any, danger. Presumably none know that the former Lady Julia Leta is in Port Kar. She was last noted in Brundisium. Moreover, almost no one, either in Port Kar, or elsewhere, would know her by sight."

"I am a barbarian," I said. "I am not native to this world. I know little of it. Please select a Gorean girl for this task. That would be far more apt for your concerns and designs. They, given their background and knowledge, would be quick of apprehension. The slightest discrepancy in speech or behavior would be instantly apparent to them. They would know thousands of things I do not. They would be much more aware than I, if Adraste were threatened, or in any form of danger."

"You will do very nicely," said the voice.

A moment or two later I heard the leather straps closing the alcove being undone.

"Master?" I said.

And then I knew I was alone in the alcove.

A few moments later the taverner's deputy entered the alcove. Shortly thereafter, he freed my left ankle of the chain and removed the hood. "Return to the floor," he said.

"Yes, Master," I said.

Across the floor, some yards away, I saw Adraste, in the yellow tunic, fetching paga.

CHAPTER FOURTEEN

Adraste and I Exchange Pleasantries

"I see no reason, Adraste," I said, "why we cannot be friends."

"That is because you are a barbarian," said Adraste.

We, with some others, were at work in the kitchen.

A girl may be demoted from the floor to the kitchen, particularly if she is seldom alcoved, this suggesting a lack of customer interest. Kitchen work, too, is often a consequence of a customer's suspected dissatisfaction. That is one thing. An explicit complaint is quite another. That would normally be followed by a whipping, that followed by an assignment to the kitchen, for a greater or lesser time. We six, however, for there were four others, had little to fear in such respects. Ho-Tosk, our master, was well enough satisfied with us. For example, we were allowed kitchen rags and our ankles were not even shackled. He, as many other taverners, who had the resources, would occasionally vary his girls on the floor, rather in the same fashion that items on a menu might be changed or adjusted. Customers, those who pay attention to such things, are quick to notice a new girl on the floor or the absence, perhaps alarming, of an expected one. Indeed, when the taverner's men notice a frequent preference for a given girl by a certain customer, she may be removed from the floor. Perhaps she is to be marketed? Fearing the loss of a favorite, the customer might then buy her. The more an object is desired the more likely its price will go up. Owners are seldom unaware of this economic probability. Indeed, the fellow had probably already reached the stage where he is annoyed when his favorite is alcoved by others. He would prefer to have her for himself. Again he is thinking of buying her. Now he is well motivated to do so. Gorean men, despite their belittling of, and mocking of, slaves, can become difficult to deal with, even unpleasantly, discourteously selfish, in such matters. Many men will die for a slave they publicly scorn. In any event, as I may have suggested, a tavern's stock of paga slaves is seldom constant. Paga girls can come and go. And often do. And what slave does not desire to be the single slave of a private master? Another reason, I suppose, for putting even a satisfactory girl in the kitchen might be to remind her that such or worse could always be her fate. With this in mind, will she not strive to be even more pleasing on the floor? In this respect, however, I think some masters, at least, might be a bit naive; they might confuse what a girl does not want with what a girl does want. It is not so much that she does not want the drudgery of the kitchen as that she does want the opportunity to obtain a master, her own master.

"Everyone needs friends," I said.

"I do not," said Adraste.

I still could not understand why my interlocutor in the alcove, when I had knelt before him, chained and hooded, had charged me as he had, with the task of being alert to possible anomalies or jeopardies which might pertain to Adraste. Why not charge a native Gorean girl with such a task? She would know thousands of things I would not about this world, its culture, history, customs, and politics. She would be aware of hints and subtleties which I, most likely, would not even note. It made no sense to me.

I had finished scouring and washing a plate, and now submerged it in the rinsing basin, after which I inserted it in the rack to my left, to drain and dry.

"Adraste," I said.

"Do not bother me, slave," said Adraste.

"I do not like you," I said, suddenly.

"Nor I you," she said, handing me a plate.

"Why are you unpleasant?" I asked.

"It pleases me," she said.

"I see," I said.

"Of course, you dislike me," she said. "I am far more beautiful than you."

"That is a matter of opinion," I said.

"That of the world," she said, "with one possible exception, if you are insane."

"I acknowledge that you are far more beautiful than I," I said.

"What is so obvious does not require acknowledgement," she said.

"I doubt that you were ever of high caste," I said.

"You probably never even had a caste," she said. "You are a barbarian. You cannot even read."

"I can read English," I said. "But, doubtless, you have never even heard of that language."

"I have heard of it," she said.

"You were once free?" I said.

"Of course," she snapped.

"Did you ever have a free companion?" I asked.

"Once," she said.

"What happened?" I asked.

"He deserted me," she said.

"I am not surprised," I said.

I did not actually think that the Lady Julia Leta had ever been companioned. Had she been companioned, it seemed certain that my interlocutor in the alcove would have mentioned this. But perhaps she had once been companioned, long before turning to her villainies.

"Adraste," I said.

"Do your work," she said.

"Do yours," I said.

I had hoped, of course, that I might find some way to relate to Adraste, in such a way as to better facilitate the charge that had been imposed on me. If I was supposed to spy on her, she, her environs and interactions, as seemed the case, the pretense of friendship seemed a plausible stratagem. Do not think the less of me. You do not know Adraste. Who, in fact, could actually like Adraste? A male might like to get his hands on her, to inform her in a thousand ways that she is in a collar, but who else? In such matters, given one's charge, one considers the means, the tools, at hand. The closeness of a friend is unquestioned; the concern of a friend is likely to be welcomed. Do not false friends betray most adeptly? Do they not make the best spies? Who is better situated to perpetrate treason than the false patriot? But my effort to relate to Adraste had been rebuffed. Again it seemed pointless to me that this task had been given to me, and not to a Gorean girl, one to whom Adraste would be less likely to object. It was difficult for me to express the intensity of my dislike for Adraste. What a liar she was, and how arrogant! In Brundisium, I recalled, she had dared to claim she had been of high caste. Thus I had been pleased to express my doubt of that in no uncertain terms. That should have stung the former Lady Julia Leta, she merely of the Merchants, to the quick! Or did she wish me to think that the Merchants was a high caste? Most did not regard it so. Gorean society is built on the acceptance of rank, distance, and hierarchy. On Gor one does not pretend such differences do not exist or are not important. Indeed, rank, distance, and hierarchy stabilize the society. Is the alternative not social anarchy, envy, jealousy, denial, uncertainty, confusion, competition, dishonesty, scrambling about, frustrated ambition, disappointment, fury, and chaos?

"Adraste," I said.

"Do not bother me," she said.

"I have heard something of interest," I said.

"I think I will go to another basin," she said.

"Not without permission you will not," I said.

"I am thinking of scratching your eyes out," she said.

"You had better settle for a bit of scratching and a handful of hair," I said, "else they will blind you, too."

"Why are you talking to me?" she said. "Do you not know you are a mere barbarian?"

"Your collar is on you as well as mine is on me," I said.

"I was once free," she said. "You were merely not enslaved."

"Let us pretend to be friends," I said. "My plainness next to your beauty will make your beauty even more dazzling."

"I need no tricks," she said.

"Why do you hate me?" I asked.

"I do not hate you," she said. "You are not important enough to hate. I merely despise you."

I had now had enough of the haughty Adraste. Did she think she was still free? Moreover, I did not regard myself as inferior to Gorean women, at least to those who were in collars. We sell quite well in Gorean markets, sometimes outselling our Gorean sisters, much to their chagrin. It was not our fault if Gorean men often found us of interest. To be sure, in the presence of Gorean men, we often strove to be found of interest. If you knew Gorean men, you would understand this. Before such men we hoped to be permitted to kneel. Before such men a woman begs to kneel. I had an end to achieve. How might one do so? If I could not win the confidence of Adraste by a feigned friendship, to achieve some measure of proximity, to further my small mission of espionage, perhaps I might alarm her, or intimidate her, to the point that she

might feel it wise to endure my company, my occasional nearness
or intrusiveness, however unwillingly. Under the circumstances I
did not think that my interlocutor in the alcove, or his mysterious
principal, would object.

"You might be interested," I said, "in something I heard, something which might be of interest to you."

"I am not interested," said Adraste.

"A sought fugitive," I said, "is rumored to be in Port Kar."

"A fugitive?" said Adraste, lightly.

"One of importance, one muchly sought, one for whose recovery money would be paid, one from Ar," I said.

Instantly Adraste stiffened, staring at the wall before her. She
clenched a plate. Then she thrust it from her. It settled into the
water.

"I see now," said Adraste, "why you are beside me."

"I was simply put here," I said.

"You she-tarsk," she whispered, not facing me. "You have been
waiting for this opportunity."

"Do not be afraid," I said.

"What do you want?" she whispered.

"Your secret is safe with me," I said.

Adraste began to tremble. She grasped the sides of the basin,
her head down, presumably to steady herself, to keep from falling.

"Perhaps you will now be more pleasant with me," I said.

"How did you find out who I am?" she asked.

"I was told," I said.

"Then another, or others, know, as well," she moaned.

"Few, I am sure," I said.

"Why should one tell you?" she asked.

"Do not concern yourself," I said.

"What do you want?" said Adraste, tensely.

"Nothing," I said.

"You see the collar on my neck," said Adraste. "I am a slave.
I am helpless. I can offer you nothing for your silence, neither
riches nor your freedom. You, too, are a slave. Be merciful."

"Your airs annoyed me," I said. "You were never of high caste.
You were only of the Merchants and, I suspect, not the high Merchants."

"The Merchants?" said Adraste, puzzled.

"Perhaps you have heard of the Lady Julia Leta," I said.

"I do not understand," she said.

"Perhaps," I said, "you have never heard of the Claudian Marcelliani, a banking family, or of its house on Ar's Street of Coins."

"No," she said, "I have not."

"I see," I smiled. "Let us continue our work, lest we attract the attention of the kitchen master."

Adraste turned to face me. "Who do you think I am?" she asked.

"Surely it is not necessary for me to tell you," I said.

"Who?" she said.

"Perhaps you have heard of a slave named 'Luta'?" I said.

"I have heard of many Lutas, and Litas, and Ranas and Dinas, and others," she said.

"I shall speak more clearly," I said. "You were once the Lady Julia Leta, of the coin house of the Claudian Marcelliani, guilty of peculation and flight, sought for public display and punishment in Ar's Street of Coins."

A sudden transformation of relief shook Adraste, and she gasped and threw back her head, covering her mouth, fighting to repress laughter.

"What is going on?" called the kitchen master.

"Nothing, Master!" called Adraste, controlling her mirth.

"I see nothing funny in this," I whispered to Adraste.

Adraste was now again the mistress of her emotions.

"Dear Zia, sweet barbarian," she said, "forgive me. I nursed my secret for so long, so well, that pent-up emotions must burst forth. I might have cried, wept, groaned, or wailed, but I dared not, for fear of the masters, for a cry of misery would surely call forth inquiry, and so, almost without thinking, my surprise, consternation, and terror, in some unusual accommodation, which must find expression, rushed forth, transformed, concealed, as laughter."

"An inadvertent substitution," I said, "mirth for dismay, laughter for distress."

"Precisely," she said.

"I find that hard to believe," I said.

"Dear Zia," she said, "tell no one that I am discovered, that I was once the Lady Julia Leta. Coin Masters are intolerant of embezzlement. They are not easily satisfied. They understand little, and conjecture much. You do not know them. They can be cruelly vengeful. What do they understand of the feelings, hopes, needs, and desires of a lowly agent, an obscure, neglected, unimportant hireling, one afflicted with want, one impoverished, one deprived, one lonely and miserable, one laboring in the midst of gold she cannot touch, one encircled by the wealth of others, wealth she is forbidden to grasp? *Ela*, I weakened. Who might not? I surrendered to temptation. I erred. I am contrite. Blame me not. Understand me. Be merciful, protect me, keep my secret, I beg it of you."

"Do not be afraid," I said.

"I think the kitchen master is watching," said Adraste, handing me a plate.

"Shall I call you 'Luta'?" I asked.

"No," she said.

"In private, of course," I said.

"Even so," she said.

"Very well," I said.

We then continued our work.

I was muchly dissatisfied with our exchange. When I had confronted the proud Adraste, who had at the time seemed much agitated, with the announcement that she was the former Lady Julia Leta, she had not responded as I would have expected, perhaps collapsing in terror, shuddering in dismay, weeping uncontrollably, moaning in despair, hysterically denying the claim, or such, but had, apparently, been amused. Indeed, she had nearly broken into laughter. Then, a moment later, it seemed she had acknowledged my claim, and wished little of me but compassion and silence. Her mirth had seemed anomalous; certainly it suggested that she might not be the Lady Julia Leta; then, a bit thereafter, too readily in my view, she had confessed to having been the Lady Julia Leta, admitted her guilt, sought my understanding, professed contrition, and begged my silence. It seemed to me reasonably clear that she could not be my interlocutor's Lady Julia Leta of Ar's Street of Coins, unless she was an actress of unusual skill and subtlety who, while actually being the Lady Julia Leta, chose to claim that identity in such a way that I would be unlikely to believe the claim. It seemed more likely that she was not the Lady Julia Leta but was pretending to be so, to amuse herself at my expense, taking pleasure in deluding a despised, ignorant barbarian. Certainly her conciliatory tone and her lavished endearments had been unconvincing. I supposed, given my interview in the alcove, there must have been a Lady Julia Leta, but I did not think Adraste was she. Rather, it seemed clear I had been misled. My interlocutor in the alcove had been mistaken. He was wrong. Adraste was not she. Given the fundamental nature of this error, I saw little reason in worrying about a Lady Julia Leta. On the other hand, it was clear that an attempt, an understandable attempt, given Adraste's beauty, had been made in Brundisium to steal her. But that was in the past, and faraway. We were now in Port Kar. I would, however, if only to avoid being thrown to the urts in one canal or another, try to remain alert to any plots or potential plots, suspicious allusions, or such, which might involve Adraste. She might not be the Lady Julia Leta but she was beautiful, and strikingly beautiful slaves are more likely to tempt thieves than plainer slaves. But, too, of course, they are likely to be more closely watched. Too, a thief in Brundisium is not likely to be a thief in Port Kar, nor a thief in Port Kar to be one in Brundisium. Strangers on Gor, particularly in smaller communities, tend to be viewed with suspicion. Indeed, in Gorean, as I noted earlier, the same word is used for "stranger" and "enemy." Incidentally, slave theft on Gor is very rare, certainly within particular communities. It is regarded as dishonorable to steal from one with whom one shares a Home Stone.

"Tonight," said the kitchen master, "the six of you, those tunicked, and not shackled, will be returned to the floor."

We would be washed, fed, rested, brushed and combed, and given fresh tunics.

As we left the kitchen, Adraste and I did not look at one another.

CHAPTER FIFTEEN

What Occurred on the Walkway

"Down on your knees, slut," said the master of the scroll shop on the Thieves' Way South. "Too often you have loitered about! I know your sort, sneaking about, sent forth by some scoundrel to steal a scroll, doubtless some client of the Golden Chain whom you hope to please. What was to be your reward, a candy, a taste of *ka-la-na*? Or were you merely to be whipped the next time he alcoved you, if you did not do this? Do you think I have not noticed you hovering in the vicinity? You have no business here. I am tempted to tie your hands behind your back and fasten a note to your collar that your indiscretion come to the attention of the Golden Chain! Scrolls cost coins, thief."

I trembled before him, on my knees, my knees clenched together. I had seen his frown on other days. But this was the first time he had stormed forth from the shop, between the street bins, to speak to me.

"I am not a thief, Master," I said. "Look upon a slave! I am not so bold! I would not dare to steal anything, even an olive or grape!"

"There are crumbs about your mouth," he said, wiping a finger across my lips and then running the finger over his tongue. "You stole a pastry from the baker," he said, "with honey!"

"No, Master," I said, "I was given the pastry by Master Leander. He is not far from here. He may be asked."

This was true, but I trusted that Master Leander would not in fact be asked. He was a jolly fellow, and I feared he might think it a delightful joke to feign ignorance of the entire matter.

There was no doubt that I was a girl of the Golden Chain. One needed not examine my collar. Some days ago we had been issued

street tunics with advertising. Concurrently our outside privileges, our opportunities to leave the tavern, which had always
been generous, had been further broadened. This lenience had
been motivated, we gathered, in virtue of the opening of a new
tavern on Palace Street, The Silken Rope, and, possibly, the reno-
vation and enlargement of the Whip and Chain, which was not
far from the scroll shop itself. Ho-Tosk had not been pleased to
have girls wandering about the Golden Chain whose tunics bore
inviting messages from the Silken Rope. Indeed, various alter-
cations had taken place amongst the slaves of these competitive
establishments. Ho-Tosk had even hired a brace of free women
with switches to keep the paga slaves of competitive establishments at a distance. Our crimson street tunics bore the small image
of a golden chain at the left shoulder, and, elsewhere, in cursive
script, one or more provocative snippets designed to appeal to
potential customers, such as, I was told, "Find me at the Golden
Chain," "I await you at the Golden Chain," "I hope to please you at
the Golden Chain," and so on. I was told the message on the back
of my tunic read, "At the Golden Chain, I am your slave." Interestingly, Adraste was not utilized in this way. I supposed this was in
accord with some directive from her mysterious master.

"And why," asked the master of the scroll shop, "would Leander give you a roll?"

"He is fond of me," I said. "He is kind. And I tell him the news.
A girl hears much at the Golden Chain."

"Rumors and gossip," he said.

"It is hard to know what is true and what is false," I said.

"It is all false," he said.

"I trust not, Master," I said.

"You have an accent," he said suddenly.

"Forgive me, Master," I said.

"It is not Cosian," he said.

"No, Master," I said.

"If it were," he said, "I would switch you."

"Master?" I asked.

"We are at war with Cos," he said.

"Yes, Master," I said.

"You are from Ti," he said, "or from west, on the Vosk."

"*Ela,*" I said, "I am a barbarian."

"Very few barbarians can read," he said.

"We are seldom taught," I said.

"Can you read?" he said sharply.

"No," I said.

"Then he on behalf of whom you act is a fool," he said.

"Master?" I said.

"Only a fool would send an illiterate slave to steal a scroll," he said. "She would not know the difference between the *Songs* of Andreas of Tor and the *Tactics* of Dietrich of Tarnburg."

"No one sent me," I said.

"You are illiterate?" he said.

"Yes, Master," I said.

"Which are the most valuable scrolls?" he asked.

"Surely Master means the most expensive," I said.

"Speak," he said.

"The more expensive scrolls," I said, "are on finer rence, with knobbed or ornamented spindles, commonly stained or varnished. Some of the most expensive are kept behind the counter; the most expensive of those have a purple ribbon tied to the spindle."

"I thought so," said the master of the scroll shop. "You were merely waiting for me to turn my back or be distracted, dealing with a customer, and then any one of them would do."

"I am not a thief," I said.

By this time I was aware that a small throng had gathered about, consisting, it seemed, of seven or eight men and three or four women.

"You stole a roll from Leander," said the master of the scroll shop, "one with honey."

"No," I said. "It was given to me."

It had not only been given to me, but it had been literally handed to me by Leander, while I had knelt before him. No longer did he cast a bun or roll to the walkway, and I must eat it, head down, on all fours, and only when given permission. A slave appreciates an occasional softening or lenience in discipline but is not well advised to confuse an act of kindness or a token of affection with weakness. The slave should take nothing for granted other than the fact that she is a slave.

"She is lying," said one of the women.

"Master Leander is kind," I said. "He enjoys what I tell him, the little things I hear at the Golden Chain."

"On whose behalf do you act?" asked the master of the scroll shop.

"I act on behalf of no one," I said.

"Beat her," said another woman.

A slave girl hovered for a moment, curious and apprehensive, at the periphery of the group but, frowned upon by one of the women, she hurried away. I knelt alone at the feet of the free.

"I have often seen you about," said the master of the scroll shop. "Why do you linger near my shop?"

"I walk, I often pass by," I said.

"You loiter," he said.

"Forgive me, Master," I said.

"Thief!" he said.

"Am I to understand, noble Brindlar," said a male voice, "that this comely slave sometimes dawdles in the vicinity of your shop?"

I caught my breath.

"Too frequently, noble Addison," said the master of the scroll shop.

"Interesting," said the male voice. "Do you not find that interesting, Lady Dorna?"

"Not particularly," said a woman's voice, as cold as the blade of a knife.

"What could explain such a thing?" asked the male voice.

I dared not turn about. My heart was racing.

"Watching, waiting for a chance to make off with a scroll," said Brindlar, master of the scroll shop.

"And where in that tunic," asked the male voice, "would you suggest she might attempt to conceal a scroll?"

This brought a burst of laughter from the men about.

"What is she doing here then?" asked Brindlar.

"It is clear," said the voice. "The vicinity of your shop, or, say, one close by, offers some coign of vantage, to lure one fellow or another, or, more likely, constitutes some agreed-upon point of rendezvous. The arsenal is close by, not even a pasang away. Perhaps she waits for some sawyer or sail maker. These collar sluts are not above clandestine assignations, even of the most casual kind."

"They are all shameless beasts," said a woman.

"How I despise them," said another.

"She-tarsks in heat," said the first.

"Report her to her master," said the second. "If the fellow wants her, let him go to the tavern and pay out his tarsk-bit."

"There is something in that," said a fellow.

"But not much," said another.

"Let her master find out, and he will beat her pretty hide off her bones," said another.

"She is not so pretty," said a woman.

"She will do," said a fellow.

"The Golden Chain," whispered another.

I dared not turn about. But he was here, Addison Steele! Tears ran down my cheeks. I wanted to leap up, and throw myself, sobbing, to his feet.

"Come, Addison," said she who had been addressed as Lady Dorna. "There is nothing here of interest."

I then sensed that they had departed. The group, as a whole, then broke up, its elements pursuing their private ways.

"Is it true, slave," asked Brindlar, master of the scroll shop, "that you loitered about, to meet someone?"

"Yes, Master," I said. "Permit me to rise, and leave. I beg it. I beg it!"

I wanted to rush after Addison Steele and, at least, if nothing else, have some sense as to where I might later find him.

"Stay where you are," he said.

"Yes, Master," I said, sobbing.

I did not know if I would ever see Addison Steele again. And I hated the woman who had been with him though I had never even seen her, the Lady Dorna. The name had been familiar. I had heard it on the voyage to Port Kar. It had been the name of the ship of the fearsome Bosk of Port Kar, said to be a slaver, trader, and pirate. It was, perhaps, a common female name in civilized Gor.

"I suspected that you had been waiting about, frequently, to meet one fellow or another," said Brindlar.

I doubted that.

"Yes, Master," I said. "Forgive me, Master. Please let me go, and I will hurry away."

"Stay as you are," he said.

"Please let me go, Master," I said. "I will no longer trouble you. I will no longer loiter by your shop. I will go away. I will stay away."

"Did you note how the men looked upon you?" he asked.

"No," I said.

"You may linger by my shop as much as you wish," he said. "Let them associate you with my shop."

"I do not understand," I said, though I feared I did.

"Perhaps I could use you behind the counter," he said.

"I cannot read," I reminded him.

"You can tell the colors of ribbons," he said.

"I would fear to touch money," I said. Commonly *kajirae* are forbidden to touch money. For such a deed one might have one's hands cut off.

"I will handle coins," he said.

"I would fear to negotiate," I said.

"I will negotiate," he said. "You stand in the background, and appear interested. Many men will do much to win the smile of a pretty slave."

I looked to the side. I could still see, far down the walkway, two figures, one of which I was sure was Addison Steele.

"May I leave, Master?" I said.

"What is the news from the taverns?" he said.

"Master?" I said.

"Surely it is not all reserved for Leander, the Baker," he said.

"No, Master," I said. I could no longer see, particularly from my knees, Addison Steele.

"Speak," he said.

I then, in misery, helpless, held in place by a master's will, recounted much of what I had earlier spread before Leander, for his wonderment, edification, and skepticism. I dared not be curt, lest I be whipped, or unduly synoptic, lest Brindlar and Leander later compare notes.

So, miserable, half in tears, I rattled on. Tharlarion races in Venna were underway, Centius of Cos, guaranteed safe conduct, had won the *kaissa* garland in the Argentum competitions; an attempt to elevate and standardize cargo fees on the Vosk had failed; the migration of four-gilled parsit fish had begun; Rencers had raised the shelter price for river pirates seeking asylum in the delta, when fleeing from ships of the Vosk League; a delegation from Tharna, visiting various towns and cities, was once again engaged on a periodic, fruitless quest of several years' standing, seeking information pertaining to the recovery of a lost child, the son of Lara, the Tatrix of Tharna, stolen when an infant; an alleged monster had supposedly been sighted in the delta. Lastly, there seemed much agreement now that the elusive Talena of Ar, the much-sought fugitive from the justice of Marlenus of Ar, had, at long last, after many subterfuges, escapes, and hazards, managed to reach the safety of her ally, Cos, where she was now an honored guest in the palace of Lurius of Jad, Ubar of Cos. This was attested to by a plethora of testimony. Indeed, it seems she frequently appeared at public functions in the company of the Ubar himself. In a recent war it seems she had much abetted the ambitions of the island Ubarates, Cos and Tyros. Without her treacheries, betrayals, and collaborations, and without the absence of Marlenus of Ar, and without the costly, ill-advised campaign in the delta of the Vosk, Ar might not have been defeated, occupied, humbled, and looted. With the restoration of Marlenus of Ar and the bloody rising of Ar's vengeful citizenry, Talena's regime had crumbled, and Talena herself had disappeared. I recalled that an enormous reward had been posted for her capture, ten thousand tarns of gold, tarn disks of double weight. Should such wealth not suffice to purchase cities? At least it might form fleets and raise armies. Now, apparently, despite hundreds of bounty hunters and vast searches, she had arrived safely in Cos.

"May I go now, Master?" I asked.

"Wait," he said.

He returned in a moment, and handed me a hard candy.

"Thank you, Master," I said.

He then turned away, busying himself at one of the street bins.

I rose to my feet and looked down the walkway, the candy grasped in my right hand. There was no sign of Addison Steele, or of the woman who had been with him.

I wiped away my tears with the back of my hand and put the candy in my mouth.

I wondered if I would ever see Addison Steele again. And I wondered if the woman with him might kill me.

I supposed that unlikely. Slaves are commonly given away or sold.

CHAPTER SIXTEEN

I Hear a Conversation, Which I do not Comprehend

I knelt beside the small, low table about which, cross-legged, sat four men, who, from their soft, brimless caps, I took to be mariners.

"He is not what he seems," said one of the four.

"Clearly," said another.

"He spoke not one word on the vessel," said another.

"He paid his passage with a golden stater," said another.

"How could one such as he have business in Port Kar?" asked another.

"Who would give him fee?" asked another.

"I fear he does not search for fee," said the fourth man.

"Who is he?" asked he who had first spoken.

"I do not know," said the fourth man. "But I fear him."

"How could one fear one such as he?" asked another.

"Only one who does not know his blade could fail to fear him," said the fourth man, whose cap bore four tiny scarlet slashes.

"You are formidable," said his fellow. "You are well known in the dark contests, in the Gambles of Blades."

"Yet I fear him," said the fourth man.

"You said you do not know him," said a man.

"I do not know his name, nor his rank, nor his station, nor even his Home Stone."

"Such a man may not have a Home Stone," said another.

"You have seen him with unsheathed steel?" asked a man of the fourth man.

"Once in Ar, early in the morning, during the occupation," said the third man.

"But he is different now, muchly helpless," said the second man.

"Inquire, if you wish," said the fourth man. "I would not do so."

I did not know of whom they spoke.

"The girl is here," said one of the men. "Let us replenish our goblets."

I held the metal pitcher with two hands, pressed it against my belly, lifted it, kissed it, and then, head down, between my arms, placed it on the table.

CHAPTER SEVENTEEN

The Delta Gate;
The Delta Market;
I am Surprised;
I Will Crave an Audience with my Master, Ho-Tosk

Port Kar is interlaced with canals, and, as one would expect, much traffic utilizes the canals, particularly in small boats. On the other hand, the city is not without its parks, plazas, markets, fields, and such. Too, there are few, if any, major parts of the city which may not be accessed by walkways and bridges. To be sure, if the bridges, which are invariably of wood, and which are usually light, carved, ornate, arched, narrow, and colorful, and lanterned at night, were destroyed, the city would become a defensible maze of fortified islands. This makes it hard to take the city, even to set it afire. A judicious burning or destruction of bridges can also isolate portions of the city, which may trap, and deny retreat, to invasive, hostile forces.

A week ago, Aglaia and I, on our way to fetch posters, had been abroad, beside the Yellow Canal, when she had cried out, pointing to her left at the water. "Look, Zia!" she cried. "Look!"

"What?" I cried, hurrying to the side of the canal.

"It is gone now," she said.

"I see nothing," I said.

"It was there," she said.

"You are teasing me," I said.

"No," she said. "It was large!"

I would have thought little of the matter except that her experience, as it turned out, may not have been as unique as I had originally supposed. I recalled reports I had heard in the tavern of an alleged monster sighted some weeks ago in the delta, something similar, save for a greater size and a silverish color, to the leatherish, black, snakelike "long tharlarion," with which the delta teems. I supposed it was, if it was real, a variety of long tharlarion, perhaps a mutant or sport, or such. It was not impossible that Aglaia had seen something in the water. As I may have mentioned, sometimes a shark, usually a marsh shark or Tamber shark, is found in the canals, but they normally find their way back to the delta or the sea. Two other anomalous events had occurred, or were said to have occurred. One claimed to have seen canal urts swimming in the vicinity of some shadowy, muchly submerged visitant to the Canal of Veminiums, presumably a shark or long tharlarion. This was unusual because urts commonly avoid sharks and tharlarion, often fleeing from their presence. In this case, they seemed to be clustering about the shape, indeed, some said, as though accompanying it, almost as though investigating it, almost as though curious. The second incident, which may have an altogether different explanation, had to do with an urt girl. She had been in the water on her rope, her hunter at hand, when she screamed in pain and the water about her swirled with blood. When she was retrieved and examined, her left leg was found to be marked by four, deep, evenly spaced lacerations. There was no sign of a shark or tharlarion attack, no indication of her having been gripped by teeth or bitten. She claimed to have been cut by daggers. This explanation was dismissed as the hysterical ravings of a distraught slave, but there was no denying the wounds. In the delta, there is an eel-like fish, the Hatchet Fish, which has a rigid dorsal fin. Perhaps four of these fish had entered the canals and, swimming together, oddly on their sides, had brushed the slave.

It was a bright, pleasant morning in late summer.

Ianthe had promised to show us something of interest, something she had discovered on one of her advertisement walks, those walks in which we made clear what delights might await customers of the Golden Chain. Accordingly we had conspired that we would, after our individual releases from the tavern, meet near the steps of the Palace of the Council of Captains, on Palace street. Aglaia and I had arrived first, and shortly thereafter, Daphne and Euphrosyne.

"Where is Ianthe?" asked Aglaia.

"She is being dramatic," said Euphrosyne.

"I do not think we should be congregated here," said Daphne. "What if a tavern's man should happen by?"

"Smile and all will be well," said Euphrosyne. "Fear rather a distemperate free woman."

I myself had thought of that. A slave tunic does little to soften the blows of a swift, hissing switch. To be sure, free women often bestow their blows indiscriminately and a slave's bared legs and arms, the sides of her neck, and such, may not be exempt from attention.

"There she is," said Aglaia.

"Come with me," said Ianthe. "I want to show you something."

"What is it?" asked Daphne.

"You will see," said Ianthe.

"I trust it will be worth seeing," said Euphrosyne.

"That you may judge for yourself," said Ianthe.

"See?" said Ianthe.

"What could do that?" asked Aglaia.

"What could twist metal like that?" asked Daphne.

Ianthe had led us through the city to the Delta Sea Gate, which is a minor gate. The largest gates are the arsenal gates and the western and southern gates, all of which communicate directly with the Tamber Gulf.

"Well," said Ianthe, "is that worth seeing?"

"Yes," said Euphrosyne, suitably awed.

"It will soon be repaired," said Aglaia.

"I hope so," said Daphne, looking beyond the gate to the trackless marshes of the delta. Outside the portal, one could see three or four of the small craft used by Rencers. These are conical and are formed of woven rence. They are commonly propelled by poling. The rence islands on which the Rencers live are also formed of woven rence. As rence rots, deteriorates, or breaks away on the bottom, new rence is added on the surface. The Delta Market is near the Delta Gate. We could see it from where we stood. Almost all local trading, fish, feathers of the Vosk Gull, favored for fletching, rence, and such, metalware, cloth and leather goods, *ka-la-na* wood for bows, wines and paga, and such, between the delta and Port Kar takes place in the Delta Market. Some produce and goods, however, come through the marsh from as far away as the towns of the lower Vosk. On the other hand, most of the trading of Port Kar is coastal, coming north from as far south as Brundisium or coming south from as far north as Kassau and Skjern.

One leaf of the gate, that on the right as one would face the gate from the city, had been lifted, bent and twisted. The other leaf hung awry on its hinges. A heavy chain, a makeshift barrier, raised and lowered by a winch, now hung between the walls where the leaves of the gate had been mounted. One of the small rence craft now exited the city, its pilot lowering his head, passing under the chain.

The guardians of the gate were still on duty, controlling traffic, coming and going.

"When did this strange thing happen?" asked Aglaia.

"Two nights ago," said Ianthe.

"I want it repaired as soon as possible," said Aglaia.

"I will inform the Council of Captains," said Ianthe.

"Who knows what could come from the delta?" said Aglaia.

"Anything could slip under the chain," said Euphrosyne.

"The gate, even when sound, is little better," said Daphne. "Every time it is open, to admit a ship or a rence boat, something could enter the city."

"Or leave it," said Aglaia.

I looked upon the ruination of the stout, heavy gate.

I think I had a better grasp of the sorts of forces which might wreak such havoc, and so easily and in so little time, than the others, but I did not think they could be found on Gor. Then I recalled how I, and many others, had been brought to this unspoiled, beautiful, dangerous world. Surely that bespoke sophistication, technology, and power.

"I have heard," I said, "of strange things, or happenings, in the city, in the canals."

"We all have," said Ianthe.

"But of things and happenings from more than two days ago," I said.

"There need be no connection between such things, if they took place, and the damage here," said Daphne.

"No," I said, "but what if all these things were true, the reports, and such, and were not unrelated occurrences, not mere coincidences."

"I do not understand," said Aglaia.

"What if there were some sort of mind here, or intention?"

"Do not be foolish," said Daphne.

"She is a barbarian," said Euphrosyne.

"If," I said, "things are connected, and some force or thing, minded or cunning, could come and go as it pleased, why would the gate be damaged, and so grievously, just now?"

"Your supposition is silly," said Euphrosyne, "but on the basis of your supposition, the matter would seem clear."

"I fear so," I said.

"To make its might, and its presence known," said Euphrosyne, "to attract attention, to send a message, to invite contact."

"Yes!" I said.

"But," said Euphrosyne, "why go to all this trouble? Why not just walk up to someone, and say 'Tal'?"

"I do not know," I said. "Perhaps, for some reason, it might not be practical, or wise, to do so."

"Too, one must be careful to whom one says 'Tal'," said Daphne. "Perhaps not everyone would do."

"Who might wish to say 'Tal' to something which can bend iron and tear gates from walls?" asked Daphne.

"Perhaps someone," said Euphrosyne.

"A message of bent iron and ruined gates would seem to be particularly addressed," said Daphne.

"Yes," said Euphrosyne, "to someone who might understand the message, and might respond."

"Let us return to the tavern," said Aglaia. "We have been absent for some time. It is not pleasant to be switched."

I glanced back to the Delta Market. As far as I could tell, things seemed normal there. There is usually less activity later in the morning and in the afternoon. Gorean markets are usually most active in the early part of the morning. On the sloping canal landing, bordering the market, I saw several of the small rence craft tied to rings fixed in the landing, sometimes more than one craft to a single ring.

We then left the vicinity of the Delta Gate. As Aglaia had noted, it is not pleasant to be switched.

On Palace Street, returning to the Golden Chain, we were crossing the square that fronts the broad steps leading up to the Palace of the Council of Captains. I glanced to my left. My body suddenly stiffened. It was some forty yards away, to the left. I caught my balance. A small sound of dismay escaped me. "What is wrong?" asked Euphrosyne. "Nothing," I said. I lowered my head a little and quickly moved to the right of Aglaia, who was

somewhat taller than I. "Zia?" asked Euphrosyne. "It is nothing,"
I insisted. The figure was large, and dark. Its movements were
awkward but purposeful. It had now passed, on our left, continuing on its way, opposite to ours. It had worn a light cloak,
despite the sun and weather. The cloak was fastened in such a
way that it concealed his left side. It had lurched as if it might
be some grotesque, powerful animal, in the semblance of a man,
half of wood. The heavy, rude crutch had struck, and sometimes
scratched at, the paving of the square. Euphrosyne stopped and
looked back. "Do not look back," I said. "Let us hurry on." "It is
only a one-legged man," she said. "It is a helpless cripple. There is
nothing to fear from such half men. Jokesters make fun of them;
children steal and hide their crutches and sing insulting songs in
their presence, keeping clear of their reach; free women will not
look upon them; such pieces of men and parts of men must smil-
ingly endure being mocked, while they hope to beg a handful of
crumbs, or a sip of bad paga. Some fellows amuse themselves at
their expense, using them as butts for humor. Some delight in
them. It gives them something on which they may look down."

"He was once whole," I said, "and, I fear, terrible."

"No more," said Euphrosyne.

"Such unfortunates should be pitied," I said.

"You still know little of Gor," said Euphrosyne. "That is the
greatest insult. Ridicule and derision they will bear, but not pity.
What Gorean would be so cruel?"

"So to some they are objects of contempt and sport?" I said.

"Of course," said Euphrosyne.

"I do not think he would prove such," I said.

"What choice has he?" asked Euphrosyne.

We then joined the others, and hurried on.

I did not think he had seen me. I had seen him once before, of
course, on board a moored ship in Brundisium. It was he who had
been referred to, but skeptically, as Bruno of Torcadino. Indeed,
I had heard that name again, during my interview in the alcove,
when I, hooded and chained, had knelt before an interlocutor
whose identity had been concealed from me. I did not regard the
so-called Bruno of Torcadino as lightly as might have Euphrosyne.
Cripple that he was he had braved and defied, even intimidated,
men both armed and dangerous. He had frightened me, as might
have a dangerous animal, unexpectedly come through a portal before one, unrestrained and baleful. Even had he seen me I did not

think he would recognize me, and certainly not in passing and at a distance. What was he doing in Port Kar? Was this a coincidence? Did he still seek his Luta? Did he suspect she was in the city? Had he intelligence of that? Had he followed her here? Where was he bound? Certainly not to the Golden Chain. Had he heard of the mangled gate at the Delta? Had that provoked his curiosity? Dared he enter the marshes? I was afraid. I must crave an audience with my master, Ho-Tosk.

CHAPTER EIGHTEEN

What Occurred One Night in the Golden Chain

His back had been turned toward me. He was in converse with two others. When I, sent to his table, knelt to inquire his order, he had turned about.

"Why did you start?" he asked. "Look up at me. Move your hair back, to the sides, slave."

I did so, and then lowered my hands.

He fastened his hand in my hair.

I lifted my hands, without thinking, to my throat, my collar.

"Hands down, palms on thighs," he said.

He then pulled my head toward him, more under the soft light of the dangling lamp.

"You know me," he said.

"No, Master," I said, unable to take my eyes from the small, triangular scar, low, at the right side of the mouth.

"I know you," he said. "I am sure of it."

"I do not think it can be," I said. "Forgive me, how could you know me? I am a barbarian."

"Brundisium," he said.

"I do not see how it can be," I said.

"The sheet, the fire, the mistake," he said.

"I do not understand," I said.

"It is she," he said to his two companions.

"Are you sure?" asked one of the three men.

"Yes," he said.

"Then she is lying," said one of them, the second man.

"But she is far lovelier now," said the man with the scar, "more beautifully curved, softer, more helpless, more vulnerable, more owned, more vital, more alive, more aware that she is in a collar. She is more of a slave now."

I did not understand how this could be. How could I now be more a slave than I had been in Brundisium? Yet I feared it was true.

"She has been longer in the collar," said one of the men.

"They cannot help themselves," said the third man. "Their bellies flame; they become more pathetically needful; they become more desperate to please; they improve."

"She would whimper and oil at a touch," said the man with the small scar.

I was grateful that he did not touch me.

"She lied, she should be whipped," said the second man.

"Please do not whip me," I whispered.

I had learned the whip early in this world, even before my serious training had begun. I recalled when I, and the others, stripped, our bodies stretched, our hands fastened high over our heads to a chain, had been introduced to its caresses.

"Do not fear," said the second man. "We would use the broad-bladed, five-stranded slave whip, suitable for female slaves. It will not mark your pretty hide."

"It is interesting that she is here," said the man with the scar.

He removed his hand from my hair.

I remained where I was, as I was.

"Three pagas," he said.

"Yes, Master," I said.

"Be quick," he said, "and return with them yourself. Do not substitute another slave. We are going to talk with you."

"Master?" I asked.

"I trust you are a charming, entertaining, informative conversationalist," he said.

I rose to my feet, backed away, turned, and hurried to the paga vat. A taverner's man, with his coin box, would collect coins. The girl goes with the price of the drink, but many men come to the tavern merely to eat and drink, meet friends, apprise themselves of news, gossip, and rumors, hear or tell stories, listen to the musicians and watch dancers, when they are performing, or even to play *kaissa* or stones, such things. A girl is seldom bound and sent to an alcove when there is more than one man at a table. Gorean men like to have slaves to themselves, and seldom hurry with what they have paid for. Men who are looking for a girl commonly come alone. In any event, I did not think the man with the scar and his fellows were interested at the moment in bringing a helpless slave to spasmodic submission.

At the paga vat I heard a slave in Alcove Seven cry out with ecstasy. Also, Daphne passed me, smiling, her wrists bound behind her back with a thrice-looped leather lace. Six other slaves were standing nearby, to the left of the heavy, colorful, beaded curtain, their backs to the wall, waiting to be picked out, or assigned to a table.

Shortly thereafter I knelt again beside the table, Table Forty-One, near the far wall of the tavern's main serving area, and placed the small tray on its surface with the three goblets. "Paga, Masters," I announced.

Each took a goblet.

I reached for the tray but a hand pressed it down on the table, that of he who had spoken of the whip.

"Remain where you are," said the man with the scar, softly.

"What is your name?" he asked.

"'Zia'," I said, "if it pleases Master."

"Do you remember Brundisium?" he asked.

I was silent.

"Shall I call for a whip?" he asked.

"I remember Brundisium," I said. "Master was kind enough to release me in Brundisium, that I might be returned to the House of Anesidemus. A slave is grateful."

"We were commissioned to obtain a slave, one once supposedly named 'Luta', now named 'Adraste'," he said. "We anticipated obtaining her from a buyer, while she was being delivered or transported. We thought things turned out more to our advantage. In virtue of an unanticipated dock fire she, and others, suitably concealed, and suitably protected from hot ash and sparks, were removed for safety from the House of Anesidemus. Our suborned contact in the house marked Adraste's sheet to facilitate her acquisition. Unfortunately for us, covering sheets were mixed, or deliberately changed, and we took you for Adraste."

"You had never seen Adraste," I said.

"No," he said. "As you know, the matter turned out badly."

"Bruno of Torcadino, the one-legged man, was your fee giver," I said.

"We received one silver stater by way of assurance and good faith," he said. "A second silver stater was due upon the delivery of the slave."

"Who was not delivered," I said.

"We had planned carefully," he said. "We had arranged a departure from Brundisium, an escape, with the first tide following the theft. Even with the theft bungled, its attempt would be obvious and noted. We did not wish to be held in Brundisium, caught in a net of investigation and interrogation. We withdrew. Later, at sea, we pondered the matter. It seemed clear that the one-legged man had not revealed his true identity. That was clear even in Brundisium. But why should he do that, unless it was important to keep that identity secret? And why should it be kept secret, if the matter was all clear, lawful, and honorable, that of bringing a slave back to her proper chains? Why not have recourse to guardsmen? And would it not be improbable to put two silver staters at risk for a single slave, however beautiful, and one vended in a low market, that of the House of Anesidemus? Why would he not have attended the auction and bid on her personally? And one who could commit two silver staters in such a way most likely has more in hand. He must know something about the slave. He must know someone to whom he can deliver her for even more than two staters. It was all mysterious. Who was he? Who was the slave? Surely there was more here than was easily seen."

I remained silent. Clearly he did not know that the true identity of Adraste was that of the former Lady Julia Leta, former agent of the House of the Claudian Marcelliani, of Ar's Street of Coins, wanted for embezzlement.

"I am surprised to see you here," he said.

"Master?" I said.

"How is it that you are in Port Kar?" he asked.

"I was sold in the House of Anesidemus," I said. "I was purchased by an agent for Ho-Tosk, my master, proprietor of the Golden Chain. I and some others were brought north, along the coast, for the tavern."

"Adraste was shipped with you?" he asked.

"No, Master," I said.

"Note that," said the second man.

The men had been drinking their paga, bit by bit.

"May I ask," I said, "how it is that Master is in Port Kar?"

I was not struck.

"We sensed that not only silver but perhaps gold might be involved in this strange business," he said. "We put about. We returned to Brundisium. We watched for the one-legged man. Days, weeks passed. We were unsuccessful. Then we learned that a one-legged man had taken ship, and recently, to Port Kar."

"Why would he have done so?" I asked.

"I do not know," he said. "But now that I find you in Port Kar I conjecture that he, perhaps having little to guide him and being desperate, thought that you, because of the change of sheets, might somehow be associated with Adraste. Surely that might be possible. He must have learned you were taken to Port Kar. Such information is easily purchased. Then, suspecting that there might be some connection or relationship between you and Adraste, and what else had he to go on, he pursued that possibility. Might you not somehow lead him to Adraste?"

"I am frightened," I said.

"We have been several days in Port Kar," he said.

"I know," I said.

"What do you know of Adraste?" he asked.

"Very little," I said.

"What is unusual or special about her?" he asked.

"She is very beautiful," I said.

"Many slaves are beautiful," he said. "That is why they are put in collars. What else?"

"Nothing that I know of," I said.

"Finally, with inquiries and silver, we located the one-legged man," he said. "We eventually followed him here. I think he had learned from some slave on the street that a slave named Adraste had served at the Golden Chain."

"She was not I," I said.

"But she, Adraste, had served here?" he asked.

"Yes, Master," I said, "until two days ago." I need not tell him that I had informed Ho-Tosk of what had occurred in Brundisium, and the current presence of the one-legged man in Port Kar. Immediately upon my disclosures, Adraste, doubtless to her consternation and confusion, had been removed from the floor. Within the Ahn she had been removed from the tavern.

"What became of her?"

"I do not know," I said. "Perhaps she was sold."

"Can you recognize her?" he asked.

"No more than many others," I said, "slaves, taverner's men, the taverner, many customers, and others."

"The one-legged man was furious," said the man with the scar.

"He was in the tavern?" I said.

"Yes," he said.

I had not seen him. Presumably I had been abroad in the city. For that fortuity I was grateful.

"Did he recognize you?" I asked.

"No," said the man with the scar. "We, having followed him, stood to the side, in shadows. His concern was with the Vat Master and the taverner's men. He cried out with rage. He demanded that Adraste be brought before him. He claimed her as his own. He shouted, he demanded, he denounced. He offered silver to any who could supply him with information as to her whereabouts. But his ranting, his offers, his cries, his wheedlings, availed him naught. With his great crutch, which must have been cored with lead, he smote tables, breaking them in two, struck lamps from their chains, swept shelves free of goblets. Then, threatened by taverner's men, armed with clubs and staves, amidst calls for guardsmen, he departed the tavern."

"I am glad I was not present," I said.

I had seen little evidence of this alleged damage. Tables must have been replaced, lamps restrung, and such. I gathered that the slaves had been cautioned not to speak of the matter. Things were apparently to be as they were before. In this way, I supposed, the physical residue of the incident eliminated, inquiries might be minimized.

"It seems Adraste, whoever she might be," said the second man, "is in Port Kar."

"And many might recognize her," said the third man.

I found myself regarded by the man with the scar. "Are you for sale?" he asked.

"I do not think so," I said. But I was well aware that I, as a property, could be bought and sold, as any other property.

"Any of these slaves will do," said the second man.

"We will find her," said the man with the scar.

"We, or the one-legged man," said the third man.

"What is the mystery of Adraste?" asked the second man.

"The one-legged man knows," said the third man.

"One other knows as well," said the man with the scar.

"Who?" asked the second man.

I sought not to tremble.

"Adraste," said the man with the scar. "We need only find her, and torture will do the rest."

I tried not to lose consciousness and collapse beside the low table.

I think then the men had finished their paga.

I heard the goblets clash together, and then, together, strike down on the table.

"Will Masters have more?" I asked, as we are instructed to ask.

I hoped they were finished.

"Paga," said the man with the scar.

"Yes, Master," I said.

CHAPTER NINETEEN

The Line

I stood with the others, my back to the wall, near the paga vat, looking at the guests, the tables, the slaves, coming and going, the serving. It was a warm evening, in the neighborhood of the Twentieth Hour, the day after I had served the man with the scar and his confederates.

My glance strayed to the door of the tavern.

The night, the tavern, the world changed.

My heart leapt, my blood raced, I struggled to regain my breath. A suffusion of heat irrupted within me. How long I had awaited this moment, hoping for it, dreading it, wanting it, fearing it.

How should I act, what should I do?

Then I straightened my body, and stood well, noting with fury, that the others did so, as well.

Surely that was expected of me. It meant nothing. I had no choice.

Should I lift my head, should I lower it? Should I look on him, or away? What should I do with my hands? Should I cross my wrists behind my back or before my body, or hold my arms to the side, or turn a little and pretend to be adjusting my collar? Perhaps I should pretend to be obliviously conversing with Aglaia on my right or Ianthe on the left?

"He is handsome," whispered Aglaia, not facing me.

"Who?" I asked. "Oh," I said, "that one."

"Yes," she whispered.

"A little, maybe," I said.

A natural, unapologetic, unassuming, unquestioned, taken-for-granted, powerful virility is common with Gorean males, presumably a consequence of the culture, which does not set itself, for political or social reasons, to diminish, undermine, cripple, and poison what otherwise would be a flourishing nature, but, as one would expect, even so, the men of Gor differ considerably amongst themselves, in judgment and appearance, in size and strength, in character and personality, and such, just as do the men of my former world.

"Would I had him for my master," said Marcia, down the line to my right.

"I, too," said Marcella.

"He would choose Adraste," said Ianthe.

"I do not think so," I said.

"Adraste is gone," said Lana.

I had no doubt that he had come at last, perhaps unable to help himself, agonized and contrite, to see me, to beg my forgiveness, to apologize for his summary treatment of me weeks ago on the Thieves' Way South, in the vicinity of Brindlar's Scroll Shop, and later in the Whip and Chain.

"He is alone," said Marcia, meaningfully.

"He is approaching," said Lana.

I stood well, and turned my hip a bit. Then I looked to the side, with indifference. I had still not decided how I would respond to his advances.

I had waited for a long time. Perhaps I should be adamant and severe with him.

We would see.

I sensed he was perusing the line.

"This one," said Addison Steele.

"Her name is Daphne," said the Vat Master.

"I will choose a table," said Addison Steele.

"When I send her," said the Vat Master, "should I wrap a leather lace about the stem of the goblet?"

"Of course," said Addison Steele.

CHAPTER TWENTY

The Message

It was early in the day.

I was arranging goblets on the shelves near the paga vat, which was now covered.

The night before Addison Steele had overlooked me in the girl line. I had wept and silently raged in my cage. How helpless one is as a slave! My pride was gone. All my pretensions, all my brave plans, had been shattered. How I was to taunt him, how I was to make him suffer, how I was to bend him to my will, how I was to manipulate him! All these aims and ambitions had vanished; how barren proved such absurd projects and programs; these tactics and formulas had evaporated; did I still think I was a free woman of Earth; did I not know I was now a *kajira*, a Gorean slave girl, an abject, purchasable animal, at the mercy of the free? Yet, too, though I, through my tears, tried to deny it, I was not dissatisfied with the collapse of my pretensions and plans. I knew that I had wanted to be defeated; in being vanquished, I was freed; in being conquered, I found the reassurance and victory for which I longed.

I wondered if I would ever see Addison Steele again.

Surely it was possible. Might he not come again to the Golden Chain? Perhaps I could see him now and then, if only at a distance.

I knew I was now a slave.

I wanted to belong to him.

But he was not interested in me.

I recalled my former life.

How different it was now.

I was now in a collar.

My pride was gone.

He had despised me as a free woman. How much more then

must he despise me as a slave! But I did not care. It was what I was and wanted to be.

My pride was gone.

I wanted to seek him out and throw myself to his feet, covering them with kisses, weeping, begging, to be purchased.

I was no longer a free woman.

I was a slave.

"Zia!" called Euphrosyne.

I turned to face her, a goblet in hand.

"I was called to the door," she said. "I was given a message, for you."

"By whom?" I asked.

"I do not know," she said. "I could not well see his face. He was muchly hooded. I do not think he is known here. I did not know him. He did not identify himself."

"Surely there is a mistake," I said.

"No," said Euphrosyne. "The message was for you."

"No one gives messages to a paga slave," I said.

"Shall I give it to a taverner's man?" she asked.

"No," I said.

"He was clear," she said. "It was for you, the slender, dark-haired barbarian slave, Zia, floor slave in the Golden Chain, the property of Ho-Tosk, proprietor of the Golden Chain."

"I do not understand," I said.

"Have you business outside the tavern?" she asked.

"No," I said. "Of course not."

"You had better not," she said.

I put the goblet with the others on the shelf.

"Tell me the message," I said.

"It is on paper," she said. She looked about, and then opened the palm of her hand. In it was a small, folded paper.

"You know I cannot read," I said. "Read it to me."

Euphrosyne unfolded the small sheet, and regarded it.

"Well?" I asked.

Euphrosyne was frowning. "I cannot read this," she said.

"But you can read," I said.

"Not this," she said. "It is unintelligible. It is not writing. It is only lines with starts and stops."

"Let me see," I said.

I seized the paper and turned away from Euphrosyne. I was shaking. I feared I might tear the paper. "Thank you," I said.

"It is writing?" she said.

"Yes," I said. "It is cursive. It is not just lines. It is handwriting. I can read it."

"It is in code?" she asked.

"No," I said. "It is in a language."

"Not Gorean," she said.

"There are other languages," I said.

"I know," she said, "but with an alphabet, languages which can be written down?"

"There are many such," I said, "elsewhere."

"What does it say?" she asked.

"I have not read it," I said.

"Read it," she said.

"Are there not tunics to be dampened and pressed?" I asked.

"That is quite possible," she said.

"Curiosity," I said, "is not becoming to a *kajira*."

"I have heard so," she said.

"Forgive me," I said.

"You will help me with the tunics?" she said.

"Of course," I said.

"You are forgiven," she said.

I waited until Euphrosyne had withdrawn, and then I took the note near the door, to read it in the morning light. It was in English, handwritten, in a bold, firm, masculine script. Its contents were as follows:

To the slave Zia,
Paga Girl at the Golden Chain,
Slave of Ho-Tosk, of Port Kar:
You are herewith instructed to be on the Walkway of the Thieves' Way South, between the Scroll Shop of Brindlar, of Port Kar, and the paga tavern, the Whip and Chain, on this day, that of the delivery of this message, at the Twelfth Ahn. Your absence from the Golden Chain has been arranged with your master, Ho-Tosk, of Port Kar. You will wear a nondescript tunic, suitable for a low slave, one which will not associate you with the Golden Chain. This tunic will be delivered by a messenger to the Golden Chain at the Tenth Ahn. Once tunicked, you will be released from the Golden Chain through a secret door. You are to discuss this matter with no one. After perusal, destroy this message.

A. S.

I understood very little about this message. The Twelfth Ahn is two Ahn past the Gorean noon. I took the message to be from Addison Steele, which thrilled me, but frightened me, as well. Had he recalled my spasmodic surrenders in the Whip and Chain and thought to amuse himself once more with my body, that of a helpless slave in his hands? But if he wished to do so, it would be much easier to avail himself of me at the Golden Chain, in a comfortable alcove where I might, stripped to the collar, serve him wine and snacks, while waiting to see what he would do with me. I wondered if he had actually written the message. Presumably he was not the only one on this world who could write in English. Gorean slavers on Earth doubtless mastered one or more Earth languages. Perhaps someone wished me to think the message was from Addison Steele. Perhaps someone simply had the same initials. At least I knew where to keep the rendezvous. I had often frequented that area. I wondered if Ho-Tosk had actually authorized my absence from the tavern. Even had I wished to escape the tavern, I would not have dared to do so. Where could one go, where could one escape to? I dreaded the marshes, with the sharks, the Rencers, the tharlarion. Were I to strive for passage from Port Kar, it would be merely to be kept, or sold, at the end of the voyage. There was no escape for the Gorean slave girl. And penalties for attempted escape could be not only painful, but grievous. Gorean masters do not care to be inconvenienced by the antics of naive or foolish slaves.

I hurried down to the office of Ho-Tosk, to crave an audience, to inquire into, and confirm, details in the message, but learned, to my dismay, that he was absent from the tavern, and would not return until tomorrow.

"Zia," called Euphrosyne, up from the laundry room below, which is on the same level as the kitchen.

"I will be with you in a moment," I said. I went down the stairs from the level of Ho-Tosk's office to the kitchen. On the way to the laundry room I surreptitiously dropped the note into one of the stoves.

"I will dampen," said Euphrosyne. "You iron."

"Why am I to iron?" I asked.

"Because you are a barbarian," she said. "Also, you did not read your message to me."

"It was not important," I said.

Several of the small irons, heated from stoves in the kitchen, were waiting on the iron plate. I grasped the wooden handle which is designed to fit the irons, inserted it into one of the irons, and set to work.

CHAPTER TWENTY-ONE

I Endeavor to Keep an Appointment; The Bridge

At a third before the Twelfth Ahn I was on the Thieves' Way South. My heart was beating rapidly. At the Tenth Ahn, a messenger, a stranger, certainly no one I knew, appeared within the tavern. In the vicinity of the Tenth Ahn, for some Ehn before, I had watched the door to the tavern, but I had not seen him enter. I did not realize he was in the tavern until I became aware of a presence behind me. He carried a small package. He indicated that I should follow him down the stairs, to the long pantry, adjoining the kitchen. There, in the pantry, he opened the package, which contained a small, gray tunic. He handed me the garment and told me to return to the pantry, in the garment, at the Eleventh Ahn. He then placed the wrapping in the wallet slung from his belt, and gestured that I should leave the pantry, which I did. Only a few steps from the pantry, however, distraught and confused, the tunic in my hand, I turned about, wildly, and rushed back to the pantry, to beg him for some intelligence as to what this whole mad business, so curious and mysterious, might be about, but the pantry was empty. Shortly before the Eleventh Ahn I donned the gray tunic, which had an odd feel about it, and returned to the pantry. He was in the pantry, waiting for me. He regarded me in the tunic and seemed satisfied. "Put your arms to your sides," he said, "and turn away from me." I complied, and a hood was slipped over my head and buckled about my neck. While I waited, he opened a portal or panel, somewhere in the pantry, one of which I was not aware. Then, his hand on my arm, conducting me, we exited the pantry. I no longer felt the flooring of the pantry or kitchen beneath my feet. The air seemed damp and musty. "There are stairs," he said, leading me. "Here. Hold the banister. Ascend." It seemed a long climb. At the end of this climb, we reached a level, floored with bricks. I heard a grating of metal, a creak of hinges, and a sliding of wood. I was conducted forward. The air was fresh. I felt warmth. The hood was removed. A door or paneling behind me closed. I found myself in the alley behind the Golden Chain. I was alone.

It was something like a third before the Twelfth Ahn. I was on the Thieves' Way South. My heart was beating rapidly.

I would hurry past the shop of Leander the Baker and that of Brindlar, the dealer in scrolls.

I did not wish to be delayed. I was not in a tunic of the Golden Chain. I did not want to be asked about this. Had I been asked, what could I have told them? The tunic had a peculiar feel to it.

I slipped easily past the bakery of Leander as two customers were at his counter. For several yards past I could still smell the fresh bread. Near Brindlar's scroll shop I waited a little, until a customer entered between the street bins. Then, looking away, toward the canal, I hurried past. Then, the scroll shop some yards behind me, I stopped. The message had told me to be between the scroll shop and the Whip and Chain at the Twelfth Ahn. I had not yet heard the bar sound for the Ahn. I was early. From where I stood I could see the sign for the Whip and Chain, small in the distance. The sign had been repainted. I was uneasy. A loitering slave may be questioned. I could walk a little, back and forth, pretending to be coming or going. There was space enough for that. On the other hand, there seemed few, if any, on the walkway. Two small boats moved past in the canal. I was uncomfortable in the tunic. This was unusual for it is hard to conceive of a garment lighter, freer, and more comfortable than a Gorean slave tunic. A free man passed and I knelt, and then, when he had passed, I rose again to my feet. Behind me was a stone wall, on which were posters and graffiti. One of the posters advertised the Golden Chain. The bar for the Twelfth Ahn rang.

I waited, in place. Of the few passing, to and fro, shopsmen and porters, none spoke to me. Some Ehn passed. Another small boat slipped by, this one moving west on the canal. Far off, ahead, I could see one of the small, narrow, colorful, wooden bridges spanning the canal. Another small boat was passing under it, approaching.

More Ehn passed.

The boat which had been far off, approaching, passing under the bridge, now passed by.

I tried to pull the tunic more away from my body.

I began to be more uneasy. Was the message some sort of hoax or joke? Had it been a ruse to lure me into an unauthorized absence? Even a single-master slave is commonly expected to request the master's permission to leave the domicile, and is expected to inform him of where she is going, what she will be doing, and when to expect her back. Was this a jest, I wondered, on the part of Addison Steele, to set me on a venture, a venture at the conclusion of which I might expect a hissing whip? Might Ho-Tosk suspect that I had tried to escape? I do not want to be hamstrung or mutilated, perhaps as an example to other slaves.

"I will wait a little longer," I thought, "then I will hurry back to the Golden Chain."

At that moment, there was a sudden noise, a bright, loud, unexpected, shocking, jagged flash of sound not a foot from my head, and a handful of stone and dust, and debris, gouged, burst forth from the wall. It was like an invisible hammer or spike had struck the wall, fiercely, and with great velocity. A moment later it seemed I recalled I had experienced a splinter of light flashing past, and then I had become aware of the noise, and the shower of debris flying from the wall, some of which pelted my left shoulder and settled on my arm. I screamed and threw myself to the ground. I did not know what had happened. I lay there in shock for a moment, and then, when I saw it, yards away, almost at the edge of the walkway, by the canal, I realized what had happened. At the edge of the walkway, by the canal, I saw a short, narrow, pointed, metal-finned, metal, cylindrical object, an arrow or missile of some sort. It was a dread, terrible object. There was no mistaking its nature or purpose. I would later learn it was a familiar article of war, a metal bird of death, the quarrel of a crossbow.

I half rose, looking about. I saw no assailant.

Was this some accident? Had I been mistaken for someone else? Who would wish to attack me? Who would wish to kill me, and why, I, a helpless slave? What had I done? Was this some terrible mistake? Was I, unknown to myself, involved in intrigues, plots, or schemes about which I knew nothing? Was I thought to be a cog or principal in some enterprise far beyond my ken?

As I saw no one about, and could discern no sign of danger,
I sprang to my feet and began to retrace my steps, to return to
the Golden Chain, but I had hardly taken a step when I saw, approaching on the same walkway on which I found myself, an unmistakable figure, large and menacing, hobbling, moving toward
me. Had he followed me from the Golden Chain? Had he been
waiting for the missile to strike me, that he might be the first
to reach the body, perhaps to examine it for messages? Was it a
mere happenstance that he was on the walkway? Surely he would
not know me, not from long ago, in Brundisium. He was moving
quickly, for his handicap. I had no immediate fear of him, as I
could move far more swiftly than he, supporting half his weight
on that stout crutch or staff. I was afraid to return in such a way
that I must pass him. I began to walk east on the Thieves' Way
South, occasionally looking back, trying not to exhibit concern. I
would cross the bridge and return to the Golden Chain by means
of the other walkway, the Thieves' Way North. But perhaps his
presence on the walkway was a mere coincidence? In the vicinity
of the bridge, when I looked again, he was much closer than I had
thought he might be. On whatever errand he might be embarked,
it was one he was prosecuting with vigor. I thought I would stand
to the side, as though not noticing him, and see if he would pass
me by. If so, there was no danger. If not, I would have time to
flee before he could reach me or strike me with that stout crutch,
that formidable aid to his balance and locomotion. He came closer
and closer and then suddenly, snarling, turned toward me. At the
same instant I darted from the wall and raced to the bridge. I was
almost half the way across the bridge when he reached the bridge.
I could outdistance him easily, and it would be easy to return to
the Golden Chain by means of the opposite walkway, the Thieves'
Way North. I was frightened, but elated. At that point, I heard a
cry, "There she is!" I turned about, and saw some five or six men
ascending the bridge from the Thieves' Way North. I recognized
he who led them. It was the man I had encountered twice in the
Golden Chain, and earlier in Brundisium, he with the tiny, triangular scar on the right side of his face, low and to the right of
his mouth. He carried a coil of rope. One of his entourage carried
what seemed to be a short rifle, surmounted transversely with
a bow of some sort. I did not doubt but what that device might
launch a missile of the sort I had seen but moments ago. "Hold!"
cried the fellow. "You cannot escape!" I looked back, and the one-

legged man, whom I knew as Bruno of Torcadino, was now but yards away. The bridge was narrow. I could not hope to elude him. I ran, wildly, helplessly, to the center of the bridge, facing west, trapped. I did not know what dangers might lurk in the water. I clung to the rail. I looked down.

"Do not jump," cried a voice. "Wait! Do not enter the water! Do not enter the water!"

A small canal boat was close.

I heard the hasty striking of Bruno of Torcadino's crutch on the bridge, nearing me. I heard the running feet of men from the other side, approaching.

"Now, jump now, into my arms," cried Addison Steele.

I sprang over the rail and was caught by Addison Steele.

CHAPTER TWENTY-TWO

What Occurred in an Apartment, Somewhere in Port Kar

"She is reviving," said a woman's voice.

I whimpered, kicked in the left thigh by a woman's street slipper.

"Awaken," she said.

Dimly, through the walls, I heard the ringing of the bar for the Fourteenth Ahn. I was in some sort of apartment. There were three curule chairs in the apartment. In one, at ease, was Addison Steele. A small table was to one side, on which reposed a fire tray, a packet or two, and a decanter filled with a transparent liquid, presumably water. There was also a large, heavy, ornate screen at the side of the room. I sensed something might be behind the screen.

"On your knees, slave," said the woman's voice.

I was bound, hand and foot. I struggled to gain my knees. Then I was kneeling before her.

She was clad in the Robes of Concealment, and veiled.

"This is the one?" she asked.

"Yes," said Addison Steele.

"You are sure?" she said.

"Yes," said Addison Steele.

"Lower your head, slave," she said.

I did so.

I sensed then the woman had seated herself.

"You may lift your head, slave," she said.

I lifted my head, and regarded her, she now resting back, sitting.

"You do not know me, do you?" asked the woman.

"Mistress is veiled," I said.

She relaxed the veil. She was quite beautiful. I wondered that there was not a collar on her neck.

"No, Mistress," I said. "I do not know you."

"But you have heard of me," she said. "I am Dorna, Dorna, of Tharna."

"No, Mistress," I said.

"She is a barbarian," said Addison Steele.

"How is it that Mistress is free?" I asked. I thought I saw her eyes cloud, angrily, for a moment. "I thought that all women of Tharna, save for the Tatrix, Lara, were slaves."

"I was first of the Silver Masks in Tharna," she said, "in the days of the Gynecocracy, second only to the Golden Mask, that of Lara. In time, I would have supplanted her, and worn the Golden Mask myself."

"The Revolt occurred," said Addison Steele.

"It seems Mistress was fortunate to escape in time," I said, "to avoid the collar."

"The capture of untold wealth," she said, "offers consolation for the loss of a Silver Mask, even a Golden Mask."

"May I ask what I am doing here, and why I am bound?" I asked. "I am the property of Ho-Tosk, of Port Kar, of the Golden Chain."

I thought I saw Addison Steele smile.

Did it amuse him, I wondered, that I, a former free woman of Earth, indeed, one of his own acquaintance, the former Miss Margaret Henderson, whom he had held in such contempt on Earth, now collared, branded, kneeling and bound, should so unhesitantly, and promptly, identify herself as what she now was, in all rightfulness and legality, a property? Let him be amused if he wished. It was what I now was, and knew myself to be.

"I will be missed," I said.

"What do you know of a slave named 'Adraste'?" she asked.

"Very little," I said. "She was purchased in Brundisium. She worked at the Golden Chain, but works there no longer."

"That is little, indeed," she said.

"Forgive me, Mistress," I said. Certainly I did not wish to reveal the true identity of Adraste, that she was the former Lady Julia Leta, of Ar's Street of Coins, now wanted for peculation.

"She is owned by Ho-Tosk, proprietor of the Golden Chain," she said.

"As far as I know, Mistress," I said. She need not know that Adraste was actually owned by someone else, whom I did not know.

"When did she disappear?" asked the woman.

"She has not been in the tavern for some days now," I said.

It seemed clear to me that the Lady Dorna, like Bruno of Torcadino and the man with the scar, though now independently, sought the former Lady Julia Leta, presumably to return her to Ar's Street of Coins, that an example might be made of her which would serve to deter others from succumbing to similar temptations. Presumably there would be some sort of recompense or reward for her return to the Street of Coins, but I did not understand the reference to "untold wealth." There are many rumors on Gor. It is well known that stories may be enlarged and embellished from telling to telling. Even if the Lady Dorna were successful in her endeavor, as Bruno of Torcadino and the man with the scar had not been, at least until now, I expected she would be disappointed in the return realized on her investment of time and money.

"Where is Adraste now?" said the Lady Dorna.

"I do not know, Mistress," I said. And this admission, at least, was true.

"You are going to tell us what you know, slave," she said.

"I have done so, Mistress," I said. "It is just that I know little."

"We shall soon know what you know," she said. "You will be unable to help yourself. There are the sensations, the powders, the fumes."

"I will untie her arms," said Addison Steele. "Her bound ankles will hold her in place. Else there might be severe rope burns."

"What does that matter?" asked the Lady Dorna. "She is a slave."

"And of some value as a slave," said Addison Steele. "We do not wish her value, as little as it is, to be lowered."

"Men are despicable," said the Lady Dorna.

"Coins are coins," said Addison Steele.

In a few moments my hands and arms had been freed. My ankles were still bound.

"Thank you, Master," I said.

"First obeisance position," he said.

I looked up. How I wanted to belong to him!

My left cheek burned, stung from his slap.

"Forgive me, Master," I said. Did I not know that the response to a command is to be immediate and unquestioning? Did I think I was still a free woman?

I assumed first obeisance position, kneeling, head to the floor, the palms of my hands on the floor, on either side of my head.

How far away was Earth!

I sensed that the Lady Dorna had risen to her feet, and was busied at the table to the side, that with the fire tray, a packet, or so, and the decanter, a rather large decanter, filled with some transparent liquid.

"Noble Addison," said the Lady Dorna. "The decanter is heavy. Perhaps you would pour?"

"Certainly," he said.

Then, to my amazement, he began, slowly and carefully, to pour a portion of the fluid in the decanter over my back. It was cold.

"Master?" I asked.

"It is water, slave," he said. "Be silent."

Very little of the fluid fell to the floor. It seemed almost as if it were sucked into the tunic.

"On your back, slave," he said.

He had not given me the "Sula" command, perhaps because the Lady Dorna was present. So I merely went to my back, my hands to the sides, palms upward. I did not spread my legs with a slave's helplessness.

My back was wet, the tunic heavy with water. Yet little, it seemed, ran off on the floor.

He then, slowly, carefully, poured water on my body, limiting his attentions to that part of my body which was covered by the tunic. I felt the water move through the tunic. Again it seemed that little of the water drained away to the floor. The material of the tunic seemed unusually absorbent. At the same time the Lady Dorna had shaken some powder from a packet into the small fire tray.

"Master?" I asked.

He returned the now-emptied decanter to the table to the side.

"Second obeisance position," he said.

Instantly I went to the second obeisance position. I did not wish to be again physically chastised for hesitation in responding to a free man's command. I now lay on my belly, prostrate before him. My hands were at the sides of my head, palms down. He did not stand close to me. If he had done so, I would have pressed my lips, reverently, to his boot or sandal.

I began to experience strange feelings in my body, where it was covered by the tunic, and then, in a bit, the feelings spread more widely, affecting my legs, arms, and neck.

"Master," I whimpered, in protest.

"I will hold her hands," said Addison Steele, crouching down, and he drew my arms forward and held my wrists. I was then stretched out before him, my ankles still bound.

I understood nothing of what was occurring.

Then I screamed, for the tunic seemed to crackle, and come alive. A myriad tiny needles seemed to penetrate my skin. It seemed I was on fire. Threads parted, and pulled away from my skin, bristling and curling, blackened, rising, twisting. The air about me shuddered, trembled, and fled, as if from flame.

I screamed again and again and struggled to escape the grasp of Addison Steele. I wanted to tear the tunic from my body.

"Mercy!" I begged, but I was held, prostrate, squirming, writhing, stretched out before him, helpless.

"Silence," he said.

"I am afire!" I cried.

"No," he said. "You are not."

It seemed to me as though I must be enveloped in a blaze of flame, but there was no flame, only, apparently, a sudden, fierce interaction of substances, freed or precipitated, I supposed, by the administration of water.

"Please!" I wept.

"In a few moments, it will pass," he said. "It will have done its work.

He had hardly said this when the pain began to diminish.

I heard the snap of a fire-maker and became aware that the Lady Dorna was igniting some of the powder she had deposited in the small fire tray.

Fumes curled up from the tray.

"Put her on her knees," said the Lady Dorna.

Addison Steele released my hands and lifted me to my knees. I was dazed, half conscious. The pain had muchly subsided.

I was aware that the Lady Dorna was approaching, holding the small fire tray by its handle. Within the fire tray there was now a small mound of powder, some of which was gray, like ash, which had apparently burned, and some of which, not yet burned, was blue. A strand of smoke rose sluggishly from the tray.

"You are on your knees," said the Lady Dorna.

"Mistress?" I said, half conscious.

"When one wishes the truth from a woman," said the Lady Dorna, "you should put her on her knees. It is hard for a woman on her knees not to tell the truth."

I was silent.

"You are going to tell us the truth," said the Lady Dorna.

"No," I said, half conscious.

I tried to lift my hands a little, but it seemed I could scarcely raise them from my thighs.

The fire tray with its burning powder, and fumes, was held before me. With the palm of her hand the Lady Dorna gently wafted the fumes toward me.

I was aware that a large male figure had emerged from behind the screen at the side of the room.

"You are going to tell the truth, are you not?" she asked.

I felt I was slipping into unconsciousness.

"Are you not?" she said softly, soothingly.

"Yes, Mistress," I whispered, and lapsed into unconsciousness.

CHAPTER TWENTY-THREE

I Awaken in Unfamiliar Surroundings

The first thing I became aware of, even before I opened my eyes, was my right cheek on the damp, cold stone. I opened my eyes, and realized that it was night. In the light of a small lamp, hanging over a nearby portal, I could make out the edge of a nearby canal, to my right. I sat up. The experiences in the apartment swept back upon me. I was no longer in the tunic which had been so impregnated with some chemical or chemicals. I shuddered. I remembered the pain, and the fumes from the small fire tray. I had lost consciousness. At least I had revealed nothing of the secrets which had been entrusted to me. I was sure of that. I sensed that my body had been washed. I was groggy, presumably from some residue of the substances, or fumes, to which I had been exposed. Where was the Lady Dorna? Where was Addison Steele? Where was I? I was sure I was still in Port Kar, but I had no idea where. The surroundings were unfamiliar. I might be anywhere in the city. Port Kar is a maze of canals and islands. Where was Palace Street? Where was the Golden Chain? I was suddenly very frightened. It was late. I would be missed! I was not in my cage. I would miss night check. What had become of me? I had not attempted to run, or escape, but how could I prove that? Would Ho-Tosk, or his men, or guardsmen, believe my story of abduction and interrogation?

I felt oddly, cumbersomely, uncomfortably clothed. I felt unusual garments about me. Again I was frightened. A slave is to be clad as a slave. In some cities it can be a capital offense for a slave to don the garmenture of a free woman unless, for some reason, she is ordered to do so. She would be terrified to be found so, clad as a free person without permission. What a vengeance might be enacted upon her by outraged, scandalized free women!

But the garmenture seemed to me eccentric, and odd. Surely it was not the Robes of Concealment, so rich, abundant, beautiful, and colorful. That relieved my anxiety. Would it not be terrible to place a slave in such garmenture, and then arrange to have her, so compromised, discovered? Who could so hate a slave? Perhaps a free woman? Perhaps the Lady Dorna? I pulled at the clothing, and feared I knew what it was, and then I rose and went closer to the small lamp at the portal. To my consternation I found that the garments that I now wore, which now seemed to me so unfamiliar, different, foreign, and strange, would have scarcely merited a second glance on my former world. I wore a large, loose, plaid, cotton shirt and a pair of jeans, the sort of commonly masculine clothing by means of which a woman of Earth might attempt to draw attention to herself, as though challenging men by donning their customary garmenture; or perhaps trying to prove that clothing is, or should be, indifferent to sex; or perhaps which might be affected by a young woman of Earth with ambivalent feelings toward her sex, or one who, for whatever reason, wished to pretend ambivalent feelings toward her sex, one who, for whatever reason, was, in effect, playing boy, or wished be thought to be playing boy, clothing more appropriately to be expected in a young, adolescent male, perhaps her younger brother. But one caveat might be lodged, for the jeans were tight, and form-fitting. It was as though one were to say, "I am not a girl, but I am a girl." I had seen no clothing like this on Gor. Oddly, it now seemed to me "barbaric." To be sure, I was still barefoot, and there were no underclothes, such as a brassiere or panties. I reeled. I strove to keep my senses, struggling against fear, disbelief, confusion, and bewilderment. Then I was even more frightened. I moved my head and neck. It could not be! What could it mean! In what danger might I now stand? Sick with fear, I put my hands to my neck. The collar was gone! I, though a Gorean slave, was not collared! I then sank to my knees, and then went to all fours, head down, trembling, and then, a moment later, shadows rising slowly about me, I lowered myself to the stones and lost consciousness.

"Lady," said a voice.

It was light.

I looked up.

Two guardsmen were standing near me, over me, seemingly puzzled.

It must have been a strange sight they found before them, a woman so eccentrically garmented.

"Masters!" I wanted to cry, but, to my amazement and dismay, no sound, escaped my lips.

My distress and fear must have been obvious.

"Be at ease, Lady," said one.

"Where are your veils?" asked the other.

"She has been robbed, and set upon," said the first guardsman.

I clambered to my knees before them, fearing I had not done so quickly enough, and moved my head, vigorously negatively. My lips moved, wildly, but no sound came forth.

"She thinks she is a slave," said the first guardsman.

I pressed my lips to his boot.

"She has no collar," said the first guardsman.

"She is witless," said the second. "Mad."

I could not understand my inability to speak. I tried to speak in the Language, and then, even, in English.

Something must have been done to me in the apartment.

I must somehow get back to the Golden Chain!

"Rise up, Lady," said the first guardsman, kindly.

I remained on my knees, shaking my head again, negatively. I tried again, unsuccessfully, to communicate.

"Perhaps she is a slave," said the second.

"No collar," said the first.

"She is a strange person," said the second. "See how she is dressed. She tries to speak, but does not speak."

"What is she doing here, so early?" said the first guardsman.

"She has had a fall, or an injury," speculated the second guardsman.

"Perhaps we should convey her to one of the Green Caste," said the other.

I put my hands on the waist of the jeans, and made as though to tear them down, to expose my left thigh.

"Stop!" said the first guardsman.

"How absurd it is," I thought. "These men and their glorious free women! He would be horrified to have the modesty of a free woman compromised, even so slightly, but they would think nothing of being served by a needful, begging slave, naked save for her collar!"

"Hold," he said.

I removed my hands from the jeans.

"We have a tablet," said the second guardsman. "Can you write?"

I shook my head, negatively.

"Perhaps she is a slave," he said.

I shook my head, affirmatively.

"Or low caste," he said.

"Come with us, Lady," said the first guardsman. "We will seek out a free woman."

I was not pleased at this suggestion, however sensible it might be.

"Are you weary or weak?" asked the first guardsman.

"Do you wish to be carried?" asked the second guardsman.

I shook my head, negatively. I was desperate to speak, and could not do so.

When they turned away, as I by gesture bade them do, I made certain to lag behind them, a step or two, to their left, heeling them. I tried desperately to speak, and was unable to do so. They did not hurry their pace, and I had no difficulty in keeping up with them. I took their pace to be a consideration, a thoughtful concession to the dignity, ease, and comfort of a putative free woman.

Some forty paces down the walkway, the first guardsman stopped before a portal where flowers grew in boxes on either side of the portal, knocked politely, and called within. His efforts were rewarded, for a free woman, hastily veiled, her companion behind her, was soon framed in the portal.

I had knelt, naturally, as soon as they had stopped. One commonly kneels in the presence of the free.

"We have a free woman here, who, I fear, is mad," said the first guardsman. "You can see how strangely she is dressed. Too, seemingly, she cannot speak. She seems to think she is a slave."

"She has no collar," said the free woman.

"Even so," said the first guardsman.

"If she is a slave, she will be marked," said the woman.

"Precisely," said the first guardsman. "We thought it inappropriate to make the determination, as, witless or not, mad or not, she seems to be free."

"I understand," said the woman. "Portus, fetch a blanket and hold it, and keep your eyes averted."

In a bit the blanket was held between the free woman and I, and the men. Her companion, Portus, even held the blanket high, gripped behind him.

I knelt.

"Stand, Lady," she said.

Commanded, I stood.

"It is all right, dear lady," said the woman. "This will not take a moment."

It did take more than a moment because the free woman had apparently never dealt with a zipper before. I managed the matter, and then put my head down, submissively.

"On your knees!" she said, sharply.

I swiftly knelt, head down.

"There is no need for the blanket," she said to the men. "She may be witless or mad, dressed absurdly, and unable to speak, but she is a *kef* girl."

Instantly the attitudes of her companion, and the two guardsmen, changed toward me.

"Who owns you? Who whips you? Where are you chained or caged? What is your name?" demanded the first guardsman.

Tears in my eyes, kneeling before them, I shook my head, futilely, helplessly.

Thanked, the free woman and her companion, together with the blanket, retired to their dwelling, perhaps to their breakfast.

"It is too bad," said the first guardsman, "that she is witless or mad, and cannot speak."

"Perhaps, under the lash, she might remember how to speak," said the second.

I drew up my jeans and followed the two guardsmen, heeling them. I received no quarter now. They strode quickly. I struggled to keep up with them.

As it was now later in the morning, the canals and walkways were more frequented. My attire, seemingly so inexplicable and absurd, attracted much attention and, I fear, some derision.

"Where are your veils?" I was asked.

"What is your Home Stone?" I was asked.

"Are you from Turia?" I was asked. I had no idea where Turia might be.

I was being conducted, as I learned, to the house of Samos, who was First Captain in the Council of Captains. On the other hand, I was not brought to Samos in connection with any business having to do with the Council of Captains. I was brought to him, rather, I gathered, because it was not clear what was to be done with me, and because Samos, aside from being First Captain in the Council of Captains, was also First Slaver of Port Kar.

CHAPTER TWENTY-FOUR

What Occurred in the Lesser Al-ka Market

"Who would want this one?" asked a man. "She cannot speak."

"Yet she is well-formed and comely," said the slaver's man. "And she is cheap."

But the fellow had turned away.

I raised my head and looked up, eyes half closed; the sun was high; the shelf was hot; then I lay down again, on the towel given us, to protect us from the roughness of the cement, my legs drawn up. I and the others, some twenty on the long narrow shelf, were naked; that is the way women are commonly sold. The shelf was not full as five rings were empty. Each of us was chained by the neck to one of the rings. When the market is crowded, more than one girl may be fastened to the same ring. Enough chain is allowed that we may be posed, and may stand, to be examined. I think I slept for a time.

It was late afternoon.

A slaver's man put one of the shallow metal bowls of gruel on the cement near my ring and I rose to all fours, put down my head, and began to feed. He then proceeded to the next ring and, from the tray carried by a slave behind him, placed another bowl on the cement, near the next ring, and blonde Kira rose to all fours.

Kira was Cosian. She had been taken at sea. She was brought to Port Kar tied at the prow of the corsair which had taken her vessel. It is not unusual for a ship, its voyage successful, to return through the western or southern sea gates, making its way slowly, in a stately fashion, through the canals to the arsenal harbor, with a lovely captive, the best of the catch, so displayed. This is a rather vaunted exhibition of a trophy, it seems, a public display of success, doubtless a vanity of sorts. Otherwise, one might have recourse to the arsenal sea gate, reaching the harbor directly. Perhaps less successful voyages when they return, if they return, do slip into the city by means of the arsenal sea gate. I do not know.

"Thank you, Master," said Kira.

I had hoped my voice would soon return, that the effect of whatever had been done to me in the apartment which might have robbed me of speech might wear off, but, as yet, I was as helplessly unable to speak as before. I feared I might be permanently deprived of speech, on a world where I was illiterate. I wondered how Addison Steele could have done to me what he did, and then I recalled I was a slave.

After a few Ehn the serving slave returned and retrieved the metal bowls.

On my walks within the city I had not passed by the girl markets. Most are located in the vicinity of the western and southern sea gates, both giving access unto the Tamber Gulf. The market in which I was now displayed was one of those associated with the House of Samos. It was near the western sea gate, but I could not see the sea gate from its location. It was a common shelf market, backed against a wall, its surface reached by shallow steps from the street.

Men and women passed by the market, but most gave it little attention. Now and then a fellow would stop to peruse the goods, sometimes with a friend. They might then share views, and comment on the goods.

Interestingly, there is a sort of culture of a market, and different markets have different cultures, so to speak. For example, the slaves might or might not be permitted to speak to one another, either on the shelf or not, or in the holding areas or not, when not on the shelf. If they are permitted to speak, on the shelf, or, more significantly, in the holding areas, a social hierarchy soon materializes, with leaders, and, say, subordinates, lieutenants, so to speak, followed by followers in their rankings, and then followers with their followers, and so on, and then, eventually, drudges, nondescripts, nonentities, outcasts, and such. Needless to say, barbarians are generally at the bottom of this social order. Markets also differ with respect to the behaviors required of, or allowed to, the slaves. In the market in which I was now displayed we were not required to accost passersby, to call attention to our charms, to wheedle a purchasing, to suggest the delights which might await a buyer, to call out, "Buy me, Master," and so on. On the other hand, we were much left to our own devices, and when a prosperous looking gentleman or a handsome, dashing fellow was in the vicinity the rings frequently became more active. Many are the strategies of the slave to secure for herself a desirable master. One might then note smiles, trembling lips, needful looks, piteous attitudes of hope, pleading expressions, and all varieties of mute petition. And, of course, one should remark posings, archings, curlings, sretchings, and such, which may range from the subtle to the blatant. A balance is commonly sought; effectiveness is the desideratum; normally one wishes to do, but not overdo. Some slaves feign indifference and, even, if they dare, distaste, or even have recourse to challenging or insolent remarks. In this way, they hope to provoke a fellow who may then be minded to buy them and then get them sobbing and begging at his feet, where, in any event, they hoped to be in the first place. There is a danger in this sort of thing, of course, for a fellow may be merely displeased and indicate that the slave is to be chastised. "No, Master!" she might cry. "Forgive me, Master!" He might then, if moved, say, "Very well then, only five lashes."

I myself had not, at least as yet, made use of such stratagems. I did not want a master now. Things might then become grievously perilous. There might be tangles of law. Blood might be shed. I had a master. Did I not belong to Ho-Tosk, of Port Kar, proprietor of the Golden Chain? I wanted to be returned to the Golden Chain, and exonerated of any charges of being a fugitive slave. I feared I might be bound and thrown alive to the urts in the canal. I watched the passersby, hoping that someone from the Golden Chain might pass by, that someone, slave or free, even a customer, might recognize me. I could not speak. I could not make my identity known.

If an individual is seriously, or even moderately, interested in obtaining a slave, or, say, adding another to his chain, he is likely to ascend the steps, examine the merchandise more closely, consult with a slaver's man, speak with the slave, and such.

This was my fourth day on the shelf.

Some six men had ascended to the shelf and had, sometimes amongst examining others, as well, paused before me. I would kneel and point to my throat and shake my head. "She is not stupid," would say a slaver's man. "She can understand, and obey.

It is merely that she cannot speak." But none were interested in a voiceless slave.

Some days ago I had been brought by two guardsmen to the House of Samos, of Port Kar, First Captain of the Council of Captains, and First Slaver of Port Kar.

I was held upright before him, by two men of the house, and turned about, so that, I gathered, he might consider the oddity of my garmenture, and then I was put to my knees before his curule chair.

He wore a lounging robe. He was a powerfully built man, with white, closely cropped hair.

I was illuminated in torchlight.

He was not.

I could not see him well.

"What strange garments are these?" asked Samos.

"I think barbarian garments, captain," said one of the men beside me. "Once, long ago, I saw something much like them at a Sardar Fair, one of En'Kara."

"She cannot speak?" asked Samos.

"Or does not speak, captain," said the other fellow beside me, to my left.

"Can you speak?" asked Samos.

I shook my head.

"Let us whip her," said the fellow to my left. "Then she will speak."

Tears ran down my cheeks; then I put my head to the floor.

"What do we know of her?" asked Samos.

"She was picked up, collarless, by guardsmen this morning, on the edge of the Canal of the Sea Sleen," said the fellow to my right.

"Collarless?" asked Samos.

"Yes," he said.

"But she is a slave?" asked Samos.

"She insists so, behaves so, and is marked so," he said, he to my right.

"The *kef*," said the man to my left.

"Can she write?" asked Samos.

"She is apparently illiterate," said the first man, he to my right.

"Raise your head," said Samos.

I looked up.

"You are a barbarian?" he asked.

I nodded.

"Knowledgeable slavers would not bring a speechless barbarian to our world," said Samos. "Such would not sell, or not well. She must have suffered some impairment here."

I was silent.

"Take off her clothes, fit her with a house collar, and put her in a pen with the others," said Samos, "those being readied for tomorrow's sales, that in the Lesser Al-ka Market."

It was now the late afternoon of my fourth day on the shelf.

Most Gorean shops open early, often in the vicinity of dawn, and close, Ahn later, in the early to late afternoon. One supposes this is to maximize the Ahn of daylight, and thus economize on candles and tharlarion oil, used mostly in lamps and lanterns. To be sure, taverns, brothels, eating houses, and some markets, slave markets, in particular, are open to the public at night. The Lesser Al-ka Market, however, was not one of these. Some homeowners mount small lamps at their gates or portals, presumably to discourage predation. Too, one supposes that more affluent households would be likely to keep later hours, and four shifts are maintained in the arsenal. There is little public lighting in Port Kar, with the exception of the bridges and sea gates which are regularly illuminated by lanterns. It might be remarked, in passing, that the Council of Captains, when meeting, commonly meets at night. Those who would go abroad at night usually carry their own light, lanterns or torches. There are concerns which, for a fee, will furnish night escorts, guards, and lantern bearers. The small, single-oared ships which ply the canals will usually have a lantern mounted at the prow.

As many shops were now closed, or closing, the shopsmen drawing the folding wooden screens across their shop fronts and chaining them in place, and many individuals were moving about, returning to homes or proceeding to one diversion or entertainment, or another, the street before the Lesser Al-ka Market was nearly as frequented as between the ninth and eleventh Ahn. Of those passing to and fro, some men, and some women, some briefly, some at greater length, paused to consider us. One of the slaver's men availed himself of this opportunity to appeal to the possible buyers, those at the shelf and those passing by. "Noble, generous masters, and noble, beautiful mistresses," he called, "consider the finest of moderately priced girl merchandise in Port Kar. Here is the Lesser Al-ka Market with some bargains beyond even those of the Greater Al-ka Market. Let your shrewd eye discern superb buys ready to be snatched away before you, before you can act. Do not hesitate. Here we have not only kettle slaves, pot-and-mat slaves, but sleek pleasure slaves, well-turned and vital, worthy of the Curulean in mighty Ar!" This assertion was met with good-humored laughter, sharing the jest. I did not find it that amusing. "Seriously, noble patrons," he continued, "you know the taste and discrimination of the noble Samos of your own city, lovely Port Kar, Jewel of Gleaming Thassa, he with whom you share a Home Stone. How then can you doubt the quality of these hand-picked *tastas*, delicacies selected with care for your delectation? And, let me apprise you that the noble Samos, as is his occasional wont, has inserted here, at one of these rings, which one, I won-der, as a challenge and surprise, a girl worthy to be the preferred slave of a Ubar!" I sensed that Kira lifted her head, and straight-ened herself. I recalled she had been a "prow girl," a trophy which had adorned a Gorean prow. I decided I hated her. Certainly, at any rate, I decided I had never liked her. "Which is she?" queried the slaver's man. "Ascend to the platform, consider taking her, or another, home with you this evening!"

Several fellows and some women did ascend the broad steps to the surface of the shelf. Many items on the shelf were examined, and posed. Kira was sold within Ehn for six silver tarsks of Ar-gentum.

I was now quite ready to be taken to the holding area, with other unsold slaves, it reached through the door at the back of the shelf, to the left, as one would face the shelf.

"How is it that you are here?" asked a woman's voice, closely, tensely, in an outraged hiss.

I was terrified of free women, and one was now confronting me.

Instantly I went to first obeisance position, but my head was yanked up, cruelly, by the hair.

I tried to scream but no sound escaped my lips.

"Yes," hissed the woman, "it is you! I thought so! How is it that you are here?"

I do not think I could have answered her, even had I been able to speak. I was terrified.

"I have been betrayed," she whispered, furiously. "The fee giver has been betrayed! The wretched sleen, the faithless tarsk, Steele, Addison Steele, what a mercenary, irresponsible, greedy scoundrel he is. His orders were clear! He disobeyed! He was to take you to the height of the delta wall and cast you over the wall, to the tharlarion below! And then I find you here! Coins are coins, I suppose! Greed! Irresponsible, stupid, dangerous, petty greed! What did he get for you, five copper tarsks?"

The free woman was well robed and veiled, but there was no mistaking the voice, nor its menace. I had closed my knees and covered my breasts with my hands. I was on my knees before an irate Dorna of Tharna, a free woman beside herself with rage.

"What is going on here?" asked a slaver's man.

"Nothing," snapped Dorna. Free women can speak sharply and unpleasantly to free men. They are protected by their freedom, and, one supposes, often, a shared Home Stone.

The slaver's man turned away, angrily.

I trembled. I felt futile and helpless. I could not cry out to the slaver's man. I was on my chain, fastened to a ring in the cement. Tears ran down my cheeks.

"Of course, you cannot speak," she snarled. "Sometimes consciousness is recovered too soon after the fumes. It would not do would it, to have you cry out, being borne away, or scream on the delta wall, before being cast down to tharlarion? What if you were to cry out secrets, or deeds, or mysteries, which are no concern of guardsmen? What if you were found on the delta wall, in the darkness, bound and gagged? Might you not be a stripped free woman? Might not murder be afoot? What was going on? What were you doing there? What if a gag had been removed? What if a collar were checked? What if a guardsman should inquire into matters? Would a report not be made? So you were made silent."

I looked wildly about.

Most of the patrons had now left the shelf. Seven rings which had formerly been occupied were now empty. Things had apparently gone well for the Lesser Al-ka Market.

"You!" called the Lady Dorna, addressing the nearest slaver's man, he to whom she had spoken earlier, shortly.

"Lady," he said, approaching. He did not look anxious to deal with the Lady Dorna.

"This one!" she said.

I shook my head, negatively, piteously, wildly, tears in my eyes, and went to first obeisance position before him.

"Do not be upset," he said. "Rejoice. You may be sold."

I trembled before him, head down.

I kept shaking my head, piteously, negatively.

"She seems somewhat less than pleased," he said to the Lady Dorna. "Are you acquainted with one another?"

"Not at all," she said. "It is merely that she, as many *kajirae*, are insufficiently cognizant of the honor and privilege of belonging to a free woman."

"I should warn you," he said. "She is a barbarian. That is clear. She has the tiny slave-world brand high on her left arm."

He was referring to the inoculation scar I had had on my arm since childhood. I had had no cavities, but barbarians may also be recognized, if one knows what to look for, by tiny bits of metal in the teeth. Language and knowledge, accents and information, may also mark a barbarian. There is so much we do not know about the world to which we find ourselves brought as two-legged beasts, cattle of a sort, bipedalian livestock. A dealer can be severely reprimanded if he does not make such sales data clear to a prospective buyer. A dealer's house can be burned to the ground for as little as not making clear the natural hair color of a slave.

"Then she should be cheap," said the Lady Dorna.

"Not necessarily," said the slaver's man, warily. "Barbarians often sell well. It seems they are starved for sex on their own world. At a master's feet, owned and mastered, they thrive."

"What do you want for her?" asked the Lady Dorna.

"I would be amiss," said the slaver's man, "were I not to call to your attention a grievous flaw in this item, one of which you may not be informed."

"I know she cannot speak," said the Lady Dorna. "What do you want for her?"

The slaver's man seemed to think for a bit. I do not think he was much pleased with the Lady Dorna.

"Two silver tarsks," he said.

"Done," she said.

This response startled the slaver's man. "But she cannot speak," he said.

"Done," she repeated. "Two silver tarsks, in the coinage of Ar."

"The coinage of Ar is rare in Port Kar," he said.

"I can access such coinage," she said.

"She is yours," he said. "Pay."

"I do not have the money with me," she said. "I will fetch it, shortly. Hold her for me."

"What do you have, to pay on account?" he asked.

"I do not have money with me," she said. "I will return shortly, money in hand. Hold her for me."

"She is not yours," said the slaver's man, in an accent that suggested some subtle sense of satisfaction.

"I have bought her," said the Lady Dorna.

"Not without money," he said.

"I will be back within the Ahn," she said. "Hold her for me."

"We do not hold slaves," he said. His response was firm. This was doubtless a matter of policy, but, I suspected, it was a matter of policy which he was more than content in this case to note and enforce.

"Dolt!" she said, and then spun about, and hurried down the steps to the street.

I watched her disappear down the street.

I pulled at the chain, jerking it against the ring.

There was much here that made me terribly afraid and much which I did not understand. Why would the Lady Dorna, a free woman, want to have an innocent slave cast to tharlarion? Was she angry that I had not revealed secrets to her, that Adraste was the former Lady Julia Leta, scion of a minor banking family, the Claudian Marcelliani, their house on Ar's Street of Coins? And why was it that the Lady Dorna, if a free woman, was without money? And, interestingly, if she spoke the truth, the funds she had access to were in the coinage of Ar, a city far distant, and inland, from Port Kar. It seemed I owed my life to Addison Steele. Were it not for him I might have recovered consciousness, if at all, only in the cold, disturbed water by the delta wall, thrashing silently, gripped in the teeth of tharlarion. I was sure, from where I had recovered consciousness and how I was dressed, that he had not sold me. Why had he left me where he had, uncollared and clad in garments strange for Gor? Why had he not taken me back to the Golden Chain? Was he in danger, for having spared me? Why had he spared me? I was only a slave. But perhaps I had been spared because I was a slave. Might it not be only that. Gorean men were fond of slaves. They knew what to do with them. They often protected them from free women. What was he doing with the Lady Dorna and the individual who had concealed himself behind the ornate screen in the apartment, presumably the "fee giver"? In what strange, dark plots might Addison Steele be involved? Clearly he was a minion of dark forces. I thought honor could not be much involved in doings so surreptitious, so deceitful, secret, and cruel, dealings perhaps extending far beyond the apprehension and returning to justice of the former Lady Julia Leta, of Ar's Street of Coins. I feared, and muchly, Addison Steele as a man, and master, but it seemed now I had misjudged him, as well, and grievously; it had never occurred to me that he might be dishonorable or a party to dealings both illicit and shameful. I remembered the pain of the tunic and the terror of the noxious fumes. How fortunate that I had revealed nothing of the secrets I knew! How disappointed I was in him. I had not seen his true self. Now I knew him. I could no longer respect him. Now, in my heart, I reviled him. Yet he had spared me.

Then I realized again, suddenly, the terrible danger in which I stood. I was naked and chained, tethered to a ring on a Gorean slave shelf. I was helpless. I could not escape. The Lady Dorna would shortly return, angry, coins in hand.

"This one," said a harsh male voice.

I kept my head down, fearing to raise it. Hope flashed within me.

"A barbarian," said the slaver's man, "comely, but unable to speak."

"She cannot speak?" asked the harsh voice.

"No," said the slaver's man. "The flaw is grievous. Let me show you others."

"No," I thought, "no!"

"Can she see, can she think, can she understand?" asked the man.

"Certainly," said the slaver's man.

"What do you want for her?" asked the harsh voice.

"Buy me," I thought, "buy me!"

"A silver tarsk," said the slaver's man.

"Ten copper tarsks," said the harsh voice.

"Forty," said the slaver's man.

"Of what use is a silent slave?" asked the harsh voice.

"Yet you seem interested in her," said the slaver's man.

"Ten copper tarsks," said the harsh voice.

"Twenty," said the slaver's man.

"Fifteen," said the harsh voice.

"Done," said the slaver's man.

I let my eye rove to the side. I saw a sturdy leg, booted. And near it, pressed down on the cement, a stout, postlike object, brown, probably of Tur wood, a heavy crutch.

CHAPTER TWENTY-FIVE

What Occurred in the Apartment
of the One-Legged Man

There were two fierce snaps of metal. I could then barely part my ankles.

"Now," he said, "you shall not run so lightly and fleetly away."

He could now easily, as I was shackled, even as handicapped as he was, move far more swiftly than I.

I was afraid to belong to him, as there was something in his carriage and attitude which suggested cruelty and violence, purpose and menace. Too, I had sensed how men had feared him in Brundisium. He, though handicapped, had not even been attacked for that next silver stater, a valuable coin, due upon the delivery of a certain slave. Despite my uneasiness, my trepidation, and such, I was muchly pleased that I had been purchased, even by such a man, before the return of the seemingly murderously intent Dorna of Tharna. I had no desire to be cast to tharlarion.

I hoped to please him.

I had little doubt that failure to do so might mean my life.

I touched the tunic I wore, nodded, and smiled. I was grateful to have been clothed, as slaves need not be clothed. He had not even made me, by days or weeks of service, prove my worthiness to be accorded a garment, small and shameful as it might be. Yet, interestingly, it was generous for a Gorean slave tunic. It was high at the neck and, if I stood, it would fall almost to my knees.

He seemed to sense my gratitude, and, perhaps, my puzzlement.

"On the walkways and streets," he said, "I do not want too many fellows turning about when you pass. Nor do I wish to be detained by officious free women who would choose to berate me should a tunic seem a bit too light or too short for their taste. I wish you to be no more conspicuous than is compatible with my designs."

I pointed to my shackles, fastening my ankles so closely together. How, so shackled, could one accompany a master on the walkways or streets? One could hobble at best, even if one could gain one's feet.

"Abroad," he said, "you will not be shackled, but leashed and braceleted."

I sat at his feet. I lifted my fingers to my collar.

"It reads," he said, "'I am owned by Bruno of Torcadino'."

I did not think 'Bruno of Torcadino' was his real name or his customary name, but I would use it to refer to him. I knew no better name for him than that.

"You are curious as to why you were purchased?" he said.

I went to my knees before him and nodded.

"You would wish to ask permission to speak," he said, "and I would allow you to do so, that you might ask questions, and such, but you cannot speak. Therefore, I will talk to you, a little, that I may find more profit in your possession than otherwise. I will get more good from you if you know certain things, and other things you need not know. First, you know me from Brundisium, do you not?"

I nodded, affirmatively.

"You are a barbarian," he said.

I nodded, "Yes."

"You know your collar, I trust," he said.

I nodded, "Yes."

I had, by now, well learned it.

"Good," he said. "Sometimes it takes days before a barbarian learns her collar. Some are stupid, and others, given the seriousness with which they might take the pathological indoctrinations of their world, so inimical to biology, feel obliged to resist, until they learn their true needs, what they most deeply crave and desire, what they cannot be women without. Then comes the collapse of walls and artifices. Then comes the weepings and cryings out, the tears of abject surrender and gladness. The most intelligent and vital are the first to come to their knees and press their lips gratefully to the feet of masters."

I thought of the radical sexual dimorphism of the human species, and the complementarities of nature.

"How foolish it would be to be ashamed of one's needs and desires," I thought. "It would be to be ashamed of oneself."

"You are unusually well-figured, and exquisitely featured," he said. "That would be more than enough for one to buy you. If you could speak, you would, I wager, have been taken off your ring before noon, perhaps on the first day you were offered. I do not know why you cannot speak, but I do not think that lack will much diminish your utility to my plans."

I did not, of course, know what his plans were, other than, I supposed, the attempted acquisition of Adraste, the beautiful former Lady Julia Leta, of Ar.

"I seek the slave, Luta," he said, "now named 'Adraste', once the noble, esteemed Lady Felitia Thaliana, of Besnit, she whom I have long sought, she whom I have followed even from the World's End. I seek to find her to free her, to return her to the glorious station of the free citizeness. I wish to return her to her family, one incidentally of wealth and standing, that she be returned to the bosom of loved ones and sheltered within the protection of her Home Stone. What is wrong?"

Much I feared was wrong, but I struggled to maintain an attitude of attention and absorbing, unqualified credulity. I sensed that my life was now in much greater danger than I had hitherto suspected. Someone, clearly, was lying or drastically misinformed. I also sensed then why I, a barbarian, might have been chosen to figure in plans about which I knew nothing. A Gorean girl, informed and perceptive, alert and wary, might have soon penetrated such machinations. Who was this supposed Lady Felitia Thaliana, of Besnit? Did she exist? What of the Lady Julia Leta, of Ar? I was sure she existed, both from my interview in the alcove, when I was hooded, and from Adraste herself. In the kitchen, she had literally admitted, however reluctantly, that she was herself the Lady Julia Leta of Ar. For what more could one ask? Clearly Bruno of Torcadino did not want me to know that he was actually in search of the Lady Julia Leta of Ar. And, too, doubtless to enlist my aid, counting on the naivety of a barbarian, he was pretending to search for his quarry to free her and return her to station and family, perhaps even wealth. At one time I might have believed that, but I had learned in Brundisium, and after that, from a thousand other asides and remarks, in the tavern and elsewhere, that Gorean society did not easily ignore the shame and dishonor which would inevitably accrue to a family's name and reputation should it be discovered that a daughter, sister, niece, or such, had been collared. The humiliating stain of slavery was not to be endured. Normally she would be kept as a slave, either in the family's house, or estates, or, more likely, sold out of the city. At best, if freed, she would be sequestered in the house, kept from public view that her shame not be broadcast.

"I have enemies, and am known to some," he said. "And it was desirable to keep secret the true identity of the slave, Luta, lest ambitious felons obtain her and not free her, but use her to extort riches from her family, threatening to otherwise make her shame publicly known. So, as you will understand, it was impractical that I, in the auction at the house of Anesidemus, should openly bid upon, or buy, Luta, even through an agent. Rather I arranged, through a brigand, Decius of Venna, to steal Luta after her purchase."

"So," I thought, "the name of the man with the scar is 'Decius of Venna'. I recalled that I had been asked about this name during my interview in the alcove, when I had been hooded and chained. At that time it had meant nothing to me.

"I am no longer associated with Decius of Venna," he said.

I did not doubt that.

"But," continued Bruno of Torcadino, "matters moved more quickly than we had anticipated. Recall the night of the great dock fire. It was arranged, given the several Ahn of the dock fire, and its ferocity, and the imminent evacuation of the slaves from the house of Anesidemus, that a particular sheet, covertly marked, would identify Luta, now named 'Adraste', the former Lady Felitia Thaliana, of Besnit."

I nodded.

"Sheets were exchanged, or confused," he said. "You were brought to me, rather than Adraste."

I nodded, again.

"It seemed that all my work, the planning and expense, and all my anxiety and suffering, and all my hopes and dreams of rescuing the former Lady Felitia Thaliana of Besnit and returning her to her waiting and loving family, had gone for naught. Adraste, as we may call her, had slipped away. You are doubtless distressed and sympathetic, but, frightened, and uncertain; you manage well to conceal your feelings."

Bruno of Torcadino then hesitated, and looked to the side, as though troubled, recalling a difficult period in his life.

"Days passed," he said. "I made inquiries. I attended to rumors. I was in despair. And then something occurred to me. What
if it had not been a coincidence, as I had hitherto supposed, that
you had been substituted for Adraste? What if it had been deliberate? What if there were some connection between you and
Adraste, a connection that even you did not suspect? What if you
were a barbarian, which it turned out you were, as I discovered,
and were an unwitting tool, one useful to my enemies, a tool chosen for its naivety and ignorance, a tool which might be useful to
them again and again, in a thousand ways, surveillance, spying,
reporting, you a slave close to Adraste, and those about her, or
interested in her, and so on? Not even Adraste would suspect you,
a barbarian. And would not one barbarian be better for such purposes than a dozen barbarians, in turn, could they be obtained,
which anomaly might attract unwanted attention? I did then, and
shortly, learn you were indeed a barbarian, and then that you had
been shipped to Port Kar, to be a paga girl in a tavern called the
Golden Chain. Slender as was this reed of possibility, I took ship
to Port Kar. Perhaps you can conceive of my delight when I, having followed you, learned that the elusive Adraste served in the
same tavern. You led me to her, and you, in one way or another,
will do it again. I see you are afraid. Do not be afraid. Surely you
wish the beautiful Adraste to be returned to the happiness and security of her loved ones in Besnit? Do not fear. I do not ask you to
recognize Adraste for me. I know her quite well, even from long
ago in Besnit. Indeed, we are dear friends. All you need do is to
glimpse her, apprising me of this fact, or report to me information
or conjectures as to her whereabouts. Indeed, you might even be
contacted by her captors, which incident might provide us with
an invaluable clue, eventually leading to her rescue. Do you understand all this, *kajira*?"

I nodded, "Yes."

I also realized that Adraste's present "captors" or "holders,"
my work and role having been compromised by my abduction
and my now being in the keeping of the one-legged man, might
not only not need me any longer, but might regard it as judicious
to have me disappear, and far more effectively than had Adraste.

"I was not pleased to learn that Decius of Venna, who failed me
so egregiously in Brundisium, was in Port Kar," he said. "I suspect
he followed me here, curious and suspicious, to cheat me of the
prize I seek. I saw him on the bridge over the canal of the Thieves'

Way. I was pursuing you, and he seemed intent, as well, to take you in hand. I, and doubtless he, conjectured you had some connection with Adraste. And why were you abroad, apparently on some errand, and not in the tunic of the Golden Chain? Was that not of interest? I noted him and he doubtless noted me. Then, before either of us could seize you, you leapt from the bridge, into the arms of some passing boatsman. What occurred afterwards? You disappeared for days. What happened? Where were you? What went on?"

I pointed to my throat, and shook my head. Tears sprang to my eyes. I could not speak. I hoped not to be beaten.

"Our quarry, the former Lady Felitia Thaliana, of—of Besnit, will be found, sooner or later," he said. "I am sure of it. Indeed, I am sure she is still in Port Kar. There is a reason for that, one that came clear to me only recently. It explains much which would be otherwise obscure. I fear only that she may be first found by others, by Decius of Venna—or others.

I knew of "others" who were interested in the former Lady Julia Leta of Ar, others who had tortured me and had sought unsuccessfully to extract secrets from me. I did not know if Bruno of Torcadino knew of them or not. There might be many, I suspected, who might wish to apprehend the lovely Adraste, the former Lady Julia Leta of Ar. Annoyed with her or not, I did not envy her, the vulnerable prey sought by intent hunters. How dreadful, I thought, to be suspended naked in a dangling cage on Ar's street of Coins, a warning to any who might contemplate making free with the resources of others. What I did not understand was why a crime, serious as it might be, against a minor banking house in Ar, far away, thousands of pasangs away, should provoke so much interest in so many parties, and generate so seemingly relentless a pursuit of its perpetrator.

"Perhaps you are curious," he said, "as to how I, with but a single leg, I, one so cruelly handicapped, might rescue the unfortunate Lady Felitia Thaliana. Yes, you are interested. There are forces about which are alien to Port Kar, and, I think, to the world, as well. Perhaps you have suspected as much. I do not know why they are about, but they are about. Presumably there is some reason for their presence. I suspect they are mighty forces. It is my hope to enleague myself with them. I sense incredible power. You look at me with wonder and fear? Well you might. Of what do I speak? Perhaps you are aware of the damage done to the Delta

Gate? I see you are. Consider the force involved. What might explain that torn, twisted metal, rent like straws in the hand of a giant, that formidable business? Might it not have a purpose? If so, what might be its purpose? Might it not be an announcement, a greeting, an inquiry, an invitation to someone, or something, to meet and parley?"

CHAPTER TWENTY-SIX

What Occurred in the Marshes

I now knelt, bound, in the bow of the small canal boat, and Bruno of Torcadino, in the stern, quietly, slowly, manipulated the single oar. The marshes were all about. We had left the city, slipping under the chain. Some men fish at night in the marshes, primarily Rencers, some trolling a small net, some fishing by means of torch and trident, the light of the torch serving to lure fish to the surface, within the range of the three-forked, barbed trident. The sky was cloudy. Both the White Moon and Yellow Moon were in the sky. Bruno of Torcadino had not lit the small lantern at the prow. There were the subtle night noises of the marsh, the calls of small amphibians, the humming of insects. At times we made our way through rence, it brushing the sides of the boat. In many places the rence is well above, sometimes several feet above, the sides of the boat. After the Rencers acquired the great bow, the peasant bow, which had taken place some years ago, the delta had become their undisputed domain. The thickets of rence provided ideal cover for mobile bowmen in their small craft, which could be deployed in their dozens. The rence islands, of woven rence, too, could be moved about, so a village located one afternoon might be gone by the next morning. In this way a rence community, a homeland or capital, a depot, camp, or outpost, so to speak, is not a fixed target. Such communities may approach or withdraw, scatter or regroup, in ways not practical for more sessile communities. This permits latitude and flexibility, both tactically and strategically.

"I am taking you with me," had said Bruno of Torcadino. "I do not want to leave you alone. I want to keep an eye on you. You could not escape, shackled and chained to your ring in the apartment, but you might be discovered. I do not wish to risk losing you."

At that time I did not know what he intended. Would one explain one's intentions to a verr, a tarsk, a slave girl?

He had rented a small canal boat.

He intended to hazard a rendezvous in the marshes, a rendezvous blind and unscheduled, an unplanned rendezvous, with whom or what was not clear.

Was this not madness?

In the canals, and when we had passed under the chain, leaving the city, I had lain bound, on my stomach, my wrists crossed and bound behind my back, my ankles crossed and bound, closely, under a canvas. In this way, bystanders, and the guards at the Delta Gate, would assume that he was alone. Slaves are property and property may be stolen; the marshes, at night, tend to be wide, lonely, and dark, and the rence in many places is high. Small boats may quietly approach one another, and bodies may be lost in the marshes.

My head had faced the bow.

Some four or five Ehn past the chain, Bruno of Torcadino stopped plying the oar, and, as the small craft drifted, pulled away the canvas. "Kneel up," he said. I struggled to my knees and was then kneeling in the bow. The single oar then began again to move in the water.

I looked back and saw the beacon on the delta wall, high and visible for pasangs. Similar beacons are mounted on the walls near the western and southern sea gates.

The oar made a soft sound in the water.

During the day in the canals that sound would most likely not be remarked.

Something large moved past in the water.

I was very still, seemingly unable to move.

The oar rested.

I could not have screamed had I wished, and not merely because of what had been done to me in the apartment of Dorna of Tharna.

I could not see it well, but there seemed an alignment of flat, triangular plates cutting slowly through the water. Such plates make it difficult to bite through the neck or spine they shield.

Bruno of Torcadino replaced the unsheathed sword which lay beside him, and resumed the oar.

"We are not going far from the Delta Gate," he said.

I squirmed in the bow, bound, on my knees.

I faced to the left. It was far off. I hoped he would see it. Let him look in the direction in which I was looking, trying to indicate what I saw.

"Do not be agitated," he said. "It is a Rencer, fishing. They do not know we are here."

The normal arrangement for torch-and-trident fishing is one torch man and one or two trident men.

We had not, as I previously noted, lit the small lantern on the prow of our canal boat. Would it not have been wise to do so, that it might have served to mark our position, announcing our arrival, so to speak, that of a party at last responding to a conjectured invitation? On the other hand, who knew who or what might see that light, and with what consequences? Dangers lurk in the marshes. I think that Bruno of Torcadino, assessing considerations, thought it best to do without the light. Perhaps whatever had the force and power to twist thick bars of metal, unhinging so mighty a barrier as the Delta Gate, did not require the dim light of a tiny lantern to be aware of our presence.

Could I have done so I would have cried out, for something rose up under the canal boat, lifting it a foot from the water, and tipping it to the side, and then, scraping the bottom of the boat, it slithered away, to the right.

"Steady," said Bruno of Torcadino, his hand on the oar.

Shortly thereafter we came on a large stand of rence, made our way through it, and came to a clearing, like a lake in the marshes.

"This is far enough," said Bruno of Torcadino. "I think this is a good place, not too close to the Delta Gate, not too far from the Delta Gate, a likely place for observation, inspection, and greeting, a sheltered place, walled by rence, yet wide and placid, a courtyard in the marshes. A fine, likely place. Here we will wait to be discovered."

I feared that we had perhaps been discovered already.

After a time, wearied, permitted, I lay down in the bow, on my back, on the discarded canvas. I could see the White Moon through the clouds. There was no abatement of the tiny, regular marsh noises. Once, when the clouds parted, the Yellow Moon shimmered brightly, unobstructed, in the sky. Then it was, again, a faint yellow disk, pale behind the mist of clouds. "Do not move," whispered Bruno of Torcadino. I lay very still. "There it is, again,"

said Bruno of Torcadino. This time I saw it. Against the bright disk
of the White Moon, shortly before clouds once more enveloped it,
half obscuring it, tattering its light, something moved across its
face. It was like an immense, dark, silent, soaring shadow. I had
seen few sights so seemingly laden with menace. "That is an Ul,"
said Bruno, "a broad-winged, claw-winged, flying tharlarion."

I did not know such things existed. Perhaps, I thought, it is
just as well that Bruno of Torcadino had refrained from lighting
the small lantern on the prow of the canal boat.

I think we must have remained better than two Ahn in that
broad, sheltered, lonely, rence-encircled lakelike stillness.

"There is nothing here," said Bruno of Torcadino, at last. "This
is all pointless, or a madness. We are fools. Yet I was so sure. But
now all is fruitless, and absurd. We have waited. We have been
patient. Were there an intelligence here, we would have been discovered. How odd are the jests of the mind; how it amuses itself at
our expense. It leads us to believe, and then it betrays us. I was so
sure. There is nothing here. We are fools. It is a mistake, and the
marshes are dangerous."

I heard the sound of that single lever, grasped, serving as both
oar and tiller, moving in its lock.

Bruno of Torcadino was bringing the small craft about.

I turned and rose to my knees in the bow.

I could see the wall of rence ahead.

But scarcely had the small boat reached the wall of rence than
Bruno of Torcadino's hand rested on the oar.

Something was different.

For a moment I did not know what it was.

Then I realized there had been an abatement of the marsh
noises.

I was hearing silence.

I recalled Bruno of Torcadino had said that the marshes were
dangerous.

Then after a moment, the noises had resumed, slowly at first,
and then, in a short while, things were as they had been earlier.

"Something passed," said Bruno of Torcadino, "perhaps a large
tharlarion."

I wondered if it might not have been something else, another
canal boat, or, say, one of the small Rencer ships, made of woven
rence.

But probably not.

As far as I knew, our passage had made little, if any, difference in the sounds of the marsh. Our passage had not silenced the marsh, as far as I had noted, however briefly.

And I had heard nothing move in the rence.

"There is nothing here," said Bruno of Torcadino. "We shall return to the Delta Gate."

He set his hands to the oar, and the boat moved. I heard the rence brush against the sides of the boat.

I turned about in the bow, to look back, past Bruno of Torcadino.

Several yards back, toward the center of that circular, lakelike clearing in the rence, something had quietly broken the surface of the water. I could not cry out, for what had been done to me days ago, before I had awakened near the Canal of the Sea Sleen. Its neck and broad head, glistening in the moonlight, shedding water, was lifted a yard from the water. It was much like a tharlarion, but I did not think it was a tharlarion. I think I would rather it had been. It seemed not to have scales, but plating of a sort. In the head were what appeared to be two large eyes, circular, and alit, as if afire.

At a distance, or hastily glimpsed, it might easily have been taken for an unusual tharlarion, but, viewed more closely, or at greater length, it was not a tharlarion, merely something which resembled, doubtless by intent, a tharlarion.

I suspected it was a vessel of sorts, or a weapon of war.

I did not know what it might be doing here, here in the marshes, less than a pasang from the Delta Gate.

I wondered if it were manned, or remotely controlled.

I wondered what sort of intelligence, with recourse to what sophisticated technology, could conceive of, and would dare to produce, so monstrous a thing, and for what purpose.

Soon we were through the rence wall and I could see the beacon atop the wall near the Delta Gate.

Bruno of Torcadino, it seems, had prematurely despaired of having been discovered in the marshes.

CHAPTER TWENTY-SEVEN

What Occurred by the Canal of the Sea Sleen

"Palace Street is too open for what I have in mind," said Bruno of Torcadino. "Here, this should serve nicely, here by the Canal of the Sea Sleen."

Several days ago, after my miseries in an apartment, at the mercy of Dorna of Tharna, Addison Steele, and, I thought, a mysterious third party, which had remained generally concealed behind an ornate screen, I had awakened somewhere along the Canal of the Sea Sleen. I did not, however, recognize this particular area.

The bar for the Tenth Ahn had not yet sounded.

The sun was warm.

Rough men passed this way. I had seen not one free woman since the ringing of the bar for the Ninth Ahn.

In the canal a canal boat passed.

I was on my leash, and my hands were locked behind my back in slave bracelets.

It was two days since our journey into the marshes outside the Delta Gate.

I was not clear as to the object of our outing. I supposed it must have one. Mostly, after hobbling about a bit, scrutinizing passersby, Bruno of Torcadino would sit to the side by, or lean against, a domicile wall, that massive crutch at hand.

"My finances," said he, "are strained. It is time to remedy the matter."

I had presumed originally that he, as is often the case with the disabled, the maimed, the helpless, and unemployable, contemplated soliciting a tarsk-bit or so from one or another of the fellows who helped compose the sparse traffic along the walkway. Yet, if this were his object, he had chosen an unusual venue for his efforts. Surely thoroughfares like Palace Street would be far more promising.

He looked to the left and right, seemingly somnolent by the wall.

Certainly I did not think that Bruno of Torcadino manifested the pathetic image of the plausible beggar. I myself would have feared to approach him.

Generally I sat or knelt at his feet.

As he regularly did when abroad, he had a cloak half about his left shoulder. This served to conceal the short sword, unsheathed, slung from the strap under the cloak, over his left shoulder.

"I must hire men," he had said. "Decius of Venna will no longer do. He is no longer a satisfactory hireling. He is suspicious and wishes to become a principal, even unsure as he must be of the nature of the project."

The project, allegedly, seemingly so generous, benign, and noble, was the acquisition of the supposed former Lady Felitia Thaliana, of Besnit, in order to free her and restore her to her family in Besnit. I now found this motivation not only hard to believe, but impossible to believe. I did my best, however, to feign credulity. I pretended to believe his account of the matter, and, I suspect, he, amused, pretended to believe that I believed it. In any event, I was no longer the naive slave, half-trained and freshly sold, I had been long ago in Brundisium. In her collar a girl learns quickly the nature of the world in which she wears it.

"Ah," said Bruno of Torcadino, looking to his right.

It was a small sound, that tiny exclamation, suggesting anticipation and satisfaction. I wished suddenly I could be somewhere else.

"Here approach three fellows," he said. "They seem good fellows, and most likely well off. I am sure they can be persuaded to share their munificence. And one coin properly invested, may become two coins, and two coins four, and so on."

"Kneel," he said, as I was then sitting, my back to the domicile wall. I knelt and he crossed my ankles and bound them tightly together, using the leash. I would have been less helpless if he had used the close shackles which I knew so well from his apartment.

I looked down the walkway.

The three men were some forty or fifty paces away.

As they approached, an unanticipated and radical transformation took place in the demeanor of Bruno of Torcadino. He seemed to struggle to maintain his balance and leaned a shoulder against the wall. He seemed to bend and shrink. He seemed weak and frail. Then he hobbled out a bit, unsteadily, from the wall. In the place of the handicapped Bruno of Torcadino, menacing and large, watchful and threatening, fierce with the great crutch, there now seemed something lost, needful, and pathetic.

"Masters!" he cried, bent over, looking up, thrusting out an open hand toward the three men. "Mercy! Pity! A tarsk-bit for a starving fellow."

"Do not approach us, disgusting, hideous creature, lest you spoil our appetites," said one of the men.

"Sell your slave," said another.

"She is dear to me, and who will care for me?" whined Bruno of Torcadino.

"Keep your distance, stay back," said the first fellow, menacingly.

"Pity, pity, have pity," begged Bruno of Torcadino, lurching forward another pace.

"Stay back!" warned the first fellow again. "I would not have you touch me, or be near me."

"Be merciful, be kind," said Bruno of Torcadino. "I am hungry."

"Liar," said the third man. "I see no dangling flesh, I see no bones protruding through your skin."

"You are a fraud, half-man," said he who seemed to be first amongst the three.

"I dislike those who are not whole," said the second man. "They make me sick, they turn my stomach."

"I hate liars and frauds," said the third man.

"They will not employ me, I have no friends," said Bruno of Torcadino, pathetically.

"Perhaps he has a coin," said the second man.

"Let us beg it from him," said the third.

"It seems there is a purse at his belt," said the second man. "Let us hope it is not empty."

"And let us sport with the slave," said the third man. "She is comely."

"She is excessively tunicked," said the first man.

"That is easily remedied," said the second man.

"Let her alone!" wailed Bruno of Torcadino.

"Let us try her lips," said the third man.

I tried to squirm back, against the wall.

"What is your name, pretty *kajira*?" asked the first man.

"She cannot speak!" said Bruno of Torcadino.

"How rare," said the second man, "what an improbable pair, a lying, importunate beggar, falsely professing hunger, with a purse at his belt, and a slave who cannot speak."

"Do not!" whined Bruno of Torcadino.

I was lifted by one man, and the tunic was torn to my waist by another.

Bruno of Torcadino put out his hand. "Please do not, kind, noble masters," he said. "Let her alone! She is a poor, helpless slave! She cannot even speak!" He hobbled a step toward me, as though he might intervene, but the first man, with a bitter laugh, and a sweep of his foot, kicked the crutch from under him and he fell heavily, awkwardly, to the walkway. Bruno of Torcadino reached out to retrieve the crutch, but the first man kicked it several feet down the walkway.

Bearded faces were thrust against mine, tearing at my face. My lips were thrust back against my teeth. I tasted blood in my mouth. My shoulders and back-braceleted hands were thrust back against the abrading wall. My body was rudely explored. My body, spasmodically, leapt in their grip. I shook my head, wildly, "No, no!" I could not help myself. My body had been honed to responsiveness by dozens of masters. I knew what I was. I was no more than a slave in her collar.

"Cut the leash from her ankles," said the first of the three men.

"When we are done with her, cast her into the canal," said the third man.

I kept shaking my head, "No," and, at the same time, my body and needs betrayed me.

A knife cut through the leash straps on my ankles, and I felt my ankles seized and parted, widely, painfully. I sunk down, sitting, my back and hands against the wall. "This one is aflame," said the second man. "So are they all," said the third man. "They cannot help themselves," said the first man. I heard laughter. I was drawn forward by the ankles, and I was then on my back, on the walkway, ankles held apart. I shook my head, "No," again. Yet I wanted their touch, their rude might. "Her head says, 'No'," laughed the first man. "But her body, says, 'Yes'," said the second. "Her body begs," said the third. "Hold," said the first man. "Is she not too pretty to be a beggar's slave?"

"How so?" asked the second man.

"She elicits insufficient pity," said the first man. "She is insufficiently pathetic."

"Yes," said the third man. "She will be a much better beggar's slave if she is mutilated, scarred, perhaps less a nose and ears."

"Let us put her to her proper slave use," said the second man, "and then attend to it."

"No," said the first man, drawing his knife from its belt sheath, "let us attend to it first."

"Good," said the second man.

"Good," said the third man.

I shook my head again, "No." Tears burst from my eyes. I wanted to cry out, but could not speak. My hair was held, holding my head in place.

I saw the knife approach my face.

I closed my eyes.

I heard the sound but did not, my eyes closed, see the blow. It was fierce, swift, and heavy. I opened my eyes, only to close them again, immediately, having caught a confused glimpse of spattered blood and half a head. The second man, he who had held my ankles, had leapt to his feet, and tried to turn about, but he had scarcely come about, when the thick, heavy, bloody crutch, like a battering ram, like lightning become timber, thrust a foot into his chest. As Bruno of Torcadino freed his crutch from the chest of the second man, the third man, in the moment, rose up, scrambled to the side, backed off, and drew a sword. No longer did Bruno of Torcadino seem cringing and weak, helpless and frail. He now, supported by the crutch, glowering, terrible in size and mien, faced the third man. The third man, clutching the sword, seemed uncertain. Clearly he contemplated flight, pondering declining to participate even in a contest so ostensibly to his advantage.

"You may buy your life," said Bruno of Torcadino. "Leave your purse, and depart."

"You are mad," said the man. "What is your stick against my steel? You have one leg. I have two. I need only avoid your first blow, feinting and circling, staying outside its compass, for you will have no opportunity for a second. I could be about you a dozen times, keeping you turning, unsteady, uncertain. When will I attack? You could not know. I could be behind you so swiftly, you could not turn without losing your balance, falling, being at my mercy."

"If you wish your life," said Bruno of Torcadino, "leave your purse and depart."

"I am not afraid of a cripple, half a man, a thing to mock and ridicule," he said.

"The decision is yours," said Bruno of Torcadino.

"Perhaps I will leave you your life," he said, the sword wavering.

"But then," said Bruno of Torcadino, "I will not leave you yours."

"You are a fool, a wretched cripple, a pathetic, suitable butt for jokes and scorn. If I do not choose to kill you now, I need only turn about and walk away. Will you follow me? Will you catch me? Will you run after me?"

"I will not run after you," said Bruno of Torcadino. "*Ela*, I cannot do so, even if I chose. But I will follow you, and some day, some night, somewhere, you will not know when, or where, I will find you. Then I will kill you."

The man's left hand went to his purse, but then he withdrew it.

"No!" he said.

"As you wish," said Bruno of Torcadino. He then turned his back to the man. I wanted to cry out a warning to Bruno of Torcadino, but no sound could escape my lips. But Bruno of Torcadino's right hand had slipped under the half cloak he wore over his left shoulder, where, suspended by its strap, hung a short, wicked blade, his unsheathed sword. It was hard to follow what had occurred for it was accomplished so rapidly, but, when it was done, it was clear what had been done. I remembered seeing it. I had heard just one sound, a small, swift sound, bright and quick, when Bruno of Torcadino, fiercely turned, leaning on the crutch, parried the assailant's blade, following which he thrust.

Bruno of Torcadino looked down, to his side, where his assailant lay on the walkway, clutching his throat, blood streaming, in gouts, a cup at a time, between his hands.

I forced myself to the side, freeing myself of sprawled, bloody weight, that of he who had been the first man, his head half broken, half torn away, encumbering me.

Then the body at the feet of Bruno of Torcadino ceased to move, and the blood subsided.

Bruno of Torcadino wiped his blade on the tunic of the fallen man and rehung it on its strap under his left arm.

I was sick. I did not try to regain my feet. I was bloody, from the blood of the man who had reached toward me earlier, knife in hand. I would not try to flee, to run, and try to return to the Golden Chain. I could not speak. I did not know how to reach the Golden Chain from my present location. My collar read, "I am owned by Bruno of Torcadino."

I was grateful to be alive. I was grateful not to have been disfigured.

I became aware of Bruno of Torcadino standing over me. I went to my knees.

"You were aroused," he said.

I put my head down.

"What a slave you are," he said.

I kept my head down.

He then turned away.

"It is a good morning's work," he said. "I found them suitable donors, with none others then about."

I looked up.

"Guardsmen rarely patrol this area," he said. "I inquired. It is too dangerous."

I then watched as Bruno of Torcadino, kneeling on one knee, in turn, beside each of the three men, gathered in the contents of the three purses. Then he, grasping the crutch, with an effort, hauled himself upright.

"I shall multiply these coins," he said, "wagering on the dark contests, the Gambles of Blades."

Bruno of Torcadino then, with foot and crutch, rolled the three bodies to the edge of the canal, and then, one by one, thrust them into the canal.

"They were brigands," he said. "Honest men would have lighter purses."

I supposed this might be true, but I did not think this consideration was such as might have entered into his calculations.

"Stand up," he said.

I regained my feet, and he pulled up the rent tunic and knotted its shreds over my left shoulder.

"Returning to our domicile," he said, "we will undoubtedly encounter, or pass, one or more free women. We must not cause them distress."

I looked toward the canal and saw a roiling of water, some thirty or forty paces from where we stood.

He turned about.

"The urts are quick," he said. "One or more of the bodies has been dragged away. See the water. Disputation is in progress. If a shark appears, they will withdraw and wait for its leavings."

I shuddered.

"You are filthy," he said, "with dirt and blood, and you will need a new tunic. In the domicile we will clean you up."

I looked at him, and I fear he read my uneasiness.

"Yes," he said, "you were aroused, and left unsatisfied. It is unpleasant. The feelings will pass but they will soon return again, and again, and more forcibly."

How helpless we are in our collars. It is done to us. We are given no choice. They do what they wish. They kindle our slave fires. Does it amuse them? They do not ask us. They do it to us. They make us the helpless prisoners and victims of our needs. How fiercely, uncontrollably, they have our slave fires burn. How can we then, made whole, full, and true women, be other than their abject slaves? We are helpless. Yet I knew I would not wish to be other than I was.

CHAPTER TWENTY-EIGHT

What Occurred After the Business by the Canal

I was in the apartment, the domicile, of Bruno of Torcadino. I had been well washed, my body and hair, and was freshly tunicked. I had been given a comb and brush, which I had put to extensive and welcome use. Such things, trivial as they seem, can mean much. A small blanket was near me, folded four times, on the floor. For that, too, I was grateful. I was not close-shackled, and my body, interestingly, bore but one bond, a loose chain, of some five feet in length, fastened to a slave ring in the floor.

It was the evening of the day in which Bruno of Torcadino, at the edge of the Canal of the Sea Sleen, had recouped his finances.

My food dish and water dish were to the side.

"I must plan," said Bruno of Torcadino, standing near the door, in a just-donned long cloak. "I must see to things. Coins are to be multiplied. Now I will proceed forth."

Seldom did Bruno of Torcadino leave me alone.

When he had done so, and I had thought him far distant, I might have screamed, and screamed, to attract attention, and plea for my return to safety, to the Golden Chain, but I could utter no sound.

He turned in the threshold. "I have seen to the assuagement of your torment," he said.

I did not understand this.

The door closed, and Bruno of Torcadino had left the domicile. I heard him descend the stairs, the strokes of the mighty crutch gradually diminishing.

About a quarter of an Ahn later the door opened.

It was not Bruno of Torcadino.

"Get your tunic off," said a voice. "Turn about, kneeling, your head to the floor, your hands clasped behind the back of your neck."

I complied, instantly.

"This will do, to begin with," said the voice.

When the figure had appeared in the threshold, I was startled and distraught. I could not cry out, from what had been done to me, days ago. But my lips had formed the word, "Master." Had I been able to cry out, my cry, its wild sound, would have been "Master!" I had learned that, long ago. A slave girl does not address a free man by his name, but as "Master." How dare she put the name of a free man on her lowly slave lips?

"This time," said Addison Steele, "I need not waste a tarsk-bit on your worthless hide. This time you cost nothing. This time you are free."

CHAPTER TWENTY-NINE

We Arrive at the Skerry of Lars

"It is said," said a fellow, "he is from the Farther Islands, say, Chios or Thera."

"From Telnus, on Cos," said another.

"Turia," speculated another.

What cared I for the origins of some young mysterious swordsman? Such may rise, like a luminous sun, and, as soon, decline like a falling star. The heroes of blades come, and go, and seek out one another. So there can be one most noted swordsman, one blade faster and more cunning than all the others? Is this not as strange as the lore and fame of the checkered caste, the Players. Who cares if a Centius of Cos or a Scormus of Ar can push tiny pieces of wood about on a hundred-squared, red-and-yellow board better than ten hundred thousand others? Is it really so superior to the planting of suls and the harvesting of Tur-Pah, the fishing for eels or parsit, the shaping and smoothing of boards or the weaving and sewing of canvas? Who is the greatest of singers, or the finest master of line and color? Who is to say it? Yet in some games the matter is not so subjective. In *kaissa* a game is won, lost, or drawn, and it is clear which is the case. It is not a matter of saying; it is a matter of seeing. And, I fear, for those who are attracted to such things, outcomes are similarly clear in the games of steel. Each city has its first swordsman. Some, misguided youths or itinerant killers, will venture from city to city, from village to village, to seek out one whose reputation they covet and would own. One need only feign insult, and blades leap forth from sheaths. So one man can kill another? Is that so important? Is that so precious an accomplishment, a guerdon to be so earnestly sought? Should one not turn one's back on so absurd a game, scorning its madness, and yet few

Goreans care being denounced as cowards. Perhaps things would be different, but swordsmen have their followers, and followers demand their champions. How foolish men are. What does it matter that one might be the provably, indisputably best at one thing or another, in a city, on a continent, or on a world? How thoughtless, unquestioned, and cruel are the imperatives of vanity! What are the vanities of women, free or slave, compared to the vanities of men, and yet we are not without fault, for we watch, and the men know we watch.

This morning, at the Southern Gate, Bruno of Torcadino, I at his heels, leashed, and front-braceleted, had boarded a game ship for the Skerry of Lars, not really a skerry, but a small island five pasangs out in the Tamber Gulf, five pasangs beyond the laws of Port Kar. The tickets are cheap, presumably subsidized in part by the Skerry of Lars itself. And beasts such as I in my collar, with my marked thigh, are conveyed for half price. In the north, muchly distant, in the vicinity of Torvaldsland, and in the waters of Torvaldsland itself, small, isolated, uninhabited skerries are often used as dueling places. In the morning, usually in a small boat, the disputants or contestants are brought to the skerry with a serving of meat and drink. In the evening, the boat returns to the skerry for the survivor. It was doubtless this northern custom which suggested not only the naming of this small islet in the Tamber gulf, so near to Port Kar, but, presumably, the enterprise for which it was best known, the Gambles of Blades, sometimes referred to as the "dark contests." The name, 'Skerry of Lars', was presumably chosen for its associations. As far as I know, none of the entrepreneurs associated with the enterprise are, or were, named 'Lars'. That name is one familiar in Torvaldsland. Indeed, some claim there is an actual, historical Skerry of Lars off the coast of Torvaldsland. If that is so, its name would seem to have been borrowed.

On the game ship, as it plied its way through the cold, choppy waters to the deemed "Skerry of Lars," I knelt at the knee of the seated Bruno of Torcadino. I was not the only *kajira* kneeling amongst the benches on which sat the masters. I noted seven. Each, like myself, was front-braceleted. On the other hand, I was the only one who was leashed. Two seemed noticeably agitated. The others seemed tranquil, or even curious. Some had presumably made this short voyage before, and others not. There were some forty men on board this particular game ship, one of sev-

eral coming and going from and to the Southern Gate, not counting the oarsmen, two to an oar, the rudder men, and he whom I
took to be the captain. The passengers were diverse in attitude
and mien, and varied in apparent wealth and status. Yet they sat
side by side, speaking to one another, and exchanging views. The
rank, distance, and hierarchy common to Gorean society seemed
in these crowded precincts to be abated or ignored. In sporting
events, there can be a leveling, one founded on wagering, a shared
community of uncertainty and anticipation, a fellowship in a de-
mocracy of risk. Many of the male passengers seemed well at ease,
and I suspected that they had made the journey before, perhaps
several times; others seemed curious, or animated or eager; it may
have been their first trip; some others, though few, seemed tense,
as though something of moment might be afoot, profit or loss, or
perhaps even ruin or redemption. Some conversed, lightly, others
with marked intent. Some perused the kneeling slaves, for few
men are unaware of the presence of visible, purchasable beauty.
I pretended not to notice, and straightened my body, pleased.
"Slave," whispered Bruno of Torcadino. Some men carried sheets
on small boards, sheets on which were lists or, at least, charac-
ters arranged in dense columns. Sometimes they conferred with
one another, and underlined or circled given lines with a marking
stick. Two men on board were Players, members of the checkered
caste. They were playing "speech *kaissa*," or "boardless *kaissa*,"
announcing to one another their moves and countermoves.

"So I was free!" I thought.

How I hated Addison Steele, whose slave I wished to be!

What an arrogant, uncompromising beast and master he was.
What could a woman be to such a man but a slave? What such
men do to us! How they treat us! How they own us! How on Earth
I had dreamed of such men, and now I was on Gor, where they
were abundant, helpless, in a collar!

But how was it that he had come to the apartment of Bruno of
Torcadino? Had Bruno of Torcadino, to assuage my needs, as one
might see to the feeding and watering of a hungering and thirst-
ing animal, and not wishing to bother with the matter himself,
merely accosted a stranger on the street, and referred him to his
apartment? Surely that seemed unlikely. And far more unlikely
yet that such a stranger would be Addison Steele, who on Earth,
as I understood it, contemptuous and displeased with me, had
first called me to the attention of Gorean slavers, a possibly suit-

able prospect for the sales block. For what else might I have been any good? So what then might be the connection or relationship between Bruno of Torcadino and Addison Steele? It did not seem to me that there could be such a connection or relationship, but yet it must somehow exist. I recalled the miseries and tortures to which Addison Steele had brought me, the tunic of fire and the noxious fumes of burning powders. Why had he done so? Cared he nothing for me? How pleased I was that I had revealed nothing of the former Lady Julia Leta to my captors! How dishonorable he must be to have subjected an innocent, helpless slave to so frightening and painful an interrogation. And how disappointed I had been with him, and how ashamed I had been for him, when I had discovered he was involved with the hateful Dorna of Tharna, and perhaps another, in a clandestine scheme to seize the former Lady Julia Leta of Ar and return her, doubtless for some reward, to a stern, vindictive justice far beyond her deserts. It seemed so cruel and uncalled for. I did not care for the haughty Adraste, but I had no wish for her to be suspended naked in a dangling cage in Ar's Street of Coins, perhaps for years, as a testimonial to a sure and implacable justice and a warning to any who might otherwise be tempted to follow her embezzling example. How could Addison Steele be involved in so ugly, unworthy, and perhaps dishonorable, a project? How wrong I had been about him! And how I longed nonetheless for his touch, and the clasp of his arms! I must dismiss him from my mind! I would do so! I must! But Bruno of Torcadino, too, I was sure, despite his tales of a fictive Felitia Thaliana of Besnit, wished to acquire the former Lady Julia Leta of Ar, and obtain some reward contingent on her delivery to Ar. But now I must wonder if Addison Steele had abandoned the Lady Dorna of Tharna and her possible colleague, and had joined Bruno of Torcadino, or if he was feigning the service of each, thus betraying both. It did not seem likely to me that Bruno of Torcadino and the Lady Dorna of Tharna, and her possible colleague, would join forces. Each I suspected would be inimical to the other, easily to the point of knives and poison. And, in either case, if serving one and betraying the other, I feared that the life of Addison Steele might be in dire peril.

Then I remembered that he was nothing to me, and that I hated him.

But he had, I gathered, spared my life, refraining from casting me from the delta wall to tharlarion.

"But that mercy," I thought, "if it be a mercy, would be typical of Gorean men." It was substantially meaningless. Gorean men do not cast slaves to tharlarion, no more than other valuable, domestic beasts, such as tarsks and verr.

Then I hated him, again.

"So I was free!" I thought. "Free! Consider that, and fume! So Bruno of Torcadino thought so little of me that he would not even charge a tarsk-bit for my use! And that arrangement was accepted without demure as appropriate by Addison Steele!"

I hated men, and wanted to kneel before them, naked, in their chains, and gratefully press my lips to their feet.

At that point the game ship drew up beside the wharf.

We had arrived at the Skerry of Lars.

CHAPTER THIRTY

The Skerry of Lars;
The Red-and-Yellow Enclosure;
I Am Informed as to the Gambles of Blades

Leashed, I heeled Bruno of Torcadino closely.

"Watch the crutch, cripple," warned a man.

"Beg elsewhere," said another, brushing forward.

But I feared Bruno of Torcadino had not come to this place to beg.

It was noisy and crowded on the islet deemed 'The Skerry of Lars'. An atmosphere of carnival or holiday prevailed.

I cried out, softly, humiliated. A slave must expect, and endure, such attentions.

There were several structures lining this muddy street, most the size of huts, shedlike, brightly painted, with backward sloping roofs, to carry rain water away from the street. Narrow apertures, trimmed, most now shuttered, served as windows. The doors of these small structures were fitted into doorways which were also trimmed. Some of the doors were closed with colorful signature knots. Most of these small structures, I assumed, were rented to visitors to the islet, some of whom might wish to have private quarters for an Ahn or so, or perhaps, even, to spend the night.

Farther down the street, perhaps a quarter of a pasang away, I could see the red-and-yellow walls of some sort of enclosure.

It was toward that structure that we seemed to be making our way.

Though there was no lessening of color and brightness along the street, a change in structures was now coming about. Most were now larger, and several might have served as dormitories. Several were open, with waist-high, flat counters. These supplied varieties of food and drink. There were also restaurants where a more leisurely clientele could avail itself of tables. One shop specialized in both the buying and selling of garmenture and footwear. There seemed to me little point in such a shop here. I also saw two paga taverns and a *kal-da* shop.

Of most interest, to most I gathered, were the large public boards covered with writing, which writing was occasionally changed by a scribe, walking back and forth on a platform, with a sponge and marking stick. I gathered from the conversations, comments, observations, and such, that these boards listed contestants, matches, and odds. Bruno of Torcadino stopped before more than one of these boards. Then, finally, he looked up at one, said, "Good," and then turned again toward the red-and-yellow structure at the end of the street. Near these boards, at long tables, men stood in lines, paying money and receiving slips of paper in exchange. Bruno of Torcadino passed these tables. "We will wait until the stadium," he said. "Things can change from day to day, from Ahn to Ahn. Fitness and tonicity, given results, news, surprise, fear, confidence, and such, can vary within Ehn. One who knows for what to look can predict much. It is more expensive but one can utilize the commercial runners, almost to the inspection of the blades."

I understood little of this.

One thing surprised me. I had noticed no free women about, either on the game ship or on the islet itself. I was not disappointed, of course, for, as a *kajira*, I much feared free women. Indeed, I was terrified of them. They much hated us, for our attractiveness to men, I suppose, and we, half naked in our collars, weak, helpless, and vulnerable, unable to resist, were much at their mercy. I wished that the masters would take them in hand, strip, mark, and collar them, and make them all slaves, no different from us, as apparently had the men of Tharna. In Tharna, as I may have mentioned, only one woman is free, Lara, its Tatrix.

One did not need a ticket to enter the enclosure. The ticket for the game ship, which, I think, is partially subsidized by the entrepreneurs of the Skerry of Lars, is, in effect, an admission fee to the islet. The entrepreneurs, on the other hand, do very well in a variety of ways. They rent the huts, like inn rooms, charge for shops and concessions, tax purchases, and, in particular, charge a handling fee for processing wagers and maintaining the public boards. To be sure, much wagering, as one would suppose, takes place amongst individuals.

The walls of the enclosure were not of stone or wood, but of brightly painted red-and-yellow canvas, suspended from high poles. Within the enclosure were circular tiers of wooden benches. There must have been seating for at least two to three thousand individuals. In the center of the enclosure, below the tiers of benches, sunken in the earth, was a wooden-walled pit, floored with sand, of some forty yards in diameter. Wooden steps, associated with aisles, led down into the pit. There were also some doors in the wooden walls themselves, connecting presumably with tunnels, through which individuals might come and go. When we entered, the stands were only partially occupied. Bruno of Torcadino took a seat on the lowest bench, and on one of the aisles. In this way he had convenient access to steps leading down to the sand. Seating was not reserved. I knelt at his knee. Even this early there were two hawkers in evidence, though they were now conversing and not yet moving about, one with small cups strung on a cord and a bulging shoulder-strap bota, now laid beside him on a bench, and another with a tray of assorted offerings, dried larma slices, nuts, dates, *tastas*, and other edibles, the tray with its straps also now resting on the bench. "There," said Bruno of Torcadino, gesturing up and behind us, to the side, "is the box for announcers and officials." "Wagers, Master?" asked a fellow with a red-and-yellow cap, and a red-and-yellow jacket, carrying papers and a mark board. "Presently," said Bruno of Torcadino. Then he turned to me. "That is a runner," he said. I nodded. "See that fellow to the right, across the aisle?" he asked. I nodded. "See the cap," he said, "two red slashes. He has stood twice in the sand, victory on his blade." I nodded, again. I wished I was back in the apartment, even close-shackled to a ring. But Bruno of Torcadino seldom let me out of his sight. "Look there," he said, "to the sand." An individual was now on the sand, a young fellow, having doubtless entered upon the sand from one of the doors in the wooden wall. He was looking about, sometimes shading his eyes and lifting his head, and sometimes looking down, as though studying the ground. Occasionally, in one place or another, he seemed to scuff sand or press his foot down. "That is Alan, of the House of Hesius," said Bruno of Torcadino. "He is testing the sand and marking the sun. It is desirable to keep the sun at your back. There are boards beneath the sand. Footing can vary considerably from one place to another. Should the sand be too deep it is harder to move within it. One is slowed. If it is too shallow, a foot may slip." I knew nothing of an Alan of the House of Hesius, of course. I did see the individual withdraw, exiting through one of the doors in the wooden wall. What I most remarked about him was what appeared to be very unusual hair. It was long, and bound back, tightly. It was red like flame, but parted with a broad band, or stripe, of blond hair on the left side. I would have supposed that such an individual, with such hair, would have sought to conceal its oddity from public view. Surely it would have been simple enough to dye one's hair or even shave one's head. At the very least one might have recourse to a hood or mariner's cap. "You are smiling," said Bruno of Torcadino. "I would not do so. That is one of the swiftest, keenest swords I have seen in dozens of cities, or on the islands."

Before proceeding, I think some expository remarks might be in order, in the light of which certain matters to follow may be better comprehended.

Many Goreans, like those of my former world, are fond of gambling, and this penchant for risk and effortless profit, with its excitements and uncertainty, takes many forms. There is little on which one cannot bet, the turning of cards and the fates of small, marked stones, the trickle of rain drops down a polished shield, the number of petals on a *dina* or *talendar*. Goreans bet on the outcomes of *kaissa* matches, not only at the great fairs or the city championships, but in the alleys, squares, taverns, and streets. What play, what declamation, what dance, what song, what song drama will be awarded a city's prize, a golden tripod and its sack of coins? Who is most skilled with the bow, the peasant bow or the riflelike crossbow, or the casting of darts or javelins? And races are popular, those of slaves, male and female, of the lofty kaiila, of tharlarion of various sorts, four-legged and two-legged, ponderous and fleet, and of the broad-winged, fierce, mighty tarns. Breeding lines are often kept in such matters. Breeding fees for champion animals can be exorbitant. There are also, of course, as one would expect, contests of physical combat, such as those of wrestling and boxing, fists often wrapped in the dreadful *cesti*, and weapon combat, amongst which would be numbered the Gambles of Blades.

Gambling amongst Goreans, as amongst those of my former world, can range from a pastime and a pleasure, something enjoyable and dismissible, to an obsession and an agony, a compulsive destructive force very much akin to an addiction, such as that to the dangerous and powerful drug, *kanda*.

The Gambles of Blades, as noted, is a form of weapon combat. One venue for such combat is the Skerry of Lars. Whereas there is, as I understand it, no standardization amongst such venues, and their activities, I would suppose that what occurred that afternoon on the Skerry of Lars might not be untypical. We shall suppose so. There was a single ring, so to speak, and the order of events was threefold. Matches in the first and second phase are posted on the public boards, and are followed by intermissions. The first phase, which is the longest and most anticipated phase, consists of "Fencing Matches." It is limited to registered swordsmen, professionals, commonly, but not always. associated with a "House," of which more will be said later. The second phase consists of "Blood Matches," which are, essentially, private duels. Some of these duels are legitimate duels, following upon sensed infringements of honor, disparaging remarks pertaining to a free woman, insults, and such. Others are rather engineered duels, fought for winnings, the enhancement of a reputation, and such. The third phase consists of "Challenge Matches," largely open at the discretion of the officials, in which the sand is, as it is said, "open." The "Fencing Matches" are "First Blood" matches. Professional swordsmen are not interested in killing one another, but defeating one another, outdoing one another, particularly with style and grace. The winner is the first to draw blood, as adjudicated by the judges on the sand. The delivery of a mortal blow seldom occurs, and would almost certainly be an accident, given the implicit understandings involved. The "Blood Matches" and the "Challenge Matches" may be either "First Blood" or "Last Blood" matches. "Last Blood" matches are duels to the death.

The colors of the Gambles of Blades are red and yellow, red for blood, yellow for gold.

"Houses" often participate in, and are often featured in, the Gambles of Blades, which "Houses" are itinerant organizations which have no essential relationship to particular Home Stones, cities, regions, or districts. They are essentially travelling teams of swordsmen which move about and participate in one arena or theater or another. Promoters vie for, and bid for, Houses, particularly well-known, successful Houses, to participate in their games. The Houses will normally spend several days in a given venue and share in the profits of the venue.

I have mentioned "registered swordsmen."

"Houses" register swordsmen, accrediting them in virtue of tests of skills. Few applicants qualify. Full members of a house will be registered swordsmen, but not all registered swordsmen are members of a house.

Several of these houses, among them the House of Hesius, are institutions several generations old. They are not only open to recruitment but sometimes acquire male children, even infants, to raise to the sword, so to speak.

I looked about.

The stands were now filled.

I was startled by the blast of a horn.

"It begins," said Bruno of Torcadino.

CHAPTER THIRTY-ONE

How Bruno of Torcadino Concluded his Afternoon

"Mind this slave," said Bruno of Torcadino.

"My pleasure," said the fellow.

I winced as the fellow put his hand in my hair, twisting it in his fist.

"You may beg not to be hurt," said the fellow.

"She cannot speak," said Bruno of Torcadino, "but she begs."

"Very well," said the fellow, loosening his grip, but not releasing my hair.

"What are you doing?" asked the fellow, for Bruno of Torcadino had lurched upward, bracing himself with the crutch, from the bench.

"The "Challenge Matches" are nearly done," said Bruno of Torcadino. "If I am to participate, I must hasten."

"Do not," said the fellow. "Resume your seat."

But Bruno of Torcadino had already accessed the steps downward, toward the sand. He descended awkwardly.

"Come back," said the fellow in whose grasp was my hair.

Each step down was gained with seeming difficulty.

"Come back," called the fellow. Then he added, "You are mad!"

I did not fear that Bruno of Torcadino was mad. I thought him coldly, calculatedly sane. I had also seen the movement of his sword at the edge of the Canal of the Sea Sleen. I had little doubt that he, when whole, would have been a most dangerous swordsman, and I had little doubt that some remnant of fearsome skills might be retained. Yet he seemed a pathetic, perhaps demented, figure as he struggled down the stairs toward the sand.

It took very little time, one man calling the attention of others to the matter, the business then coursing through the crowd, before his descent was marked. Awe and disbelief, astonishment and even alarm, were the first reactions of the crowd. Most, doubtless, thought him confused or mad.

On the sand, he hobbled to the judges' table, which was below the officials' box, the place of the announcers and supervisors, higher in the stands.

He turned to the crowd, and cried out, "Challenge!"

After a moment of incredulity, someone laughed, and, a moment later, the stands roared with laughter.

There were three judges at the table. One seemed angry, very angry, perhaps thinking Bruno of Torcadino's presence mocked the games. Another judge gestured that he should leave the sand. The third judge gestured, almost surreptitiously, to two attendants to approach, presumably to escort him back to his seat, if not from the high-walled, canvas enclosure as a whole.

Bruno of Torcadino held up a silver tarsk, which flashed in the sun, and then placed it on the judges' table.

He lifted his head to the amused crowd.

"Challenge!" he cried once more.

The judges conferred.

Bruno of Torcadino could no longer be dismissed.

A coin had been placed.

"One coin, a silver tarsk, has been placed," called the judge. "Is it matched?"

The stands were silent.

I knew that yesterday's looting had netted Bruno of Torcadino several coins, many of comparable value. I also knew that his wagering, abetted by the runners, during the "Fencing Matches" and the "Blood Matches" had been unusually successful. He seemed to have an uncanny sense of degrees of prowess, even before the first bright contact of steel. Too, several times before my purchase, I later learned, he had frequented the Gambles and familiarized himself with the bouts of several contestants, though then refraining from betting, perhaps to avoid calling attention to himself. At this point, today, despite his remarkably successful wagering, he had not yet turned his winning slips into coins. That could be done later at the guarded money tables, if one were able, if one were alive. I suspect that he had placed but one tarsk on the table to suggest either limits to his affluence or some diffidence as to his skills. On the other hand, a silver tarsk is a coin of not inconsiderable value. For many Goreans, a silver tarsk might represent the savings of several months.

After a time, a voice from the stands called, "It is matched."

Bruno of Torcadino seemed to slip for a moment, and then recover his balance. He then shrank down, and seemed weak, and frail.

I would have been overcome with pity, save that I knew Bruno of Torcadino. I felt cold.

"The challenger is a cripple," called the judge to the stands. "Withdraw your match!"

"It is not withdrawn," called the voice back.

This announcement was met with some derisive commentary. Too, there was some hissing, and some sounds reminiscent of the bleating of verr and the grunting of tarsks.

"It is not withdrawn," repeated the voice, belligerently.

"That will be an easy tarsk," called a fellow.

The judge then called again to the man in the stands. "Will you be content with first blood?"

"Yes," said the fellow.

This concession was met with approval in the stands.

The judge then turned to Bruno of Torcadino. "Do you find First Blood acceptable?"

"Of course," said Bruno of Torcadino, as though gratefully.

This acquiescence was met with laughter, and, I think, some relief, in the stands.

Bruno of Torcadino and the acceptor of his challenge, he now descended from the stands, and a second tarsk put beside the first, stripped away their garments to the waist.

One of the judges cautioned the acceptor of the challenge, "Do not wound or mark deeply. A scratch will do."

"We shall see," said the man. "Sometimes a blade slips."

A second judge regarded the weapon of Bruno of Torcadino, uneasily. It was short, double-bladed, light, and heavily oiled. It is common to oil swords, lightly, to protect them from rust. When a blade is heavily oiled it seems clear that something may be in mind which goes beyond simple maintenance. An oiled blade enters and withdraws from flesh more easily. This is an advantage in First Blood contests, where a light touch may be sufficient for a win. The oiled blade is also easier to pull free should the blade be jammed between ribs. This can be an advantage in Last Blood contests, particularly if more than one contestant is involved. The third judge held up a small hollow bar, on a cord, and took a light hammer in his hand.

The combatants faced one another, at a distance of three paces.

Scarcely had the bright note of the light hammer on the small bar rang out than Bruno of Torcadino apparently lost his balance and fell at the feet of the acceptor of his challenge.

"First Blood," said Bruno of Torcadino.

The acceptor of the challenge stepped back, puzzled. "Of what does he speak?" he asked. "He fell. The dolt cannot even stand. Both tarsks are mine."

"This is that of which he speaks," said the adjudicating judge, wiping a finger across the abdomen of the acceptor of the challenge. At the tip of his finger was a red streak.

The acceptor of the challenge cried out in disbelief, and rage. "It is an accident," he cried. "I did not even feel it! It is a fluke, luck, chance, a mishap!"

"You did not see the blade," said the judge.

The acceptor of the challenge, furiously indignant, howling with rage, uttering objections and imprecations, denied redress, was politely escorted by two attendants from the sand.

Bruno of Torcadino then hobbled, lurching, to the judges' table, and placed one of the two silver tarsks on the other.

Then, coughing, wavering, seemingly finding it difficult to speak, he lifted his right hand, sword grasped, in the air. "Challenge!" he burst out, and then his body shook, with coughing. To speak briefly, four men, in turn, initially assured and eager, each confident, each intending to win several tarsks at the risk of one, such stakes generously granted, responded to the challenges of Bruno of Torcadino. After the second of the four men, the crowd became silent and watchful. Clearly more was going on than was evident on the surface. Bruno of Torcadino was no longer a joke. It was no longer clear that he was a fool or mad. Each blood he drew he drew from a wound wider and deeper than its predecessors. Challenges ceased.

Bruno of Torcadino went to the judges' table, and scraped his winnings into his purse.

"Challenge, and Last Blood! Last Blood!" screamed a distraught figure, disheveled and agitated, racing down the steps to the sand, a sword in hand.

"Stop!" cried one of the judges.

"Away, off the sand!" said another.

"Last Blood!" screamed the man.

Bruno of Torcadino turned to face the newcomer. It was he who had first been on the sand with him, who had been led away by attendants, dissatisfied, howling with misery and rage, screaming of misplay and injustice, drunk with hate, unwilling to accept defeat, humiliated by the loss of a drop of blood, the token of an ocean of shame, convinced of trickery, deceit, and chicanery.

Bruno of Torcadino regarded the man, evenly. Then, after a moment, he spoke. "Shall I accept your challenge?" he asked.

There was a long moment of silence.

It was hard to know what passed between the two men at that time.

Then, suddenly, the man turned about and fled away, up the stairs, and disappeared in the crowd, which then began to disperse.

"Who is that man?" asked Bruno of Torcadino.

"Do not mind him," said one of the judges. "He is a knave, a killer, a fugitive from five cities, and a coward."

"His name?" asked Bruno of Torcadino.

"Vas, of Anango," said a judge.

"I may be able to make use of him," said Bruno of Torcadino.

"Avoid him," said the leader of the judges.

"How can I do that, if I am going to kill him?" asked Bruno of Torcadino.

Silence divided the space between the judges and Bruno of Torcadino.

"You may wear a cap with five red slashes," said a judge.

"I shall not do so," said Bruno of Torcadino.

"To such a cap you are entitled," said the second judge.

"I do not advertise prowess," said Bruno of Torcadino.

"That is your first move?" said the leader of the judges.

"Yes," said Bruno of Torcadino.

A short time later Bruno of Torcadino joined me on the bench. The fellow in whose charge I had been placed released my hair. Sometimes, as events on the sand below had ensued, his hand would tighten, this communicating his interest and excitement to me.

Men drew aside now as Bruno of Torcadino passed amongst them. Some smiled. None ventured to touch him. Some drew back in fear.

He had turned in his slips at the money tables and filled his purse.

"Now," said Bruno of Torcadino, "our finances are repaired. I can hire men, and have them in readiness."

We then made our way to the crowded pier, to wait for one of the game ships, to return to the Southern Gate.

"Swordsman," said a voice.

We turned about, and I knelt.

It was the young man with the strange hair, Alan, of the House of Hesius.

"I congratulate you," said Alan. "I wished to tender you respect."

Bruno of Torcadino nodded.

"I watched," said Alan. "Your skills are formidable. I could learn much from you."

"I do not teach," said Bruno of Torcadino.

"Guard your secrets," said Alan.

"And you yours," said Bruno of Torcadino.

"You did not kill," said Alan. "You did not change the challenges."

A changed challenge allows a contestant to withdraw without penalty.

"Once I killed for sport," said Bruno of Torcadino. "I no longer do so."

"Your handicap?" said Alan.

"Of course," said Bruno of Torcadino.

"May I see your sword?" asked Alan.

"If you wish," said Bruno of Torcadino.

This accession surprised me, but no quarrel was afoot, many were about, and there seemed a sort of fellowship, a kinship, or understanding, between these two, both of whom, I gathered, was a master swordsman, fellow citizens, as it is said, "in the city of blades."

"A fine weapon," said Alan. "It is muchly oiled."

"One must be ready," said Bruno of Torcadino. "Can you read?"

"Ahh," said Alan, softly, awed, holding the sword to the light. "I suspected this."

I gathered that there was some tiny inscription on the blade.

"The Taurentians," whispered Alan.

"Once," said Bruno of Torcadino.

"The palace guard, of the Central Cylinder of Ar," said Alan, "the private guards of Ubars, of Ubaras."

The blade was then returned, almost reverently, to Bruno of Torcadino.

Clearly the young man was awed.

"I have watched your play, more than once," said Bruno of Torcadino. "Your blade is worthy of the Taurentians."

"Surely not," whispered Alan.

"Take your sword to Ar," said Bruno of Torcadino.

"Board, board now," called a pilot. "Board for the Southern Gate."

"I wish you well," said Alan.

"I wish you well," said Bruno of Torcadino.

As the game ship, well oared, smoothly rowed, clove its way through the choppy waters toward the Southern Gate, Bruno of Torcadino spoke. "I am going to recruit men," he said. "I shall find them in taverns, some of which you know, the Golden Chain, and the Silken Rope."

I put my head down, that he not read my features.

I was excited, exhilarated. I must not betray my emotions.

I trusted that he would not, as usual, let me from his sight. How I had longed for an opportunity to reach the Golden Chain! Surely he knew that I had been owned there. Doubtless he deemed my collar and my silence would be enough to keep me in his keeping.

I trusted he was mistaken in this.

I was sure that if I could reach the Golden Chain, all would be well. I would then be free of Bruno of Torcadino. I would then be safe.

CHAPTER THIRTY-TWO

What Occurred in the Apartment of Bruno of Torcadino When Bruno of Torcadino was Absent

I rolled in frustration and fury, from one side to the other, naked, on my blanket, on the floor of the apartment of Bruno of Torcadino. Tears scalded my eyes. My shoulders and thighs were sore. I could move little before I was caught up by the chain. I was close shackled and my shackle chain was chained to the slave ring in the floor. My wrists were fastened behind my back, in slave bracelets.

It was the evening of the day following our visit to the Skerry of Lars, in consequence of which Bruno of Torcadino had muchly repaired his fortunes.

My hopes were dashed, my plans ruined.

"I go to buy men," he had said, standing by the door, before leaving the apartment, "men who can be bought. You will remain here."

I had hoped that he, as was commonly the case, would have kept me with him, not wishing to risk my loss. I wore his collar, I could not speak. He could have chained me to a wall in the vestibule of a tavern, if it had a vestibule, or outside a tavern, to a slave ring, as some masters did with their girls, before entering a tavern. He could even have had me hooded. What had he to fear? But, of course, if all went well, I might have been recognized, certainly at the Golden Chain, did he patronize it, or I could have, in some way, surely at the Golden Chain, did he wish to recruit within it, even at the risk of the lash, called attention to myself, created

some commotion, enough to warrant an inquiry. Then Bruno of
Torcadino might have been detained and questioned, and I, pend-
ing the outcome of an investigation, could have been seized and
returned to the security of my cage. I was sure the tavern's legal
claim to me would be upheld by the scribes of the law. But now
these trembling, glowing possibilities, as tenuous and uncertain
as they might be, had closed their wings and were still.

I rolled to my back, arching my spine, and stared angrily at
the ceiling, and then, uncomfortable, was going to turn to my
side once more when I stopped, moving not a muscle. The ceiling
white, ill-painted, and cracked, flickered in the light of the tiny
tharlarion oil lamp to the side, the single source of illumination in
the apartment. There was a sound on the stairs, and then someone
was on the landing outside. It seemed much too early for Bruno
of Torcadino to have returned from his venture to enlist cohorts.
Too, I had heard nothing of the crack or scraping of his stout
crutch. Perhaps someone was confused or mistaken, had entered
the building by mistake, but the sounds had suggested stealth.
I went to my left shoulder, drew up my legs, and made my body
small. I was afraid. I heard the door tried, twice. Had I been able
to speak, I would have called out, to inquire, or inform an inter-
loper that the apartment was not empty, or cried out, to utter a
warning or sound an alarm, anything to somehow rid myself of an
unwelcome, unseen presence outside the door, anything to discourage an intrusion.

There was silence in the hallway outside the door.

Then suddenly, there was a sharp, loud, splintering crash as
the door was kicked open. I jerked back, in my bonds. I could not
well see the figure outside.

Then Addison Steele stepped into the room.

"As I recall," he said, "there is no point in warning you to silence." Then he said, "Are you not in the presence of a free man?"

I squirmed, trying to get to my knees.

He lifted me to my knees before him. His proximity made me
uneasy.

I put my head down.

"Look up," he said. "I will read the subtlest expression on
your face, the least movement of your body."

My former world had not prepared me for the intentness and
care with which a Gorean male can look upon a woman. How few
women on my former world, I thought, have been truly seen by

a man. I did not think the men of my former world, as a whole, no matter how much they might look at a woman, really saw a woman.

I lifted my head but I dared not meet his eyes.

I felt his fingers touch the side of my throat, gently, above the collar, and then he withdrew his hand, and straightened up, and backed away.

I still could not speak.

His touch, as light as it was, had made me very much aware of him.

"You have become *kajira*," he said. "It is an incredible and marvelous improvement in a woman. I suppose it goes with the mark and collar, the whip and chains, and learning you are a woman."

I looked down.

"You are where you belong," he said.

I kept my head down.

"Look up," he said.

I again lifted my head.

"I was present," he said, "when silence was imposed upon you. You were unconscious, and yet, in a way, conscious. You seemed to understand, in some vacant, abstract way. I have some sense as to how it was done, and yet have little understanding of the mechanics involved. Others, doubtless, would know more. I do have some sense as to how speech could be restored to you, that is, under what conditions it could be restored to you, but, again, I understand very little of the mechanics involved."

I understood very little of what he was saying.

Yet I was profoundly excited to hear that I might once again be able to speak. I recalled the powders and fumes of the apartment of Dorna of Tharna. Perhaps there were other powders and fumes, a vial of chemicals, a restorative drug, or such?

"You will note," he said, "I have entered unannounced, and, I suspect, unanticipated. I have damaged the door. It is splintered, it hangs awry. I find that suitable. There is a reason for this unusual ingress. Doubtless you are curious. I will tell you a little, but not enough for you to understand. It is better that you do not understand. If you did, your life would be in greater jeopardy than it is now. I wonder if you realize your life is in jeopardy? You do remember, I am sure, that I was instructed to cast you from the delta wall to tharlarion but neglected to do so. Why should one waste a slave, even one as miserable and worthless as you, a shallow creature extracted from a desecrated, unloved world? I have broken in, rudely, leaving blatant evidence of a forced entry, in order to convey to Bruno of Torcadino the impression that his premises have been violated by a thief, presumably a slave thief, a thief of slaves, that, as I shall not rifle or disturb the room. Surely many must have noticed you in his keeping, here and there, on the walkways, and so on. Would it not be simple to steal from a cripple, thus to secure an easy acquisition, even if the quality of the loot might be less than would be desired? A slave thief would be likely to bring with him tools, at least adequate to open a link and free a girl from a ring. So why then, when he returns, will he find you still here? Perhaps the slave thief is a rank amateur, hoping to find you unsecured, as slaves often are, or the keys conveniently about, in the apartment, perhaps in a drawer or chest, perhaps dangling just outside your reach? More likely, he was interrupted, or alarmed, in his work, sounds within the building, conversations in the street, or such, and feared discovery, or despaired of carrying you away, bound and gagged. Thus Bruno of Torcadino returns and finds you as he left you, chained to the ring, shackled and back-braceleted. Upon his return, he will doubtless ask you many questions, to which you will indicate "Yes" or "No," by nodding, shaking your head, and such. To such questions you will give no indication whatsoever of my identity or the nature of my intrusion. Rather you will feign ignorance, and respond along the lines I have suggested, the withdrawal of an alarmed slave thief, or such. In this way you will protect my life and, in the long run, I assure you, increase your own chances of survival. Now, you will wish to know the reason for my intrusion. I wish to induce a fear in Bruno of Torcadino that he may lose you, and even that others may be interested in your acquisition, either for the procuring of information, or, as in the case of the Lady Dorna of Tharna, the removal of a witness. If my plan proves successful, he will wish to keep you under surveillance at all times."

I looked up at Addison Steele, standing apart from me, across the room.

"Bruno of Torcadino is an extremely intelligent and dangerous man," continued Addison Steele. "He realizes from the unusual affliction dealt to you that others, significant and informed others, other than Decius of Venna, who would presumably not have the resources to bring about such a result, seek the same goal as himself, obtaining the slave, Adraste. She is a common quarry."

I understood little of this.

"Bruno of Torcadino," said Addison Steele, "from your earlier disappearance and silencing, realizes his immediate competition in the hunt for Adraste is likely to be both sophisticated and formidable, and he also realizes that you can recognize them. This is a boon for him and a peril for you. I am privy to some of the plans of Bruno of Torcadino. Surely you have suspected that much from my earlier visit to you."

I had, indeed, suspected as much. Was not Addison Steele treacherous and disreputable, dishonest and dishonorable, a stranger to loyalties? If one is on all sides, how can one help but be on the winning side? Yet this was a dangerous role to play. If one is on all sides, how can one help but be on the losing side, as well? Few people who knew Bruno of Torcadino, for example, I was sure, would have cared to betray him.

"Bruno of Torcadino," said Addison Steele, "tomorrow night, or the next night, or the next, sometime in the near future, depending on his success in gathering followers, plans an outing. I want you to be with him in that outing. If my plan is successful, you will be with him. He will not wish to leave you alone. I want you on that outing. You will be on that outing—as my spy."

I shook my head wildly, negatively. I wanted no part in such matters, matters I did not understand, which were seemingly fraught with danger.

"You do not have a choice in this," said Addison Steele. "You are *kajira*."

I regarded him, with misery.

"You look well," he said, "naked, kneeling before me, marked, and in a collar, shackled, your small wrists locked behind you, in slave bracelets."

He then approached me, and stood before me, closely. I was torrentially aware of his presence. I pulled weakly at my imprisoned, braceleted wrists, held behind me.

"You are, as I recall," he said, "the former Miss Margaret Henderson, of Earth."

I put my head down.

"Is that not true?" he said.

I nodded.

"Look up," he said.

I lifted my head.

"Now," he said, "former Miss Margaret Henderson, of Earth, please me."

I then pleased him.

CHAPTER THIRTY-THREE

A Harrowing Night is Spent in the Marshes

Bruno of Torcadino and I did not even have to lower our heads to pass under the chain at the Delta Gate.

We were no longer in one of the single-oared canal boats.

"These craft," said Bruno of Torcadino, "are well-woven, light, and sturdy. Two slaves could lift one. They are ill-adapted to the open water but well ply the marshes."

That afternoon, Bruno of Torcadino, at the market quay inside and near the Delta Gate, the Delta Market, had purchased a rence craft.

"But maintain your balance carefully," he said. "They may be easily capsized."

I could have found my way back to the Golden Chain from the Delta Gate, but I had no opportunity to do so. How often I had hoped to flee from him! It was not merely that I was leashed, but, when passersby were about, or we forded crowds, a simple cry from Bruno of Torcadino, "Stop her," or "Running slave," or such, would have put a dozen men, swift, long-legged brutes, after me. Within Ehn, bruised and disheveled, my hands thonged behind me, I would have been returned to him, cast at his feet. Too, if I were alone, guardsmen might have summoned me to them for a collar check, as is often done, following which my hopes of reaching the Golden Chain would have been considerably diminished.

I now knelt in the bow of the small rence craft, my hands and feet free.

I gripped one of the two light paddles. Rence craft may be either paddled or poled. Rencers commonly stand in them and pole them, but this was not practical for Bruno of Torcadino.

My leash strap was now wound about my throat.

The previous few nights Bruno of Torcadino had essayed this journey, as previously, in a canal boat. This afternoon, however, he had bargained for and obtained a rence craft.

"Too easily," he had told me, "I was discouraged by my first effort in the delta. The mystery of the Delta Gate is still unsolved. I am sure its solution is to be found in the marshes. The canal boat is too large. A rence craft is smaller, and is almost part of the marsh itself. Rencers come and go like shadows. Why can we not do so, as well? A canal boat is easily seen and avoided, a rence craft not so. If we are not to be contacted, we may be fortunate enough to detect one who is contacted. I suspect a rendezvous is afoot, one perhaps of several. Would it not be interesting to look in on such a meeting?"

The delta is vast, of course. Armies might be lost in it. But Bruno of Torcadino, reasoning that the considerable damage done to the Delta Gate was a demonstration of power, and an invitation to parley or confer, reasoned further that a projected meeting point must be convenient to the city. He further surmised that, assuming that matters had not been prearranged, a straight line perpendicular to the center point of an imaginary line connecting the two sides of the delta portal would be the simplest, most likely line on which a meeting might take place. Lastly, the rence-encircled "lake" in the marshes, located in our first trip several days ago, concealed, and secluded, lying on that line, seemed an ideal venue for a clandestine encounter.

We were now, again, as we had been the past several nights, concealed within its encircling rence.

"Success has not hitherto crowned our efforts," he had said, "but do not despair. That crown will yet be theirs. Hunters are patient. Within that marsh there are wonders."

One doubtless supposed that that which had wrought such ruination at the Delta Gate was within, or associated with, the marshes.

I had made no effort, either by gesticulation or drawing, to convey to Bruno of Torcadino what I had glimpsed on our first trip into the marshes. I recalled what I had seen as we were returning to the city, those two, luminous, fiery disks, like eyes, burning in the darkness behind us, lifted over the scarcely disturbed, placid water. I did not even know what it was. I was frightened. I did not wish to see that thing again, whatever it was. Certainly I did not wish to intrigue Bruno of Torcadino, nor

stir his curiosity, nor confirm his speculations. I wished only to
escape from him.

"We must be patient," whispered Bruno of Torcadino.

I gathered that he had, some days ago, one night, visited various taverns and taken several men into fee, most likely cutthroats
and brigands, men who saw no point in inquiring into the nature
of an employment, if it paid well. I did not know what he needed
these men for. None had been brought to the apartment. I did
not know their numbers. Decius of Venna, as I recalled, had had
something like ten men. I did not think Bruno of Torcadino's hires
were now engaged in any activity. I conjectured they were on
"retainer," so to speak, and, in some way, were readily summon-
able, perhaps within an Ahn, or two. Among his hires, I was sure,
would be the master of a ship. He would need some way to bring
Adraste, or Luta, the former Lady Julia Leta, to some point on the
continental coast, prior to carrying her overland to Ar.

"Patience, patience," whispered Bruno of Torcadino. I suspected that he was talking more to himself than to me. He was not
really a patient man. But, too, he was a man of stern will. I trusted
he would abide by his own counsel.

The slender rence craft rested lightly on the water, nestled
within the rence. We had laid aside our paddles. Both the White
Moon and the Yellow Moon were in the sky. Not since our first
trip into the marshes had I seen any sign of an Ul, that gigantic,
winged tharlarion. How terrifying had been that sight, that monstrous, silent, soaring form briefly silhouetted against the White
Moon. Tonight, I had sensed little of the presence of tharlarion
about, of any sort. The difference, I suspect, was in our vessel,
the rence craft as opposed to a canal boat. When we had availed
ourselves of a canal boat, we were far more aware of tharlarion
in the vicinity, turning in the water, emerging and submerging,
sometimes circling the boat. Sometimes they brushed against, or
prodded, the boat. One had risen up under the boat, tipping it. I
was not sure what the difference was. I supposed it had to do with
rence; rence would be familiar to them, a part of the marshes, here
snagged, here floating, here loose, there massed, there tangled and
rotting. I think they did not associate rence with the prospect of
possible food. Whatever the explanation was, I was grateful.

By now the smell of the marshes and the marsh noises were
familiar.

We had been long in our place of concealment.

I was ready to return to the city.

I recalled Addison Steele.

He had ordered me to please him.

I had then pleased him.

I could not have done otherwise. I was *kajira*.

Nor would I have cared to do otherwise. I was *kajira*.

I was profoundly grateful to have been permitted to please him, he a free man, I only a worthless *kajira*.

"Be absolutely still, do not move," whispered Bruno of Torcadino.

Suddenly I became very afraid. I remained motionless. I feared I could not move, even if I wished to do so.

Several yards to our left, through the rence, I saw two lights.

I heard a breaking, and parting, of rence.

Then I could see, in its own lights, one at the stern, one at the bow, a large canal boat. In the canal boat were some seven or eight men, mostly sitting. I saw no women, slave or free. I wondered if it were wise to carry a light, let alone two. A large man, cloaked, standing, was in the bow. Something in his carriage seemed familiar. I wondered if I had seen him before. Two men were in the stern, one standing, propelling and guiding the boat with its single oar and one near him, cloaked and hooded, sitting. Only two men were standing, the oarsman, and he in the bow. Each of the men, save the oarsman and he who was sitting by the oarsman, wore sable garb. I wondered if that were because it was night. But then why were the oarsman and he beside him not similarly garbed? Then he who had been sitting by the oarsman, cloaked and hooded, rose to his feet, steadied himself with a hand on a stanchion, one of four to which a canopy might be fixed, and pushed back his hood. I think I could then have recognized him in any light, at any distance. It was Addison Steele!

"Do not move," whispered Bruno of Torcadino.

The man in the bow, not looking back, lifted his hand, and the oarsman ceased to ply his oar, and the boat drifted a few yards forward into the lakelike clearing in the rence.

Everything was still, save for the familiar marsh noises.

We were well concealed, I was sure.

After a time then, the man in the bow, seemingly satisfied, motioned that the oarsman should proceed.

About a quarter of the way into that lakelike clearing in the rence, the man in the bow indicated, with a slight gesture, that the oarsman should still his oar.

For about an Ehn the boat rocked in place. I could see the two lights reflected on the water, unsteady, shimmering.

Then the man in the bow reached within his cloak and raised his hand to his mouth. There were then three soft, birdlike notes.

"Those are the sounds of the nesting marsh kite," whispered Bruno of Torcadino. I had heard of this bird, but had never seen it or heard its cry. It weaves its nest of rence, which floats on the water. Some speculate that the humans who had long ago taken to the vast, formidable delta marshes, perhaps fleeing to them, might have realized the possibility of rence islands from the nest building of the marsh kite. Certainly the vast, trackless, treacherous marshes would discourage invasion or pursuit; would they not constitute a barrier more immense and impenetrable than a thousand walls of stone?

Shortly thereafter the three notes were repeated.

But I had not seen the man in the bow lift his hand to his mouth.

"The signal has been answered," whispered Bruno of Torcadino, with satisfaction.

The hair on my forearms and the back of my neck rose.

Some yards before the canal boat the waters stirred, swelling up, and then parted, revealing, shedding water, a rising, monstrous head. It suggested a gigantic reptile of metal. The two glowing disks seemed to be eyes. They were set forward on the head, as is common with predators. There were wide metal jaws which briefly opened and closed. The grip of such jaws could tear loose the side from a canal boat, or bite a rence craft in two. In the light of the forward lantern on the canal boat I saw the reflection of light on metal teeth and fangs.

To my horror I felt the rence craft move.

"We must approach, we must hear," whispered Bruno of Torcadino. "We must make ourselves known."

"He is mad," I thought.

The rence craft is light, quick, and maneuverable. It could easily evade and outdistance the canal boat. But what of the monstrous thing in the water, a vessel, ship, engine of war, or such? I had no idea of its speed, power, or capabilities. And I had no idea of the nature of the intelligence that guided or animated that emergent metal beast, nor what might be its values, priorities, and purposes. I feared it might be alien, far from human. It might not feel, care, think, or act as a human. It had responded to the signal of the man in the bow of the canal boat. That surely bespoke intention and prearrangement. But it was unlikely the presence of Bruno of Torcadino had been anticipated, nor was it likely it would be welcomed. Stealth and secrecy were afoot in the marshes. Those who seek stealth and secrecy are unlikely to view exposure and intrusion with either tolerance or equanimity.

Very gently, I remaining still, Bruno of Torcadino moved our rence craft closer to, but to the right side and behind, the canal boat. None in the canal boat, as far as I could discern, were aware of our presence. I did have the eerie sense that the monster, or something within the monster, or something associated somehow with it, might have remarked our presence.

I wondered what might be the depth of the marsh at this point. I was not a strong swimmer. On my former world, I had frequented beaches and pools less for the joys of the water than for the pleasures of being admired. In many places in the marsh one can wade, in depths as shallow as the ankles, as high as the waist. Bars are frequent. Occasionally canal boats are stranded on a bar and one must disembark and thrust the craft free. This inconvenience seldom attaches to rence craft because of their shallow draft. Patches of quicksand, which are rare in the marshes, are sometimes marked by Rencers with yellow-tufted wands. Given the physics of quicksand, comparative densities, and such, it presents one with little danger of drowning. By far the greater danger is entrapment. If one is unable to free oneself, perhaps by spreading out, getting to one's back, and working one's way to more solid ground, one might drown in rising tides, fall prey to tharlarion, or even, eventually, die of exposure or hunger.

"I give greetings to the nameless lord, he rightfully foremost amongst his people, wrongfully banished from a far world, planner of deep deeds, master of lightning and fire, bender of iron, terror of the delta, ruler of the marshes, dispenser of largesse," called out he who was in the bow of the longboat.

"You are late," I heard.

I first heard the sounds only as mechanical noises, much as one might note whirs, or clicks, in a machine. A moment later, this half freezing my blood, I realized these sounds were surrogates for, or facsimiles of, Gorean phonemes.

"You are late," I had heard.

These words seemed to emanate from the large, hideous metal object before us, only yards away, partially risen, head and neck, from the dark water, the ship or device crafted in such a way as to suggest the features of a fearsome aquatic tharlarion. Given its immersion, I was not sure of its actual size.

"Much cannot be helped, great lord," said the fellow in the bow of the canal boat. "Messages come and go. We are at the mercy of the strength of birds, the stamina of kaiila, the beat of the long oars and the accommodations of congenial winds. Time takes time. Expedition is afoot."

Despite the might and horror of the object to which he addressed himself, there was neither reluctance nor apology, nor cringing, nor fear, in the tone of the man in the bow of the canal boat. He spoke as might a Ubar to a Ubar. I sensed he might rule a realm, though one subtle, dark, and concealed in shadows. I had the sense I had seen him before, even if not directly.

Once again then I heard sounds seemingly emanating from the large, frightening artifact in the water, that formed so much like a predatory, aquatic beast. Knowing now what to expect, I had no difficulty in following its Gorean.

"I am impatient of excuses," it said. "Resources are limited. I cannot now draw on the goods of a world. Delay is unwelcome."

"I make no excuses," said the man in the bow of the canal boat. "I do but report matters as they stand. However unwelcome might be delay, it is inevitable. I cannot control the speed of tarns, the pace of kaiila, the strength of men, the whims of winds."

The two lights on the canal boat, one at the stern, one at the prow, were reflected in the water, shimmering there, and were reflected, as well, from the metal plates or scales, of the hideous monstrosity but yards away. I wondered if it were wise to have the lanterns on the boat lit. Who knew what might note such things, what might lurk in the marshes? I recalled that Bruno of Torcadino had never entered the marshes in such a way. Perhaps the difference was the size of the canal boat, the number of men aboard, or even the complacency, or confidence, of those aboard. Presumably their numbers would be more than sufficient to deal with any curious, or even aggressive, tharlarion.

"I trust those of the sable caste do not betray their fees," said the thing.

"Did we do so," said the man, "fees would not be forthcoming."

"I could kill you now," said the thing.

The mechanical noises were evenly spaced and uniform in sound. In them there was no indication of emotion. In the absence of cues of tone, volume, and pace, it took me a moment to realize I had just heard a dire threat. Never before had I been so explicitly conscious of the enormous role in communication and understanding effected by how a thing is said as opposed to what is said. Meaning, unnoticed, far exceeds the meaning of words.

"But you are too wise to do so," said the man.

"Evidence has been assessed, probabilities calculated," said the thing. "I am sure the quarry is nigh, almost at bay."

"I deem it so," said the man.

"Time does not dally," said the beast. "It is relentless, and may be short. Each Ahn is precious. We are not the only ones who seek our quarry. Men in a hundred cities scour mansions and high holdings, prowl roads and byways, follow hints and rumors. He who would obstruct our efforts is brilliant. Who would have dared to conceal the most coveted of jewels in the setting of a metal collar? And who, while thousands sought her in secret places, would dare to place her where she would least be suspected, in public, in a public tavern, almost within his purview, as a common slave?"

"Few would know her face," said the man in the boat.

"Some would," said the beast.

"With him," said the man in the bow of the boat, "I have an ancient score to settle."

"Not with blades, I trust," said the beast.

"You are well informed," said the man.

"He is thought to be the finest sword on Gor," said the beast.

"He is undoubtedly skilled," said the man.

"Who should know better than you?" asked the beast.

"The swiftest, sharpest, and most cunning of swords is innocuous in its sheath," said the man. "What defense has it against a quarrel loosed from the darkness, a knife in the back, a dram of poison?"

"I do not understand," said the beast, "why he who would obstruct our will, having access to the quarry, has not reaped the reward of himself returning it to Ar."

"On this world," said the man in the bow of the boat, "there is a quaint social artifact, taken seriously be some. Perhaps that is involved. It is called honor."

"Interesting," said the beast. "I trust you are not inhibited by such a pointless, mundane trammel."

"It is overcome in the third of the Nine Steps of Blood," said the man in the boat. "One betrays a comrade."

"I see," said the beast.

"It is done but once," said the man. "Else the sable caste could not prosper. To do it a second time means death."

"Then you, too, have an honor," said the beast.

"Of a sort, to the caste," said the man.

"A narrower, darker honor?" said the beast.

"If you like," said the man.

"He who would obstruct our will," said the beast, "is a dangerous foe, quick in thought, astute in judgment."

"But fallible," said the man in the boat. "He erred grievously."

"Fortunately for us," said the beast.

"At the World's End, he permitted the supposed mercenary, Rutilius of Ar, who could recognize the quarry, to live."

"Rutilius of Ar," said the beast, "is one of the few who could recognize the quarry. He is almost certainly Seremides of Ar, the former captain of the Taurentian Guard."

"Who is wanted as a traitor to Ar, a betrayer of its Home Stone, a fugitive from proscription," said the man in the boat. "He was recognized in Brundisium, attempting to recruit men, to steal a slave."

"Doubtless the quarry," said the beast. "Luckily his attempt was foiled."

"We needed only keep him under surveillance," said the man in the boat. "Thus we were led to Port Kar."

I sensed agitation in the rence craft, behind me, for Bruno of Torcadino, as I shall continue to refer to him, stirred, angrily.

"I think there is one place the quarry must be," said the monstrous metallic beast, the two disks, so like eyes, alit in the darkness.

"It will require men to storm that place," said the man in the boat, "several men."

"You are marshalling such means, obtaining that commodity," said the beast.

"From four cities, and three towns," said the man, "from the darkness of forests and the caves of mountains, from dismal alleys and crowded *insulae*, from the camps of bandits and the lairs of pirates."

"If he who would obstruct our will is apprised of these preparations the quarry may be moved," said the beast.

"To whence?" asked the man in the boat. "The harbor is under surveillance, and each gate of the port, and even the skies are watched, for the darting, message-bearing vulo, returning to a far cot, for the majestic tarn."

I was not pleased to hear this, as it suggested that the delta errands of Bruno of Torcadino, in which I perforce must accompany him, might have been remarked.

"Bounty hunters are plentiful, frustrated seekers are desperate, human sleen await scent, failed soldiers of fortune despair of their fees," said the beast. "Recruit them."

"And the common thread amongst them, soon suspected, would be the undoing of our hopes," said the man in the boat. "We would have a nest of *osts*, a chaos of traitors, each determined, sooner or later, to have the quarry for himself alone. Better to recruit the naive, expecting no more, and interested in no more, than the fruits of common brigandage."

I was terrified in the bow of the tiny rence craft, so near now to the canal boat, and the dread thing of such terrible mien, illuminated in the light of the two lanterns. I had not realized how important, and to so many, might be the recovery or acquisition of the former Lady Julia Leta of Ar, nor how widespread and diligent, how complex, and how costly, might be the efforts to achieve that aim. I could not understand how the peculations of a larcenous clerk, petty and vain, could warrant such concern and attention. How zealous are Goreans! I supposed a principle must be involved, one to be satisfied at all costs, to warrant such a disproportion between expenditure and achievement, between cost and value, between effort and success. Did I not know that the muchly sought, heinous, treasonous daughter of Marlenus of Ar, Talena of Ar, was safe in Jad, under the protection of Lurius, Ubar of Cos, whose schemes she had done so much to forward and abet, I might have dared to suppose it was she, and not a Lady Julia Leta of Ar, who was spoken of so obliquely as the "quarry." "Poor Adraste," I thought, "how content you might have remained in your humble, modest station, had you but known that your petty vanity and greed might lead to a dangling cage in a Street of Coins."

"How long until you have assembled those required?" asked the beast.

"Not every brigand will do," said the man in the boat. "And agents must be planted, contacts made, spies ensconced, patrols and watches noted and recorded. Later some must know the broad-winged tarn, others the craft of siege work, mining and ascent, the management of ladders and the planning of waves of attack. We must have vessels, too, shallow-drafted and broad of beam, some large enough for the conveying of men, some small enough and quick enough for close work, armed with springals to launch javelins of fire, some sturdy enough to support catapults, for boulders and cauldrons of flaming oil."

It seemed to me that considerable forces were being marshaled, even a small army, acting in concert with some form of naval support.

"How long will this take?" inquired the beast.

"Much has already been arranged," said the man in the boat.

"He who would obstruct our will," said the beast, "has already withdrawn the quarry from the Golden Chain. He is thus apprehensive. In a hundred ways at a hundred times, despite our utmost watchfulness, the quarry could be moved, and concealed even more effectively."

"I think neither easily nor too remotely," said the man in the boat. "Each pasang of separation increases his risk of losing it."

"I trust," said the beast, "he has no inkling of our project."

"Surely none," said the man in the boat. "Given surprise, in an Ahn of invasion and fire, before aid could be mustered and organized, the holding could be stormed and the quarry seized."

"I fear delay," said the beast.

"It takes time to craft a crossbow, the stock and trigger, the sheaves of metal, the cable," said the man in the boat, "but, once built, its quarrel may be loosed in an instant."

"My resources, once those of a world," said the beast, "are much depleted."

"The quarry in our power," said the man in the boat, "much, thereafter, could be restored."

"And when can you loose your quarrel?" asked the beast.

"From now, some days," said the man in the boat.

"I remain uneasy," said the beast.

"Time takes time, expedition is afoot," said the man in the boat.

"Ho!" cried Bruno of Torcadino, to my dismay, his voice ringing across the water.

The man in the boat spun about, suddenly. Consternation shook within the boat. Men cried out. Weapons were seized. In that moment, seeing the man in the boat, turned about, his face illuminated in the light of the bow lantern, I realized I had seen him before, in the apartment of Dorna of Tharna, the Proud. It was he who had emerged from behind the screen.

"I wondered when you would speak," came from somewhere within the metal shape quiet in the water. There was no agitation in the machine, or thing, either in its sounds or in its demeanor.

"Whatever vast intelligence resides within or speaks through the dreadful housing before me, know that I have long sought your acquaintance," called Bruno of Torcadino. "I understand your invitation to parley, announced in the destruction of the mighty delta gate. I respond. Do not trust others. I alone am trustworthy."

"Quarrels," said the man in the boat, and quarrels were set in the guides of bows.

"Do not fire," said Addison Steele, clutching the rail of the canal boat. "Clearly he who chooses to cloak himself in a guise of metal has been well aware of these others, a free male and a female slave."

I then suspected that Addison Steele might well have been aware of our presence. I remembered he had some sort of relationship with Bruno of Torcadino. Perhaps he feared to lose one source of fee.

"Do not, mighty being, trust those of the sable caste," said Bruno of Torcadino. "They are treacherous, exploitative, and greedy for gold. They are thieves and killers, loathed and despised even at the World's End. They proffer empty promises and drain your resources. There is no search for men, no seeking of ships, no gathering of tools of war."

"Prepare," said the man in the boat.

"Hold your fire!" cried Addison Steele.

"We have much in common, mysterious intelligence," said Bruno of Torcadino. "I too, seek the quarry you seek. I do not deem you stupid nor do I foist delay upon you, rich with excuses, to demand more gold. You need men. I have men, ready, able men, waiting, who can strike within the Ahn, should you so wish."

"Aim!" said the man in the boat, and I saw the crossbows of his followers align themselves, most on Bruno of Torcadino, two upon me. I resisted the impulse to hurl myself into the marsh. A scream of terror welled up within me which I could not utter.

"Who are they, what do they know, who sent them?" cried Addison Steele. "Mysteries abound. Our most secret and finest plans may be in jeopardy!"

"We need not fear what they know," said the man in the boat, "if it perishes in the marshes."

"And how then can we learn what others know?" asked Addison Steele.

"Lower your bows," came from the device in the water.

"Bows down," said the man in the boat, his voice sullen with rage.

"Who are you, what do you want?" came from the machine.

I glanced upward and saw, briefly, this time silhouetted against the Yellow Moon, that fearsome shape which I had seen once before, long ago, silhouetted then against the White Moon, on our first venture into the marshes, when we had first happened upon this quiet, secluded, rence-encircled bit of water, so ideal for clandestine meetings.

"I call myself Bruno of Torcadino," said Bruno of Torcadino. "I conceal my true name for private reasons. I am of Glorious Ar. I wish to return to the city of my Home Stone in honor and glory. If I might be instrumental, even in some small way, in returning our common quarry to Ar, I would be favored in the eyes of my Ubar, the great Marlenus. Confusion as to my past would be dispelled. I would be acquitted of false charges. I would once more be welcomed and esteemed."

"For whom do you work, who are your colleagues?" came from the metal thing.

"I work for myself, and have no colleagues," said Bruno of Torcadino.

I wondered if this were true.

In any event, I feared that Bruno of Torcadino had made a false move. Are not even the wisest occasionally the dupe of their vanity?

"You claim to have men?" said the thing.

"They are ignorant of the purport of their fee," said Bruno of Torcadino.

"What would you ask for your help?" asked the beast.

"Nothing, of course," said Bruno of Torcadino, "other than the redemption of my name and the glory of contributing to so noble an end."

"You would serve me without recompense?" inquired the beast.

"Yes," said Bruno of Torcadino.

"There is nothing to fear from him, noble Pa-Kur, whose very name bespeaks confederacy with my people," said the beast. "He is both a liar and a fool. You may kill him."

"Spare the slave," said Addison Steele, "her lineaments are not without interest. Do not cast away tarsk-bits, even so few."

"Aim!" cried the man in the boat, he who had been addressed by the name 'Pa-Kur'.

I heard the cry "Fire!" almost at the same moment that Bruno of Torcadino capsized the tiny rence craft and plunged us both into the water. There was a mad, incomprehensible moment in which the cold water of the marsh swirled about me and Bruno of Torcadino disappeared. I was blinded with water, and, emerging, spit water from my mouth. I could hear shouts, and I heard something tear through the rence of the capsized craft. Something else sped past me and entered the water not a yard away. "Light torches!" I heard. To my amazement, soaked and slipping, I had my feet under me. I was standing! The water was only to my waist! I saw no sign of Bruno of Torcadino, and I saw no sign of the metal monster, so like an aquatic tharlarion. "Look for him, look for him, kill him!" I heard, the voice of Pa-Kur. Some men, with torches and drawn swords clambered over the side of the canal boat and were wading about. Two others, with armed crossbows, surveyed the water from the canal boat. Pa-Kur was still at the bow. The oarsman and Addison Steele were toward the stern. One of the men with a torch was close to me. He prodded the turned, soaked, capsized rence craft with his sword, and thrust his blade through it several times. There was much stirring about. "Find him, kill him!" screamed Pa-Kur. Again I saw nothing of Bruno of Torcadino nor of the metallic monstrosity which had been visible but moments ago. I wiped my eyes and mouth. The water in the marsh, at this point, was mostly fresh, from the great Vosk river, feeding the delta. "Fetch the slave!" I heard, the voice of Pa-Kur. I saw one of the bowmen on the boat discard his bow and slip over the side of the boat. I turned wildly away. I would flee, moving through the water toward the encircling rence, within which I hoped to conceal myself. Then a man with a torch was before me, and I turned aside. In a moment I again saw the bright flare of a torch before me, and I turned aside again. I realized I was being forced back toward the canal boat. I looked wildly toward the rence. I then heard someone plunging through the water, close to me. I turned about. It was the fellow who had slipped over the side of the boat a few moments ago. He was almost upon me. I was frantic. I decided to throw myself into the water and try to swim. I turned about again, away from my pursuer. I had no more than cast myself forward into the water when a large, masculine hand gripped my ankle. I was captured!

I was drawn back, thrashing, twisting, my belly in the water. Then his hand was thick and heavy in my wet hair. He turned me to my back and held me before him. I put my hands on his wrist helplessly, futilely. I looked back, and up at him. I shuddered. He was Gorean, and I only a woman of Earth, here *kajira*. He then pulled me up by the hair, and I was half standing in the water, him behind me. I wanted to beg for mercy but could utter no sound. I then felt the sand of the marsh beneath my feet, and between my toes. He then bent me backward. I knew myself considered. I was held, as in the "slave bow." I was assessed, as the slave as I was, a purchasable female, curvaceous, vendible meat, fit to be exhibited on the slave block. How vulnerable this makes a woman feel, and yet, startlingly, reduced to the raw female of her, how thrilled she is, so aware then of her enticements and excitements, her desirability, her worth, that men may buy her, steal her, even kill for her, anything to own her, to number her amongst their possessions. "Yes," said he, "not without interest." He then straightened my body, shook my head, cruelly, roughly, burning my scalp with pain, and thrust my head under water. I do not know how long he held my head under water, but I am sure it was a very short time. Yet I feared I might drown. Then my head was drawn up, out of the water, and I gasped for air. "You are going to behave, are you not, worthless, branded, collared slut?" he asked. I could not speak. Again he shook my head, causing me much agony. Tears burst from my eyes. I wept, bitterly. "Are you not?" he demanded. I was terrified to displease a free man, but I could not speak. I shook my head, wildly, the little I could, as it was held. Its tiniest movement caused me pain. "Speak!" he snapped. "She cannot speak!" called Addison Steele. "Bring her here!" called Pa-Kur. "Noble Pa-Kur," said Addison Steele, "she cannot speak." I was half carried, half dragged, to the side of the canal boat, and men reached down and hauled me aboard. I knelt amongst the feet of the men, my head down to the deck of the canal boat. I drew my sopped hair down, about my face, for I feared that he spoken of as Pa-Kur might recognize me from the apartment of Dorna, of Tharna.

"What of he who named himself Bruno of Torcadino?" demanded Pa-Kur of his men, who were now muchly returned to the canal boat.

"No sign," said a man.

"He drowned," said another.

"Bring me the body," said Pa-Kur.

"We found no body," said a man.

"He must have drowned," said another.

"I want the body," said Pa-Kur.

"Tharlarion, swamp fish, knife-teethed fish," suggested another.

"He has escaped," said Pa-Kur.

"Surely not," said a man.

"We shall find him through the slave," said Pa-Kur.

"She is impaired, she cannot speak," said Addison Steele.

"Women speak freely when they are naked, on their knees, and chained, and in the presence of a whip," said Pa-Kur. "Unfortunately we have no chains with us, as we did not anticipate encountering a *kajira*, particularly one so lovely, one who would look so well in chains."

I trembled, kneeling, head to the deck.

The torches were extinguished, one by one.

"Women enjoy chains," said a man. "They know they belong in them."

"As for a whip," said Pa-Kur, "a sword belt, wide and supple, double buckled, will do."

"She cannot speak," said Addison Steele.

"Strip her, kneel her before me, and hold her head up," said Pa-Kur.

The tunic was torn from me. Even the miserable, shameful scrap of a slave tunic, so revealing and humiliating, is something. How precious it is to a slave, so little. I was lifted and placed, kneeling, before Pa-Kur. One man held my head up, his hand fastened in my hair. Tears ran down my cheeks. I knew enough not to try to shield my body or close my knees. "How *kajira* I had become!" I thought. Out of the corner of my eye I saw that one of the men had freed his sword belt, the sheath put aside. The belt, doubled, swung from his hand. I did not wish to feel its lash.

"Noble leader, great Pa-Kur, confederate of beasts, Lord of the Black Caste," said Addison Steele, "the slave will be of little use, as she cannot speak."

"She will know the habits and haunts of Bruno of Torcadino," said Pa-Kur. "She will know more than enough to enable us to find him."

I could not help, held as I was, but look up, into the face of Pa-Kur, leader of these men. His back was to the bow lantern. The stern lantern was some feet behind me. It was night and the light was poor. Clouds, too, now obscured the moons.

I feared to look into such a face, like ice and stone. The eyes shone almost as if light blazed through glass. It was hard to tell, in the light, the color of the skin. The complexion seemed neither fair nor dark. I did not think it could be as I seemed to see it. It seemed now, in the light, as though it might be gray. It was of no shade or color to be expected in human skin; it was of a shade and color to be expected only in fur, in the pelt of an animal, or in the hide of a shark. I wondered if what I knelt before, so helplessly, was wholly human.

"Release her hair," said Pa-Kur, kindly, "lest you cause her discomfort."

My hair released, I put my head down, and swept my wet hair about my face.

"Do not be foolish," said Pa-Kur. "Do you think I do not recognize you, from the domicile of Dorna, once of Tharna? Look up."

I raised my head. I had hoped he would not know me. I did not understand why he had spoken of the Lady Dorna, as "once of Tharna."

"You are pretty," said Pa-Kur.

"She is a barbarian slave," said Addison Steele, "from the world, Earth."

"I have heard of that world," said Pa-Kur. "It is an excellent source of slaves. "Its women are taught to betray and deny their nature. They are without the masters for which they long, and without which they cannot be complete. They are starved for sex. Then some, selected from amongst the most beautiful, intelligent, and needful, are brought to the collars, chains, and whips of Gor."

I feared for Bruno of Torcadino.

Surely he had perished in the marshes.

"You are unlikely to know me, *kajira*," said he at whose feet I knelt. "Do not be concerned. Many do not know me. Many have not even heard of me, save for brief, whispered words, spoken in private. I am Pa-Kur, of the Black Caste, the Caste of Assassins, Master of a hundred Black Courts. The Black Caste is the noblest and most essential of castes. It eschews borders and repudiates Home Stones. It knows no city as its own, and thus claims all cities. Without it, how could justice be done and wrongs righted?

Where law fails and judges err, what but the blade and quarrel can speak? Let insult be answered and slander avenged. The verdict of steel is sufficient and conclusive."

I knew too little of Gor to understand this. I had heard of the sable caste, of the black caste, but, until this night, I had never knowingly met a representative of the caste. Do they not mingle amongst men unnoted, until the hunt is nearly concluded, until the black dagger is placed on the forehead? Certainly he who called himself Pa-Kur spoke highly of the caste. Why then, if its aim was so exalted and its ideals so high, was it so dreaded, feared, and shunned?

"Bruno of Torcadino," said Pa-Kur, "has intruded into matters beyond his ken. His interference could be costly. He places in jeopardy a project of great moment. We must discuss matters of importance with him."

I saw one of the men smile.

"You will help us find him, that we may speak with him," said Pa-Kur. "He will have fled his domicile, but that is of little matter. You know him, are familiar with him, are aware of his doings, his movements, his tastes, his preferences, his choice of taverns, his routes and itineraries, the precincts he frequents, and so on."

One light was at the stern of the canal boat, the other at its bow. We were much secluded in our small lakelike enclosure because of the thickness and height of the surrounding rence. On the other side of the rence, I doubted that the light of the lanterns could be seen. There was, of course, another direction, one seldom thought of, one which would be marked by no compass, one which would appear on no map.

"Now, pretty *kajira*," said Pa-Kur, "you will tell us all you know of Bruno of Torcadino, his true identity, his antecedents and background, his Home Stone, his caste, his past, his business in Port Kar, his plans, how he came to the marshes tonight, what he was looking for, and what he might know of us, our intentions, preparations, and plans."

I was terrified.

I knew almost nothing of what he wanted.

I was, perforce, silent.

"You will speak," said Pa-Kur. "It would be easy, to begin with, to cut off your ears and nose."

"She cannot speak, noble Pa-Kur," said Addison Steele. "She is bereft of speech."

"She will speak," said Pa-Kur.

"She cannot," said Addison Steele.

"She will," said Pa-Kur.

"Noble Pa-Kur!" protested Addison Steele.

"Noble Addison," said Pa-Kur, "be silent. You know nothing of what transpires here." Then Pa-Kur bent down, seized my hair with two hands, and lifted my head to his fearsome visage. "Look into my eyes, fully, deeply," he said.

Held, I could not turn my head away.

"There was a room by a canal," he said. "You remember the room. You remember a tunic, the burning tunic, the tunic of fire, you remember the packets, the powders, and the fumes."

I tried to force such terrible memories from my mind, but could not do so.

"You have heard my voice before," he said. "You remember it, from before. Was it so long ago?"

Tears ran down my cheeks.

"It was I who forbade you to speak," he said. "I now rescind my command, that command which only I could rescind. It is re-scinded. You may now speak."

My eyes opened, widely. I trembled. I had the odd sense, surely mistaken, that I could now once more speak.

At that moment it seemed chaos broke out havoc loose down striking gigantic form dreadful fierce scarcely glimpsed out of darkness descending splintering wood lantern struck aside sink-ing into marsh shouting men curses cries leather wings broad wide vast alive beating once twice long narrow jaw so quick hardly seen snapping seizing hideous scream water splashing a woman's scream was it mine weapons brandished quarrels hissing from bows and the Ul's wings smote wind torrent rushing about blast-ing hard to see now Yellow Moon emerging from clouds man held in jaws writhing it rose yards into the air slashed wounded blood like rain frame bristling with the metal fins of quarrels hung mo-tionless save for beating wings yards from the canal boat hovering another flight of quarrels striking into the large body a man's leg falling into marsh head gone body limp hanging from jaws shaken thing turns hissing darts away lost over the rence.

I found myself waist deep in the water.

I had slipped through the gouged, splintered wood, to the side, the boat tilting. I forced myself away, toward the rence.

The canal boat was then behind me, listing.

I must wade or swim.

I must reach the delta gate.

I forced my way through the rence.

I pressed on.

I was now elated for where I trod the water was only ankle deep. With such footing I could reach the gate in a quarter of an Ahn.

To be sure, I did not recall such shallowness on earlier ventures into the marsh.

Once again the moons were obscured by clouds. I welcomed this darkness as it made my recapture less likely. Too, the shallowness of the footing reduced, I was sure, the possible attacks of fish and tharlarion. I must try to reach the Golden Chain. I did not even think of obtaining freedom. How absurd that was! There was nowhere to escape to. Naked and collared, branded, I was only too clearly *kajira*. Too, I knew myself. I knew I belonged in a collar. How startling, precious, and welcome had been that insight! How grateful I had been to accept that recognition, so at odds with all I had been taught to profess and iterate! I did not want freedom but a strong, fine master whom I might submissively and helplessly love and serve, with my whole being and heart, forever, a master in whose keeping, he so strong and powerful, I could never forget I was a slave, only a slave, the slave I was and wished to be.

I was much pleased.

I remembered the scream I had heard.

It had been mine.

How startled I had been, to hear it, realizing only a moment after I had heard it, that it was mine.

I did not understand.

It had been mine!

It was the first sound I had uttered in many days.

How could it have been that I could scream?

Suddenly my right foot sank to the knee and I nearly fell. I tried to pull my foot free but my left leg then sunk to the thigh. I tried to remain upright. Then I was in the marsh to my waist. I became alarmed and struggled and I sank further. I was held fast. I could not free myself.

The clouds parted and the light of the moons again bathed the marsh and rence. To my right, some feet away I saw a wand, a tufted wand. I knew the meaning of that marker. I could not well tell the color in the light, but I was sure it would be yellow. Rencers sometime set such markers in the marsh to warn of quicksand.

I was alone.

I could see nothing about which I could grasp.

I sunk no further.

My arms and hands were free.

Given the comparative densities, the physics of displacement, and such, I was in no danger of slipping beneath the surface. Initially, of course, I was less sure of that than later. The longer one remains held fast, of course, the greater is the danger. One is in the most immediate danger from long tharlarion whose body shape distributes its weight in such a way that it has little to fear from quicksand. A second danger has to do with tidal levels. In my situation the rising tide in Thassa and the Tamber Gulf will wash back into the marshes. In such a case, depending on the levels, which I did not know, it might be possible to drown. A more remote possibility, but not one to be ignored, was death by exposure or from a simple lack of sustenance.

Then, again, clouds obscured the moons.

My feelings, after my first terror, were less of alarm than of frustration and futility. I was angry with myself and the marsh. I felt helpless, and stupid. I had managed to escape, I was sure, from terrible danger. How fortunate I had felt. How elated I had been! And now I might as well have been publicly caged, in a cage others might open but one in which I was a helpless prisoner, in a cage at the mercy of whomsoever might happen by. And then I was very afraid, and for the first time since I was trapped. What if no one should happen by?

I was afraid to cry out, for fear Pa-Kur and his men might hear me.

Surely they could not be far away.

The sand about me grew slick and wet. Water washed against me. I scooped up a bit of water and tasted it. It was sea water. The tide was rising in the Tamber. I had no idea how high the tide might rise, inches, a foot, a yard, several feet? Tides vary considerably, even to the number of tides a day. They are influenced by a number of things, such as the primary of the planet, the size of the planet, the period and nature of its rotation, the size and number of the planet's moons, winds and storms, and the configuration of coastlines and tidal basins. My body felt cold in the dark as the water rose slightly. The Yellow Moon then broke free of clouds and I could see its light reflected all about me in the rising, surrounding water. I tried to go to my stomach, to force myself prone, and then to my back, to force myself supine, distributing my weight, but I could not do so. I could not draw my body upward, my legs free. I could not free myself!

I could feel the encircling water rising.

I suddenly became aware that I was screaming, hysterically, heedless of who might be listening.

I do not know how long I cried out.

It may have been a quarter of an Ahn.

The water was rising, slowly, inexorably.

I stopped screaming.

I caught my breath.

My throat was sore.

I was cold.

I looked about, wildly, at the moonlit water, at the tufted wand, less of which could now be seen, at the rence to the side.

I must try to cry out, again.

"Please, help!" I whispered, hoarse, scarcely capable of hearing my own voice. "Please, help!"

At that moment I felt something strike against my back. My first thought was that it was the investigatory prodding of a marsh shark or a Tamber shark. I screamed in fear. I took it to be the first of two or three such proddings, prior to the turning and the strike. But the water was too shallow for that. Then I cried out again, certain that it was the snout of a long tharlarion, moving easily through the shallow water. But it could not be so, for such a beast seizes its prey, precipitously, and then drags it under water to drown it, after which it feasts. But what had struck my back had seemed inert, wooden, thick, wide, afloat, and curved. It was debris of some sort. Then it seemed about to turn about and drift away. I wrenched my body about and caught at it. It slipped from my hand, and I struck at it, dragging my hand across it, moving it back toward me. Then I had one hand on what seemed part of a rail. I suspected it had come from the side of the canal boat, from the right side of the canal boat, in the darkness, and somehow, in the mix of waters, that of the exiting freshwater flow of the Vosk, draining through the marsh, and the incoming, rising tide of the Tamber, had turned and moved behind me. I was desperate that it not drift away, behind me, in the tide. I fear I was not thinking clearly. I pulled it around, before me, one hand tight on the rail, the other hand, as it could, grasping the edge. It was large, and wooden. It was some three by four feet, and curved, consisting of narrow planks fastened to a curved rib. I pressed it down, fiercely, against the sand about my waist. Given its breadth it moved only an inch or so into the sand. By its means I obtained purchase, something anchored in terms of which I could press down and lift myself, inch by inch, upward, free of the grip of the sand. In a few Ehn my body was much across the object, and then the object was caught in the incoming tide, and it floated, supporting me. I wept with gladness, freed, thrashing to the side now, back amongst the rence. I do not know then if I fainted, or, overcome by my ordeal, exhausted, fell asleep. I awakened in the early morning, half lying across my makeshift vessel, to the sound of marsh birds. In the attack of the Ul, the night before, the canal boat of the Assassin, Pa-Kur, had been muchly damaged. Portions, from the impact and the blows of the struggle, the beating wings, had been splintered free. It was one of these remnants in virtue of which I had managed to free myself. From where I was I could still see the tufted wand, the yellow efflorescence at its summit. The tuft was limp and sodden. The water then, I knew, had risen some four or five feet, to a level at which, had I been unable to free myself, I would have surely drowned. Some of the canal boat's debris, given currents and such, had apparently taken much the same course that I had followed in my flight.

I could see the walls of Port Kar in the distance.

I supposed that Bruno of Torcadino had perished in the marsh.

I did not know the fate of the others.

I suspected that, together, and armed, they would survive.

I thought of Addison Steele.

I found myself hoping, desperately, fervently, for no reason I understood, that he had survived. Why should this be? He was a rogue and a villain, dishonest, corrupt, and untrustworthy, even treasonous. How I hated him! He had dared to treat me as a slave, I, once the well-stationed, proud Margaret Henderson, of Earth, as the slave I now am! He had treated me with disdain and contempt, albeit a disdain and contempt which I knew, as a slave, I richly deserved. He had treated me as a meaningless beast, a luscious, purchasable object worthy only of serving a master's pleasure. How dared he treat me so? How dared he treat me as a beast! And then I recalled that I, as a slave, was a beast, only a negligible beast. I hated him! I wanted to wear his bracelets, his collar, his chains, and feel his whip, if he should choose to whip me!

Again I looked to the walls of Port Kar.

I had little hope of surviving in the delta, not for long, nor did I wish to do so. It was my hope to return to the Golden Chain.

I must avoid Rencers.

Unattended slaves are taken, reasonably enough, as fugitives.

Most commonly, if one manages to survive for a time in the delta, there are two alternatives, other than being cast to tharlarion or staked out for an Ul.

One is kept or returned.

If one is kept one's forehead is branded and one is kept as a rence slave. If one is not kept, one is nearly concealed with ropes, thrown into a rence craft, and taken back to Port Kar for punishment. In such a case, to whom would I be delivered? Rencers expect, as I once noted, to receive a tarsk-bit for returning a less beautiful slave, and two tarsk-bits for returning a more beautiful slave. I did not know if they would ask one or two tarsk-bits for me. It is men who decide such things. If masters are unwilling to pay the tarsk-bit or tarsk-bits, the girl is taken back to the delta to be forehead-branded and made a rence slave. Alternatively, if free rence women have their way, she may be thrown to tharlarion or put out for an Ul. That fate is also one which may be visited upon a slave who is found displeasing to her master.

I then began, while keeping a careful watch, to make my way back toward the city.

CHAPTER THIRTY-FOUR

I am Again at the Golden Chain

Brushed and combed, washed and rested, watered and fed, freshly tunicked, I knelt before Ho-Tosk, my master, proprietor of the Golden Chain, in his office.

How else should a slave girl be before a free man?

"It is an interesting story, you tell," said he.

How different I was now from the filthy, disheveled, exhausted, naked, hungry slave, braceleted and leashed, who had been yesterday delivered by guardsmen to the portal of the Golden Chain!

"Much occurred," I said. "I have related matters as well as I can."

"It was your understanding," he said, "that you left the Golden Chain with my permission?"

"So the message said, explicitly," I said.

"You should have checked with me," he said.

"You were unavailable," I said.

"The timing of the message doubtless took that into consideration," he said.

"I suspect so," I said. I saw no point in informing him that the message had been signed with the initials 'A' and 'S' which I took to stand for "Addison Steele."

"You were abducted, questioned, and abandoned?" he said.

"I revealed nothing," I said. I was confident that the secret of Adraste, that she was the former Lady Julia Leta, had been well kept. I was sure that Ho-Tosk was party to this small conspiracy.

"You spoke volubly and willingly," said Ho-Tosk. "You revealed everything that you thought to keep secret."

"No, Master!" I protested.

"You do not remember it," said Ho-Tosk, "but you spoke amply and informatively, to the best of your ability."

"Surely not, Master!" I said, dismayed.

"You are not to be blamed," he said. "The fumes, the chemicals, the suggestions and instructions. How could they be resisted? You could not help yourself."

"Then I revealed all, unknowingly?" I asked, miserable.

"You revealed what you took to be the truth," he said, "as it was intended you would, should the circumstances arise."

"I do not understand," I said.

"Nor need you," he said.

"Yes, Master," I said.

"What you heard in the delta is important, and of great interest," said Ho-Tosk.

"I have recounted it to the best of my memory," I said.

I had had little difficulty in returning to the Golden Chain from the delta. I had allowed the guards at the gate to suppose that I was a returning fugitive from the Golden Chain, convinced of the horror and hopelessness of surviving in the delta, begging to be returned to her appropriate chains.

"You will be well lashed, if not hamstrung," had said one of the guards.

"Yes, Master," I had said.

"Many, convinced of the terrors of the delta, return," had said another guard.

"Those who are not eaten, drowned, or caught by Rencers," said another.

"You are pretty," said another. "Perhaps they will not cut off one of your feet."

My hands were then fastened behind my back in slave bracelets, and the leash of Bruno of Torcadino, which had been wrapped about my collar, was unwound, and I was led to the Golden Chain. I had muchly feared they would read the collar, the leash unwound, which identified me as the property not of the Golden Chain, but of Bruno of Torcadino, but they did not do so.

"After you were abandoned, unable to speak," he said, "you were picked up by guardsmen, delivered to Samos, First Slaver of Port Kar, and, subsequently, sold in one of his outlets."

"Yes, Master," I said, "to the one-legged man, he who calls himself Bruno of Torcadino."

"We know of him," said Ho-Tosk.

I no longer wore the collar of Bruno of Torcadino. Shortly after I had arrived at the Golden Chain, the Golden Chain's collar had been placed on my neck and Bruno of Torcadino's collar had been removed. In that way there had been not even a single moment in which I was not in a collar. This is common with slaves.

"Bruno of Torcadino bought me," I said. "He will think he has a claim on me."

"My claim," said Ho-Tosk, "has priority. The matter is clear in the law."

"I could not speak," I said. "I could not explain matters."

"I understand," said Ho-Tosk.

"He paid fifteen copper tarsks for me."

"You are worth more," said Ho-Tosk.

"I could not speak," I said.

"Even so," he said.

"A girl is pleased," I said.

"Do you understand why you could not speak?" he asked.

"No, Master," I said.

"I do not understand the mechanism fully," said Ho-Tosk, "but it is done through the mind. One is told one cannot speak, one is convinced that one cannot speak, and then one cannot speak. Then, normally, it is included in the matter that only he who has brought about this condition can dispel the condition. This is useful, as one might wish the subject to be able to speak again, later, perhaps to answer questions, or such."

"But the chemicals, the fumes," I said.

"Doubtless they have their role," said Ho-Tosk, "perhaps to weaken resistance, to induce a greater susceptibility to suggestion, or such."

"I was at great risk in the delta," I said, "helplessly caught in quicksand."

"You managed to seize upon a bit of flotsam, some debris," he said, "enabling you to free yourself."

"Yes, Master," I said.

"It seems you were very fortunate," he said.

"Very much so, Master," I said.

"Such a happenstance seems very unlikely," said Ho-Tosk.

"I was very fortunate," I said.

"It seems so," said he.

I was uneasy, distraught before my master. As far as I knew I had revealed nothing in the apartment of Dorna of Tharna, but

Ho-Tosk apparently believed I had fully satisfied my interrogators, but yet, amazingly, he did not seem concerned with the matter. I gathered then that there was little importance now attaching to the former Lady Julia Leta, of Ar, or, more likely, given Adraste's recent withdrawal from the tavern, that I had been given false information, and that Adraste's former identity was not that of a Lady Julia Leta, of Ar. What then might be her former identity? Given what I had heard in the delta, I had gathered that the "quarry," as they spoke of it, must be considerably valuable. If I was not aware that the fabulous Talena, of Ar, so despised and hated, so grievously sought, the treacherous Ubara, the scheming traitress to her city, the betrayer of her Home Stone, the colleague of mortal enemies to Ar, was now safe in Cos, the guest of Lurius of Jad, I might have dared to entertain the suspicion that the "quarry," however unlikely such a prospect, might be she.

"Where is Bruno of Torcadino?" asked Ho-Tosk.

"I do not know," I said. "I suppose him to have perished in the marshes."

"And the Assassin, Pa-Kur, and his men?"

"I do not know," I said. "As there were several of them, and armed, I suspect that some, at least, managed to return to the city."

"They did so," said Ho-Tosk.

I was pleased to hear this, as Addison Steele had been a member of their party.

"And have now disappeared within the city," he said.

"Am I soon to be returned to the floor?" I asked.

"It is not clear that Bruno of Torcadino perished in the marshes," said Ho-Tosk. "And it is clear that Pa-Kur, and others, did not."

"Master?" I said.

"I think you know more than it is wise for a *kajira* to know," he said.

"I have already spoken," I said.

"And to how many others might you speak?" he asked.

"Surely to none, Master!" I said.

"It would be easy enough to cut your throat," he said.

"Master!" I protested.

"But it is not our way," he said.

"A girl is pleased," I said.

"You are no different from thousands of others," he said, "dark-haired, shapely meat, block goods, begging, moaning beasts, juicing at a snap of the fingers, melting and ready as soon as a master deigns to look upon you. You have learned your collar well and your meaning in chains."

I knew it so. How else could one be on Gor, in the hands of Gorean men?

I was not discontent.

I knew I was now where I belonged, on my knees, in a collar.

"We could change your name and lose you in any one of a hundred markets, markets as far south as Schendi, as far north as Torvaldsland."

"Yes, Master," I whispered.

I could belong to anyone!

How aware I was then of the vulnerability of a slave girl, a property, to be done with as others pleased.

"But you may yet be of service," he said. He then reached into a drawer at hand and drew forth from it a folded object, one of belted leather. He cast it against my body. "Hood yourself," he said, "and crawl to me. I will buckle the straps."

"Yes, Master," I whispered, drawing the object down, over my head.

In moments I was before him, on all fours, my head down, the device snugly buckled.

"May I ask where I am to be taken, and what is to be done with me?" I asked.

"No," he said.

CHAPTER THIRTY-FIVE

I Have Been Removed from the Golden Chain;
My Tunic is Changed;
Florian;
I am Informed as to my Whereabouts

"Stand still," said the male voice, "I will remove the hood."

I felt hands at the buckle, at the back of my neck.

My hands were behind me, fastened together in slave brace-lets. I pulled weakly at the linkage. I had no hope of freeing my-self. Such bracelets are light, simple, comfortable, and wholly effective. One knows well how well one is held. One does not slip such bracelets. One listens for the metallic sounds, one reminds oneself by so simple a test of how closely together one's wrists are fastened. One knows oneself helpless, and one is aroused.

"One wonders if your features and hair are as attractive as your lineaments," he said.

Doubtless he would soon know, as I would be tacitly assessed.

I had been taken, hooded, my limbs free, from the Golden Chain this morning. I was walked, a tavern's man's hand on my arm, to one of the nearby canals, where I was handed down into the arms of a fellow. "You may hold to the rail," I was told, and my hands were placed on the rail. A moment later the propelling oar moved, and the canal boat was underway. Given the noises of various males, presumably on occasional walkways, or possibly even in other canal boats, passing, I soon realized why I had been permitted to stand. I was still in a tunic of the Golden Chain and Ho-Tosk was not averse to displaying me, even hooded, as one of his girls. Similarly, as noted before, he sometimes let us roam about the city, suitably tunicked, as living advertisements, so to speak. "She is an Ahn girl," I had heard cry, and more than once. But I was not an Ahn girl, and the Golden Chain did not supply Ahn girls. An Ahn girl, usually a paga slave, is delivered to a given address for an Ahn or so, or even an evening, a morning, or a night, and is then, later, picked up and returned to her master, a tavern or such. Ho-Tosk, and the proprietors of the better taverns, seldom furnished Ahn girls. The major reason for this, as I understand it, is the "monitoring problem." A slave out of reach may be a slave at risk, or even a slave stolen. Given my hooding and the twistings and turnings of the canals I soon had no idea of my location. Then, after something like an Ahn, I no longer felt the sun and breezes on my arms and I had the sense that we might be making our way in narrower, less traveled canals, darker canals, between or behind close buildings. The air was less fresh. It was cooler, damper. I heard no sign of activity on walkways. "Down, *kajira*, belly," I heard. I lowered myself to my belly and felt my hands drawn behind me. A moment later I felt curved metal quickly, expertly, encircle my wrists and heard two snaps. I then wore slave bracelets. A sheet or cloth was then thrown over me. No longer could I be seen. Few, if any, would see where I was taken. Shortly thereafter I sensed we were once more abroad, somewhere in the maze of Port Kar's larger and more traveled canals. After several Ehn we paused, apparently at some gate, which, with a rattle of bolts and chains, was opened. We passed through this gate, which was then closed behind us. I guessed we were then within the water walls of some holding, in some small, private harbor, presumably near a mooring and landing.

I was lifted from the canal boat and felt stone tiles beneath my feet. "There are steps," said a male voice. "I will carry you." I was then, in strong male arms, carried up several steps. I wondered what it would be, to be carried so by Addison Steele. How weak I would have felt, how hopeful, how ready. I would hope that he would be kind, and touch me. I would tie the bondage knot in my hair, whimper, and put myself to his feet, *kajira*. Then I must wait, to see what, if anything, would be done with me. The master is all. I then recalled how despicable he was, and how much I hated him. I was then placed again on my feet and, a hand on my arm, was guided through several doors and down several passages. Four times I was lifted and carried up flights of stairs. I supposed the steps leading up from the landing had brought me to the ground floor of the holding itself. If that is the case I would then be on the fifth floor of the holding, which, in addition to the passages traversed, would testify to the size of the holding. It must belong then to an important person, perhaps even a member of the Council of Captains, the body sovereign in Port Kar. I would later learn that its high porch and parapet were literally one, as was the case with several other large buildings and holdings, with a tiny portion of the city's walls. This holding, I would discover, was at the delta wall.

"Stand still," had said the male voice, "I will remove the hood."

I felt hands at the buckle, at the back of my neck.

The hood was pulled away, and I shook my head, loosening my damp hair. He pulled the hair away from my face, smoothed it, and put it back, behind my shoulders. I did not meet his eyes. Sometimes meeting the eyes of a free person directly is construed as an impertinence, a challenge, an insolence or defiance. Much depends on how it is done, of course, and the master. What master does not like, upon occasion, to look long, and deeply, into the eyes of a lovely slave?

The corridor in which I found myself was well lit, with light streaming in from high, narrow windows.

"Yes," said he, to himself, musingly, "a Golden-Chain girl."

I took this to be a compliment. When I had first encountered Addison Steele on this fresh, strange, beautiful world, on the Thieves Way South, I recalled he had expressed skepticism that I might be a girl at the Golden Chain. I trusted he would no longer be surprised.

A tiny key was put into the locks of the slave bracelets, and they were removed.

"Do not kneel," he said.

The key and bracelets were then placed in his wallet, slung from his belt.

"Remove your tunic," he said.

I slipped from the tunic, which he then took and placed in his wallet, as he had the key and bracelets.

When a slave is told to remove her clothing, she does not hesitate, protest, or cavil. She obeys without reluctance or reservation. She obeys unquestioningly, instantly.

"You may now kneel," he said.

I knelt, knees closed, back straight, hands on thighs, looking ahead, down the corridor. He paused, standing behind me for a moment, and then withdrew. I did not break position to look after him.

I remained as I was for perhaps a quarter of an Ahn.

As I was still in the collar of the Golden Chain, I gathered I had not been sold, or given away.

If this is done, the girl is often the last to know.

Then a door opened, several feet down the corridor, to my left, and a young man, blond, brush bearded, of medium height, clad in a house tunic and sandals, emerged, and then stood in the corridor, regarding me.

I kept my eyes ahead.

Clearly he was free.

Too, there was a whip at his belt.

He approached to within some seven or eight feet of me.

"What is your name?" he said.

"Whatever Master pleases," I said, a common response.

"What have you been called most recently?" he asked.

"'Zia', if it pleases Master," I said.

"Who whips you?" he asked.

"I am the slave of Ho-Tosk, of Port Kar, Master of the Golden Chain," I said.

"Who whips you?" is a common way of asking a slave girl her master's name. Slave girls, on the whole, are seldom, if ever, whipped. That is because they strive to be pleasing and there is no reason to whip them. Sometimes they beg to be whipped, to be reassured that they are only slaves. Ho-Tosk, for example, had never whipped me, or had me whipped. Perhaps the inquiry had rather be, "To whose whip are you subject?" One does expect, of course, to be punished, if one is not pleasing. Who could respect a master who does not keep us in our place, at his feet? One soon learns not to test the limits of one's discipline, as it is quite real, as real as hissing leather and weighty chains. One does not forget one is a slave.

"In this house," he said, "your use is ours. You will think of our discipline as your discipline, of your collar as our collar. Do you understand?"

"Yes, Master," I said.

In this house, then, I would be full slave, no quarter or concession given.

I did not even know in what house I was.

Something seemed familiar about his voice, but I could not place it.

He removed a bit of cloth from his wallet.

"Do you beg clothing?" he asked.

"Very much so," I said. Slaves treasure their tunic, perhaps even more than the smug, jaded free women of the high cities their veils, hoods, and robes.

"This is a tunic," he said, shaking out the bit of cloth in his hand.

That was obvious.

"It is a rather common tunic," he said. "It lacks the color, texture, and quality of the tunics of the Golden Chain."

I was silent.

I was now sure I had heard the voice before.

But where?

"It is said," he said, "that the girls of the Golden Chain think quite well of themselves, that they are proud, that they are haughty, that they look down on other slaves, that they regard themselves as special."

"We are only slaves," I said.

To be sure, not every girl was regarded as fit to be put on the floor of the Golden Chain, or, indeed, on certain others of the taverns of Port Kar.

"Perhaps you deign to serve the rabble," he said.

"If we were not pleasing, we would be well switched," I said.

"I have had many slaves who were quite as good as those of the Golden Chain," he said.

"Yes, Master," I said. I did not doubt it.

It was not my fault that I had served in the Golden Chain.

"Do you think you are special?" he asked.

"No, Master," I said.

"What had he," I wondered, "against the Golden Chain?"

"This tunic is of nondescript gray," he said, dangling it from his right hand. "It is loosely woven, light, thin, and short. It is far from the grade, color, and splendor of the fine tunics of the Golden Chain. It is a common tunic, for a common slave. What is your brand?"

"The *Kef*," I said.

"A common brand for a common slave," he said.

"Yes, Master," I said.

Kef is the first letter of the most common Gorean expression for a female slave, '*Kajira*'.

"You are thus a common slave," he said.

"Yes, Master," I said.

"As many others," he said, angrily, "in the Golden Chain."

I was silent.

"But you did serve in the Golden Chain," he said.

"Yes, Master," I said.

"Perhaps then," he said, "this tunic is far beneath you. I shall replace it in my wallet."

"No, Master," I said. "I beg it!"

"You would be clothed?" he asked.

"Yes, Master," I said.

"You, such a woman, beg a tunic, a mere tunic?" he asked.

"Yes, Master," I said.

"Do so," he said.

"I beg a tunic, a mere tunic," I said.

"What sort of mere tunic?" he asked.

"The mere tunic of a slave," I said.

"Why?" he asked.

"Because I am a slave," I said.

He cast me the tiny garment and I hastily, gratefully, slipped it over my head. It was split at both thighs.

"The tunic does not make the woman beautiful," he said, "it is the woman who makes the tunic beautiful."

I remained silent.

"*Nadu*," he snapped.

Instantly I went to *nadu*, knees spread, widely, back straight, head up, hands palms down on thighs.

"Now perhaps you understand what sort of slave you are in this house," he said.

"Yes, Master," I said.

"Now you do not seem so proud, so lofty, Golden-Chain girl," he said.

"I am not proud and lofty, Master," I said. "I am a slave."

I gathered that he might have had an unsatisfactory experience at the Golden Chain. If this were the case, I was puzzled. It was not our fault if he was defeated at *kaissa* or lost a game of stones at the Golden Chain. Had one of the girls showed him insufficient deference, or dared to prove less than satisfactory? That was hard to believe. Every alcove was furnished with disciplinary devices. Had he been reluctant, for some reason, to make use of them?

"Now you are as a woman should be, before a man, on your knees," he said.

I did know it was where I belonged, and other women, too, in whose heart they knew they were, and should be, slaves.

"I will not make the same mistake with you, as I did with another," he said.

I did not understand these words.

"In this house," he said, "you are available to any free man who wants you, immediately and unquestioningly, instantly and without the least demur, when, where, and however he might want you. Do you understand, Golden-Chain girl?"

"Yes, Master," I said.

"And there will be no wasting of a tarsk-bit for your use," he said.

"No, Master," I said.

I sensed that his hostility had nothing to do with me personally.

I was sure of the voice. Surely I had heard it somewhere, but when, and where?

Then I, kneeling before him, in *nadu*, uneasy beneath his scowl, aware of his whip, was suddenly no longer sure I had heard it before. How could I truly know? Might I not be mistaken? Perhaps what I had heard was merely a similar voice? Might I then have conflated the two? It is easy to invent fictions which masquerade as memories, often plausibly, even vividly. Memory itself, with its gaps, substitutions, and distortions, is often unreliable. How painful can be its comings and goings, its games, tricks, and jests! And how can one distinguish between an authentic memory and a seeming memory? Falsity would not be falsity did it not hide under the claim of truth.

"And do not think you will not be worked heavily as well," he said.

"I will try to be pleasing to the masters in all ways," I said.

"Should you now be whipped?" he asked.

"That is the decision of the master," I said.

"Later perhaps," he said. "The tunic might mitigate to some extent the blows of the lash."

"May I ask the name of Master?" I asked.

"'Florian'," he said.

"Master appears to have reservations pertaining to the tavern, the Golden Chain," I said. "May I ask why?"

"No," he said.

"Yes, of course," I thought, suddenly, wildly, it all now so clear, "the Golden Chain!"

"What is it?" he asked.

"Nothing, Master," I said.

"Speak," he said.

"It was you who addressed me in the alcove in the Golden Chain, when I knelt before you, chained and hooded!"

"The hood can affect hearing," he said.

"I am sure it was you," I said.

"Does Euphrosyne still serve at the Golden Chain?" he asked.

This question startled me.

"To the best of my knowledge," I said.

"The girls of the Golden Chain," he said, "should be stripped, shackled, and switch-driven to the steps of the palace of the Council of Captains, there to be publicly whipped, that they may then the better learn that they are slaves."

I did not deem it judicious for me to dispute the matter.

"And you," he said, "are a Golden-Chain girl."

"I was bought by the Golden Chain," I said.

"Only three slaves in this house," he said, "are reserved to the Holding Master, those named 'Vella', 'Cecily', and 'Adraste', the latter named slave known to you."

"The former Lady Julia Leta, of Ar," I said.

"You will follow me," he said. "I will take you to your cage and add your name to the rosters."

"The "rosters,"" I said.

"The work roster and the girl roster," he said.

"May I ask," I asked, "in what house I wear my collar?"

"Of course," he said, "this is the house of Bosk, he of the Council of Captains."

He then turned about and strode down the hall, and I leapt up, and hurried after him.

CHAPTER THIRTY-SIX

I Learn More of the Holding, In Which I Wear my Collar

"Paga!" called a fellow, and I hurried to him, to replenish his goblet.

"Hold," he said, and I remained still.

He lifted the hem of my tunic, to the waist.

"A *Kef* girl," he said.

"Yes, Master," I said.

"I thought you were from the Golden Chain," he said.

"I am owned by Ho-Tosk, proprietor of the Golden Chain," I said.

"A *Kef* girl, a common slave?" he said.

"I was bought for the Golden Chain," I said, a bit arrogantly I fear.

Most of the girls at the Golden Chain were "*Kef* girls." The *Kef* might be a common brand but that did not entail that the girl who wore it was a common slave. Many preferred slaves and high slaves wore the *Kef*. As far as I knew, the *Kef*, the cursive *Kef*, was the most common brand for a female slave on this world. I was angry. I strove to repress my annoyance. I supposed I was, in some sense, a common slave. That did not make the matter less annoying. If anything, it made the matter more annoying.

His hand did not release my tunic.

"What are you doing here?" he asked.

"Serving paga," I said.

"Are you insolent?" he asked.

Some heads at the table turned toward us.

"No, Master," I said, quickly. I feared, suddenly, my cleverness might buy me a lashing. I would not care for that, at all. I think that few would, who had had such an experience. It is one thing to be subject to the whip, and be thrilled and aroused by this subjection, and quite another to be subjected to its explicit attentions. "I do not know why I am here," I said. "I was brought here. We are taken and done with as masters please. Curiosity is not becoming to a *kajira*. Please forgive me, Master."

"We will see if you are insolent in chains," he said.

"I assure Master I am not insolent," I said. "I beg Master's forgiveness."

"She is on the Girl Roster," called Florian, from his chair near the head of the table. "Her name is 'Zia'." The chair at the literal head of the table, a large, sturdy, armed chair, was empty. The head of the holding, I gathered, was not present. This was a dining hall for crews and various crews were at sea.

The fellow released my tunic. "You will be summoned to my quarters later, at my convenience," he said.

"And to mine!" said a man.

"And to mine!" said another.

"And she will not cost you a tarsk-bit!" called Florian.

"I must replenish the pitcher, Masters," I said, and hurried from the room.

There was much laughter behind me.

I knew little of Bosk, of Port Kar. Certainly I had not seen him, at least not to my knowledge. Little seemed to be known of many of this city. I wondered if this were a heritage from the days when there was no Home Stone in Port Kar, when she was known broadly as the "Scourge of Thassa," a den of thieves, pirates, and cutthroats, rather than as she now chose to speak of herself, as the "Jewel of Gleaming Thassa." Bosk, I gathered, had come to Port Kar as a stranger from the marshes. His sword had won him a crew and ship, and thus it had begun. Who knew what names were his earlier, or what deeds might have led one such as he to a city with no Home Stone. He was said to be a paga fellow of Samos of Port Kar, who was First Slaver of Port Kar, and First Captain, or High Captain, in the Council of Captains, which body, as earlier noted, was sovereign in Port Kar. His holding, five stories in height, was large and its wide sea wall, with parapet, formed a tiny part, some fifty yards or so, of the long, irregular, sprawling delta wall itself. I did not know how many crews or ships he had. I supposed he had some three to four hundred men and some seven or eight ships. My inquiries into particulars were ignored or rebuffed. I soon desisted, lest it be suspected I was a spy. Cities are often wary of one another, even if they are not actually at war. Agents tend to be multifarious and diverse. And even within a city, rivalries might exist amongst houses and holdings. Who knows what might be heard, even by a slave? Too, it is well known that a jumble of words which is meaningless or of little import might, if joined with other words, be formed into coherent sentences. Sometimes small things, inconsequential things, say, pieces of a puzzle, may be assembled into meaningful wholes, say, pictures, or other things, things intended not to be seen or understood. Tatters of discourse may be woven into tapestries of information. I had no desire to be taken for a spy. Curiosity may not only be "unbecoming to a *kajira*," but might, I suspected, particularly if satisfied, be fraught with peril. One of the ships of Bosk of Port Kar, incidentally, was the *Dorna*. This was the vessel which had engaged, and destroyed, the Cosian raider on the voyage north from Brundisium to Port Kar. I did not know, of course, if there might be any relationship between the name of the ship and the Lady Dorna whom I had encountered so unpleasantly some weeks ago. I still remembered the terrible tunic of pain and the noxious fumes she had inflicted on me in her apartment. It did not seem likely to me, on the whole, that there would be a connection between the two names, that of the woman and the ship. Ships are often given a feminine name, and, for all I knew, 'Dorna' might be a familiar woman's name on this world. Bosk of Port Kar's smallest ship was the swift *Tesephone*, it also bearing a woman's name, though one of a rather Cosian ring.

"You had best return to the tables," said Portia. "If the men must call for you, you may be beaten."

"What is the master like, this Bosk of Port Kar?" I asked.

"You have never seen him?" she asked.

"No," I said.

"You are a Golden-Chain girl?" she said.

"Yes," I said.

"What are you doing here?" she asked.

"I do not know," I said. "I think I am here that I be protected, or employed somehow. I saw strange things in the delta."

"What?" asked Portia.

"Nothing," I said.

"You do not wish to speak?" she said.

"It is nothing," I said. I wanted to speak, but I suspected I had said too much already.

"Much is strange now," she said. "There is the problem of the Delta Gate. How could it have been damaged, so twisted and torn, with no siege, no attack? Why has it not been repaired?"

"Strange traffic is abroad," said Renata. "Night voyages into the marshes."

"The masters seem different, of late," said Ina. "I fear something may soon take place. We hear little. They tell us nothing."

"They seem rowdy enough now," I said.

I smoothed down the hem of my tunic.

"Tell me of the master," I said.

"If you are not owned here, are you free of the attentions of the men?" asked Sophia.

"I gather not," I said.

"She is on the girl roster," said Portia.

"He is a large man," said Renata, "but there are many larger. He is clear of eye and keen of ear. He has the boldness of the larl and the agility, tenacity, and reflexes of the sleen."

I had never seen a larl or sleen, but I had acquired a vicarious knowledge of such animals, and others, from various chain sisters, overheard conversations in the tavern, and such.

"He may be of the scarlet caste," said Ina. "It is said he is adept in the *kaissa* of the sword."

"It is said," said Renata, "that the point of his blade conceals itself within its own movements, until, like the ost, it chooses to strike."

The ost, I had heard, was a serpent, one whose bite was commonly fatal.

"He is a mariner," I said.

"He has ships," said Ina.

"He has favored slaves," I said.

"Cecily," said Renata, "and sometimes Vella, when he calls for her."

"And Adraste," I said.

"As far as I know, he has never laid eyes on Adraste, nor so much as touched her," said Portia.

"She is not on the girl roster," said Ina.

"There is something different and special about her, but I do not know what," said Sophia.

I was not now as sure of the former identity of Adraste as I had been, some days earlier.

"Certainly she is worked well enough," said Portia.

I had no doubt but what that was true. Yesterday, when I was bringing Florian's list of, and inventory of, *ka-la-nas* of Market of Semris upstairs from one of the wine cellars to the office of Luma, a free woman, the only free woman in the holding as far as I knew, who was seemingly the accountant and business manager of the holding, I had encountered Adraste. She was in a hallway on the third floor, naked, on her hands and knees, shackled, scrubbing tiles under the supervision of a guard. She threw me a look of unbridled fury. How humiliated must have been the lofty Adraste, to find herself put to so miserable a servile task. Was it not far more fit for one such as I? I was even a barbarian. Yet, why should she object? Did she think she was a free woman? She was a slave. I would not stop to speak with her. I was afoot and she was on her hands and knees. Her mood was one of shame and rage. It would have been very difficult to speak to her under those conditions. Too, I had my errand to run and the guard was present. I hurried past.

"Are the slaves here allowed into the city, to wander about freely?" I asked Portia.

This was common enough with the girls of the Golden Chain, though, to be sure, advertising often seemed to be involved.

"Surely, frequently," she said.

"And Adraste?" I asked.

"No," she said. "Adraste is confined to the holding."

"I think I am to be confined to the holding, as well," I said.

"Do not be too sure," she said.

"Paga, paga!" we heard cry, from the dining area.

"Your vessel is replenished," said Portia.

"Coming, Masters!" I called, and, vessel steadied in two hands, hastened back to the dining area.

CHAPTER THIRTY-SEVEN

I Prove to be of Service to Masters

The smooth tiles of the walkway, one of many in Port Kar, some-where in the city, were warm to my feet.

I was in the short gray tunic I had been given in the house of Bosk. My neck was still encircled with the collar of the Golden Chain.

"I do not understand, Masters," I said.

"You will walk in this area," said Florian, "past that entrance way, as though on an errand, and then return similarly. You will do this, back and forth, again and again, until summoned to our feet or until you deem it wise to run toward us."

"That I understand, but why am I to do this, what is the point of this?" I asked.

"Are you asking a master for the rationale of a command or an explanation?" he asked.

"No, Master," I said. "Forgive me, Master."

"You wanted to be free of the holding, to have an opportu-nity to enjoy the sights, the wind and sunlight, of the city, did you not?" asked Miles, colleague of Florian, a guardsman from the holding.

"Yes, Master," I said. "Forgive me, Master."

I had seen little of Florian's colleague, Miles, in the holding of Bosk of Port Kar. I did have the sense, occasionally, that I had seen him, or might have seen him, or someone much like him, some-where before.

At this point, the bar began to sound the Tenth Ahn, the Gorean noon.

Both Florian and Miles were in street robes, seemingly two gentlemen at leisure.

"You do not even know where you are, do you?" asked Florian.

A worker in the livery of the arsenal passed.

I raised my voice, the bar ringing its reverberating, measured notes, that it might be easier for the masters to hear.

"No, Master," I said.

"Golden-Chain girls are so stupid," said Florian.

"I do not think so, Master," I said, trying to make myself heard, wisely or not.

"They are all worthless," said Florian.

"But some, I hear," said Miles, "are troubling."

"That will do," said Florian.

It was not easy to talk or hear, with the strokes of the great bar.

"You have been here before," said Florian.

"Not to my knowledge," I said.

"She is a Golden-Chain girl," said Florian, "—stupid."

"Certainly," I think Miles said, as the sound of the bar made it hard to hear. Certainly he could speak more clearly or raise his voice, or at least wait for the interval between the strokes of the bar.

How should I know where I was? I had been brought here, hooded, in a canal boat and only relieved of the hood on the walkway. As far as I knew, I had never been here before. I did not recognize the area. It could have been any one of a hundred walkways bordered by canals in any one of the numerous districts of the city.

I was not braceleted or shackled. What did they mean 'until I might deem it wise to run toward them'?

We waited until the bar had stopped ringing.

The sound of the ringing seemed to continue, even past the last stroke, ringing in my memory, seemingly unwilling to vanish.

"If our surveillance is accurate," said Florian, "it should be nearly time."

"There is variation," said Miles. "Sometimes it does not occur at all."

"If necessary," said Florian, "we could come back tomorrow, and the next day, and so on."

"Masters?" I asked.

"Start walking," said Florian.

I had trodden the appointed course, as directed, back and forth, several times. I was now well ready to be relieved of this burdensome, pointless task, but the two fellows down the walkway gave me scant attention. Only occasionally did they seem to so much as notice me. I resisted the temptation to call out to them when near them. I sensed that that would be very unwise. I walked briskly enough for a time, but gradually, wearying, I slowed my pace. Even the lofty kaiila or a sturdy saddle tharlarion can tire.

"Have I not seen you here earlier?" asked a free woman.

I dropped to my knees. "I trust not, noble and beautiful Mistress," I said.

"Perhaps not," she said, and continued on her way.

Gratefully, I rose and continued to perform my assigned task.

I was pleased that I wore a nondescript tunic. Had I been in that of the Golden Chain, I think that her curiosity would have been piqued, and she might have looked into the matter further. *Kajirae* are seldom interested in coming to the attention of free women. The switch hurts.

There was not much traffic here, even in the bordering canal. This may have had to do with the time of day in this particular district, as the busy times in a district can vary with the occupations and interests of the locale, for example, with the change of shifts in the great arsenal, the deliveries to markets, the freighting and departure of ships, having to do with tides, and so on. The district, too, of course, may have been simply sparsely populated, though I did see several of the three- and four-story common-wall dwellings typical of Port Kar. Indeed, my ambulations took me regularly past the portal, coming and going, of one of these buildings. This was the "entranceway" which had been designated by Florian. Many such buildings, incidentally, lack walkways, and can be reached only by water. They usually have a narrow landing with mooring cleats, but often they will have one or two vertical, colorful, thick, capped, metal poles, rising from the canal itself, to which boats may be tethered. One then steps from the boat directly into the house. Sometimes several boats are tethered to one pole. Occasionally there is a sea gate leading through walls to a landing. This was the situation at the holding of Bosk of Port Kar. I had never seen an *insula* in Port Kar, but they might exist somewhere in the city. The *insulae* are essentially tenements, often seven or eight stories high, crowded with dozens of tiny, low-ceilinged, narrow, often-unlit, one-room apartments.

A peddler pushing a two-wheeled cart, filled with bundles of rags, passed by. Too, later, a scribe went past, his kit on its strap over his shoulder. He was calling out, in a droning, chanting voice, to see if anyone might wish something read or something written.

I had passed the entranceway, approaching it, again, and now, having turned about, I had just passed it, again, on my way back toward where Florian and Miles were dawdling about. They were not even looking at me. Let them do all this walking, I thought, and let me stand around down there or sit there in the sun with my back to the wall. Certainly I could spend my time doing nothing just as well as they.

I stood still for a moment.

I looked about.

This was surely not a busy district, at least at this time of day, but too, it did not seem lonely, unsavory, or dangerous. I had the sense that it was gentile, in a slightly shabby way. I supposed that if one wished to be in an area where one might be comfortably ensconced and relatively inconspicuous, it would be hard to have made a better choice. One placing oneself here would not be likely to suffer from the noticeable prominence of affluence nor the meddling, critical scrutiny of inquisitive, crowding, perhaps suspicious or hostile, neighbors. Here, I supposed, one would attract little attention. Now who, I asked myself, would be likely to favor such an arrangement? And why, I asked myself, would I be here, doing what I was doing? And I was suddenly very afraid.

"Hold, slave!" I heard, a fierce, commanding woman's voice. Surely that of a free woman! What slave would dare speak like that? "Hold!" she screamed.

I knew the voice!

I was terrified.

"Hold! Do not move!" she cried.

For a moment I could not move, for fear. It was she who had not pitied me in the tunic of fire, she who had subjected me to the stifling, acrid, horrid fumes of interrogation, she who had wanted me cast from the delta wall to tharlarion, she who had tried to buy me at the Lesser Al-Ka Market, doubtless to fulfil the murderous intention which had been frustrated by Addison Steele, reluctant to "waste a slave."

I broke into a wild, desperate run, away, anything to escape she who styled herself Dorna of Tharna. I had no desire to be cast from the height of the delta wall into the jaws of waiting, clustered, thrashing tharlarion, churning about, anticipating fighting for a part of the wall's offering.

"Hold!" she shrieked.

I could easily outrun Dorna, encumbered as she was in the voluminous splendor of the multicolored robes of concealment. Such garmenture attests to importance, dignity, station, honor, and display; too, it may intrigue the curious, appraising male to speculate about the wonders and treasures it may conceal; but it does little for freedom of movement, say, on occasions in which a fleet departure might be advisable. Indeed, a ribald joke heard in the taverns, where no free woman is present, is to the effect that the point of the robes of concealment is not only to pique male curiosity but to render their occupant easier to apprehend. If this is the case then an interesting covert parallelism would exist between the concealment of the free woman and the exposure of the slave.

"Fugitive slave!" screamed Dorna. "Fugitive slave! Running slave! Stop her! Stop her!"

I was just to speed past Florian and Miles when Florian stepped before me, and seized me. I struggled helplessly in his arms, my size and weight so small compared to his, helpless in his grasp. "Let me go, Master!" I wept. "You do not understand! She wants to kill me!"

I was miserable as I, now held by the arms, facing her, saw Dorna hurrying toward us.

"Let me go!" I begged. "Protect me! Please! She wants to kill me!"

"Be quiet," said Florian.

"My gratitude, noble masters," said Dorna, breathing heavily, her street veil reacting to the intensity of her breathing. "Naughty Mira," she said to me, scolding me. "You have been gone for two days. I was worried about you. You are naughty! I fear I must give you five strokes of the switch for your antics."

"That is too little," said Florian. "A solid lashing, and then close chains, and biscuits and water for five days, would be better."

"I fear I am too gentle and permissive a mistress," said Dorna.

"I gather this is your slave," said Miles.

"Can you read, noble masters?" asked Dorna.

"No," said Florian.

"Do you take us for scribes?" said Miles, apparently offended.

"No, no, forgive me," said Dorna.

This exchange will be better understood if it is understood that many Goreans cannot read, particularly in the lower castes, and, interestingly, in the scarlet caste, the caste of Warriors, as well, a high caste. Indeed, who would be so bold as to claim that the Warriors was not a high caste? It would help, too, to understand that, unlike on my former world, an inability to read is not taken as particularly regrettable or shameful. One does not expect the metal worker to be skilled at baking or the baker to be adept at metal work. So why should bakers and metal workers be expected to be skillful or adept at reading and writing, the expertise of the scribe? Indeed, some castes rather look down on the scribes. What do scribes know about baking or metal work? Indeed, some Goreans who can read, particularly amongst the Warriors, feign an inability to read, considering it embarrassing or unseemly for their caste.

"See the collar," exclaimed Dorna. "It reads 'I am Mira, owned by Dorna of Tharna.'"

"No, it does not!" I cried.

"Can you read?" asked Miles.

"No," I said.

"Then how do you know what it says?" asked Miles.

"You should not tell lies, Mira," said Dorna. "I shall have to consider giving you an extra stroke of the switch for that."

"I am not Mira!" I cried.

"Be silent, Mira," said Florian, shaking me by the arms.

I was afraid he would break my neck. I remined still, helpless, held, tears in my eyes.

"Please hold her for me, noble masters," said the Lady Dorna. "I shall return momentarily with men to take her off your hands."

"Business presses," said Florian.

"I will be only a moment," said Dorna.

"No need," said Florian. "We will conduct her to guardsmen and you can claim her later."

"No, no!" she said.

"Surely you do not fear her theft," said Florian. "Who would want so woeful and pathetic a slave?"

I did not think that that remark on the part of Florian was necessary or indeed accurate.

"First you take us for scribes and now for thieves," said Miles, reprovingly, seemingly offended.

"No, no!" said the Lady Dorna.

"I am sure there is a guard boat with guardsmen about," said Florian. "I recollect seeing one in the vicinity."

"To the east," said Miles.

"Yes," said Florian.

I did not recollect seeing such a boat. And, normally, guardsmen, where practical, as here, are afoot.

"Please hold her, and wait," said Dorna. "I can return almost immediately."

"We have other things to do," said Florian.

"Hold!" said Miles. "What luck! Approaching even now is a guard boat."

"Excellent," said Florian.

"The entire matter can now be smoothed out, simply and neatly," said Miles.

"Perhaps one of the guardsmen can read," said Florian. He then released my arms and fastened one hand in my hair, his left hand, and bent my head down to his hip. I was then in Gorean leading position. In this position, the slightest resistance or recalcitrance on the part of a slave, or even an unintentional failure to exhibit perfect submission, can result in agonizing pain. One hopes to accommodate oneself as perfectly as possible to the least signal from the captor's grasp, to the least whim or caprice of his will. Too, one is not only vulnerable and helpless in such a position, but so held, in such awkwardness and humiliation, so amusing to the free, one is well reminded of one's slavery.

Miles raised his hand, waving, summoning the guard boat to the edge of the canal.

"Once a determination is made," said Florian, "I am sure a guardsman or so would be happy to deliver the slave to your domicile."

"I think I shall withdraw," said Dorna.

"Guardsmen are often overburdened, and do not wish to be taxed with unnecessary, onerous duties," said Florian. "I understand they are sometimes sympathetic, particularly if a consideration might be involved."

"I see," came from somewhere within Dorna's veiling, a brief utterance suggesting both interest and speculation.

The boat came gently to the side of the canal.

"How may we be of service?" I heard.

"Can one amongst you read?" inquired Florian.

"Publion," said the fellow.

"Noble guardsmen," said Dorna, "these two noble masters have been of great assistance to me. They have kindly apprehended my escaped slave, Mira. I am the Lady Dorna of Tharna. I trust I need not verify my identity."

"Your robes proclaim your freedom," said the fellow, "and it is offensive and discourteous to question the word of a free woman."

"My slave's collar shows her mine," said Dorna. "It reads, 'I am Mira, owned by Dorna of Tharna.'"

"That should do," said the fellow.

"I will need a man to bring her to my domicile," said Dorna.

"Understood," said the fellow.

"It is nearby," said Dorna.

"Good," he said. "But first we must read the collar."

"Is that necessary?" said Dorna.

"A mere formality," said the man.

"I am a free woman," said Dorna.

"Nonetheless," said the man. "Routine requires some corroboration in such a case, however minimal. Please, forgive us."

I, bent over, my hands on Florian's wrist, was conducted to the edge of the canal. Two fellows had already disembarked and were waiting.

I suddenly recognized one of the fellows still in the boat. I had carried paga to him, not in the Golden Chain, but in the house of Bosk!

"Are you Publion?" asked Florian, of one of the fellows on the walkway, he closest.

"Yes," said the man.

"We have a runaway girl here," said Florian. "And this," he said, indicating the Lady Dorna, "is her mistress. Please read the girl's collar and see that she is returned to her proper chains."

"Certainly," said Publion.

"Probably you should keep her shackled and leashed," said Miles to the Lady Dorna.

"An excellent suggestion," said the Lady Dorna, uneasily.

Florian then raised his arm, lifting and straightening my body, his hand still in my hair, until only my toes were on the walkway. "Put your head back," he said, "far back, and cross your wrists behind your back."

In this way a girl's collar may be easily read.

Publion stepped forward.

"Hold," said the Lady Dorna, "I think we can dispense with the formality."

"Lady?" asked the other fellow who had emerged from the boat, who seemed the senior of the two who were now on the walkway.

"You have my word that she is mine," said the Lady Dorna. "Perhaps we can overlook certain unnecessary details of this transaction—"

"Lady?" asked the man.

"—for a small remuneration," she said.

"Do you seek to bribe guardsmen of Port Kar?" asked a man in the boat, bearded, with a silver slash on his helmet.

"No, no, officer," said the Lady Dorna. "I thought only to furnish a gratuity, betokening my appreciation."

"That is different," said the man.

"I thought it might be," said the Lady Dorna.

"Come closer," said the officer.

The Lady Dorna went to the edge of the walkway.

"How much?" asked the officer.

"Would a tarsk-bit be sufficient?" asked the Lady Dorna.

"No," said the officer.

Florian had now returned me to leading position. I do not think the Lady Dorna realized that Miles had now moved behind her.

"Two," said the officer.

"Very well," said the Lady Dorna.

"Two—silver tarsks," said the officer.

"Do not be absurd," said the Lady Dorna, angrily. "That is far more than the slave is worth."

"Two silver tarsks," said the officer, adamantly.

"Very well," said the Lady Dorna, in fury, reaching into her purse, slung at her hip.

Apparently the Lady Dorna now had coins at her disposal, a least to the sum of two silver tarsks. I recalled that, earlier, at the Lesser Al-ka Market, when she had wished to buy me, she had been without funds, as much so as a slave might have been, lacking even something which might have been put down on account. I gathered now, however, that that contretemps was no longer to be repeated. Currently she seemed supplied with considerable resources.

"Hand them to me," said the officer, "one in the palm of each hand."

"Have no fear," said the Lady Dorna. "There are two."

He raised his hands from the canal boat, toward her, and she bent down, extending her hands, parallel, to hand him the coins.

He did not take the coins, however, but gripped her wrists. "Take the coins," he said to a subordinate, who removed the two silver disks from her hands.

"You may release me," she said, acidly.

"Note the small, soft palms of her hands," said the officer to his subordinate, regarding them as they were held.

"Such palms look well in *nadu*," said the subordinate, "when a naked slave dares to put the back of her hands on her widened thighs, mutely begging a master to be put to his use pleasure."

In the usual position of *nadu* the palms of the slave's hands are placed down on the thighs. Slaves can be beaten for boldly daring to beg for use in such a way, exposing the delicacy of their palms to the master. Similarly tying the loose bondage knot in her hair may bring discipline. Many masters do not care for such blatant, piteous behaviors, such insolent boldness, resenting the slave's attempt to appeal to them, to plead for the satisfaction of her needs. Who cares for the needs of a slave? Do the brutes, the monsters, I wonder, not know what they have done to us? It is they who, perhaps to their amusement, saw to the kindling of our slave fires, they who have made us the helpless prisoners of our needs. Do they understand what it is to be in a collar? Do they understand our torment, its depth, its urgency, its rage, its heat, and pervasiveness? How it puts us at their feet! Do they not understand that the strongest of a slave girl's bonds, more stringent than the coarseness of swathed ropes, more obdurate than the clasp of weighty shackles, are her needs?

"Release my wrists," said the Lady Dorna, sternly.

At that point the subordinate seized the Lady Dorna's veils, wadded them, and thrust them back, deeply into her mouth, and then secured them behind the back of her neck. Her wrists were still held by the officer. Her eyes were startled, and wild. An instant later Miles had slipped a slave hood over her head, drawn it down, and buckled it shut. The subordinate meanwhile slapped slave bracelets on her held wrists, and the officer pulled her down, into the canal boat, and put her to her stomach. The subordinate, with his foot on her back, held her in place. "I think we may now be off," said the officer. His two men descended from the walkway, slipping into the boat. Miles followed them. Florian, looking about, released my hair. I was facing the boat. I felt Florian's sandaled foot against my fundament, pressing, and he gave me a vigorous push, and I, so impelled, half stumbled, half fell, into the canal boat which, even then, as Florian boarded, was drawing away from the walkway.

CHAPTER THIRTY-EIGHT

The Incarceration of Dorna the Proud, Once High Silver Mask of Tharna

"It will begin shortly," said Florian. "I expect you will be interested in watching."

Something in his voice or mien made me uneasy.

Too, I had work to do, within the Ahn, in the laundry. I would not care to be late and face the First Girl's switch.

"I do not think so, Master," I said. "I beg to be excused."

"*Lesha!*" he snapped.

Automatically, reflexively, instantly, without thinking, I turned away from him, stood straight, lifted my head, tipping it back, and placed my wrists behind my body. I had done these things, and only a moment later realized I had done them. The response had been unquestioning and instantaneous. We are trained so.

Slave bracelets were snapped about my wrists, pinioning them behind my body. A moment later the leash collar was buckled about my neck.

"Do you think you have a choice?" he asked. "Do you think you are a free woman?"

"No, Master," I said.

"You are a beast, an animal," he said, "worthless and meaningless, goods, an object, a property, no more than vendible collar meat."

"Yes, Master!" I said.

"What are you?" he said.

"*La kajira! La kajira!*" I said. "I am a slave girl! I am a slave girl!"

"Anything else?" he asked.

"No, Master!" I said. "Only that! Only that!"

"Do not forget it," he said.

"No, Master," I said.

"Perhaps you should be whipped," he said.

"Please do not whip me, Master," I said.

He then came in front of me, and gripped the leash just inches from my neck, and, by its means, pulled my head toward him, closely. I could feel his breath on my lips. I went to "slave lips" and tried to press forward, but it was not permitted. I could move forward no more. I was but an inch from his lips, held in place. "No," he said. "Another wants you, but I cannot understand why."

So close to him, my wrists pinioned behind my body, so lightly and briefly tunicked, I was dreadfully uneasy.

"You would placate me, would you not?" he said.

"Yes, Master," I said.

"And in the Golden Chain," he said, "did I pay my coin, you would please me well, would you not?"

"I am *kajira*," I said. "I must. I would have no choice."

"And you would enjoy it, and do it to the best of your ability, would you not?" he asked.

"Yes," I said, "yes, Master."

"And you would helplessly beg more, and want more?" he said, angrily.

"Yes, Master," I said.

"Slave," he sneered.

"It is what I am," I said, "and what I want to be."

"Are all the slaves at the Golden Chain like you?" he said.

"Yes, Master," I said. "We are slaves."

He drew back his hand and I feared I was to be cuffed, but he lowered his hand angrily, loosened the leash, turned about, and began to make his way down the hall. I hurried to follow, on my tether.

What could be his concern with the girls of the Golden Chain?

"Master," I called. "You said another wanted me. You know how vulnerable and helpless a slave is! Who wants me?"

"Curiosity is not becoming in a *kajira*," he said, not slackening his pace.

"Master," I called. "Where are you taking me?"

He stopped, and turned about, angrily.

"Forgive me, Master," I said, putting my head down. "Curiosity is not becoming in a *kajira*."

He then continued on his way, I after him.

Shortly thereafter we turned from the hallway and began to make our way downward, descending steep, ill-lit, narrow stairs. He slowed his pace, presumably that I would be in less danger of falling. Aside from the wine cellars, I knew little about the forbidding, labyrinthine passages below the house. They were not such as to invite or encourage exploration.

It was four days ago that the men of the House of Bosk had abducted she whom I had understood to be the Lady Dorna of Tharna, the colleague of the dreaded Pa-Kur, high amongst the Assassins.

It had come as a great surprise to me when the hooding and veils of she whom I had taken to be the Lady Dorna of Tharna were torn aside, and her splendid robes drawn down to her shoulders, to discover that the beauty of her lovely neck was much set off and enhanced by the locked, close-fitting circlet of bondage. Dorna was collared!

I think it would be helpful, even advisable, at this point, to pause, to supply certain details, historical and otherwise, in the light of which ensuing events might be better understood. These have to do, in particular, with history, espionage, and inaction.

The city of Tharna was once ruled by a gynocracy. Convention, education, culture, and law, seemingly the very air one breathed, from the cradle on, was engineered to demasculinize men, to make them fear their nature, to betray their blood, to suspect and be ashamed of their most natural interests, desires, impulses, and urges. It was a travesty of biology, a meretricious, loveless, frustrated world. Thwarted drives and suppressed desires led to hypocrisy, belligerence, impatience, cruelty, and war. Women were victims, too, being unwittingly estranged from their own natures, taught to be what they were not; instructed to rejoice in their own misery, to see riches in their own self-denial and poverty. In public, women wore masks, one supposes designed to portray uniformity, contentment, serenity, remoteness, and beauty. Conformity reigned; difference and individualism were abhorred. Each must be alike, changeless, and perfect. And who will dare to look behind a mask? The masks in Tharna were silver, save one, that of gold, that of the Tatrix, Lara. Dorna, Dorna the Proud, stood high in Tharna, was indeed the highest of the "Silver Masks," and was covetous of the Golden Mask, that of the Tatrix. As might be sup-

posed, beneath the loveless, unhappy, sterile placidity of Tharna
were the stirrings of a seething discontent. As the result of a particular confluence of historical circumstances, which need not be
recited here, the storms and flames of revolution unexpectedly
burst forth, resulting in a radical transformation of Tharnan society. Masks were torn away, melted down, and forbidden. Today
there is only one free woman in Tharna, Lara, the Tatrix. During
the revolt, one gathers that some of the "Silver Masks," those not
captured and collared, fled the city, presumably, undefended and
unprotected, to soon find themselves in foreign chains. Amongst
these, I suppose, was Dorna the Proud. She was now the slave
of Pa-Kur, of the Assassins. I did not know how she had come
into his possession, where or how he might have seized or purchased her. But now, clearly, it was his collar on her neck. I did
not doubt that he had "found her flanks of interest," as the masters say, but I suspected her value to him went far beyond her
desperate attempt to please him fully and perfectly in the furs.
She was beautiful, brilliant, and unscrupulous, a suitable participant in clandestine plots and villainies. Too, she was resource-
ful and talented. For example, she could assume the disguise of
a free woman with aplomb, whereas most slaves, whether previously free or not, would be terrified to do so. I myself would not
only be terrified to do so but I could not do so if I wished, at least
without help. I was unfamiliar with the number and layering of
robes, the arrangement of veils, even the mysterious hooks and
fastenings which somehow managed to bring together and secure
the often-sumptuous ensemble of the Gorean free woman. In some
of the more extreme cases, the free woman cannot even dress herself, but requires the assistance of a skilled "woman's slave." Such
"woman's slaves" tend to be expensive.

Secondly, in the context of these background remarks, I think
some reference to espionage would be in order. Espionage is ancient; it may antedate the human species. What predator does
not acquaint himself with the habits and gathering places of
prey? Might not keen-eyed, shambling creatures before humans
have looked in secret on one another, noted comings and goings,
scouted numbers, weapons, and defenses; does the pleasant beast,
feigning amity, have more in mind than trading shells and claws?
On Gor, there were, as far as I knew, no concealed cameras, no
electronic listening devices, no reconnoitering satellites, or such,
but, as in the ancient world, espionage, in its quiet way, was per-

vasive and rampant. Pharaohs and emperors, kings and caliphs, had their secret forces, their networks of spies and informants. Knowledge is often more precious than gold, information more valuable than jewels. Who means you well, and who means you ill? What are the parameters of time and space? How swiftly may troops be moved, and over what distances? Where is water in the desert? When, given ice and storms, can mountain passes be negotiated? Should one attack or defend, advance or withdraw? The dark is dangerous; one seeks to buy light. The gambits of espionage are many and ancient. Among them, often unnoted, are the meretricious diversion, the false trail, the calculated deceit, the sowing of lies, the deliberate misdirection. Markers can be turned or moved; maps can lie. Falsity believed can draw blood and conjure disaster. The role of the spy or informant, witting or unwitting, is not always the acquisition of information; it can extend, as well, to the propagation of misinformation.

Thirdly, lastly, one might speak of inaction, presumably, in this case, as the result of a misplaced satisfaction or complacency. I think that I mentioned earlier, that the mysterious Bosk of Port Kar, a high captain in the Council of Captains, he in whose holding I now wore my collar, was not now within the holding. He was presumably somewhere at sea, and had been, for some time. I did not know the import of his absence, the nature of his voyage. I had heard several conjectures, which convinced me that no one knew anything more about it, really, than I did. Also, I did not wish to pry into the matter. Already, due to some earlier inquiries I had made, mostly having to do with other matters, I feared I might be taken as a spy. Certainly I would not be the first slave to be inserted into a household for the purposes of obtaining information. Too, I was under no delusion as to what might and might not be becoming to a *kajira*. One conjecture was that Bosk of Port Kar was off to Brundisium, on a trading venture, dealing with amber; another was that he had gone to Torvaldsland, to the north, to buy furs; other conjectures had him inspecting the arsenal reserve in the great northern forests, establishing a trading station at Skjern, even mapping the coastline and taking soundings south of Kassau. It was also speculated he might be "fishing," namely, doing the business of piracy, scouring the seas for shipping to seize and loot. Another had him engaged in burning and raiding towns amongst the Farther Islands, west of Cos and Tyros. He seemed, by repute, a formidable man. I did not know his true

nature. Within some men there are many men. I had never, personally, seen him, at least to my knowledge. His men spoke highly
of him, sometimes in awe. His ship, interestingly, the *Dorna*, had
departed from the arsenal sea gate several days ago, before I was
brought to his holding. I do not know, of course, if what soon occurred, which was not anticipated, would have eventuated as it
did, if the master of the holding, this Bosk of Port Kar, had been
present. What if he had been present? Would things have turned
out differently? How could one know? Some men look deeper into
things than others. Some men are more wary, more suspicious,
than others. Some men accumulate and prepare more assiduously
than others. And some men, when the twig snaps and the branch
moves, when birds rise unexpectedly from the grass, when the
calls of the marsh kite and the Vosk gull cease, are more attentive than others. What might an unfamiliar scent or step portend?
When an unseen hand casts the dice, who will read them first?
Men differ. How is one to conduct oneself, when the flames break
out, when the earth trembles and shakes, when the predator appears? Men differ.

Would what soon occurred have turned out differently, if Bosk
of Port Kar had been present. One does not know. How could one
know? But he was not present.

As mentioned, it had come as a great surprise to me to discover
that she whom I had taken to be the Lady Dorna of Tharna, when
her hooding and veils were torn aside, and her robes pulled down
to her shoulders, was collared. She, in fury, standing amongst the
men, lost no time in drawing her robes up, again, about her throat,
and rearranging her hooding and veils. "Free me, return me to
my domicile, instantly," she said. "Do you not know who I am? I
am Dorna, Dorna the Proud, first of the Silver Masks of Tharna!
You will be roasted alive on spits, and your flesh cast to sleen! You
will be thrown alive to leech plants! You will be fed to tharlarion,
boiled in honey, caged with starving urts!"

"Take her to her cell," had said Florian.

I was one of three slaves who had been assigned to attend the
prisoner.

Dorna's cell was comfortable, if not large: it was well-lit, and
airy. It was on the fifth floor of the holding. It contained certain amenities, including bedding and a couch. It was clearly
the sort of incarceration chamber which might be occupied by a

free woman, not a slave. Despite her collar, she was not chained, penned, or caged. I think we, the slaves, were not clear as to how to relate to her. She spoke as, and behaved as, a free woman. Too, in the beginning, she was permitted the raiment in which she had been captured, the hood, veils, and robes. The first time I attended upon her I was cuffed afterward by Florian, for I had knelt in her presence.

"She is not First Girl to you," had said Florian. "Why did you kneel?"

"She seems so much like a free woman," I had said, looking up at him from my knees, my hand to my stinging cheek.

"She is a slave," said Florian.

"I was present when she was captured," I said. "How she was handled, scarcely like an apprehended free woman. Did you suspect, then, she was not free?" I could not conceive of a Gorean male treating a free woman in the rude, efficient fashion she had been handled and subdued.

"Surely you noted, instantly, that her hands were bare," said Florian.

"I did not think about such things," I said.

"Stupid barbarian," he said.

"Many free woman," I said, "do not wear clothing on their hands."

"Particularly amongst the less affluent," he said. "But she was in street robes, and consider their sumptuous nature. In such regalia to be without clothing for the hands is much the same as being barefoot. Her master did not want her to forget she was a slave."

"I see," I said, learning more of the subtleties of Gor.

One item in the cell of Dorna I neglected to mention. It was a holding pole, which, in the case of Dorna, served as a feeding pole. Whereas holding poles differ amongst themselves, depending on accouterments, such as belly chains, neck collars, and bracelets, and the purposes to which they may be applied, the device in Dorna's cell was rather typical. It was some five feet in height and four inches in diameter. It was anchored solidly, vertically, in the stone flooring of the cell. It lacked a collar arrangement, but it did have a belly chain and adjustable bracelets. The pole in Dorna's case served primarily as a feeding pole. As it was used, in her case, the slave is knelt and her back is fastened closely against the pole by the belly chain. Her wrists are then lifted, and fastened well back, and well over her head by the bracelets. In this way she is knelt, held in place, and cannot feed herself. In its way the pole is a rather severe reminder of one aspect of a pervasive understanding in Gorean culture—slave dependence. For example, consider merely three aspects of slave dependence. One, the slave may not speak without the permission of the master, and though many slaves have a standing permission to speak, that permission may be revoked at any time. Two, the slave has no control over her own clothing. If she is clothed, at all, it will be when the master permits, and as the master directs. Three, the slave has no control over her own food. Although she commonly prepares and serves the food, she must wait until the master permits her to eat. The first bite, of course, the first sip, and such, will be taken by the master. Needless to say, it behooves the slave to prepare ample, nourishing, and tasty meals. Commonly the slave participates in, and enjoys, the same meal as the master, he sitting and she kneeling. Occasionally she must be content with porridge or slave gruel, and water, these taken from bowls placed on the floor, to which she must address herself on all fours without the use of her hands.

When a slave would attend on Dorna, a man, usually Florian or Miles, was always present, even when they were not putting her at the pole or relieving her of its restraints. I only realized the reason for that later.

"I will not eat!" had cried Dorna, kneeling, fastened to the pole, her wrists shaking the bracelets high above her head.

"Do as you please," said Florian.

This was the third time I had come to feed her.

"Bring me water!" she said.

"No," said Florian.

"No?" she said.

I knew little of the plans and intentions of the masters, but I suspected they had something in mind, and would not care to spend a great deal of time with Dorna.

"No food, no water," said Florian.

"I do not understand," she said.

"It requires very little time to thirst to death," said Florian. "Three or four days should be sufficient. Enjoy the indescribable horrors and torments of thirst, such as the desiccation of the body and the agony of cramping muscles."

"I have changed my mind, you monster," she said.

"Excellent," said Florian.

"What are you doing?" she cried.

"Removing your hood and veils," he said.

"The veils need only be lowered slightly, modestly, and delicately, for a slave, a female slave, to administer me food and drink," she said.

"Nonetheless," he said.

She shook and squirmed angrily in her restraints.

Veiling is common with Gorean free women in public. The removal of a veil or veils without the owner's consent is referred to as "face stripping." In some cities this is a crime punishable by death, particularly if the woman shares one's Home Stone. Bodies tend to be similar, but features tend to be individual, personal, and unique. Many Gorean free women, interestingly, if forced to choose, would prefer body stripping to face stripping. In a sense, to them, body stripping is more impersonal and less revealing than face stripping. Doubtless this is a cultural matter. One of the reasons that Gorean men tend to think of the women of my former world as at best uncollared slaves is the blatant and brazen way in which so many of them allow their features to be looked upon. Is not a face, with its delicacies and subtleties, its myriad expressions, a thousand times more revealing than a body?

"You were discourteous," he said.

"Sleen!" she cried.

"Again," he said.

He removed the knife from his belt.

"What are you doing?" she cried.

"As you are in a collar," he said, "you are doubtless pleasant to look upon—in all ways."

"Stop! Stop!" she screamed.

I gasped, waiting, standing to the side, with the tray of drink and provender for Dorna.

Florian, with his knife, had cut away her outer robes, and now had them looped over his left arm.

Dorna was fuming but had the wisdom not to provoke Florian further, at least at that time. She was now in two or three light, sliplike garments. I saw enough to realize that she would doubtless bring a high price in a market.

"You may now feed the prisoner," said Florian.

"Get on your knees, slave!" said Dorna.

"Do not," said Florian.

"I may not," I said to the prisoner.

I then began to serve Dorna.

The food was of the finest in the holding, from the tables of the masters themselves. There was even a white *ka-la-na*. I was not permitted to sample the food and drink myself, and I refrained from doing so, even when Florian, or another, was not looking. It was not so much that Dorna might have called this act to the attention of her jailer, whoever he might be, as that I found satisfaction in my obedience. I wanted to obey. I was a slave. It pleased me, and fulfilled me, to obey.

It was on her third day of captivity that I think I learned why slaves were not left alone with Dorna, why a male of the house was always present. Florian had been called away, as I understood it, and I found myself alone with Dorna. I was gathering up the plate from which I fed her and the cup from which I gave her her wine, and was about to return these wares to the carrying tray, when she spoke to me. "Slave," she said, "seek out the men of Pa-Kur, he of the Black Caste. You know the place, the dwelling near the place of my capture. Inform them of my captivity, that I am held prisoner in the holding of Bosk of Port Kar. They will seize hostages or bribe me free. I will then be safe!"

I regarded her, startled.

"Do this," she said, "and you will be richly rewarded. I will see to it personally. You will receive your freedom, and a gold tarn disk, of Ar, of double weight! Many men do not see that in a year. You will be free, and can buy yourself a house, a business, and slaves."

"You need not respond to that solicitation, slave," said Florian, reentering the cell. "There is no point in doing so." I gathered that he had been listening, that he had been close, unseen, immediately behind the wall, to the right of the bars.

Dorna shrank back in her restraints.

"I think it will be best for you, sweet, pleasant prisoner," said Florian to Dorna, "if the noble Pa-Kur does not know your location. Let him think you the victim of a pedestrian abduction, and on your way to a market. If he knew you were in the keeping of his enemies, what would your life be worth? In such a case, I would avoid the windows, for a quarrel, sped from the saddle of a gracefully soaring tarn might slip between the bars. Too, you might receive a packet of poison, with instructions as to how to make use of it. And might not an ost, so small and deadly, move one night toward the warmth of your body while you sleep?"

"I am indispensable to Pa-Kur!" she said.

"Are you?" asked Florian.

"He loves me!" said Dorna.

"He loves blood, steel, and power," said Florian, "and you, while beautiful, are only a slave."

Dorna regarded Florian. In her eyes were doubt, and terror.

Florian then turned to me. "You have permission," he said, "to deliver the message requested by the prisoner to Pa-Kur."

"No, no!" said Dorna. "Do not do so. I must think! I must think!"

"You may remove the tray, the plate, and cup," said Florian.

"Yes, Master," I said, head down, putting things in order, "Thank you, Master."

"Would you have complied with the prisoner's request?" he asked.

"No, Master," I said.

"I did not think so," he said. "Too, it is unpleasant, I would suppose, to have your chest cut open and, while you live, have the molten gold of a tarn disk, of double weight, poured upon your heart."

I hurried from the cell.

I knew I would not have complied with the prisoner's request. Dorna had wanted me dead, and I feared her, and did not trust her. Of what value would my life be had I had complied with her request? Too, even if I could be free of the house to wander about, there would have been terrible dangers attendant on such an action. Even if successful, I would live in fear. I might be hunted down and, after my capture, find myself subject to an intolerable vengeance. Too, I did not hunger for freedom. I had known freedom, its loneliness and emptiness. I did not want freedom. I wanted a master, a master whom I might love and serve, wholly and devotedly, who would subject me to the authority, warmth, passion, strength, and domination which I, a slave, wanted so much, for which I so much longed.

I looked back once, and then hurried down to the kitchen.

After Dorna would feed, Florian, Miles, or another, would free her of her restraints. It was difficult for Dorna to control her temper, with the masters, and certainly the slaves. Too often she spoke abruptly, and failed to be pleasing. By the fourth day of her imprisonment her slippers and hose had been removed, and her garmenture had been reduced, piece by piece, to a short sliplike garment that might easily have been mistaken for a slave tunic. As this gradual diminution of garmenture took place it became more and more evident that slavers would be likely to find her of more and more interest, if not for keeping for themselves, for a sales item on which they would be likely to realize a handsome profit.

"It will begin shortly," had said Florian. "I expect you will be interested in watching."

Something in his voice or mien had made me uneasy.

Too, I had work to do, within the Ahn, in the laundry. I would not care to be late and face the First Girl's switch.

"I do not think so, Master," I had said. "I beg to be excused."

I had shortly thereafter found myself leashed and braceleted, and following him down steep, ill-lit, narrow stairs. Save for the wine cellars, I knew little about the chambers or passages below the house. They were not such, as I noted earlier, as to invite or encourage exploration.

CHAPTER THIRTY-NINE

The Observation Panel

My hands were still braceleted behind my back, but the leash had been released, and it dangled before me, occasionally touching my breasts or a thigh.

Florian was some two yards before me.

He had slowed his pace, doubtless because of the footing.

I stifled a scream as something, small and furtive, scurried by, claws scratching on the stones.

"Do not be concerned," said Florian. "It is a tiny urt. You have little to fear from such quick, ugly, little things unless you are bound helplessly and left for their attentions."

The stones of the passageway were damp beneath my feet. Occasionally I stepped to one side, to avoid puddles. The passage, well below the house, was lit no better than the stairs, only a small tharlarion-oil lamp every few yards. The air here was damp and musty.

Then Florian stopped before a stout, wooden door.

"We will observe from within this chamber," he said.

He entered, and I followed, after which he closed and bolted the door. The room was lit by another small tharlarion-oil lamp.

I was apprehensive that he had bolted the door. What woman, even a slave, would not be? As he was of the household, he was as master to me, but he was not my legal master. Ho-Tosk of Port Kar, proprietor of the Golden Chain, was my legal master.

I did not know what I was doing in this small, dank, closed-in place. He had spoken of something which was to begin soon, something which I might be interested in watching.

I should be at the laundry.

The door had been bolted.

One gathered he did not wish to be disturbed.

He turned to face me.

Had his words been a pretext to get me to this place? That seemed unlikely. Surely I was on the "girl roster."

Was there actually something which was to begin shortly?

Perhaps so.

Might he amuse himself while waiting?

Was I to be put to use?

I did not know.

Sometimes it pleases the masters to have us beg use.

If I were ordered to beg use, I would do so, of course. I would have no choice.

How different was this world from my former world! How often I had, on my former world, subtly hinting the prospect of favors I had no intention of bestowing, been escorted to expensive clubs for dining and dancing, following which, returned to my apartment, I would, given my escort's hopes or expectations, feign surprise or shock, and even rage. I had had my evening. Why should I pay for it? Later, alone in my apartment, I was much satisfied. I would congratulate myself on my cleverness. I received much pleasure, much gratification, from such behaviors. How stupid and foolish were such males! How easy it was to make fools of them! But now I was at the mercy of men. Now I was on Gor, in a collar!

A slave need not be ordered to beg use. More often we are ordered not to beg use, as the master has no time for us. I wonder if they understand the torment of our needs.

"We shall watch something together," said Florian. "You, in particular, should find it of interest."

"I should be at the laundry," I said.

He went to a side of the chamber and slid back a small, narrow, rectangular metal plate.

"Come here," he said. "Look through the aperture and tell me what you see."

I went to the aperture. "We are apparently above the next level," I said. "I look down into another chamber. It is much better lit than this one."

"Describe the chamber," he said.

"It is large, but empty," I said. "To one side is what appears to be a sunken pool. To the side of the pool there is a metal fire basket, lit, with its wooden-handled heating tray. Near the fire basket is a box. Something is on the box, perhaps envelopes or papers. It is hard to tell. Toward the center of the room is a metal holding pole with a belly chain and wrist shackles."

I then turned about, to face him.

"Open your mouth, widely," he said.

I sank to my knees before him, complying.

"Get up," he said. "Who told you to kneel?"

I looked up at him, puzzled. I could not speak for my mouth was open, widely. I had not been given permission to close it. I pulled at my wrists, braceleted behind me.

"Get up," he said. "How vain you are. Do you think you are in an alcove at the Golden Chain? Do you truly think I would be interested in allowing myself to be served by so inferior a slave and slut as you, only another worthless Golden-Chain girl?"

I struggled to my feet, keeping my mouth open, widely. Once again I was aware of his seemingly inexplicable animosity toward the Golden Chain, and its slaves. Surely the Golden-Chain girls were amongst the loveliest and most helplessly responsive slaves in Port Kar. That reputation was ours, at any rate, and I did not doubt but what it was well founded. The tavern was popular and often crowded. Our girls were often thonged and sent to an alcove. And surely I, amongst them, had wept for more, and begged for more, many times, in my chains in one or another of the tavern's alcoves. I recalled that he had said that another wanted me, but would tell me no more. Was that why he had never put me to his pleasure? Was that why he was not putting me to his pleasure now? But, if so, who wanted me? As a slave, I knew that anyone who wanted me might have me. I need only be bought. But who wanted me? Florian, the beast, would not tell me. Did I know him, had I ever seen him before? Was it someone who had merely looked upon me, whom I had never seen? How vulnerable and helpless are slaves!

A wadding was thrust in my mouth and held in place by straps, these cinched behind the back of my neck. Alarm must have shown in my eyes.

"You are to observe, Golden-Chain girl," said Florian. "You are to do so in absolute silence. You are not to cry out, you are not to speak."

He then, by the leash, drew me to the opened observation panel. There were two rings near the bottom of the aperture, one on the left, one on the right, fixed in the stone. He threaded the leash through the left ring, pulled it tight, and fastened it in such a way that my head was held in place, at the opened observation panel. In this way, I could not draw away from the panel, even should I wish to do so.

"It will begin, shortly," said Florian, coming to stand beside me, to my right.

At that moment, from somewhere, below, in some passageway, I heard a long, wild, wailing woman's scream. A few moments later a door, below, was thrust open. "No! No!" I heard, a woman's voice. "What is the meaning of this? Let me go! Free me! What are you going to do? Stop! Stop!"

One of the guards entered, one I recognized from the canal boat, carrying Dorna in his arms. Her body was wrapped tightly, from ankles to throat in several layers of gray cloth. In this wrapping, she could barely squirm. It was fastened about her by what seemed numberless loops of coarse rope. There was a light sheen about the wrappings, the blankets, sheets, or whatever they might be. It reflected the fire light in a way unfamiliar to me, certainly not like common rep-cloth, a cheap, common material often used for the garmenting of slaves. It did not occur to me immediately, but I conjectured, a moment later, given the terror of Dorna, and the situation below me, the fire, the pole, the pool, and such, what must be occurring. I wanted, desperately, to pull away from the ring to which I was fastened. I regarded the material in which Dorna was wrapped. It must have been treated, perhaps saturated, with some unusual substance or substances. In full daylight, I suspected it might have proved indistinguishable from common rep-cloth. Yet, I was sure, even then, that if one wore it, it would have had a different feel to it. There was, in any case, no mistaking the terror of Dorna. She may never have felt that feel on her body before, but she doubtless suspected its nature, and purpose. I tried to pull away from the ring but could not do so. "Steady, slut," whispered Florian.

Two more men entered the room below, Miles, whom I knew from the holding, and he who had been the seeming officer on the canal boat, whom I shall refer to as "the officer."

"Put her on her knees," said the officer.

Swathed as she was, she knelt stiffly within the ropes and layers of material. Her arms were helpless within the swathing. She could not have spread her knees, even if commanded to do so. Tower slaves and free women commonly kneel with their knees together; pleasure slaves commonly kneel with their knees spread. In this way, they are more conscious of the nature of their slavery.

I recalled that a woman was supposedly more likely to tell the truth when she was on her knees. Perhaps this was because of a greater sense of vulnerability, which sense enhances the fear of punishment. Kneeling, of course, also induces a sense of helplessness. Too, it is a posture of submission, and thus appropriate for slaves. To me, as a natural slave, which I now knew myself to be, it felt right and proper to kneel. I loved to kneel. I knew I belonged on my knees before a master. I suppose many women feel they belong on their knees before a master. If they are slaves, is that not where they belong? How else can they be themselves and have their fulfillment? How I pitied the poor slave who has no master.

Dorna looked wildly about her. "It is not necessary to proceed further, noble masters," she said. "I will speak volubly and honestly. I will tell you all you wish to know, freely and in detail. To be sure, this puts my life in mortal jeopardy. Thus I beg of you, but do not seek to bargain, that you will have the mercy to sell me secretly far from Port Kar, that I will be spared the vengeance of those I am now ready to betray."

"You," said Miles, "though your neck is encircled with a collar, are an esteemed colleague of, and informed confidant of, Pa-Kur, of the Caste of Assassins."

"Yes, Master," said Dorna.

"And thus, you are privy to the most secret plans, programs, and schedules of Pa-Kur and his associates, particularly pertaining to possible designs having to do with this house?"

"Yes, Master," said Dorna.

"Speak," said the officer.

"Pa-Kur," she said.

"Your master," said the officer.

"Yes, my master, Pa-Kur," she said, "has designs upon this house. I fear to speak, but must. He believes that somewhere in this house is a golden cup, worth perhaps two tarn disks of gold, of double weight. He hopes to take the cup as a trophy to the Black Court of Brundisium, that to prove his temerity and skill. He has enlisted two men to assist him in secretly entering this holding with the intention of locating, and absconding, with the cup."

"Do you think you are a free woman?" inquired the officer.

"Master?" she said.

"Free women may lie," said the officer. "Slaves may not."

"I do not understand," she said.

"You have lied long enough," he said. "Immerse her."

"No!" she screamed, but the guard who had introduced her into the chamber, in his arms, lifted her and plunged her into the pool. He even, three or four times, held her head fully, briefly, under water. Then he drew her soaked figure dripping from the pool and laid her near the fire. Oddly enough, there was no great pool of water about her soaked figure. It was as though her tight, wrapped layers of sheeting, within the ropes, sucked the water into its fibers.

"Cut the ropes!" she screamed. "Free me! Now! Now! Tear away the cloths!"

"But you are bare within the layers," said Miles.

"No, please!" she cried.

Her eyes were wild with terror. She struggled within her bonds. She tried to roll toward the feet of the officer, doubtless to press her lovely lips pleadingly upon his high, bootlike sandals, but the guard, interposing his own bootlike sandal, did not permit this. "Mercy, mercy!" she wept. "Take pity on a mere slave!"

"'A mere slave'," said Miles. "Interesting."

"It will begin soon," said the officer.

"Mercy, Masters!" begged Dorna.

Then she shrieked in horror. Even yards above the floor of the chamber, where Florian and I were at the observation panel, one could hear the crackling, the fierce whisper, of precipitating, interacting chemicals.

I was held at the observation panel, tightly, by the leash, fastened to the ring. I could not pull away. I wanted to cry out in misery and protest, but, the prisoner of a Gorean gag, could not do so. I jerked at the bracelets that held by hands pinioned behind my back. "Steady, worthless, well-formed she-tarsk," said Florian. I turned my head piteously toward him, but he thrust my head, held by the hair, back to the panel. "Doubtless you have some sense of her torment," said Florian, quietly. "Were you not yourself once clad in a tunic of fire? Fire cloth is interesting. I would not mind clothing one of your collar-sisters from the Golden Chain in such an attractive little outfit. Perhaps she might then learn to better please a paying customer. It might be pleasant to have her at my feet, weeping and begging to please me, in the way of what she is, a worthless, miserable slave."

Florian then removed his hand from my hair.

"Look well," he said.

Below, Dorna was writhing and screaming.

"After this," said Florian, "she will be well primed for the powders."

"It burns, Masters!" wept Dorna. "Have mercy! Beat me! Lash me! But free me of the ropes! Cut away the cloths! I beg it! It hurts! It hurts! It burns! It burns!"

"Perhaps you are now docile, and are prepared to be cooperative?" asked Miles.

"Yes, Master! Yes, Master!" she screamed.

"Be patient," said Miles. "In a few Ehn the reactions will subside, and then cease."

"Though the pain will linger for some time," said the officer.

Well above the floor of the chamber below I could still hear the crackling from the cloths, though now it was less fierce.

I think Dorna then fell unconscious.

"Remove her impediments," said the officer. "Put her at the pole, belly chain and high-wrist shackling."

The guard then undid the swathing of ropes which had held the treated cloth so tightly about her body, and put her, kneeling, she held by Miles, at the pole, her back to the pole. The guard then cinched the belly chain about her, pulling her back, tightly, against the pole, and then drew her wrists up, high, over her head, and shackled them to the pole.

"I think she has slept long enough," said the officer. "Awaken her."

The guard went to the pool of water, and returned with a pan of water, which he dashed over her body.

She awakened, instantly, screaming, "Not water! Not water!" Then she struggled in the belly chain and shackles. Links of metal scraped the iron pole. As she was fastened, she could not rise to her feet.

"You need fear water no longer," said the officer.

"She is a pretty little slave," said Miles.

"Please do not speak of me so demeaningly," she begged.

I recalled that she had once held a high position in Tharna, that of First, or Highest, Silver Mask, in the time of the Gynocracy.

"How is it now?" asked the officer.

"It still burns," she said.

"But not so much," he suggested.

"No," she said. "Please give me clothing."

"You are a slave, a beast, a domestic animal," said the officer. "You are not entitled to clothing. Surely you know that."

"Yes, Master," she said.

"Perhaps you would be interested to know what is going to be done with you," said the officer.

"Sell me secretly, far from Port Kar," she begged.

"After we are done here," said the officer, you will be sedated, and will sleep for several hours. "You will awaken in a disreputable part of the city. You will learn, presumably shortly thereafter, that the collar of a well-known, popular tavern, the Golden Chain, was put on your neck and that of Pa-Kur removed. You will also discover that you are clad in a tunic of the Golden Chain. You will be taken as a runaway slave and will be returned to the Golden Chain for punishment, and service."

"'Service'?" she said.

"That of a common paga girl."

"No!" she cried.

"There you will better learn you are a slave," he said, "waiting on masters, bringing them food and drink, and pleasing them, should they find you of interest, in the alcoves."

I had little doubt that many would find her of interest.

"No, no!" she said. "I would be seen, tunicked and unveiled. Sooner or later, I would be recognized. My life would be forfeit. I have been in the power of enemies of Pa-Kur. He would find me and kill me!"

"We trust he will try," said the officer.

"You are bait," said Miles.

"Following your capture," said the officer, "we anticipated that Pa-Kur and his cohorts would vanish, and it has proved so."

"He has done you no harm," said Dorna. "It would be unlawful to seize him."

"He might be legitimately seized for the attempted destruction of property," said the officer.

"Or its destruction," said Miles.

"The destruction of what property?" said Dorna.

"You," said Miles.

"Now, my dear," said the officer, going to the box on which reposed some envelopes or packets, "it is time for you to tell us all about the secret plans of Pa-Kur."

"You cannot make me speak," she said.

"Of course not," said the officer, "but the powders in these packets, suitably mixed and administered, will do so, easily."

"Never!" said Dorna.

The officer shook powders from certain of the packets unto a piece of paper, creased the paper, and then went to the metal fire basket, where he deposited the contents of the creased paper unto the fire basket's wooden-handled heating tray. Shortly thereafter tiny curls and wisps of smoke began to rise from the heating tray.

"I will never speak!" cried Dorna.

An Ehn or two later the officer held the heating tray close to the prisoner. He wafted the fumes toward her. "Never!" she said. But she had to breathe.

"You have seen enough," said Florian, undoing my leash from the ring fixed in the stone beneath the observation panel. He then drew me away by the leash, and carefully, silently, slid the panel shut. He then removed my gag, unbolted and opened the door, and led me by the leash from the chamber.

CHAPTER FORTY

The Feast;
I am Belled;
Early Morning

The dining hall in the holding was loud with conversation and song.

The crews of the holding, those who were in port, amply gathered about the long, broad table, were in a raucous, high-spirited, boisterous mood.

Paga flowed and trenchers were heaped with slabs of roasted meat. Grasping hands pulled bowls of nuts and fruit across wood. I heard knives plunged, slicing, into flat, rounded loaves of bread.

"Paga!" called a fellow.

A celebration of sorts was in progress.

This had to do, I gathered, with information obtained yesterday from the interrogation of Dorna the Proud, though so lofty an appellation was scarcely appropriate for a collar girl. She was now simply "Dorna," and 'Dorna', of course, was a mere slave name, put on an owned beast at the discretion or whim of masters. She would have awakened this morning, cold and on stones, struggling to consciousness, initially distraught and confused, somewhere in Port Kar, finding herself in the tunic and collar of the Golden Chain. As it was now evening, she may already have been picked up and returned to her "master," Ho-Tosk, possibly for a lashing as a runaway slave and doubtless for a "return" to her service in the tavern, her service as a lowly, available paga girl.

"Paga, paga!" called another fellow.

I was not serving.

I, and three others, Cella, Korinna, and Ianthe, a different Ianthe from she whom I knew so well from the tavern, unclothed save for our collars, on all fours, were beneath the table. Men occasionally like women so, captive women or slaves. In the case of the captive free woman, she is fully clothed in her regalia, save for being deveiled, face-stripped. This is to convey to her that she, though free, is far less in worth, station, and value than the free women of the captor's city. If the free woman will eat, she must ask for food. She will then be hand fed or a bowl will be put under the table from which she must feed, on all fours, without the use of her hands. In this way, she is given to understand that she, despite being free, does not have the status of the free women of the captor's city. Later, she can be stripped, marked, and collared. In the case of slaves, men, of course, like them naked under the table, as is appropriate for them, as the animals they are. Too, so situated, the slaves are well reminded of their status, that they are beasts, purchasable, vendible beasts. They, too, are commonly hand fed, but they may not ask for food articulately. They must make small, pleading animal noises, and hope that the master will give them something. Sometimes the master requires that he must first be pleased. In spite of what some in my former world might think, most slaves, sincerely and profoundly, want to be pleasing, and wholly pleasing, to their masters, domestically, socially, and, in particular, sexually. Many slaves, it must be understood, love their masters with a love that few free women, with their concern for status, self-image, self-containment, balance, commensuration, and proportion, could equal. The slave abandons herself to the master; she is his, not hers. Perhaps it pleases us even more than the masters to find ourselves naked beneath their tables. We are then near our masters. And why should we be elsewhere, or otherwise? We are slaves. Indeed, it is in the nature of a privilege to be beneath the masters' tables. Indeed, this was only the second time I had been allowed beneath the table. I recalled that after Addison Steele had put me to his pleasure in the cheap, dingy tavern, the Whip and Chain, he had referred to seeing me on Earth, from time to time, dining with, and exploiting, "one weakling or another," and had thought that I might make an acceptable slave, naked and collared, crawling under a table, at a man's knees, hoping to be fed. I thought of Addison Steele, faithless and duplicitous. How I despised him! And how I longed to be beneath his table!

As I mentioned earlier, this dinner, or feast, at least as far as its tone and nature were concerned, seemed to have something to do with what had been learned from the interrogation of the slave, Dorna.

I did not know what this might be, as Florian had removed me from our chamber of observation before her interrogation had commenced in earnest.

And, naturally I suppose, slaves were given little, if any, sense of the content of her responses to whatever questions may have been asked. Would one discuss such matters with verr or kaiila? But what if a verr or kaiila, or, say, a sleen, might be in such-and-such a place, or vicinity, and overhear such matters? How could they be blamed for what they might accidentally hear? The job of the beast then, if it should be interested in such matters, however improperly, is to see to it that it places itself in a position where there is something to hear, however accidentally. Accordingly, I began to crawl, bit by bit, toward the head of the table. The captain's chair, at the head of the table, was empty, because the master of the holding, Bosk, of Port Kar, was at sea. On the other hand, near the head of the table, were the places, side by side, occupied by Florian and Miles, who, I took it, from their position at the table, and other indications, stood high in the holding.

The motivation for my crawling forward, toward the head of the table, was that I had heard that the *Alexia*, one of the ships of Bosk of Port Kar, had recently anchored in the arsenal harbor, just this afternoon, from far Bazi, bearing tea, as the enterprises of Bosk of Port Kar were varied and widely flung. A newcomer, one I did not recognize, in the rimless cap common to mariners, had just been admitted to the hall and had been called to the head of the table. I took him to be most likely the captain, or a captain's officer, from the *Alexia*. If this were the case, might he not be soon apprised of new and important developments having to do with the holding?

"How went the voyage, noble Astron?" inquired Florian.

"As reported, well," said the newcomer. "Our hold is bulging. Too we have bales and boxes of six new teas, unknown, I think, even in Brundisium or Jad. They may yet rival black wine in preciousness, at a quarter the cost."

"This may mean war with Thentis," said Miles.

"The captain, even now, is giving an accounting to Luma," said the newcomer. "How stands the holding?"

"Securely," said Florian. "Why should you ask that?"

"No reason," said Astron.

"Were there no reason," said Florian, "you would not have asked."

"One hears many things," said Astron, "some perhaps innocuous or irrelevant, some perhaps surprising or puzzling, some perhaps darkly minacious."

"Rumors?" said Florian.

"Rumors have wings, even at sea," said the newcomer. "They soon reach far ports."

"What rumors?" asked Florian.

"Say," said the newcomer, "that Talena, the traitress Ubara, sought by the justice of Ar and a thousand bounty hunters, has been located."

"Where?" asked Florian, muchly concerned.

"Safe in Jad," said the newcomer, "the honored guest of her former ally, Lurius, Ubar of Cos."

"Rumors may have wings at sea," said Florian, then relaxed, "but it seems some fly slowly. That is an old rumor."

I myself had heard that rumor, several times, in the Golden Chain.

"And some rumors, it seems," said the newcomer, soberly, "spread their wings closer to home, in the arsenal itself."

"Such as?" asked Miles.

"That the Delta Gate was sundered, and has not been repaired."

"Those are not rumors but facts," said Florian. "It is not clear how the gate was damaged. It is thought that a large tharlarion may have been responsible."

"One of iron, the size of a ship?" asked the newcomer.

"The cause is not clear at this point," said Florian. "Until the matter becomes clear there is little point in repairing the gate. What was done once may be done again."

"Port Kar is in jeopardy," said the newcomer. "An ineffectual gate invites attack."

"The gate is under surveillance and there are no fleets in the delta," said Florian.

"An attack would strike at the gate," said the newcomer.

"Undoubtedly," said Florian. "Why else should the gate be rendered useless."

"And it is said there are strange lights, and sounds, mysterious doings, in the delta," said the newcomer.

"One always hears such things," said Miles. "Rencers often contrive such things to discourage penetration into the delta."

"One must be vigilant," said Astron.

"Concern," said Florian, "may be postponed."

"I do not understand," said Astron.

"It is not important," said Florian.

"This is no holiday, at least no common holiday," said Astron, "and yet I see no seaman's supper before me, bread, meat, porridge, larmas and paga. Are those not decanters of *ka-la-na*, ruby red and tawny, like the wet pelt of a fresh-foaled kaiila? Do I not see flasks and vessels common to the liqueurs and syrups of Turia? Might those not even be tospits, short-stemmed and long-stemmed, from the lands of the Wagon Peoples? And do I not smell the aroma of hot, steaming black wine? That must have cost the holding a shiny tarsk-bit. For a common day, is the board not unusually laden, so heavily and lavishly? You even have girls under the table, unclothed."

"It is always pleasant to look upon comely slaves," said Florian.

"They prove a lovely addition to the décor," said Miles.

"Particularly if they are naked," said Florian.

"Their presence does much to improve the appetite," said Miles.

Hearing this I drew back a bit.

"Surely this is no ordinary meal," said Astron.

"Very well, dear friend," said Florian. "The matter is well known within the holding and you are of the holding."

"I attend you, and with great interest," said Astron.

"Given our harboring of an elusive personage, one whose acquisition would be considerably profitable to certain parties, we have long feared an attack in force upon the holding. This attack would presumably be mounted by our most powerful and dreaded enemy, Pa-Kur, of the Assassins, who is bent upon the seizure of our harbored personage. Lately, however, we have captured one who, though a slave, is privy to the most secret details of his most secret plans. She has been interrogated by means of the cloth of fire and the fumes of truth."

"The subject of such an interrogation is not to be envied," said Astron. "Their consciousness is numbed and their will is seized. Chemically subdued and docile, they are helpless to resist, whatever might once have been their most earnest intents and harrowing fears. They answer questions clearly; they speak fully and

honestly; they cannot help themselves. Their cooperation is assured. These things are as inevitable as the heat of fire and the
cold of ice."

"And they will have no recollection of what they have said and
done," said Florian. "Commonly they believe themselves to have
successfully resisted the interrogation, and are confident that they
have revealed nothing."

I was less than pleased to hear this remark.

"Given this celebration, the *ka-la-na*, the black wine, and
such," said Astron, "I gather that the outcome of the interrogation proved favorable to the interests of the holding."

"Certainly, for the time being," said Florian.

"The projected attack, then, is not imminent," said Astron.

"Far from it," said Florian. "It is beset by difficulties of recruitment and supply. It is currently scheduled, tentatively, for the
tenth day of the tenth month, Se'Var."

Se'Var, or Se'var-Lar-Torvis, follows the Ninth Passage Hand,
the last day of which is the winter solstice. Se'Var-Lar-Torvis is the
"Second Resting of the Central Fire," the sun, Tor-tu-Gor, Light-
upon-the-Home Stone.

"That is more than six months," said Astron.

"Which is far more," said Florian, "than even the conjecture
of our spy in the camp of Pa-Kur, which was in the neighborhood
of two months."

I had not realized that the holding had managed to place a spy
in the camp of Pa-Kur. It was hard to conceive of a post more perilous. Certainly I, myself, would not have cared for such a role. Too,
crouching under the table, I was suddenly frightened. It was like
feeling a cold wind. Perhaps it might not be wise to know such
things. Did I not know that curiosity was not becoming to a *kajira*? Perhaps I had heard much that I was not supposed to know. I
recalled that Florian had removed me from the observation chamber before the crucial portion of Dorna's interrogation had begun.
I suddenly regretted having been afflicted with so insatiate a curiosity. Yet, how can we help it? As is common knowledge, *kajirae*
are amongst the most inquisitive of beasts. Why should we not
be? We are told so little and are so helpless. I decided it would be
wise to discreetly withdraw. At least, I thought, I had not been
belled.

"By six months," said Miles, "if all goes well, Bosk, lord of the
holding, should be well returned."

"I see now the point of the black wine, and such," said Astron.

"And," said Florian, "you see how it is, that concern may be postponed."

"Yes," said Astron.

"So join us, noble Astron," said Florian.

"Gladly," said Astron. "Yet I would feel better if Bosk were closer at hand."

"He is often at sea," said Miles. "Most of us are."

"When did Bosk put out to sea?" asked Astron.

"Some twelve days ago," said Miles.

"What is he about?" asked Astron. "Does he hope to fill his hold with gold or slaves?"

"It is strange," said Miles. "To his ears rumors came that Bosk of Port Kar, he himself, was spreading terror west of Cos and Tyros, that he was mercilessly preying upon the towns and shipping of the Farther Islands, Chios, Daphna, and Thera."

"Absurd," said Astron.

"Impostors, ships, flying false flags," said Miles.

"Why should anyone do that?" asked Astron.

"To conceal their identity?" suggested Miles.

"Bosk was angry," said Florian.

"The wrath of Bosk is a terrible thing," said Miles.

"Few would risk it," said Florian.

"So Bosk is at sea to investigate?" said Astron.

"In fury, with three ships," said Florian.

"I wish him well," said Astron.

"As do we all," said Florian.

I decided to crawl slowly backward. I had heard enough. I feared I had heard too much.

"So now let us feast, dear Astron," said Florian. "Beverages and viands abound. We shall all eat and drink heavily and sleep late."

"Be it so," said Astron.

I began to crawl backward.

"Clumsy slave!" said a voice.

"Forgive me, Master!" I said.

"Do not strike her," said a man. "She only wants to put her cheek on your knee, look up at you piteously, and be fed."

"The girls under the table are fed only what they are given," said another man.

"Let her beg elsewhere," said the fellow whom I had apparently discomfited.

"Come here, slave," said Florian. "Crawl forth."

I was then before him, on all fours.

"Well?" he said.

"Forgive me, Master," I whispered.

"It seems you must have heard much," he said.

"Where I was," I said, "I could not help hearing—a little—a tiny bit."

"And why were you where you were?" he asked.

"Forgive me, Master," I said.

I feared I had angered him, and that my transgression might be deemed grievous. It is not a light thing to anger a master. What slave girl does not know that? Too, had I not heard what might not be for the ears of a *kajira*?

I went to my belly, in misery, pressing my lips to Florian's feet, fervently, again and again. It is a common way in which slave girls attempt to placate a master.

"Well, Miles," said Florian, after a bit, "what shall we do with her? Boil her in oil?"

"No," said Miles. "In water. It is cheaper."

"We could throw her to leech plants," said Florian.

"What if they threw her back?" said Miles.

"Feed her to sleen?" said Florian.

"And risk the welfare of fine animals, not to mention the wrath of sleen keepers?" said Miles.

I lifted my head. "Masters are not angry?" I asked.

"I suspect that a lengthy and splendid lashing would be sufficient," said Florian.

"Perhaps," said Miles.

"I trust not," I said, uneasily.

Surely they knew the nature of *kajirae*, what we are like. Our curiosity is legendary, partly perhaps because it is so often frustrated. I think sometimes the masters enjoy tormenting us so. We can do nothing about it. We are in collars.

"Did you really think, little idiot," said Florian, "we would not know you were about, a naked slave at our knees?"

"Did you snatch up a crumb of fact, lap up some news?" asked Miles.

"Forgive me, Masters," I said.

"What you heard is no longer sensitive," said Florian. "It is common knowledge in the holding. Even the slaves know."

"I did not," I said.

"You are a barbarian," said Florian.

"But the matter of the spy," I said.

"The spy has been recalled," said Florian.

"That is a good-looking slave," said Astron.

"Thank you, Master," I said. "A slave is pleased if Master is pleased."

"She is not only worthless, but excessively plain," said Florian.

"Worthless, yes," said Astron, "but consider the fineness, the delicacy, of the features, the dark-brown hair, the soft lips, which might be easily bruised by the violence of a master's kiss, the sweet shoulders and vulnerable belly, the trim ankles, which would look so well in shackles, and the eyes. I suspect tears could be easily brought to those lovely eyes."

"Women are marvelous, naked, and in collars," said a man.

"Women are troublesome," said another.

"Not when they are stripped, and collared, and on their knees, in the shadow of a whip," said another.

"True," said another.

"That is how they should be," said a man.

"That is where they belong," said another.

"Nonetheless," said Florian, "she is excessively plain. She is a Golden-Chain girl."

"A Golden-Chain girl?" said Astron.

"Yes," said Florian.

"I can believe it," said Astron.

"Thank you, Master," I said. Then I faced Florian. "May I speak, Master?" I asked.

"Yes," he said.

"I fear I am not so plain as Euphrosyne," I said.

A burst of laughter escaped Miles.

"Do you court a lashing?" demanded Florian.

"Not at all," I said.

"Compared to Euphrosyne," he said, "you are no more than an ill-bred, mottled she-tarsk!"

I remained silent, but my silence, I assure you, did not betoken agreement. It was true, however, that Euphrosyne was one of the most popular girls in the tavern.

"I gather," said Astron, "that Ho-Tosk remains adamant."

I recalled that Astron had been long at sea.

"I would not have Euphrosyne if she were given to me," said Florian, angrily.

"Of course not," said Astron.

"That is well known," said Miles.

I had long suspected that Florian's belligerent animosity toward the Golden Chain, and all that might appertain to it, had something to do with lovely Euphrosyne.

"Master," I said to Florian, "I am hungry. May I be fed?" I hoped to be fed by hand, but, often enough, some food is thrown on the floor under the table, which is to be taken on all fours, without the use of our hands.

"Not now," said Florian. "Perhaps later, if you are fortunate. You have been too inquisitive. We will have to find a way to keep closer track of you. I do not like the way you sneak about. Perhaps, one time or another, we might not be aware of your presence. Crawl to the kitchen. I shall send instructions to the kitchen master."

"Yes, Master," I said.

I was very hungry. I should have remained away from the head of the table. Had I done so, I am sure I would have been nicely fed by now. Too, I was annoyed that my presence had apparently not been as unobtrusive as I had thought, and that the information I had obtained, congratulating myself on my subtlety and cleverness, had been public knowledge, at least within the holding. No one had told me. To be sure, I was not a familiar member of the household. I do not think the matter really had to do with my being a barbarian. My Gorean was now quite good, and many of the slaves in the holding, as far as I could tell, though unsure of my accent, uncritically accepted me as a native speaker, a mistake which I thought it needless to rectify. If my original Earth name 'Margaret' had been put on me, though then, of course, as a mere, perhaps mocking, slave name at the whim of masters, things might have been different. Earth-girl names, incidentally, are sometimes put on native Gorean girls, perhaps to punish them, belittle them, demean them, humiliate them, or so on. They must then answer to that name, of course, promptly and perfectly.

I heard the irritating tinkle of the bells, changed my position, and then lay as still as I could, so as not to jangle the bells, the blanket clutched about me. I had been sleeping, for some Ahn. I supposed it now must be something like the second or third Ahn. I was not sure what, if anything, had awakened me. Perhaps it was the bells. One of the girls, laughing at the bells, told me that after the second night or so I would ignore them or not hear them when asleep. I was not sure why I had awakened when I did. I was naked in my cage, as we, most of us, at least in this holding, are commonly slept. The blanket was large and warm, and served as both mattress and bedding. Sometimes, as a punishment, a girl is denied the blanket. In many establishments, the girls are chained to rings at night. If one has a private master, one is often slept at the foot of his couch, chained there by a neck or ankle, usually the left ankle. In this way, the master, awakening, has the slave at hand, to put to use whenever and however he might wish. A small tug, once or twice on the chain, alerts us to awaken, that we may kneel, head down, awaiting the master's pleasure. Some slaves with private masters are allowed to share the master's couch. This is a sign of great favor, and often a slave must serve long and well before being granted so great a privilege and honor. She kneels beside the couch, humbly lifts and kisses the bedding two or three times, and then ascends the couch. Often slaves, as other animals, are not allowed on the furniture. I heard the bells again, to my irritation. They were, in their three rows, locked about my left ankle. I could not remove them. How the other slaves had laughed, that I be so humiliated. The bells were not the sensuous bells whose rustle drives masters wild, not the sort worn by many dancers, where coins are cast to the dancing floor, usually to be retrieved later by a taverner's man, not the sort sometimes fastened on a slave's ankle before her use, that they may record her least tremor, and resound to her wildest passion. No, they were tiny, clanking bells, of the sort that might be fastened on a rooting tarsk or a grazing verr, that their location might be more easily noted by local tenders. It seems I had been too inquisitive. "We will have to find a way to keep track of you," had said Florian. It seemed he did not care for the way I "sneaked about." How frightful if, at one time or another, they might not be aware of my presence! How bothersome that would be! Well, they had little to worry about now! I could not move a step without those bells marking my every move! As instructed, I had crawled, unfed, to the kitchen. There, chained by the neck to a ring, I had waited while hearing the noises of the feasting, the songs and shouts of men, the glad cries of slaves, rejoicing in their sharing of the feast. At last, the instructions for the kitchen master had reached the kitchen. I was to be given two spoons of slave gruel, after which I was to be belled and put to bed in my cage. Soon, belled, on all fours, I was walked to my cage by a guard. Behind me I could still hear, for some time, the sounds of the feast. The feasters would, I gathered, as Florian had suggested, "eat and drink heavily and sleep late." Then the cage door was locked behind me.

I do not know why I awakened when I did. Perhaps the bells had sounded, and awakened me. I did not know.

As I lay in the cage, warm in the blanket, trying not to move, many thoughts, as they will, came and went. I thought of my former life on Earth. How free, truly, had I been, without a master before whom I could at last be myself? Was I, or others, really so free then? Had I not been subject to a thousand restrictions, pressures, and forces, not been governed by a thousand bondages of compliance and convention? Had I not been informed how I was to speak, behave, and think? How perilous it had been not to conform! How many falsities and lies were imposed in the name of truth and honesty? Were we truly so free, swarming about, coming and going, in those immense, shimmering hives of steel and glass, their walls blazing in the sun? Was nature, with its wind and sunlight, its rain and snow, its grass and mountains, really so inferior to crowded, noisy thoroughfares, small and narrow at the foot of artificial cliffs and canyons? Was it so wonderful, really, to scratch and fight, to plot and plan, to climb stairs leading to nothing? Is it the best of bargains to spend a life on parties and restaurants, theaters, and night clubs? Is one well advised to seek out for oneself glittering traps? What wise animal would knowingly hasten to enmesh itself in snares, even golden snares? On Earth my life had been shallow and frivolous, pretentious, hectic, and meaningless. How vain I had been! How satisfied, how proud, I had been of myself! How brightly I had sparkled amongst similarly worthless baubles! And then I was brought to Gor, and made a slave. Was it not fitting? Why should one such as I, so cheap and worthless, so meretricious and petty, not be a slave, not be owned and mastered? What else could one such as I be good for? And so I had found myself stripped and sold from a block in Brundisium. At last I had some value, small as it was, the value of a slave. It is lonely in a cage, and collar. How I wanted a master, to fulfill my worthless womanhood!

I do not know why I had awakened when I had.

I wondered about Dorna.

She must have awakened somewhere in Port Kar, and discovered herself in a tunic of the Golden Chain and a new collar, doubtless also of the Golden Chain. She might try to hide. But where might a tunicked, marked, collared slave hide? Perhaps she had already been picked up by guardsmen and taken to the Golden Chain, there to serve as bait for her master, Pa-Kur, of the Assassins. I trusted that Ho-Tosk would not have her beaten, as she was not truly a fugitive slave. The lash is very painful. But, I thought, to preserve the charade that she had attempted to flee the tavern, a beating might be in order, lest suspicions be aroused otherwise. In the light of this view, particularly as I recalled her treatment of me, I was prepared to view the beating of Dorna with complete equanimity.

I recalled that Florian, while we were proceeding to the observation chamber, had informed me, in his casual way, that someone wanted me. This muchly piqued my curiosity and apprehension, but, as is the way with masters, he did not elaborate on the matter. I did not know who this mysterious someone might be, but I conjectured it might be one of the men in the holding, for several had perused me well, or one fellow or another who had seen me, and perhaps tried me out, in the Golden Chain. I wondered if Ho-Tosk would sell me. I supposed it would depend on the offer.

I also thought of Adraste, whom I had occasionally seen in the holding, put to one servile task or another. It did not seem that her beauty had managed to purchase her an exemption from the common chores of slaves. She seemed to be treated no better or worse than the other slaves. I suspected that that, if nothing else, would have infuriated the arrogant beauty, to be treated so casually, so routinely, so indifferently. I was now reasonably sure that Adraste was not the former Lady Julia Leta of Ar, given my adventure in the delta as the slave of he who spoke of himself as Bruno of Torcadino. The metal monster in the delta, the talk of recruiting men, of the gathering of equipment and the accumulation of resources, and the presence of Pa-Kur, of the Assassins, suggested an enterprise and project far more important and weighty than the mere capture of a lovely, embezzling thief from Ar's Street of Coins. So I supposed that the identity of Adraste was other than that of the former Lady Julia Leta of Ar. It must be that of someone far more important. Though the thought alarmed me greatly, I might have been tempted to fear that she might actually be the former Talena of Ar, the fabulous, bitterly sought, widely sought, long-sought, treasonous Ubara of Ar. That possibility, of course, was ruled out as Talena of Ar was now safe on Cos, under the protection of her

former ally, Lurius of Jad. In my wandering thoughts, I also considered my annoyance with Florian, which went far beyond his
reticence to reveal to me even the name of one who was supposedly "interested" in me and his radical and unaccountable dis-
paragement of me and the Golden Chain. He had also, it seemed
reasonably clear, though presumably under orders, made me an
unwitting participant in political intrigues I did not understand.
When I had been chained and hooded in an alcove of the Golden
Chain, he had informed me that Adraste was a peculating thief,
the former Lady Julia Leta of Ar, sought by the justice of Ar, and
had enlisted me in a project to spy upon her, and alert Ho-Tosk
to any unusual or suspicious behaviors, inquiries, contacts, and
such, which might involve her. Now I suspected that I had been
lied to, given false beliefs not only to mislead me, personally, but
beliefs which I, say, under torture or interrogation, might convey
to enemies, that they, too, would be misled. I recalled my ordeal
with the tunic of fire and the fumes of truth. I had been convinced
that I had revealed nothing, but I had learned, later, from Addison
Steele, to my dismay, that I had spoken fully and volubly. Now,
clearly, it seemed likely that I had conveyed nothing but false information, whose only value, if any, was to mislead enemies.

It was quiet in the holding. The feast was now long over. I
tried not to move my ankle, with its humiliating bells, such as
might bedeck a tarsk or verr. How amused the other slaves would
be in the morning! I was pleased that few, if any, knew I was a
barbarian. That would have been almost too much to bear.

I do not know why I had awakened when I did.

I knew little of the politics or intrigues of Gor, or of Port Kar. I
did gather, however, that yesterday was an important day for the
holding. Did the feast not signal that? Much intelligence of interest had apparently been gained from the interrogation of Dorna.
No attack or onslaught on the holding was imminent. The tunic
of fire and the fumes of truth could not be resisted. I, myself,
had learned that. Indeed, some spy within the camp of Pa-Kur
had even been recalled, doubtless to lessen that agent's jeopardy
which, as time went on, might be expected to increase, perhaps
exponentially.

How quiet it was.

I was careful not to move my ankle.

There had been much relief in the holding following the rev-
elations of Dorna, particularly as Bosk of Port Kar, master of the

holding, was absent. As far as I knew, I had never seen or met him. He was apparently at sea, looking into reports that he himself was at large, preying on shipping and ravaging towns on the Farther Islands.

I would now try to return to sleep.

I myself had undergone the ordeal of the tunic of fire and the fumes of truth, in much the same way as had Dorna. Dorna, then, and her confederates, would be well aware that the tunic of fire and the fumes of truth could not be resisted. I had spoken, I gathered, fully and volubly. But what had I revealed, only what I had been told, only what I took to be the truth.

I did not know why I had awakened when I did.

Bosk of Port Kar was far away, at sea. One could understand that. Why would he not, in rage and fury, inquire into depredations enacted in his name?

He was not in the holding.

Suddenly I realized, in terror, why I had awakened when I had. I rose to my knees with a jangle of bells and seized the bars of my small, sturdy cage, clutching and shaking them wildly, futilely. "Masters, Masters!" I screamed.

And almost at the same time I heard shouts and cries, from the corridor outside, running feet, and the clash of weapons.

CHAPTER FORTY-ONE

How Events Proceeded
In the Holding of Bosk of Port Kar

It was late morning, the Ninth Ahn, when a stranger, in a scarlet scarf, bearded, sword drawn, kicked open the door to the room in which my cage was kept. He looked about, swiftly, taking in the room, and then strode to my cage. I quickly knelt, with my head to the floor of the cage. "Why are you alone?" he demanded. "Are you being punished?"

"I have been kept alone," I said. "I do not know why. I think it is because I am in the custody of the holding, but not of the holding. I do not think I am being punished."

He lifted the lamp.

"Put aside the blanket," he said.

I did so, immediately. Slaves are to obey unquestioningly, instantly.

"You are belled," he said, "though clumsily."

I could not help the bells which had been put on me.

"Kneel up," he said, "head high."

I did so.

"You are a pleasure girl, are you not?" he said.

"Yes, Master," I said.

"Why then," he asked, "if you are belled, are you not in pleasure bells?"

"I do not know," I said.

"Get your knees apart, widely," he said.

I did so.

"You are a well-curved, little beast," he said.

"Thank you, Master," I said.

"Are you privately owned?" he asked.

"No, Master," I said.

"Who is your master and what is your collar?" he asked.

"I am owned by Ho-Tosk, of Port Kar," I said, "and my collar is that of the Golden Chain."

"That is a tavern?" he asked.

"Yes, Master," I said.

So then he was not of Port Kar.

He sheathed his sword.

"Where is the key to your cage?" he asked.

"On the wall, to the right," I said.

In moments then I was released from the cage and stood before the stranger.

"Turn about," he said, "and cross your wrists behind your back."

With two quick loops of thong and a knot jerked tight, my wrists were fastened behind my back.

He then freed his blade of its sheath.

"May I speak?" I asked.

"Yes," he said, "but if I am not pleased, you will be beaten."

"The holding is captured?" I asked.

"Besieged," he said. "Fighting continues."

"What is going on?" I asked.

"Slave raid," he said. "This house is rumored to contain luscious fruit for the markets. And from what I have seen, it does."

"He does not understand," I thought. "He does not know what is going on." I was sure that this was no ordinary slave raid. The central concern of this attack, I was sure, was not a general harvesting of slaves, but the acquisition of one particular slave, Adraste. I was sure he did not know that.

"And you yourself," he said, "are quite acceptable."

"Thank you, Master," I said.

"Leading position," he said.

I bent over, and he fastened his left hand in my hair.

I was then, my head at his hip, conducted from the chamber.

I found myself soon added to a rope-coffle. At that time I was one of ten slaves, and was she most recently added to the coffle. The rope was looped twice about my neck, knotted, and then dropped behind me, ready for the next to be its prisoner. If my coffle sisters had been tunicked earlier, that was no longer the case. I myself had been brought naked from my cage. Slaves are commonly stripped when in coffle. Each of us was bound as I was, my hands fastened behind me. We were alone, in a corridor on the fourth level.

From somewhere, seemingly far off, I heard the shouts of men and the clash of blades. Then it was quiet.

"Speak to me," I begged of Cella and Ianthe, those closest to me in the coffle.

"Before dawn," said Cella. "Five mighty tarns, draft tarns, each with a string of ten men, hovered at the parapet. These raiders discharged, they seized the parapet, hurling secured rope-ladders down to barges, by means of which more assailants reached the parapet. Vigilance was sparse and relaxed, if present. A guard or two was swiftly done away with."

I knew little of tarns, and had never seen one. I gathered that they were gigantic, dangerous, avian monsters. Few would dare to approach them. Those rash enough or mad enough to risk ascent to their saddles were called "Tarnsmen," an unusual and fearsome breed of men. These swift, terrible, broad-winged monsters were rare in the vicinity of Port Kar.

"Port Kar is surely under attack," said Ianthe.

"Not Port Kar," said Cella. "It would take fleets, hundreds of tarns to threaten the city."

"Then the holding is under attack," said Ianthe.

"The masters were unready," said Cella. "Apparently they suspected nothing."

I recalled the optimism, the mistaken sense of security, which had characterized the masters. How unwisely they had eaten and drunk "heavily," and had intended to "sleep late"! What a miserable awakening, then, must they have had, to rise, groggy and confused, to find enemies in the corridors. I wondered, had Bosk of Port Kar been present, if things might have been the same. How furious he might be, to learn of so egregious, though understandable, a lack of readiness.

"How many attacked?" I asked.

"Many," said Cella, "I am sure, six hundred, at least."

"We are told nothing," said Ianthe, "but some of us have seen fighting, and one hears the enemies crying out, informing one another, issuing orders."

"It seems the intruders hold the parapet and the top three levels of the holding, and are at the canal gate below," said Cella.

If that were the case, then resistance must have stiffened. The men of the holding must have rallied and taken a stand. The intruders had not managed to seize the holding in a single, fierce sweep of force. I supposed some corridors had been barricaded. We were on the fourth level of the holding. I thought the men of the holding, crews not at sea, might number a hundred or so men. It made sense to me that the intruders were also at the holding's canal gate. That would prevent Adraste from being hastened from the holding. The intruders would presumably have reached the vicinity of the canal gate from the roof, by descending rope ladders similar to those used to reach the parapet. I heard no alarm bars from the city, so I gathered that there was, as yet at least, no general awareness of the raid in the city.

Within a few Ehn of my coffling, four more slaves were added to the coffle, Mira, Lana, and the two Litas, referred to in the holding as blonde Lita and brunette Lita. 'Lita' is a very common slave name on Gor.

"Listen," whispered Cella.

"I hear it," I said, "swords."

It was then quiet for some Ehn; then there was again, briefly, the sound of swordplay. Then it was quiet, again. The noise of war, as nearly as I could tell, had come from the floor below.

This suggested to me that the men of the holding had attempted to challenge the intruders on the third level, but unsuccessfully. Given the likelihood that the men of the holding were outnumbered, say, six to one, it seemed inevitable that the intruders, if only by weight of numbers, would not only maintain their hold on the third level but soon control the second, and descend to the first. The defenders then would be trapped between the intruders within the holding and those outside, at the canal gate.

"Masters!" suddenly cried Renata, who was second in the coffle.

Instantly we fell to our knees.

Four men, with red scarves, surged into the corridor, descended, I supposed, from the fifth level, the level above us, from which the parapet could be reached.

I turned my head away.

I recognized he who was first amongst them, Pa-Kur, of the Assassins!

"Lift your heads!" he screamed.

He strode down the coffle line. "She is not here!" he screamed. "She is not here!"

"Who is not here?" asked one of the men with him.

"These slaves are comely," said another. "Let us get them over the wall, down to the barges."

"I want her, her!" cried Pa-Kur, looking about, wildly.

"Who?" asked one of this cohorts.

"We will look further!" cried Pa-Kur.

"Hold!" said one of the men with a red scarf. "The city may soon rise. Danger looms. Do not delay. We have been misled. This is no slaver's house, with crowded pens! I doubt there are more than twenty slaves in this holding. You are not interested in slaves! You are interested in a single slave, or in an act of vengeance!"

And then he was silent, and wisely so, for the sword of Pa-Kur was poised at his heart.

"Shall we search further?" asked Pa-Kur.

"By all means," whispered the man.

"For whom do we search?" asked another man. white-faced, stepping back.

"Can you recognize her?" queried another.

"Yes," said Pa-Kur. "She was once my prisoner, as unveiled as a she-tarsk."

He then proceeded down the corridor.

He had not said where she had been his prisoner nor under what circumstances, nor what might have ensued.

The fourteen of us were then again alone.

"I hear swordplay," whispered Cella. The sound was faint but audible.

A little later we could hear the bar for the Tenth Ahn ringing over the city. Shortly after that, Portia was added to the coffle, and we were then once more alone.

At one end of the corridor, now, though no masters were present, we remained on our knees. Who knew when a master might emerge into the corridor?

How fitting this seemed to me, that I should be kneeling, neck-roped, my wrists tied together behind my back.

I, and the other slaves, would abide the outcome of the doings of men, as the sort of cattle we were.

The intruders wore red scarves. This informed me that they were not associates of long standing. They did not really know one another. It seemed they had been gathered for a single task, a single mission. The men of the holding, on the other hand, were familiar with one another and would easily recognize one another on sight.

I knew little of the holding of Bosk of Port Kar. I was not really a member of its household. I supposed it did not make much difference when one is a slave. One is sold in one market or another, one is in one cage or another, one is on one chain or another, one is in one collar or another. Yet how important is the master! So much depended on the master! Did it matter, really, if the master was a good master, whether he was of Ar or Brundisium, or far Turia or even Port Kar? Did it matter, really, whether he was of Cos or Tyros, or of the mainland? I knew that docilities and submissions were endemic, pervasive, universal, in the animal world, and were not humans a part of nature, natively as real and honest as any other form of life, selected for in the course of evolution, formed in the light of the same tendencies, habits, and forces that governed all life and meaning? How can we be fulfilled before we are kneeling at the feet of our masters? In nature we are their possessions. I wanted a master who would be to me as master to slave, who would be kind to me, and yet would have a whip, and would use it on me if I were not pleasing, a master whom I would obey, and must obey. How I wanted to be owned by Addison Steele!

How would he treat me?

I knew he despised me, muchly so, and rightfully so.

I would try to be a good slave to him.

I would try not to be too often beaten.

We were at the long edge of a corridor which ran parallel to the delta wall. Light entered the corridor from narrow arrow ports in the wall.

I had not seen Adraste recently. I surmised, however, that she was still in the holding.

I wondered what might be the relationship, if any, between her and the mysterious Bosk of Port Kar.

Perhaps she had already been located by Pa-Kur and his confederates.

Pa-Kur had not seemed interested in our coffle, save to examine it, to see if it might contain she whom he sought, doubtless Adraste.

One of his cohorts, I recalled, had suggested that we be put over the wall and lowered down to the barges. On the other hand, it seemed Pa-Kur had had no interest in the mere acquisition of a small number of attractive beasts, to be disposed of in one market or another. He was relentless in his search for one slave. From my point of view, this was just as well. I had little enthusiasm for the prospect of a most perilous, swinging, dizzying descent into the arms of delta brigands or, worse, being cast bodily over the wall, hopefully to be retrieved from the water before being seized by tharlarion!

I think it was shortly after the eleventh Ahn that some thirty or forty red-scarfed intruders emerged into our corridor. Several bore vessels and plate; some had rolled rugs or tapestries in their arms or draped over their shoulders; some had wrapped about themselves robes and cloaks. "More loot," said one of the new-comers, noting the coffle. "Forget them," said another. "We have searched well," said another, "and none of the slaves satisfies the captain." "Let us withdraw," said another. "The city cannot long remain in ignorance of our presence." "It knows nothing," said another. "No alarm has sounded," said another. "It is only a mat-ter of time," said another. "Let us make haste," said another. "No," said another. "Let us first gather up these slaves."

We shrank back in our bonds. We, too, were loot, with our market value, in that respect no different from vessels, plates, and such.

Two men with knives began to slash the ropes from our necks. The haste and vigor with which this was done made us fear that our throats might be cut.

Then, to the side, from another portal, emerged another man, short-tunicked, sword in hand, wearing a red scarf.

I gasped.

It was Addison Steele!

Why was I startled? Was it not to be expected? Was he not a minion of Pa-Kur? Had he not been present, in the retinue of Pa-Kur, at the interview with the metal monster in the marshes? Had he not been present in the apartment of Dorna the Proud, an ally of Pa-Kur, when I had been so terrorized and discomfited, when I had suffered in the tunic of fire, when I had been forced to breathe in the noxious, harrowing, penetrating fumes of truth? But, too, he had been enleagued, it seemed, with he who called himself Bruno of Torcadino, surely a rival to the schemes of Pa-Kur and his colleagues. Was his heart then not for hire? Did I not know him as duplicitous and faithless, as venal and untrustworthy? How easily he might turn his coat! How I hated him! How I loathed and despised him! And I wanted so much to be chained at his feet!

One of the fellows who had entered the corridor with the men bearing loot, he perhaps first amongst them, looked up from the rope he had just severed, that which had neck-confined Ianthe. "Welcome," he shouted, and then he said, warningly, "but beware. Do not challenge us. This loot is ours. Seek your own!"

I was startled to see Florian and Miles, and others of the holding, some four or five others, following Addison Steele, each in a red scarf. Were all these as unconscionable and traitorous, as disloyal and opportunistic, as Addison Steele?

"Defend yourselves!" cried Addison Steele.

In that moment loot was strewn about, slaves screamed, men cursed, and swords flashed. The men who had followed Addison Steele, including Florian and Miles, fell like beasts of prey on the laden crowd of intruders who fell against one another, stumbling, losing their balance, buffeting and impeding one another. Surely the intruders considerably outnumbered the new red-scarfed arrivals but they had not been set for the attack nor had they expected it. The advantage of surprise was with the new arrivals. Too, how many might be behind the new arrivals? Who knew? Most of the intruders, confused and terrified, loot cast aside, turned their backs, and fled, seeking nearby exits. Some were jammed in the portals, and strove, even to the attacking of their fellows, to reach safety. Some, before they could turn to protect themselves, died in the threshold. The thin line of intruders who sought to resist the new arrivals were cut down in place.

"They are divided," cried Addison Steele, looking after the departed intruders. "They cannot communicate with one another. They do not know our numbers. They descend to a lower floor. They are not led."

"For now," said Florian. "They will soon be regrouped, and led."

"Perhaps they have had enough of this holding by now," said Miles. "They demanded troves of slaves. It seems they were lied to, told that this was a slaver's house."

"They will wish to extricate themselves from the holding," said Florian. "They are numerous, far more so than we, and dangerous. And men will fight more fiercely for their lives than coin."

"Free the slaves," said Addison Steele. "Slaves," said he, "uti-lize the back stairways, and make your way to the first level, to the inner vestibule of the canal gate."

I recalled hearing that intruders were in the vicinity of the canal gate, presumably to guard against Adraste's being slipped from the holding to safety.

The slaves stood.

Those who were still coffled, as I was, had the coffle rope cut away.

One of the men then began, swiftly and carefully, with a knife, one by one, to cut away the thongs which bound our wrists.

"No," said Addison Steele. "Not that one. Leave her tied."

The man then passed on to the next slave.

"I like to see her that way," said Addison Steele. "Too, it will help her to keep in mind that she is a slave."

I looked angrily at Addison Steele. As if I needed anything to remind me that I was a slave! Was I not naked, marked, and collared? I pulled angrily, pointlessly, at my wrists, thonged so snugly behind me. I was helpless, utterly helpless. Yes, before him, as before the males of Gor, I was well aware that I was a slave. How different he was from so many of the men of Earth! Before one such as he how could one be but a slave? And yet, I suspected he might be a man of Earth. Surely the humans of Gor were of human stock, descendants of humans of Earth. And then I real-ized, shocked and awed, how the men of Earth might be.

"To the parapet," said Addison Steele. "We can outnumber them by hundreds to one."

"If we can rouse the city," said Miles.

"Ignite the smoke beacon of danger," said Addison Steele. "Ring the alarm bar."

"Can they be reached?" asked a man.

"Follow me," said Addison Steele.

"Yes, Captain," said Miles.

CHAPTER FORTY-TWO

An Alarm is Given;
A Ruse is Enacted;
The Bridge of Boats;
A Large Canal Boat Casts Off

"I hear it!" said Cella. "Listen!"

"It is the holding's alarm bar, on the parapet!" exclaimed Portia.

"The masters have been successful!" said Ianthe.

"Doubtless then," said Cella, "the smoke of danger rises from the delta wall, as well."

"Time is short then for the enemy," said Korinna.

"We need not concern ourselves then with new collars," said blonde Lita.

"How can the enemy withdraw, if the parapet is held?" asked brunette Lita.

"There are many of them," said Cella. "There would be more than enough to retake the parapet and reach the barges."

I was alarmed to hear this, for I feared that Addison Steele, Florian, Miles, and the others would be swept aside in a routed enemy's frantic effort to reach the safety of the barges at the foot of the wall.

But perhaps Pa-Kur's martial acumen and force of will would somehow manage to consolidate the enemy and delay its withdrawal until its mission was completed. Then, would there not be time to reach the parapet, crush resistance, and reach the safety of the waiting barges?

I and the other slaves, by means of a narrow, obscure stairway, one of those different from the open, broader stairwells which a column of men might ascend abreast, had now reached the inner vestibule of the holding, adjacent to the outer vestibule, that closest to the canal gate. I was the last to reach it, and be admitted through the hastily constructed barricade which essentially sealed it off from the holding as a whole, for, being bound, I had been obliged to move with great care on the steep, narrow stairs.

"Be with the other slaves," had said a man, gesturing to the side of the inner vestibule. I had then hurried, belled, to join the others, kneeling in the shadows. A few were tunicked. They, I gathered, had not required a rescuing from the intruders. Some slaves I did not see. I assumed they were in hiding, or had been apprehended and were still in the custody of the intruders. Perhaps they had already been lowered, or cast, over the delta wall and were tied in one or another of the waiting barges. Amongst the tunicked slaves kneeling against the wall of the inner vestibule, one stood out amongst them, one in a modest, white-silk tunic, dark-haired, green-eyed, olive-skinned Adraste! How beautiful she was! Surely men might kill to possess such a woman, even if there were not some mysterious emolument attaching to her ownership. Of all the slaves in the inner vestibule only I was bound, my wrists tied behind my back. Addison Steele, the monster, had seen to that!

"What is that sound?" I asked.

"Pounding on the gate of the outer vestibule," said Cella. "They have a beam. They want to crush it in."

"So," I thought to myself, "the intruders within the canal gate are no longer content to wait, watching the portal, lest Adraste be ushered through to safety in the city. They are now intent upon forcing an entry. How limited now is their time!"

Then I realized that the alarm bar, high on the parapet, was no longer ringing. Did that mean that the parapet had been retaken by the intruders? Did that mean that Addison Steele, Florian, Miles, and the others were now dead? I had gathered from the character of the intruders that they were unlikely to take prisoners. Too, I suspected that they, in their frenzy and frustration, and now perhaps fear, would not be likely to leave wounded antagonists behind them.

I continued to hear the pounding on the gate to the outer vestibule.

Some men hurried past us.

"They go to reinforce the gate," said Cella.

I estimated that there had been some twenty men in the inner vestibule, to guard the barricade, and presumably some others, doubtless fewer, in the outer vestibule, to monitor the portal within the canal gate which, until moments ago, had not been approached.

"Listen, listen!" cried Cella.

"The city bars sound!" cried Portia.

We heard the ringing of bars throughout the city.

"Port Kar rises!" said Mira.

A man called back, from the barricade, "Torches approach and a green flag of parley!"

He was joined on the barricade by some ten or so defenders. Given the size, weight, and height of the barricade, that militating against its swift dismantling, and the unreliability of its footing should one attempt to climb it, a small number of men was sufficient, at least for a time, to defend it against a much larger force of attackers.

"Parley, parley!" called a voice from down the corridor, from beyond the barricade.

"Let no more than three approach!" said a defender, half concealed, on the barricade. "And let them be he bearing the flag, one carrying a torch, and one to speak!" Then, a moment later, the defender called out, "That is close enough. Stop! Speak."

"Do you value your lives?" inquired a voice, powerful, arrogant, and belligerent, from outside the barricade.

I was frightened. I knew the voice. It was that of Pa-Kur!

"Far more than yours!" responded one of the defenders.

"We mean you no harm," called Pa-Kur. "Let slaughter cease. Our interest is paltry. We seek nothing of great value, only something of personal interest to us, a worthless, stolen slave. Her name is Adraste."

At this point, Adraste rose to her feet, but was gestured back to her knees by a defender.

"Surrender the slave to us," called Pa-Kur, "and we will promptly withdraw, nursing no grudges and wishing you well."

"I cannot hear you," called out the defender on the barricade.

"Behold," called Pa-Kur, "I fling over your mountain of wood, rugs, and rubbish a purse. It contains three silver tarsks, far more than the slave is worth. Deliver her to us. Let it be a simple sale. Thus the bargain is yours and you live, your honor untarnished!"

The small sack, seemingly containing something metal, doubtless three silver tarsks, struck on the floor, not feet from where
we knelt.

A moment later one of the men on the floor retrieved it and
hurled it back, over the barricade.

"It is difficult to hear you," called out the defender on the barricade. "Can you speak more loudly or clearly?"

More bars throughout the city had now joined those sounding
the alarm. Their sound, of course, was much subdued, given the
thick walls of the holding.

"We will fire the barricade!" screamed Pa-Kur.

"You will find it difficult to attack through flames," said the
defender.

"I have better than four hundred men behind me, ready to assault your puny barricade," said Pa-Kur.

"Those will be few compared to thousands in the city," called
the defender. "The city awakens! Men arm themselves! Can you
not hear the ringing of the bars? What if they think you are
threatening a Home Stone? What then will be your fate?"

"Let us flee!" cried a man on the far side of the barricade.

Then there was a cry of death, and he was heard no more.

"I conclude this parley now," said Pa-Kur. "You have made
your choice. Die with it!"

There was then a silence, save for the ringing of the bars over
the city.

"Prepare for an onslaught!" cried one of the holding's men
from his position on the barricade.

Then from the other side, from the outer vestibule, there was
a sound of splintering wood.

"We cannot hold the portal!" called a man.

"We are lost!" cried another.

Then, from the other side of the barricade, now back several
yards, I heard Pa-Kur cry out, "Be done with it! Swiftly! Sweep
them aside like vulos, trample them like urts! Kill all! Spare none!"

There was a scrambling, the sounds of slipping, of breaking
wood, cries of anger, and death.

It seemed not many had assaulted the barricade, and few, if
any, had reached its pinnacle. The barricade was high and thick,
and the footing treacherous and unreliable. Defenders were steady
of footing, and muchly shielded, for the barricade had been constructed with such things in mind. Climbers, struggling upward,

must risk darting spears and descending axes. Defenders had the advantages of both height and security of position.

"They are resisted, driven back, dismayed!" called a defender, elated.

But I did not think so few men could long withstand larger numbers, and prolonged strife.

Meanwhile, from the court of the outer vestibule, I heard the cries of men, the rending of wood, perhaps the collapse of a gate, and the clash of blades.

"Fire the barricade!" I heard Pa-Kur cry.

"There is no time!" shouted a man. "Hear the bars!"

Then, to my amazement, I heard a voice from the other side of the barricade cry out, "Hold! Hold! Withdraw, brothers! Save yourselves! There is little time. The parapet is clear. The way is free. Back to the parapet and down to the barges. They are your only hope, for time is short, and they will soon be scattered and set afire, for ships even now hurry forth from the arsenal!" What so amazed me, and delighted me, was that the voice was that of Addison Steele! He lived! And then, from elsewhere on the other side of the barricade, other voices cried out, as well. "Save yourselves while you can!" "You were betrayed!" "There are no crowded pens of slaves here!" "You were tricked!" "Do not die for the whim of another!" "Escape! Escape while you can!" "The way to the parapet is clear!" "The road to safety will soon be closed!" "Hear the bars!" "Beware the ire of the men of Port Kar! Expect no mercy. It is not their way. Flee! Flee while there is still time." "Do not let your bodies rot for months on impaling spears, raised on the walls of the city, a warning to others, a testimony to the displeasure of the Men of Port Kar!"

Amongst these voices I recognized that of Florian, and perhaps of Miles, and surely others.

"Stop! Stop!" cried Pa-Kur. "Rally, rally! Attack, attack!"

But I gathered that Pa-Kur, buffeted and ignored, surrounded by frantic, desperate, running men, soon found himself deserted in the corridor.

Addison Steele, Florian, Miles, and others, in their donned red scarves, blending in with the intruders, had strewn disorder and discord, confusion and terror, amongst the cohorts of mighty Pa-Kur. His men fled, seeking stairwells, climbing, rushing, gasping, unopposed to the parapet, there hoping to avail themselves of the rope ladders by means of which the barges, were they still there, might be reached.

"Sleen! Sleen!" screamed Pa-Kur, and then it seems that he himself withdrew.

A moment later a path through the barricade was opened, and Addison Steele, Florian, Miles, and some others entered the inner vestibule.

They did not so much as glance at the slaves.

"The outer vestibule is taken," said a man. "We have sealed off the inner vestibule, but we are too few to hold the inner gate. I fear there is little hope."

Even as he expressed this sober assessment one could hear the sudden pounding of a beam on the inner gate.

"The enemy, how many?" asked Addison Steele.

"Observations taken Ahn ago, from the second floor of the holding, conjectured fifty or sixty, captain," said the man.

"Too many," said Addison Steele. "We shall withdraw to the other side of the barricade, and defend a stairwell. We need only hold out until the citizens of Port Kar, in their hundreds, enter the holding and relieve our distress."

"Time is on our side," said Florian.

"Let us hope we can survive until its arrival," said Miles.

"Get the slaves to safety," said Addison Steele. "They are not to be lost or, in war, accidentally cut and bloodied."

"Yes, captain," said a man. "Slaves up!" he snapped. We rose instantly.

At the same time a panel in the inner gate broke inward. Then the beam smote another panel loose.

But oddly, then, we heard cries of anguish, fear, and pain at the gate. Then the beam pounded no more. Through the ruptured paneling we could see men turned about to face others, streaming in from the broken canal gate at the outer vestibule. There was a brief interval of swordplay and then weapons were being cast to the ground, and intruders were kneeling, head down, the backs of their necks exposed to the stroke of swords. In such a way they surrendered, mutely begging for mercy.

We heard a voice cry out, "Strip, brigands. To your bellies, hands behind you! Await your chains!"

"Open, open in the name of the Council of Captains of Port Kar!" called a voice.

"Guardsmen!" said Florian.

Miles ran to unbolt the half-ruined door to the inner vestibule.

"We are safe," said a man.

"Down, slaves," said another.

We knelt in place.

Men from outside crowded into the inner vestibule. There were glad cries. Weapons were sheathed. Red scarves were cast down. Their work was done. One could sport such a token now only with jeopardy. Warriors embraced. It was joy, madness, and tumult. I felt a hand seize my hair, and draw me to the side. It was not the hand of Addison Steele! I was drawn up and felt a knife's edge at my throat. "Be silent," said an ugly brute. For a moment I did not recognize him, and then I remembered him from the Skerry of Lars. It was Vas of Anango, and I recalled that Bruno of Torcadino had said that he might have use for him, and that he had intended to recruit men in Port Kar. A moment later I was startled to see Bruno of Torcadino himself. He was standing, head bowed, close to Adraste, who was now standing, though in the presence of a free man. Bruno of Torcadino's sword was blood-ied. I suspected he had cut his way through to the inner gate. He spoke to her softly, as in awe, almost reverently. "Noble, glorious Ubara," he said, "hope of Ar, light of the world, most beautiful of all women, we are in great danger. Accompany me. Outside a cloak and hood are waiting. Surely you recognize me, Seremides, once first sword of the Taurentians, your beloved servant, always loyally at the foot of your throne. At my plea I have been commis-sioned by the Ubar of Cos, the noble Lurius of Jad, to bring you safely to Cos, our ally in the venture to save Ar from the tyranny of Marlenus."

"Are you truly my friend?" asked Adraste, or whomsoever she might be.

"How horrid that the beautiful Talena of Ar, freest of all free women, most noble and most splendid of all free women, rightful Ubara of Ar, should be clad in a mere tunic and that of a slave, that her graceful, regal neck should be encircled so closely, so obdu-rately, with the shameful, degrading badge of servitude, a collar. I avert my eyes. I struggle not to faint with the impropriety and indignity of it all."

"You would have surrendered me in Ar," she said, "in the hope of winning amnesty for your own crimes against the state."

"Never," he said. "It was a ruse. My true intent was always to contrive a way to save you, to deliver you to your friend and ally, noble Lurius of Jad."

"I would sooner believe an urt," she whispered.

How dare she speak so to a free man?

That she had not spoken aloud to him suggested to me that she was uncertain as to what was occurring.

"If you will not trust me, trust the great Lurius of Jad," he said. "I have here, regard it, recognize it, the seal of Jad. I could receive this only from the hand of Lurius himself. It confirms my commission."

"Perhaps you would betray me to Ar, for your own wretched skin," she said.

"Do not forget," he said, "that I, too, am on a proscription list, and that I fear and hate Ar. Rather than enter Ar I would gladly enter a cage of rabid, starving sleen. Moreover, to assuage your concerns, should I betray the commission of Lurius, my own life would be forfeit. I would be hunted down and slain, following lengthy, grievous tortures. My life depends on my fidelity to the commission of your beloved friend and colleague, Lurius of Jad. You have seen the seal. You know it. How else could I have come by it, were it not from the very hand of Lurius himself? Come quietly with me. A cloak and hood await, and a swift ship, ready to bring you in honor to Cos."

"It is rumored," she said, "that I am already in Cos, honored and protected."

"We shall turn the rumor into fact, noble lady, beautiful Ubara," he said.

Then, sheltered and unnoticed, at the wall of the inner vestibule, as men milled about, bustling, hearty and hale, laughing and joking, now free of the neighborhood of death, Talena, as I may now speak of her, accompanied by hobbling Seremides, as I shall now speak of him, made their way along the wall toward the shattered portal of the inner vestibule. In a moment they would be in the outer vestibule and making their way toward the landing of the holding's inner harbor. I had no doubt that the sea gate there had been breached long ago. Vas of Anango spun me about jerking the knife from my throat. I opened my mouth to scream, even though I might not have been heard in the midst of revelry, but his large hand pulled me back against him, capping my mouth tightly, and I felt the point of his knife in my side. "Cry out," he said, "and you die." I nodded my understanding, as I could, a small pressure on his hand. How helpless I felt, naked, collared, my hands tied behind me! "Move," he said, removing his hand from my mouth, thrusting me ahead of

him. Then a second pair, again a slave and a master, made their
way from the inner vestibule. I gathered that Vas of Anango had
not wished to risk killing me in the press of the celebrants. The
sound of the bells on my left ankle, if heard, was ignored. It
was only that of another belled slave. Then we were making our
way through the outer vestibule, threading our way amongst
standing men, some still with bared weapons. We stepped about
fallen bodies, those of red-scarfed intruders and those, doubtless, of men of Port Kar. Blood, here and there, now brownish
red and sticky, was drying on the tiles. Living intruders, on
their bellies, hands behind them, were being fitted with chains.
Then we were through the opening that had held the remain-
der of the timbers of the outer portal and were on the landing
of the holding's small harbor. The canal gate, which had been
forced inward by the rescuing men of Port Kar, hung awry on
its hinges. The holding's harbor itself, and the canal beyond the
harbor, was bristling with canal boats. Some had been aligned,
hull to hull, to afford a passage, a bridge of boats, to access the
landing. "That slave is naked," said a man, interposing himself
between a canal boat and Vas of Anango. "Suitably," said Vas of
Anango. "She is belled," said the man. "She is a stray, a kitchen
slave, picked up by the men of the holding of Bosk," said Vas
of Anango. "I am returning her to the Silken Rope. We bell our
kitchen slaves thusly." Vas of Anango then sheathed his knife,
lifted me from my feet, and stepped about the fellow who had
impeded his progress. "Say nothing, give no token of distress,"
he whispered to me, "or I will break your neck." He was a large
man, and I had little doubt he could easily break my neck, or
back, or strangle me in the crowding and stirring, his act possibly escaping notice. I had inadvertently been close to Talena
when Seremides had approached her. I had witnessed their interaction, even to the overhearing of their words. Seremides had
perhaps indicated to Vas of Anango, his fellow, that I was to be
taken in hand. Otherwise might I not interfere, give warning, or
sound an alarm? I was miserable with fear that I had heard far
too much for my own good. At the first opportunity, in privacy,
might I not be done away with, to protect a secret I had no wish
to share? Commonly the slave's protection is her collar, and her
standing, or lack of standing, as a domestic beast, her market-
ability, and such. She is not a free person. Indeed, legally, she
is not a person. Who would be so stupid as to cast aside seized

loot or destroy a snared, vendible animal, particularly one likely
to be attractive? Now, however, in virtue of what I had heard, I
feared that such common assurances, so often relied upon, might
no longer obtain.

Vas of Anango, then, I in his arms, stepped on the planking
lying athwart the bridge of boats, that linking the aligned canal
boats, that wooden paving which might be trodden by two men
abreast. By such a route, a relieving force, the lifters of a siege,
men not crowded in hurrying canal boats, might approach, almost at a run, the landing of the holding of Bosk of Port Kar.
We made our way boat by boat, on this planking, twice turning
corners, and then reached a walkway. On this walkway, amongst
some men and women, waiting, gathered perhaps for news, was
Seremides, Talena, and a slave in the livery of the Golden Chain,
holding what appeared to be a flat, soft, folded bundle. "Euphrosyne!" I thought. Tethered at the side of the canal, near them,
was an oared, half-covered, half-canopied, canal boat containing
some nine or ten men. Vas of Anango lowered me to the walkway
and I found myself in leading position, my head at his hip, his
hand twisted in my hair. Seremides then, steadied by the crutch
under his arm, took the bundle from Euphrosyne, and shook it
out, revealing a long, opaque cloak with an attached hood. This
garment he draped carefully about the head and shoulders of
Talena, with ceremonial dignity, almost reverently. He then motioned to two men from the boat, and they helped Talena down
into the boat, to a place under the canopy. As I approached,
bent over, perforce, at the side of Vas of Anango, I saw Seremides
pass something to Euphrosyne. I took it to be some recompense
for a service tendered. She thrust it in her mouth. I assumed it
was a hard candy. Such things are often used to reward a slave
girl. Sweets are precious to a female slave. We covet them. We
hope for them. We will work so hard, so very hard, for one. Free
women find that amusing, but they are not slaves, not in collars! Euphrosyne, turning slightly, saw me. She was clearly surprised, and confused, to see me here, on the walkway. Her lips
silently framed the question, "Zia?" In the meantime, Seremides
had apparently said something to one of the men in the boat
because he had ascended to the walkway. "Master!" exclaimed
Euphrosyne. "Be silent," said Seremides. Then Euphrosyne, to
her obvious astonishment and consternation, was seized and literally cast down into the arms of two of the men. In a moment

she was bound and gagged, and thrust under the half-canopy of the boat.

I was forced to my knees before Seremides, Vas of Anango's hand still in my hair. "This one," said Vas of Anango, looking about, "shall we kill her now?"

"Do not be foolish," said Seremides. "She, like the other, is attractive. Were the matter open, we could sell them. I might even give you your choice."

"But the matter is not open?" said Vas of Anango, suspiciously.

"No," said Seremides. "The prisoner whom we have rescued, who is of high birth on Cos, wishes to have them as personal serving slaves."

"All served in the Golden Chain?" said Vas of Anango.

"Yes," said Seremides, "and thus they witnessed our noble prisoner's humiliation and shame, and perhaps even had the effrontery to think of themselves as her equals. She will thus enjoy having them at her feet. They are to suffer, as proxies, for our prisoner's former discomfiture. Doubtless they will be deprived of the touch of masters, so agonizing for a needful *kajira*, worked long and hard, fed little, and beaten frequently."

How mixed were my feelings! I was elated, almost weeping, to learn that I was not to be summarily slain and, almost as much, filled with dismay that I might soon become a victim of the proud, vengeful former Adraste. I could remember from my training in Brundisium the terror of my female instructors when a master might threaten them with being given to a mistress. And I had no doubt but what the former Adraste, with all her rancor and resentment at her former status, afflicted with the memories of her perceived degradation, would be a most demanding and formidable mistress. I particularly feared for vain, short-tempered Euphrosyne, for she was somewhat haughty and impatient for a slave, and had regarded even the former Adraste with small respect. Indeed, it was said, she had even, in the alcoves, occasionally dared to prove less than fully pleasing. Also, I was startled to hear that Talena, the former Adraste, was alleged to be of high birth on Cos. Thus, I gathered, that the men of Seremides, including Vas of Anango, did not realize the importance of their rescued prisoner, did not understand that they had in hand the fabled, muchly sought Talena, sought by a thousand bounty hunters, she who had once been the Ubara of Ar.

At a gesture from Seremides, Vas of Anango lifted me up, and, with a jangle of bells, cast me into the arms of a fellow on the canal boat.

"Tie her ankles, gag her, and display her," said Seremides. "Those who look upon us will see her, be pleased, and think little of what cannot be seen."

A single thong was looped about my ankles, and they were tied closely together. A slave may be held with perfection by even so slight a bond. I was then knelt before a thwart near the tiller. A heavy wadding was then placed in my mouth and fastened in place. I could no longer articulate speech. I could then make only the tiniest of helpless sounds. They needed have no fear that I might cry out, interfering with their plans.

"Help me on board," said Seremides, "and cast off."

CHAPTER FORTY-THREE

We Seek the Southern Gate;
We Encounter Difficulties;
A Tumultuous Passage;
We Arrive at the Skerry of Lars

"Row evenly, lads," said Seremides. "Be patient and smooth. Waste no time, but show no visible haste. Attract no attention. We are unhurried, sober fellows about some unhurried, sober business. None must suspect our errand. But do not dawdle. Our lives will depend on unnoted expedition."

Vas of Anango was at the tiller.

A small, single-oared canal boat, of the sort typical of Port Kar, was passing us. "The alarms are silent!" called its pilot.

"There is peace at the wall," said Seremides, pleasantly.

The pilot, in gliding past, noticed me, and obviously found me of interest. Slaves must put up with such scrutiny. Yet it pleases us. Who does not thrill to be so noticed? I was kneeling, bound, stripped, and gagged. He grinned, approvingly. Most masters keep their slaves on a short leash. What slave would have it otherwise?

One of the men in our craft came from the bow, making his way about the low, sunken, closed, canopied area, and stood over Seremides, who was seated rather amidships, somewhat behind the canopied area. The man wore a short-sleeved jacket of sleen-skin and a mariner's cap of the same material. I took him to be the leader of the small crew.

"I trust you have planned well," said the man.

"Even from the strife in Ar," said Seremides, "even from the time of flight and terror, even from the restoration of Marlenus, even from the World's End and back."

"This day is yours," said the man.

"At last," said Seremides.

"You were patient," said the man.

"One must needs be so," said Seremides.

"You lay in readiness to exploit the inevitable attack on the holding of Bosk of Port Kar," said the man.

"What choice had we?" asked Seremides. "We lacked the strength for an assault on the holding."

"Let others do battle, for the spoils you seize," said the man.

"Of course," said Seremides.

"Pursuit must be feared," said the man.

"We are underway," said Seremides. "Pursuit incapable of obtaining its object is equivalent to no pursuit."

"The canals are largely clear," said the man.

"Traffic sped to the wall," said Seremides.

Occasionally we saw a woman in a window of one of the buildings lining the canal. Usually they looked upon us, idly. Occasionally Seremides, smiling, waved to one or another of them. "Give me that one," called one of them, pointing down to me. "I will teach her what it is to be a slave!"

Like all female slaves I had a great fear of free women. How cruel they are to us! How they hate us! And I feared that I, and haughty Euphrosyne, were soon to be given to a freed Talena. I did not think that Euphrosyne would be so haughty then.

Another canal boat slipped past us, presumably on its way toward the delta wall, perhaps even to the delta-gate market.

"Soon lads," said Seremides, calling to the rowers, "we will be at the Southern Gate, and from thence to the Skerry of Lars, near which a swift, ready vessel, foreign and unmarked, awaits."

"We are but Ehn from the Southern Gate," said the man, he whom I took to be the leader of the crew.

"Hear that, fellows?" called Seremides. "The Southern Gate is nigh. And once the Southern Gate is behind us, then it is only five pasangs to safety, only five pasangs to riches and success!"

"The sky darkens," said an oarsman, "the wind rises. I fear the open water will be choppy. Waves will be high, the valleys deep."

"As much so for others as for us," said Seremides. "Row on, lads, row on."

"There," said the man whom I took to be the leader of our crew, pointing forward, "the Southern Gate!"

A long canal boat, much like ours, was near the Southern Gate, at a pier to its right.

"Rest oars," called he whom I took to be the leader of our crew.

"Do not dally," said Seremides. "The sleen of vengeance swim in our wake. Press on!"

"But look," said he whom I took to be the leader of our crew.

"What?" said Seremides.

"That boat," said the man, pointing.

Seremides struggled up, supported by the heavy crutch. "It is moored," he said. "Press on!"

"But see," said the man. "It casts its moorings!"

"Just now?" asked Seremides.

"It has been waiting," said the man.

"How do you know?" asked Seremides.

"This boat is not armored," said the man. "We do not carry mercenaries."

"So?" asked Seremides.

"It must have been waiting," said the man.

"Who would wait?" said Seremides.

"Who knows?" said the man.

I feared I knew.

"I brook no interference," said Seremides.

"If they approach, we must negotiate, or turn back," said the man.

"Do so, and die," said Seremides, removing the hitherto concealed wicked short sword from beneath his cloak.

"Perhaps they mean us no harm," said the man, "meaning merely to cast off and be about some business."

"I fear we are their business," snarled Seremides, lifting his sword to the man's throat.

"I did not sign on to fight," whispered the man. "I am of the mariners, not the scarlet caste."

"Shall I thrust?" inquired Seremides.

"No," said the man, backing away.

"If all goes well, reluctant one, you need not fight," said Seremides. "When I hired this boat, I anticipated the possibility of such a contingency. This boat may not be armored, but it is heavily timbered, and the bow is reinforced with iron."

"The boat is going to pass us," said an oarsman, looking about.

Seremides turned to Vas of Anango, at the tiller. "You, tarsk of Anango," said Seremides, "will follow my directions explicitly, immediately."

Vas of Anango growled something back to Seremides, which I took to be a token of begrudged understanding and agreement.

"I am sure that there is nothing to fear," said he whom I took to be the leader of our crew.

"Press on," said Seremides. "Each Ehn is crucial. By now eager ships, like tenacious sleen, hungry for blood, hurtle in our wake."

But no stroke was called.

"Stroke, stroke!" screamed Seremides.

Almost at the same moment the ship to our right changed course, as though to come alongside.

"Look, another ship, another ship, too!" called an oarsman, forward, twisting about, pointing.

It was true, another large canal boat, which had apparently been lurking outside the Southern Gate, now made its appearance, to the left.

"Steady, men," said he whom I took to be the leader of our crew.

"Press on!" said Seremides.

"Oars, at ease," said he whom I took to be the leader of our crew.

"Are you mad?" said Seremides.

"I understand the rescued prisoner is valuable," said he whom I took to be the leader of our crew. "Why should she be yours? We can sell her back and share much gold."

"You have dealt with my enemies," said Seremides. "You have betrayed me!"

"You, but not gold," he said. "And put away your sword, cripple. In a moment we will be boarded. You are helpless. If you cause the least difficulty, you will be slain. Perhaps Decius of Venna will allow you to have two or three silver tarsks, for your help in delivering the slave to him."

Perhaps it was well that his last words were so proud. Thus he perished happily in his moment of triumph. The body, a moment later, toppled into the canal. This occurrence was not missed by several of the oarsmen who, naturally, all faced the stern of the boat.

"I am now captain," said Seremides. "I was once first sword of the Taurentians in Ar. You are unarmed, save for mariner's knives.

My sword is thirsty. In two Ehn I could kill all or most of you. The others might go overboard, and trust that the canal sleen and the Tamber sharks have not yet scented the blood in the water. Oars ready! We are going to shear the oars of the vessel which suspects nothing, coming alongside. Now, stroke!"

The boat lunged ahead. I was thrown back against the thwart before which I knelt. "Shear!" screamed Seremides a moment later to Vas of Anango. I drew to the side as I could. I saw our oars on the right lifted. Almost at the same time there was a hideous wrenching and scraping of wood, a snapping and splintering of oars, and the cries of startled, angry, dismayed men. Then we were beyond the turning, crippled boat, pathetic, like a bird with a broken wing.

Our oarsmen cheered.

"You could not have done this without me!" shouted Vas of Anango.

"Nor others, as well!" said Seremides.

I saw Decius of Venna standing, clinging to a rail, shaking his fist, then his figure, growing smaller, was dropping behind.

"To the Southern Gate!" said Seremides.

"The other ship comes about!" said Vas of Anango. "She blocks the gate!"

"Strong oars, fellows!" cried Seremides. "Stroke!"

"Can you not see?" cried Vas of Anango. "The gate is blocked!"

"Hold your course, or die," said Seremides. "Stroke, lads, stroke!"

"What if they do not draw away?" said Vas of Anango.

"They may or may not, as they please," said Seremides. "If they draw away, we pass freely. If they do not, we pass, as well."

"Back oars!" cried Vas of Anango.

"Stroke!" cried Seremides.

"You are mad!" said Vas of Anango. "See, they do not believe you. They call your bluff! They do not draw aside! Back oars! They remain in place!"

"On!" said Seremides. "Stroke!"

"We are doomed!" said Vas of Anango. "Two ships perish. There will be kindling in the water, glad feasting for sharks!"

"Stroke!" cried Seremides.

The oarsmen, their backs to the bow, sweating, strained at the oars. The strokes were deep and powerful.

I could not scream, for I wore a Gorean gag. I fought my bonds, wildly, futilely. My efforts were unavailing. I was absolutely helpless, a slave who had been tied by Gorean masters.

There was a sudden rending of wood and the iron-reinforced prow of our canal boat rose out of the water, climbing the gunwales of the other boat, and then, after a terrible moment, plunged back into the water, scattered planking and timbers on each side.

"Well done, lads," cried Seremides. "Now, on, on, through the gate, to victory, to safety and riches, to the Skerry of Lars! Stroke, lads, stroke!"

I looked back. There was a debris of timbers and oars in the water, and men, too, some swimming, some clinging to wreckage.

I saw the barred leaves of the Southern Gate, fastened back, high on each side, slip past. Then the boat shook and rolled, free in the troubled, stirring waters of the Tamber Gulf. The wind was cold and the sky dark.

"Behind us!" said Vas of Anango. "The first boat comes about, pursues!"

I looked back. The shearing on the one side of the boat of Decius of Venna had snapped oars but not torn open the strakes. Half the oars on the uninjured side of the boat had been repositioned to provide the craft with a symmetry of leverage.

"Do not fear her," said Seremides. "Her wings are clipped. She can move but cannot fly. She cannot overtake us. She cannot match our speed. Fear rather terrible ships yet unseen, narrow ships, swift and long oared, even now coursing in our wake."

The canal boat was buffeted to one side, and was washed back, and then, again and again, it was lifted, and then fell back, dropping between waves. Spray was whipped by the angry wind, and lashed the oarsmen and we who were behind the canopied area, Seremides, myself, and Vas of Anango. I thought those under the canopy, the beautiful Talena of Ar, and the lovely, gagged, bound slave, Euphrosyne, were scarcely more protected than we. Many times, were I not gagged, I might have cried out in alarm, for I saw on either side waves higher than the rails of our craft, as we dropped into troughs, and then, a moment later, pitching, sprang up, seeing only sky, and a storming horizon.

"I do not like the sea," said Vas of Anango. "We will ship water. We will be swamped. We will founder."

"It is as dangerous to go back as forward," shouted Seremides.

"Ask the men!" demanded Vas of Anango.

"Ask my sword, and weigh its response," said Seremides.

"You are mad," said Vas of Anango.

"Turn back then, to decorate an impaling post," said Seremides.

Vas of Anango, with his leaning weight and two arms, struggled to keep the tiller steady.

"Yes," said Seremides. "Do you think we are making off with a trinket, a bauble hidden in our purse, a vulo tucked beneath our arm? You do not understand the gravity of the venture in which we are embarked. You do not grasp what deed we are about. More ensues than you suspect."

"Speak!" demanded Vas of Anango.

Seremides hesitated, and then said, quickly, "We rescue a high-born maid of Cos, even a cousin to great Lurius of Jad."

"She is in a collar, sell her," growled Vas of Anango.

"Great Lurius will pay well for her safe return," said Seremides.

"She is in a collar," said Vas of Anango. "They are no good for freedom after that. Once a slave, always a slave."

That was a common Gorean saying. I knew it true of me. I knew I was born for the collar and now I wore one, on Gor. I wanted more than anything to love and serve a master, helplessly and rightlessly, one who would own me and treat me as the slave I was.

"We shall let great Lurius decide," said Seremides.

It then, in the darkness and wind, began to rain, heavily.

In the instant before it began to rain, I detected, it frightening me, what I took to be a momentary flash of sinister illumination on the coarse features of Vas of Anango, and then it vanished, as deliberately as the closing of a drawer, the descent of a panel, the locking of shutters, the closing of a door, the dropping of a curtain.

"Vas of Anango suspects," I thought. I was sure, as well, that this was recognized by Seremides.

"It is true that some slabs of collar meat sell for more than other slabs of collar meat," said Vas of Anango, offhandedly.

"True," agreed Seremides, apparently unconcerned, squinting his eyes against the rain. He returned his sword to its concealed sheath.

"But I do not like the darkness, the sea, the rain," said Vas of Anango.

"Rejoice," said Seremides. "It obscures vision, it impedes pursuit."

Somewhere behind, I supposed, the handicapped canal boat of Decius of Venna struggled in our wake. I wondered if it had stopped to take aboard the men in the water, the crew of the boat which had sought to block our passage through the Southern Gate. That would cost time, but would gain him men who might later prove to be sorely needed. Too, I was sure that, by now, boats from Port Kar, and perhaps even vessels from the arsenal harbor, would have passed the Southern Gate, intent upon our apprehension.

"You are shivering," said Seremides.

I could not control the trembling of my body. I was cold and drenched. I could hardly see for the rain. My hair was about my eyes, disheveled and sopped; rain ran down my cheeks, and over my face and gag. The thongs which bound my wrists and ankles were soaked. The canal boat was not only tormented by the rain and spray, but, from the splash of the waves, had shipped water. As I knelt my knees were in water.

"I will take the tiller," said Seremides. "You, wretch of Anango, put her under the canopy with the cousin of great Lurius and the tunicked slave, Euphrosyne."

"Surely," said Vas of Anango, with mock skepticism, "you do not wish slaves to share the shelter of a cousin of great Lurius of Jad."

"Do not concern yourself," said Seremides. "As you noted earlier, the noble cousin of great Lurius is in a collar."

"Ah," I thought, "on this world men put us in collars, as it pleases them to do so. They put us in collars for they like us that way. We have nothing to say about it. They seize us, and put us in collars which we cannot remove. Does this not tell us what we are? We must wear them, for masters will have it so. They put us in collars, where we belong. We are then in our place, at their feet. We are thrilled then, owned, rightless, helpless, subject to their whips. We are obedient, content, fulfilled, and happy, and hope for their caress. If they are not men, how can we be women? If they are not master, how can we be slave?"

Seremides pulled himself to the tiller. "Under the closure of the canopy," he said, "there are blankets. See that she is covered, and warmed."

"Solicitation," asked Vas of Anango, "for a slave?"

"As for a sleen or kaiila," said Seremides.

I doubted that the canopy would afford much relief from the elements. Its drenched sides were shaking and snapping in the wind, and water must have seeped under its curtains. Nonetheless, I would be grateful for any attention. I would be particularly grateful for a blanket, even if, as was likely, it would be damp.

Vas of Anango lifted me, carried me, unsteadily, almost losing his balance, to the canopy, and deposited me within its folds.
Talena, free of bonds, covered in a blanket, was sitting to one side,
her knees drawn up under her chin, her arms about her knees.
Euphrosyne, bound hand and foot, and gagged, covered, half
lay to my right. Vas of Anango put a blanket about me, rudely,
roughly, and withdrew through the rain-pelted curtains. I lay on
my side, on the thick, flat mat which floored the canopied area.
Talena did not speak to me, and Euphrosyne, misery in her eyes,
looked away. I, too, though grateful for the warmth of the blanket
and the shelter of the canopied area, was, as was Euphrosyne,
miserable. I was desolate with fear and grief. I was to be carried to
far-off Cos, to be a woman's slave, the slave of proud Talena, once
a Ubara, whom we had had the foolish temerity, unwitting as it
was, to treat as an equal in Port Kar. How terrified are slaves of free
women! How they hate us! How it pleases them to make us suffer!
What would be done with us? I was aware of the storm, the pour-
ing of rain, and the shaking of the curtains of the canopied area.

Twice I heard Seremides call, "Pause, wait, be ready, lads, now,
now stroke," when, I suppose, the rhythm of the oars had begun
to lapse from some desiderated regularity.

I heard Seremides once inquire as to pursuit.

"None that I can see," called Vas of Anango.

"Watch for the pier lantern of the Skerry of Lars," said Seremides.

I think I then, helpless in my bonds, exhausted, forlorn, and
frightened, racked with fatigue, fell asleep.

I awakened to a cheer, and, half an Ahn later, our canal boat
scraped against wood.

I heard oars being brought inboard, and several oarsmen clambered ashore. Lines were being fastened to mooring cleats.

"The Skerry of Lars," said Talena.

Outside, and above, presumably on the pier, I heard Seremides
say, presumably to a confederate who had been awaiting our arrival, "Raise a blue lantern and a yellow lantern, on the pier pole."

The wind and storm had abated. It was cool and cloudy, but
calm.

"I see no pursuit," said Vas of Anango.

"It will come," said Seremides.

"Are we not to be met?" said Vas of Anango.

"We are met," said Seremides.

"I see no ship," said Vas of Anango.

"It is there," said Seremides. "Green, difficult to detect, low in the water, long-oared, swift, two masts down, to be raised and mounted, if the wind for Cos be fair."

"The lanterns, one blue, one yellow, ascend the pier pole," said a man.

"I see no ship," reiterated Vas of Anango.

"They have a glass of the Builders," said Seremides. "The lanterns will be easily noted. Even now oars are outboard and enter the water."

"I hear no beat of the *keuleustes*," said Vas of Anango.

"She approaches," said Seremides, "as silent as the sea sleen."

"Should not your lads be rewarded?" asked a voice, that which I had taken as that of a confederate of Seremides. "I have arranged free paga at one of the taverns here."

"I have no objection," said Seremides. "Go lads, drink now, if you will, and return soon. In the meantime, I will draw your pay, that waiting for you at the Coin House, good pay, a gold stater of Brundisium for each."

I heard the men leaving the pier.

"Are you not going along?" asked Seremides.

"I think not," said Vas of Anango. "The paga will be drugged."

"Of course," said Seremides. "But each will awaken with a gold stater of Brundisium in his wallet."

"Why waste the gold?" said Vas of Anango.

"I was once of Ar, even captain of the Taurentian guard," said Seremides.

"And you might meet one of these men again, somewhere, on one day or another, at one Ahn or another," said Vas of Anango.

"Scan the sea," said Seremides. "Look to the horizon, whence we came."

"Ho!" said a voice, that of he whom I took to be a confederate of Seremides, who had been waiting on the Skerry of Lars. "A ship approaches, from the west. It is unmarked. It flies no flag or pennons."

"It is a knife ship of Cos," said Seremides, "built for reconnaissance and speed."

"It turns," said the man. "It remains away."

"Wise, wary captain," said Seremides. "It will lower a longboat."

Almost at the same time, Vas of Anango called out, "Boats! Canal boats! Six! Others, I think, behind them. I can see them! Many! Far off! They approach!"

I heard the crutch of Seremides strike on the pier, four times, as he must have changed his position to reconnoiter.

"The near ship lowers a longboat!" called the confederate of Seremides.

"Excellent," said Seremides. "We have ten Ehn, at least."

"Worthy officer, noble Seremides," called Talena, putting aside her blanket and parting the curtains of the canopied area.

"Glorious, revered Ubara," intoned Seremides.

"Give me a knife," she said. "I wish to teach these sorry personal slaves, both of whom I have found displeasing, that it is not a light thing to displease their mistress."

"A knife, Ubara?" said Seremides.

"I have a score to settle with these worthless sluts," she said. "Both esteemed me too little in the Golden Chain. Each dared to think themselves my equal."

"Officious, pretentious she-tarsks, indeed," said Seremides. "But is not owning them enough?"

"No," said Talena.

"Would not a sound lashing be sufficient, to inform them of their foolish error?"

"The knife," she said. "A lashing might be forgotten. I want something they will not forget, something they will remember every time they look in the mirror."

"What are you going to do?" asked Seremides. "Scar them, to lower their value?"

"I am not satisfied so easily," said Talena.

"Ah!" said Seremides, "you will cut off the ears and nose of each, a punishment worthy of a free woman of high caste."

Vas of Anango uttered a harsh laugh.

Euphrosyne and I recoiled in horror and struggled, but could not free ourselves.

Seremides bent down and handed his belt knife, handle first, to Talena, who then withdrew into the canopied area, and closed the curtains.

"Kneel up, worthless sluts," she said, and dragged us up, with her left hand, one at a time, by the hair, to our knees.

We were then, terrified, gagged, bound hand and foot, helpless, our scalps wild with pain, kneeling before her, she, too, on her knees before us, in the low canopied area.

"The longboat approaches!" called the confederate of Seremides.

"So, too, the boats from Port Kar," said Vas of Anango.

"We have at least five Ehn," said Seremides. "The men from Port Kar are unaware of the longboat. There is time."

Talena, kneeling, held the knife.

"I am less than fully pleased with you," she said.

We could not speak. We shook our heads, desperately, negatively. As we could, we pleaded for mercy. Tears ran down our cheeks.

She lifted the knife.

CHAPTER FORTY-FOUR

What Use Talena Made of the Knife of Seremides

"Do you really think I would keep slaves such as you, mere she-tarsks?" asked Talena.

We looked at her, stunned.

"I do not understand how either of you were accepted as paga girls at the Golden Chain," she said.

I think neither of us could have spoken, even if we had not been gagged.

"And you are both so stupid," she said. "Sometimes I could not sleep for Euphrosyne crying out the name of Florian in her sleep, begging for his touch. Were you so afraid, Euphrosyne, of your need of a master that you treated him dismissively, so haughtily, with coolness and rudeness? Did you know that he wanted to buy you, to own you and punish you, but Ho-Tosk, seeing his infatuation, is holding out for a higher price? How do you think you would fare then, in a leash at his feet? And you, Zia, an ignorant barbarian, untutored and illiterate. Were you to dance, you would be whipped from the floor. You cannot play the *kalika*. You are bereft of songs. What is to be said for you other than the fact that you, like Euphrosyne, look well in a collar, and obviously belong in one?"

Euphrosyne and I, astonished, exchanged mystified glances.

"Men from Port Kar will soon be here," said Talena, "perhaps within Ehn, and I, before their arrival, will be embarked in a Cosian longboat, to be freed and honored in Cos, the guest of noble Lurius of Jad, my former ally and now my benefactor. At last I shall be safe, and occupy a rightful high station. You two, of course, as is proper, will remain what you are, worthless, meaningless slaves. Now I shall sever your bonds, and cut away your

gags. Give no sign of this, lest the men on the pier suspect my action. When the opportunity presents itself, flee onto the Skerry of
Lars. Seremides is a cripple and he cannot catch you. The others
will have no time to pursue you. Time is short. The men of Port
Kar are near. The rendezvous must be kept. When I am finished,
be silent and wait your chance to run."

Talena then, with the knife, which was exquisitely sharp, freed
us, even of our gags, and we crouched in the canopied area, waiting, frightened, shocked, trying to understand what had occurred.

CHAPTER FORTY-FIVE

What Occurred on the Skerry of Lars

"Men gather, curiously," said the confederate of Seremides, uneasily, "attendants, employees of the Skerry, itinerant licensed swordsmen."

"Go back," shouted Vas of Anango. "Nothing here concerns you."

"We must depart, glorious Ubara," called Seremides. "Come forth, with your punished slaves, to the longboat."

"Leave them here," said Vas of Anango. "Who would want them now, without noses, without ears? Next she will have their heads shaved."

"They will do nicely as a woman's slaves," said Seremides. "Their mutilation will serve as a warning to other women's slaves, encouraging them to be more diligent in their service. Too, so ugly, their appearance will pose no threat to the beauty of their mistress, and, by contrast, will even enhance it. Too, so ugly, they will not be attractive to men, always an inconvenience for a mistress. And, too, lastly, they will not suffer from the airs of a good-looking collar slut. They will have nothing to live for, but to humbly and lovingly serve their mistress."

"A moment!" called Talena, from within the canopied area. Then she turned to us, whispering. "I shall try to draw the men to the side," she whispered. "Part the curtains in the rear of the canopied area. When I give the signal, flee."

"Noble passenger," said Seremides, earnestly.

"I am coming," said Talena.

We watched Talena exit the canopied area. We crept to the back of the area. I held one fold of the curtains there, and Euphrosyne the other. We were tense, ready to leap forth, and spring to the pier.

"How shall I clean this knife?" asked Talena.

"Clean it later," said Vas of Anango.

I gather she must have held the knife in such a way that it could not be well seen.

"No," said Talena. "It is soiled with the blood of slaves. It must be cleaned now."

"I shall wipe it clean on your hair!" cried Vas of Anango, and he must have rushed to her side.

"Hurry!" wailed the confederate of Seremides.

"There is no blood on this knife!" cried Vas of Anango.

"Run, run!" screamed Talena.

Euphrosyne and I, as one, leapt through the rear curtains of the canopied area, were amongst the stern thwarts of the boat, and scrambled over the rail, and onto the pier. I heard Vas of Anango cry out with rage. Talena's stratagem had well drawn him and the confederate of Seremides to the side. But, *ela*, no way was open before us! We had scarcely sped three or four mad, wild, desperate yards when we were intercepted by the gathered men, seized by the arms, and faced back, toward the moored boat. I struggled futilely. How well reminded I was then of the difference between my slightness and its dramatic contrast with the size and strength of men. Sometimes Gorean males, in the absence of Gorean free women, speak of the Master Sex and the Slave Sex. When one is in a collar and on one's knees one well understands this. Perhaps free women understand it as well. Nature had decided long ago which was to be the Master Sex and which was to be the Slave Sex. Should the master not be a master and the slave a slave? How can one be fulfilled, if one cannot fulfill one's nature?

"Hold them!" called Vas of Anango. "I will cut their throats."

"There is no time!" cried the confederate of Seremides. "See the horizon! Ships approach, rowed with earnest purpose! A dozen craft will land within Ehn! The longboat will pull away!"

Vas of Anango growled with fury, but, wavering, uncertain, did not approach us more closely.

"This one," said a man, he who held Euphrosyne, "wears the collar of the Golden Chain."

"I, too!" I cried.

"We are stolen!" cried Euphrosyne. "Return us to our master!"

"Yes," I cried, "Ho-Tosk, of Port Kar!"

"I know him," said a man.

"Save us from thieves!" cried Euphrosyne.

"Please, Masters," I cried.

"They are ours, duly purchased," snarled Vas of Anango.

"An inquiry will be made," said one in the crowd.

"It seems you can afford bells, but not a tunic," called a man from the crowd.

I had been belled from the night of the celebration, before the attack on the holding of Bosk of Port Kar. I had not been tunicked since my caging on the same night, and had been commanded forth, as I was, unclothed, from my cage early this morning by a red-scarfed intruder. It is not unusual to keep a captive slave stripped. Indeed, captive free women are likely, as well, to soon find themselves fully bared. Due to the danger of inadvertently encountering concealed poisoned pins or knives, they are usually stripped by the sword or knife, or ordered to tear away their own clothing and place themselves naked in a posture of submission before their captor. Commonly this act is performed in something of a frenzy for the unfortunate captive is given very little time in which to accomplish this act, the time being determined by a tiny sand glass or the captor's measured counting. This helps her to understand that a command is to be obeyed immediately and unquestioningly. This stripping of the free women, however it may be accomplished, helps them to better understand their imminent fate, that they will soon be marked and collared. As a slave, I had very little sympathy for free women. I was pleased to think of them, once so haughty, so lofty and arrogant, now on their knees, stripped and collared, subject to the switch or whip. How their life is changed! Will they be given permission to speak? Will they be given a rag to wear? Will they be fed? When they were free, did they ever anticipate that they would one day crawl to a master, a switch in their teeth? They soon learn, as we all do, to throw their legs apart at a snapping of fingers.

"Come away," said the confederate of Seremides to Vas of Anango.

"You did not mutilate the slaves," said Seremides to Talena.

"No," said Talena.

"Ubara," said Seremides, in awe.

She returned his knife to him, and he returned it to its sheath.

"Haste!" said the confederate of Seremides. "Pursuers will dock momentarily!"

From where I was held, I could see several of the boats from Port Kar. The longboat from the Cosian ship was across the skerry.

I did not think it could be seen by the approaching pursuers. I did not doubt but what it would make its departure, laden or not, shortly before or after the pursuers had reached the pier.

"Hurry, Ubara," said Seremides to Talena.

"Hold!" said Vas of Anango.

Seremides turned about.

"My fee," said Vas of Anango.

"You were paid," said Seremides. "This morning, the morning of the action, as was agreed, two gold staters of Brundisium."

From this I gathered that Vas of Anango was somehow preeminent amongst the others. Perhaps he had assisted in their recruitment.

Surprise coursed amongst the men present. I knew little of Gorean coinage, but, from the reaction, I gathered that the gold stater of Brundisium was a coin of considerable value.

"I raise my fee," said Vas of Anango.

"Very well," said Seremides, with an anxious glance to the sea. "A third stater."

"The slave," said Vas of Anango, drawing his sword.

"Approach," said Seremides.

"I am content where I am," said Vas of Anango. "I do not care to step within the compass of your blade."

"Have you gone mad?" said Seremides. "Look to the sea!"

I could now hear men in the approaching boats, shouting to the shore. Men were crowded in the bows. The note of a guards-man's canal trumpet carried across the water to the pier.

"Noble Vas," cried the confederate of Seremides, hurrying to Vas of Anango. "Reconsider, I beg of you!"

"Do not touch me," said Vas of Anango. Then he addressed himself once more to Seremides. "I shall deliver the slave to Cos," he said. "You have delegated me in to act in your place. Who shall gainsay that? What are two or three gold staters, even of Brundisium, compared to the wealth I suspect you seek, for which you risk so much, for which you strive and gamble?"

"Great lady," said Seremides to Talena, "to the longboat! Now!"

"Surely not, Captain," said Talena. "It is you, not he, who have done all this to save me."

"To the longboat, noble lady," said Seremides, "hasten, hurry to safety, security, honor, privilege, and station!"

Talena hesitated, looking from the longboat to Seremides, to Vas of Anango, to the crowd, to the nearing boats, but yards from docking.

"Now, worthless slave!" screamed Seremides. "Are you un-aware you are tunicked? Are you unaware of the declamatory mark characterizing your thigh, informing the world of what you are, a purchasable beast? Are you unaware of the collar on your neck, that you are a mere property? Run, to the longboat, now, lest, as you deserve, you be publicly stripped and lashed!"

"Hold, slave!" said Vas of Anango. "We are not done here!"

Talena wavered, sobbing, distraught.

"Let her go!" cried Seremides.

"Cast your crutch aside," demanded Vas of Anango, "and your knife and sword."

"Do not do so, noble friend," begged Talena.

Angrily Seremides slid the crutch to the side, fell heavily to the planks of the pier, and shoved his knife and sword out of reach.

"Now, run!" commanded Seremides.

"Yes, run, slave," laughed Vas of Anango.

Talena, weeping, hurried toward the waiting longboat.

"You have won," said Seremides. "Hasten, be off!"

But Vas of Anango did not move.

"Go!" cried the confederate of Seremides.

"I was humiliated in the contests," said Vas of Anango. "I was publicly shamed."

"You have taken fee," said the confederate of Seremides.

"As is my right," said Vas of Anango.

"Honor!" said the confederate of Seremides.

"Do you think I would leave such an enemy behind me?" asked Vas of Anango.

"I see," said Seremides.

"Last blood," said Vas of Anango.

"Be quick," said Seremides.

"Do not!" cried the confederate of Seremides, clutching at the arm of Vas of Anango. But Vas of Anango angrily shook himself free, turned, and thrust his weapon into the heart of the con-federate of Seremides. Men cried out in protest. "He sought to interfere," said Vas of Anango. He laughed then, and turned back to Seremides. But a figure had interposed itself between Vas of Anango and Seremides.

"I seek to interfere," said the figure.

"Get out of the way," said Vas of Anango.

"See," said Seremides to the figure, "that your blade touches his no more than three times."

"Get out of the way!" screamed Vas of Anango.

"Last blood," said the figure, quietly.

Vas of Anango, in fury, lunged forward.

I did not hear a single interaction of steel, but saw Vas of Anango crumple to the pier.

The figure which had interposed itself between Seremides and Vas of Anango wiped its blade on the tunic of Vas of Anango, and then sheathed its sword.

"Excellent," said Seremides.

"Master," it said.

At the same moment I heard shouting, and a note from a guardsman's trumpet, and two or three boats sliding against the pier, and saw men scrambling out of them, variously armed. I caught sight of Decius of Venna, emerging from one boat, followed by men, and Addison Steele, from another, with Florian, of the holding of Bosk of Port Kar, and Miles, too, of that holding. And other boats were docking.

The figure which had interposed itself between Seremides and Vas of Anango spoke sharply, authoritatively. "Those of the red company," he said, "screen us." He then, gently, almost tenderly, lifted the body of Seremides in his arms and began to walk toward the pier at which the longboat yet lingered. I saw nothing further then because men of the "red company," one of the companies of itinerant, licensed swordsmen currently competing at the Skerry of Lars, rushed forward to greet the newcomers.

Men crowded together, pushing and shoving, smiling, grinning, holding to one another, buffeting one another. "Welcome!" I heard. "What occurs?" "What do you seek?" "Let us tell you what we have seen!" Mightily must the newcomers have been frustrated. I heard Florian cry out, "Where is the slave, Adraste. We seek the slave, a stolen slave, Adraste, Adraste!" An Ehn or two later I saw again the figure, now returned, which had interposed itself between Vas of Anango and Seremides. It was the young swordsman, Alan, of the red company, he of the unusual hair, so red with the incongruous slash of blonde, he of remarkable blade skills, who had been called to my attention by Seremides weeks ago. The newcomers, freeing themselves of the attentions of the crowd, began to search the buildings, housings, domiciles, emporiums, and barracks of the Skerry of Lars. I saw no sign of the crutch or weapons of Seremides. I did not know what had become of them. It was explained to those to whom it might be of interest that Vas of Anango had murdered a man, and that a member of the red company, attacked, had defended himself and slain the murderer. The purse of Vas of Anango was cut loose from his belt and given to the young swordsman, who refused it, on the grounds that its contents had not been well won, having been tainted with dishonor. The coins were later distributed amongst the lower workers of the Skerry of Lars. "But," said Alan, to a fellow of his company, "I do have a gold stater of Brundisium." He then displayed the coin. "Where did you get it?" he was asked. "It was given to me," he said. "It will pay my way to Ar." When the pier was less crowded, many of the men dispersing, some arm in arm with the newcomers, to the skerry's taverns, I looked to the far pier. There was then no sign of either a longboat or the waiting, low-in-the-water, easily unremarked galley which had been visible earlier. I also noted that the blue and yellow lanterns had been removed from the signal pole of the skerry. Shortly after the arrival of the contingents from Port Kar, Euphrosyne and I had been released. We then knelt in place, on the pier, where we had been released, waiting to be claimed. "Tell me of the wind," said a man. "It is a fine, fair wind," said another. "And how does it blow?" asked the first man. "To the west," he was told. "Then it seeks the shores of Cos," said the first man. "Yes," said the second.

CHAPTER FORTY-SIX

Paga Grows Short;
The Arrangement of Distractions;
I am Conducted from the Tavern

Restless, loud, and rowdy were the patrons of the Golden Chain. Goblets were struck on the low tables. Men shouted. Tables had been overturned. Four mariners had been ejected into the street.

"Hear the patrons," said Ho-Tosk. "Things grow ugly."

I hurried past him, a goblet in hand, anxious, the paga swirling. I was barefoot and briefly tunicked, as is common with a paga girl. Happily I no longer wore the three rows of tiny, clanking bells, suitable for a tarsk or verr, which had been placed upon me by order of Florian, supposedly to make it easier to keep track of me, days ago, in the holding of Bosk of Port Kar. They had been, in effect, of course, more than anything, punishment bells, put on me for the amusement of masters, to punish me for my curiosity, a trait which was, as is well-known, despite its ubiquity, allegedly unbecoming to a *kajira*. How eager we are to understand and know! How cruel are the masters to keep so much from us! How amused they are to treat us as the mere slaves we are! We are nothing, only *kajirae*, owned objects, kept for their service and pleasure. Would one discuss plans with tarsks? Would one wish to keep kaiila or verr informed of what is to be done with them? How helpless one is as a slave!

"Paga, paga!" called a man.

Euphrosyne hurried to him.

It was ten days since the repelled attack on the holding of Bosk of Port Kar, who was apparently still at sea, supposedly in the

vicinity of the Farther Islands, intent on investigating depreda-
tion and carnage wrought in his name. But, for all I knew, he was
himself a pirate and marauder. Might it not be clever to pose as
one's own imposter, to rob and burn, pretending to be one's own
self? How cunning to seize loot for oneself and meanwhile feign
outrage over the supposed exploits of a masquerading other!

I knelt and served paga to a table, lowering my head and extending my arms.

It was late in the low-ceilinged, lamp-hung hall of the Golden
Chain.

It was crowded, as was often the case toward the end of a week
or the end of a passage hand, that having to do with the paying of
wages. There are twelve months in the Gorean calendar, each consisting of five five-day weeks, each followed by a five-day passage
hand. The only exception is the five-day "Waiting Hand" which
follows the Twelfth Passage Hand, and precedes the first day of
the month of En'Kara, or En'Kara-La-Torvis, which is the vernal
equinox, the first day of the Gorean New Year. In addition, a con-
voy of merchant ships, the grain fleet, five ships from Brundisium,
guarded by three longships, were moored in the arsenal harbor.

"Away," said a fellow, with a gesture of his goblet, he sitting
cross-legged, at the table, much engaged in conversation.

I rose up, and returned to the vicinity of the Vat Master.

My tunic was torn at the left hip, the result of a patron's
drunken grasp.

No one had recently bound my hands behind my back and
sent me to an alcove, to await his pleasure. The alcoves were currently in use, each belted shut from the inside. Gorean males do
not hasten with their pleasure. A private master will often devote
several Ahn to his slave. After all, she is his to do with as he
pleases, and he owns her. Sometimes a day and a night are spent
in this fashion. Commonly a morning, an afternoon, or an evening
is devoted to such a pastime. The Gorean master does not hurry.
The slave, when not bound, chained, writhing, or such, serves
him, cooks for him, and brings him food and drink. Often she
must pose and dance, frequently naked. How lovely she is! How
exciting she is! How desirable she is! How proud he is to own such
a possession! What male would not care to own such a property?
Occasionally, brought mercilessly to the delicate, tense brink of
a wild, cataclysmic, global yielding, the slave orgasm, unknown
to free women, concerned with their integrity and personhood,

she must wait, and beg her master's permission to yield, which situation can be fiercely, painfully, keenly frustrating, particularly when the slightest touch of a finger or tongue will set off the explosive charge which makes clear and confirms her unmistakable bondage. How well she then understands herself a slave, and how precious is the release when granted! But, mercifully, such torment is rare. Commonly, as her body is played upon, as a musical instrument, she is brought to successions of crescendos of ecstasy. Several times, as the master pleases, she may be forced to endure such inordinate, unspeakable pleasures. Do not feel sorry for her. She is not a free woman. She has nothing to say about it; she is a slave. The alcoves were occupied. My belly was restless.

"We are busy tonight," I said to the Vat Master.

"Your tunic is torn," he said.

"Yes, Master," I said.

After the business on the Skerry of Lars, Euphrosyne and I were returned to the Golden Chain.

For some reason we had both been fitted with new collars. They were both typical, common collars, flat, light, comfortable, closely fitting, and locked. How lovely are Gorean collars. How well they look on us. I wondered if free women envied us our collars. Also, of course, they are extremely efficient custodial devices. A girl could not even think of slipping one. I had learned that my first day on Gor. They are on us.

In the taverns, paga girls hear much. This cannot well be helped. Masters may not care for this, but facts, allusions, loose talk, rumors, and such, abound amongst the tables. As a consequence, I suspect that in most cities, the average paga girl is likely to be more informed, or misinformed, than the average citizen. The attacking force which had beset the holding of Bosk of Port Kar had withdrawn, largely unimpeded, into the delta. To be sure, it was not clear how it would fare in those trackless marshes or at the hands of territorial Rencers. It had doubtless purchased its way to Port Kar. Whether or not it might manage the same in a retreat to the Vosk was not clear. The Delta Gate, I heard, had been repaired. Nothing more had been heard, to date, of the metal monster rumored to frequent the marshes. Decius of Venna, and his men, undetained, had left Port Kar. They, interestingly, in the same way as hundreds of others, had naturally been taken as volunteers in the effort to recover a stolen slave named Adraste. Apparently it was not understood, at least generally, that he himself

had wished to obtain the slave, whoever she might be, and whatever worth she might have, for himself. It was generally accepted
that the slave, Adraste, had been carried away. Her importance, if
importance she truly had, was not generally understood. It was
accepted that she did have some interest to those of the holding of
Bosk of Port Kar. Little, if anything, was known, at least by most,
of a cripple named Seremides. It seemed few, certainly amongst
the newcomers, had noted the departure of a longboat from one of
the piers of the Skerry of Lars, and fewer yet had noted what may
have been its mother ship, a quiet, soft-oared ship, masts down,
soon moving westward.

"I do not like it," said Ho-Tosk. "The alcoves are filled. Tem-
pers flare. Paga grows short. Mariners, long at sea, are ashore. They
are hungry for food, drink, and slaves. The tables are crowded.
Men press at the threshold. Where shall we seat them? Dare we
turn them away? They do not share our Home Stone. They may be
reckless, careless. What will they do?"

"Send them to the Silken Rope," said one of his men.

"Many at the gate," said Ho-Tosk, "have been turned away by
the Silken Rope."

"Paga, paga!" called a fellow from across the room.

"There," said the Vat Master, pointing to the fellow, and he
then dipped a goblet into the paga, lifted it, dripping, and thrust
it into my hands. "Thread your way amongst the tables," he said.
"Be quick. And do not spill a drop or you, barbarian slut, will be
lashed across the back of the thighs."

"Yes, Master," I said.

Shortly thereafter I returned to the Vat Master.

A moment later, Daphne, shaken and red-eyed, her tunic
half torn away, threw herself to her knees before the Vat Master
and kissed his feet. "Master," she wept, "permit me to withdraw
through the beaded curtain!"

"You are half-naked," he said.

I gave no sign of any reaction, but I found his remark piquant.
Even in an intact slave tunic, is a woman not already half naked?
Is it not the point of a slave tunic to leave little doubt as to the
charms of its occupant?

"I was put on my belly, on the table!" she said.

"Did he pay his coin?" asked the Vat Master.

"Yes, Master," said Daphne.

"No matter then," said the Vat Master.

"What transpires?" asked Ho-Tosk.

"This is the third one this evening," said the Vat Master.

"We cannot have this," said Ho-Tosk.

"The alcoves are occupied," said the Vat Master.

"Still," said Ho-Tosk. Then, looking about, he turned away.

"Master," pleaded Daphne.

"Very well," said the Vat Master. "Withdraw, but return anon, freshened and retunicked. If you are not back within ten Ehn you will be fetched and whipped."

Daphne leapt up and disappeared through the thick, dangling, colorfully beaded curtain.

There was a woman's cry of distress from somewhere in the semidarkness.

"There is another one," said the Vat Master. "And the paga grows short."

Off to one side two fellows were scuffling.

"Should guardsmen not be summoned?" I asked.

"They are busied in the streets," he said.

When I had been returned to the cages of the Golden Chain from the Skerry of Lars, I had, of course, recalled the beautiful slave, Dorna, once, in her freedom, called Dorna the Proud, once the highest of Silver Masks in Tharna, second only to the Golden Mask, Lara. It was my understanding that she had been remanded to the Golden Chain, not only to be treated as the slave she was, but to serve as bait for the capture of Pa-Kur, master of the Assassins. However, I did not encounter her. She was not on the premises. It seems that no effort had been made, either to silence her, or to acquire her, which might have led to the capture of Pa-Kur. Upon reflection, this did not surprise me. She had, although unwittingly, played her part well, misleading Florian and others as to the timing of the assault on the holding of Bosk of Port Kar. Too, what secret knowledge, or such, could she have now that would be relevant to the designs of Pa-Kur? Was she not now worthless to him, save perhaps as collar meat? Surely, in any market, he could buy *kajirae* who might do quite as well as Dorna, squirming, moaning, whimpering, thrashing, gasping, and panting in his arms. Why should he risk himself or an agent in her acquisition? Surely, as astute as he was, he would suspect a trap. And he could always wait and, if he wished, pick her up later. Too, I suspected he had other things on his mind after the unsuccessful assault on the holding of Bosk of Port Kar. Indeed, had he managed to escape the marshes alive? In any event, Dorna was no longer the property of the Golden Chain. I did not know what had become of her. I had heard that she was purchased, loaded with chains, and taken away. We must expect such things. We are slaves. Incidentally, I understand that masks, whether of silver or gold, are no longer permitted in Tharna.

There was a stir amongst the tables, and I noted that an alcove had opened up. A taverner's man called out a number and a fellow raised his hand, clutching an ostracon. In this way, as honor was implicitly involved, contention was eliminated.

I wished more alcoves were free. I wished Addison Steele was present. I knew he held me in contempt. Yet might he not want me? Might he not thong my hands behind me and command me to an alcove, where I would kneel, head down, bound, awaiting him? I knew that every bit of me was his. Even from Earth and the cocktail party I had sensed that I belonged naked at his feet! How I had fought this, I, such a stupid, foolish, willful, wayward girl! How could I admit that I was a slave, and his slave! How deep was biology, and the secret of my being! How alien this was to all that I had been taught! I tried to resist, on Earth, and even on Gor! But I could not do so. I wanted his collar on my neck! How I had tried to hate him, and despise him! But I loved him, wholly, helplessly, hopelessly. I knew I was worthless, an illiterate barbarian slave girl. How rightfully he would look down upon me, I, who had been so vain, shallow, petty, and pretentious on Earth. What could I be good for, but to be slave? I trembled in his presence. Before him I could hardly stand. Before him I was weak. I wanted his domination. I wanted to kneel before him, and look up at him, adoringly, and beg to press my lips submissively and gratefully to his whip. He was the master of my heart and belly. How far he was above me, he a free man and I only a slave! Yet I would not have wished to be a free woman. That would have been too little for me. I wanted to love him a thousand times more than could a free woman. I wanted to love him with the selfless, marvelous, abject, wonderous love of a slave. *Ela*, I was not even a high slave, only a cheap, common girl, easily affordable, purchasable even by men of modest means. I knew I was nothing to him. But I loved him with every particle of my owned, marked, and collared body, with every particle of my heart and belly.

"Ho-Tosk," called the Vat Master, anxiously.

The proprietor, distracted and concerned, was soon at his side.

"Look," said the Vat Master, pressing a goblet down in the vat. The paga scarcely covered the base of the goblet.

"I have sent word to the warehouse," said Ho-Tosk. "I did not anticipate this early shoring of the ships from Brundisium."

"Nor did others," said the Vat Master.

"We cannot command the winds and the waves," said Ho-Tosk. He then, with a hurried gesture, summoned one of his men, one with the jangling coin box at his belt. "Paga grows short," he said. "More is ordered. Men must be entertained. We must give them something to think of other than empty goblets."

"We do not want the tavern dismantled," said the Vat Master.

I could understand his concern. He, aside from a few slaves who would doubtless be cuffed or slapped about, would be the likely focus of a rapidly rising, widely spread disgruntlement.

"I will summon musicians," said the taverner's man.

"And will they play to an empty floor?" asked the Vat Master.

"That is true," said Ho-Tosk. "Our patrons, frustrated enough already, will not be likely to tolerate that."

"Shall I summon the musicians?" asked the taverner's man.

"Yes," said Ho-Tosk.

The fellow then disappeared through the beaded curtain.

"And who is to be put upon the floor?" asked the Vat Master. "What should we do for dancers? Adraste is gone. Ianthe is indisposed, Aglaia has a sprained ankle. Who else would you dare risk before such a crowd?"

Sensing the urgency of the matter, another taverner's man had joined the group, he who had chained and hooded me long ago, for my interview with a stranger, in the matter of the alleged Luta, supposedly the former Lady Julia Leta, of Ar, the stranger who had later turned out to be Florian.

"You need a dancer," said the fellow who had recently joined the group.

"There is none," said Ho-Tosk.

"You had a dancer on your want list, recently submitted to Samos, First Slaver," said he who had recently joined the group. "Is she not caged below, even now?"

"She has not been delivered," said Ho-Tosk, despairingly.

"One of the finest dancers in Port Kar," said he who had recently joined the group, "is Sandra, a slave of Bosk of Port Kar, housed in his holding."

"Send for her," said Ho-Tosk. "We have good relations with the holding of Bosk of Port Kar."

The fellow then hurried away.

"He will not return in time," said the Vat Master.

"We are lost," said Ho-Tosk. "Let us hope the tavern is not set afire."

Another alcove opened up, and a taverner's man, he governing the ostraca, called out a number, and another fellow, clutching an ostracon, rushed forward, losing no time in delivering it to the taverner's man. "You!" he cried, looking about, to a passing, startled slave, "come here!" In a moment he had tied her hands behind her back. He then pointed to the now-opened alcove. "There!" he said. The slave hurried to the alcove and knelt within it, head down. We could see her silhouetted outline, delineated by means of the tiny tharlarion-oil lamp beyond her. In a moment he had joined her, drawing shut the leather curtains behind him.

"Paga, paga!" called two other men.

"May it be the will of Priest-Kings that the paga speeds to our door," said the Vat Master.

"There may be hope yet," said Ho-Tosk.

The musicians arrived and took their places at the side of the dancing floor. There was a *czehar* player, two flutists, and a drummer, with the small *tabor*. They were followed by the taverner's man who had gone to fetch them. "There are no dancers," said the *czehar* player, who was the leader of the small group. "Ianthe and Aglaia are unavailable."

"One has been sent for," said Ho-Tosk, "from the holding of Bosk."

"Let us withdraw," said the leader of the group.

"Play something," said Ho-Tosk.

Daphne, freshly tunicked, then returned to the floor.

"Can you dance?" asked Ho-Tosk.

"No," said Daphne, hurrying away.

"She fears the whip," said the Vat Master.

Often, when a girl dances, unless her skills are familiar, recognized, and indisputable, a taverner's man, with a whip, is discreetly in the background. If he, or the patrons, a commonly discriminating and demanding audience, fond of the provocative subtleties and beauty of slave dance, are dissatisfied, he applies the admonitory, hissing leather to the slave. Under these circumstances it is clear that it is in the best interest of the slave to do her best, to be as pleasing as possible. She is, after all, a slave. In a sense, this sort of thing is typical of, and pervasive in, Gorean bondage. The slave, being a slave, and not a free woman, is subject to the whip. The average slave is seldom, if ever, whipped, for she is commonly zealous to be found pleasing, knowing well she will be whipped, if she is not. To be sure, an occasional stroke of the whip is an excellent reminder that she is not a free woman but a slave; and, indeed, she may even, upon occasion, beg for a stroke or two, that she be reassured of her servitude. It might be mentioned, in passing, that being marked and collared, being naked, or clad as a slave, obeying, needing permission to speak, kneeling, being subject to bonds, kissing the whip, being owned, and such, is incredibly arousing to a slave. Even performing small, domestic tasks can be arousing for a slave, for she knows she is owned. She is a special thing, a property, a possession. Bondage is not only her way of life, but her fulfillment. She would have it no other way. She is where she wants to be, at the feet of her master.

The musicians began to play.

Euphrosyne arrived at the vat, and looked with dismay into the vat. "I cannot return with half a goblet," she said.

"Paga!" called a man.

"Paga!" called another.

"They will beat me!" said Euphrosyne.

"Can you dance?" asked Ho-Tosk.

"No," said Euphrosyne.

"Here," said the Vat Master. "A quarter of a goblet of paga. We can do no better. On your way!"

"They will beat me," said Euphrosyne.

"Perhaps they will merely stretch you across the table, as they have done with others," said the Vat Master.

Whimpering, Euphrosyne took the goblet pressed into her hands, and sped back amongst the tables.

"What of Sucha, Tamira, and Fina?" asked Ho-Tosk.

"Not dancers," said the Vat Master.

"Several serve in the alcoves," said the fellow who had gone to fetch the musicians.

"None are dancers," said the Vat Master.

"We are lost, lost," said Ho-Tosk.

At that point a burly fellow, presumably of the Arsenal, for he wore a sawyer's brown and yellow smock, made his way to the paga vat. He held a paga goblet in his right hand, and his left hand was knotted in Euphrosyne's hair, her body bent down, her head held at his left hip, in leading position. "What is this?" he said, lifting the goblet. "The bottom of this goblet is scarcely damp."

"*Ela*," said Ho-Tosk. "It was a mere quarter cup. I am sorry. It could not be otherwise. The slave is not remiss. Behold."

The fellow stared groggily, only half comprehendingly, into the paga vat. "There is no paga left," he said, slowly, trying to grasp what doubtless seemed to him a most unexpected anomaly.

"Very little," said Ho-Tosk.

"Then you are truly short of paga?" said the man.

"Yes," said Ho-Tosk. "The girl spoke the truth. She is not so unwise as to be deceitful. It will not be necessary to lash her."

The fellow released his grip on Euphrosyne's hair, and she rushed about the vat, to station herself behind the Vat Master and the vat.

"There will be no charge, of course," said Ho-Tosk.

"Paga has been ordered," said the Vat Master. "It will doubtless arrive momentarily."

"Ho!" cried the sawyer. "Beware, brothers! The vat is drained! There is no paga! Who has made off with the paga? Where is it hiding now? Who is hiding it? We know, do we not? What price will they charge now? A silver tarsk for a cup? Search the tavern! Find it! Tear up the floors, pull apart the walls!"

Fortunately, the incoherent suggestions, the reeling, drunken importunings, the inflammatory proposals, of the belligerently tottering sawyer were not taken seriously, particularly as he almost immediately lapsed into unconsciousness and was carried to the side. On the other hand, his obstreperous, ranting analysis of the situation did serve to apprise the tables of a hitherto generally unrecognized problem, one which might soon prove acute, particularly as a number of patrons were on the point of beginning, or continuing, their evening, rather than prematurely terminating it.

"Be patient, noble friends," called Ho-Tosk, "dear sharers of a Home Stone, and esteemed guests of Port Kar; it is true we are a bit short of paga now, for which deprivation I accept all responsibility, but more is even now hurrying to our portal. Wait a moment, a moment. Shortly there will be a free round of paga for all!"

This information did much to calm the tables.

Some of the patrons, at four adjoining tables, then broke into a song extolling the great harbor of Brundisium. Almost simultaneously, local mariners and workers from the arsenal, not to be outdone, added to the ambiance by contributing a competitive medley of tavern songs. It was not long then until disputes arose having to do with the comparative merits of the ships and slave girls of Brundisium vis-a-vis those of Port Kar. This might have grown ugly, save one fellow insisted on the greater beauty of the slaves of distant Ar. He was struck unconscious, which seemed to satisfy both parties, those of Brundisium and those of Port Kar.

"Where is the paga?" asked the Vat Master of Ho-Tosk.

"Perhaps the scoundrels of the Silken Rope have waylaid the delivery," said Ho-Tosk. "They, too, must be crowded, and needful."

"I think we shall withdraw," said the *czehar* player.

"Stay where you are," said Ho-Tosk.

"I fear insurrection," said a taverner's man, he who had fetched the musicians. "If it were in the streets, we could nail boards across the portal."

"Perhaps," said the *czehar* player, "you should do so anyway, to keep it from reaching the streets."

The portal was now muchly open, for those who had crowded about seeking entrance, having learned of the dearth of paga, had, at least for the most part, departed, presumably intent on taking their custom elsewhere.

Doubtless this was disconcerting to Ho-Tosk.

At that point, Addison Steele, and Florian, of the holding of Bosk of Port Kar, in casual street tunics, appeared in the threshold.

Both seemed surprised, at least momentarily, by what they had come upon. The paga girls were not hurrying about amongst the tables, but gathered together, somewhat apprehensively, near the paga vat. Taverner's men, with coin boxes at their belt, were inactive, standing to one side. There was little bustling about, little laughter, no shouting, no busy, genial hum of conversation, no coming and going. Ho-Tosk was on the floor but not mingling with customers. One had the notion of something like a tense restraint at the tables. A fragile, unwilling, sullen acquiescence seemed pervasive. Might there not be an unseen tempest brewing? Matters seemed calm, like the stillness of a crouching sleen before it pounces.

Ho-Tosk, who seemed to recognize and know the two new guests, summoned them to his side, anxiously, but discreetly. He took Florian by the sleeve. "Where is Sandra?" he said.

"The dancer?" said Florian.

"Yes," said Ho-Tosk, "the property of noble Bosk, of the Council of Captains."

"I conjecture," said Florian, "she is in the holding, perhaps being put to slave use."

"You did not bring her with you?" said Ho-Tosk.

"No, should we have?" asked Florian.

"We know nothing of that," said Addison Steele.

"I sent for her," said Ho-Tosk.

"Then she is doubtless on her way," said Florian. "What did you want her for?"

"Paga is short," said Ho-Tosk. "I fear looming disruption, unmanageable unruliness. We want to entertain, pacify, and distract the clientele."

"Make the alcoves available, *gratis*," said Florian. "Who would not prefer a slave in one's arms to a goblet in one's hand?"

"See how crowded we are," said Ho-Tosk. "Not one alcove is free."

Florian looked across the wide, low-ceilinged, lamp-lit room.

"They are all belted shut," said Addison Steele.

"Every one," said Ho-Tosk, disconsolately.

"You have sent for additional paga?" said Florian.

"Certainly," said Ho-Tosk, somewhat shortly.

"Paga, paga!" said a fellow at one of the tables, striking his empty goblet on the table. This call was picked up at other tables, as well. And there were more impatient crackings of goblets on the small, square tables, about which men sat cross-legged.

"Where is Sandra?" asked Ho-Tosk.

"Doubtless someone is bringing her, even now," said Florian.

"Paga!" called another man. "Yes, paga, paga!" called another.

"You have slaves, unemployed, unused, unbusied, loitering shamefully about the paga vat," said Addison Steele.

"They are not dancers," said Ho-Tosk.

"No matter," said Addison Steele. "Put them on the floor. See which one is commended and applauded. See which one is disparaged and hooted. Let the whip master use his own judgment or be responsive to the mood of the crowd, or both. Let men take bets on whether this one or that one will be whipped, or how long before this one or that one is whipped. Wagering commands attention. Gambling reigns. When stakes are placed and the fate of coins is uncertain, who thinks of paga? Courage, noble Ho-Tosk. Dismiss unease and perplexity. Sought distraction, so coveted, is at hand. Safety, so fearfully sought, is before you. Rejoice, your floors, furniture, and walls are safe."

"Noble patrons," called out Ho-Tosk. "Paga will soon be here, but, in the interim, let us appeal to those of you with sporting blood, who do not fear to try your luck, who relish risk and hazard, who would not fear to bet a tarsk-bit, to win a copper tarsk."

Curiosity sprang up amongst the tables.

"Who amongst you," said Ho-Tosk, "is not a superb judge of the lineaments of slaves, the trimness of ankles, the curves of calves and thighs, the latitudes of bellies, the sweetness of bosoms, the softness of shoulders, the beauties of features, eyes, and hair, the excitingness of a lovely throat closely encircled with an owner's collar? I thought so! Yes, experts and authorities abound. We will put girls upon the floor, to writhe, pose, and dance for you. First, let them stand before you, one by one, being considered, while you make your bets; then, the bets made, they will perform. All are beautiful, of course, else they would not be at the Golden Chain, but none are skillful, trained dancers. Each, in her way, is inexperienced and ignorant. Pity the poor things, to be so challenged. Doubtless the whip will crack frequently. Will she be adequately pleasing to the crowd or not? Will the crowd be patient with her nor not? Will she be soon whipped from the floor, or later whipped from the floor, or will she finish her performance acceptably, or even to acclaim, her back, legs and arms untouched by the lash?"

"Begin, begin!" called more than one man.

"Put that one before us, first," said Florian, pointing.

"Please, no, Master!" cried Euphrosyne to Ho-Tosk. "He knows I cannot dance."

"Nonsense," said Florian. "Despite her numerous lacks, failings, shortcomings, flaws, and faults, she is a female. Of that, obviously, there is no doubt. Thus, slave dance resides within her hereditary coils. It lies within the pelvis, hips, heart, blood, and belly of every woman."

"He does not care for me," wailed Euphrosyne. "He wants me punished!"

"Why?" asked Ho-Tosk.

"I did not care to please him," said Euphrosyne.

"What?" cried Ho-Tosk.

"He found me insufficiently pleasing," said Euphrosyne, wisely modifying her remark.

"It is your business to be far more than merely pleasing," said Ho-Tosk. "It is your business to be a perfection of pleasingness, a begging, yielding dream of pleasure."

"I am tunicked," wept Euphrosyne. "I have no silks, no bangles, no bracelets, no bells, no necklaces, no veils!"

"To the floor," said Ho-Tosk.

Euphrosyne then stood on the dancing floor, before the men.

She regarded Florian, reproachfully, accusingly. "It is you who have done this to me," she said.

I saw coins exchanging hands, and bets being brokered.

The musicians looked at one another.

"Play," said Ho-Tosk.

"Dance, slave," said Florian.

"He cannot command me!" cried Euphrosyne.

"You are mistaken," said Ho-Tosk. "He is your master. I have sold you to him."

Euphrosyne regarded Florian wildly, disbelievingly.

"You, taverner's man," said Florian, "uncoil your whip, stand near, and have it ready."

Euphrosyne trembled.

There was a swirl of music from the musicians.

"Girl," said Ho-Tosk, "must a command be repeated?"

Euphrosyne then began to dance, before the men, and her master. The taverner's man with the whip lifted it twice, looking to Florian, but each time Florian indicated that he refrain from employing that supple tool. Euphrosyne, at the beginning, was desperate to please. But soon, suspecting that she might be immune from the attentions of the leather, perhaps due to the weakness or indulgence of Florian, she began, subtly, to test him. This alarmed me, for I suspected that I, from my time in the holding of Bosk of Port Kar, knew the nature of Florian better than she. It began with a suggestion of impudence, and a hint of disrespect. Then it seemed she danced an insolent arrogance, even a contemptuous, challenging defiance.

Men looked from one to another.

Then Euphrosyne, obedient to the music, ended her dance and sank, weary and sweating, smug and triumphant, to the surface of the dancing floor.

"Lash her, ten strokes," said Florian.

"No!" she wept.

Then she recoiled from the first blow.

"Please, no, Master!" she cried. "Forgive me, Master!"

"Nine more," said Florian. "Then strip her, and bind her, hand and foot and put her on the floor of the waiting canal boat, that bearing the design of the holding of Bosk. Tonight I will muchly pleasure myself with her."

Two or three men profited considerably, given the changing of odds during the dance. Few had anticipated that, as the dance went on, that Florian would make his disapproval explicit. Euphrosyne had tested her new master, and had not found him wanting. I knew she had wanted strength in her master, and now she had been reassured. She had found it. Florian was gentle in mien, and softly spoken. It was his way. But he was not weak. He was Gorean. Euphrosyne would now know herself owned, now understand that she had a master. As she was being bound by a taverner's man, I sensed that she, even in her discomfort, could not have been more pleased. I suspected she would make him an excellent slave, perhaps even a love slave. I wondered how long he had secretly owned her.

"Next!" called Ho-Tosk. "Daphne!"

"These girls are not dancers," said the Vat Master. "And even so, we shall soon run out of them."

"The paga must arrive shortly," whispered Ho-Tosk, uneasily, to the Vat Master. "A surcease of demand can be but temporary."

Daphne began to dance.

I shuddered, hearing the whip cracking.

Few girls were available for the dancing floor. Samos had not delivered a dancer, as yet, and, as noted, Ianthe and Aglaia, two plausible dancers, were unavailable. Several paga girls were alcoved, and, even had they not been, none were dancers. There was, as yet, no sign of the dancer, Sandra, from Bosk's holding.

"May I speak?" I inquired of Ho-Tosk.

"Yes," he said.

"I am not a dancer," I said.

"That is known to me," he said.

"I am a mere, worthless barbarian," I said.

"That is known to me," he said.

"I would not wish to reflect badly on the quality of the Golden Chain," I said.

"You just do not wish to be whipped," he said.

"That, too," I said.

"Do not concern yourself, conniving she-sleen," he said. "I had already decided to put you at the end of the line. Not only are you not a dancer, but, worse, you are an ignorant barbarian. I would not like to see the tavern shamed, nor a comely property, one perhaps too clever, lashed beyond its deserts."

"Thank you, Master," I said.

Following Euphrosyne and Daphne, and discounting myself, there were but seven paga girls available, and, hopefully, paga would arrive before most of them were put on the floor; these were Sucha, Lais, Tamira, Fina, Relia, Renata, and Phyrne.

I heard Daphne cry out in misery and she collapsed to the floor after the second stroke of the whip.

"Off with her! Away with her!" cried men.

I was muchly disturbed, and frightened. I had thought Daphne was doing quite well. Surely she was beautiful. Does that not count for a great deal? To be sure, she was not a dancer, no more than the rest of us. Too, might not Gorean males be overly discriminating in such matters, and, familiar with the performances of skilled dancers, fail to be accepting of less skilled performances?

The whip fell again on Daphne, as she crawled hurriedly from the floor.

Money was exchanging hands, and there was an undercurrent of disgruntlement. The audience, I feared, was displeased.

"Where is the paga?" called a voice, from somewhere amongst the tables.

"Next," called a man. "Next!"

"I am sorry, noble patrons," said Ho-Tosk. "Daphne, though beautiful, is not a dancer. Blame the house. We have not paid to have her so trained. But her alcove skills, as doubtless some of you know, are considerable."

"Next!" cried several men.

I trusted the paga would arrive, surely before the next dancer, or victim, or two, might be presented before the audience.

"Behold," called Ho-Tosk, "the lovely Lais, graceful and lithe, eyes as blue as the skies of En'Kara, lips as red as the scarlet dina, hair as yellow as ripe sa'tarna. How she will please you!"

Lais, I noted, did not look as confident of this as Ho-Tosk. I had little doubt but what she would prefer to be below in the kitchen or back in her cage.

"Later!" called a loud voice, with the authority of a distinguished, preferred customer, one whose right to be heard could not be lightly gainsaid.

All attention was on the figure who had risen from a nearby table.

"We hear with pleasure," said Ho-Tosk, "the voice of the noble Addison Steele."

"All due respect," said Addison Steele, "to the lovely Lais, whose performance we eagerly await, but let our appetites be whetted by some brief delay."

I heard grumbling from amongst the tables.

"You would first see another?" inquired Ho-Tosk.

"Yes," said Addison Steele. "That one!"

I tried to move away, unnoticed, to slip through the beaded curtain, but the Vat Master's sudden grip on my upper left arm held me in place.

"Surely Master will reconsider," said Ho-Tosk. "Already the tables are displeased."

"Lais, Lais," I heard, a murmuring amongst the tables.

"No, dear friend," said Addison Steele. "That one."

"She is a barbarian," said Ho-Tosk. "She is ignorant and stupid. She cannot read. She knows nothing. She could not name the four Wagon Peoples. She would think nothing of picking up a squirming ost. She could not tell Turia from Kassau. Let us get around to her later, if there is time."

I did not think Ho-Tosk's assertions were quite fair to me, although I could not, indeed, name the four Wagon Peoples.

"She!" said Addison Steele.

I would have sunk to my knees, unable to stand, were it not for the grasp of the Vat Master.

"Here," said Addison Steele, "is a coin."

Ho-Tosk caught the coin, expertly. Then he looked at it. "A copper tarsk-bit," he said, grinning, "a most copious remuneration."

There was laughter amongst the tables.

"Do you accept it, dear friend?" inquired Addison Steele.

"Yes," said Ho-Tosk. Then he turned to me. "To the floor," he said.

"Please, no, Master," I begged.

"Now," he said.

Lais gratefully fled from the floor, but dared not leave the room.

I made my way to the floor, and knelt, head down. I did not know if I could rise. I hoped for mercy, to feel only a few strokes of the whip, as I struggled, shamed and back afire, to crawl from the floor. I remembered Talena's words to me, on the Skerry of Lars. "Were you to dance, you would be whipped from the floor."

"Ready?" asked Ho-Tosk to the musicians.

"This will not take long," said the *czehar* player.

I lifted my head, and saw, some feet away, Addison Steele, in repose, sitting cross-legged at his table. Florian was with him. Euphrosyne was doubtless on the floor of a canal boat, moored nearby, supine or prone, stripped, and bound hand and foot. Florian would let her wait, as the slave she was.

My eyes briefly met those of Addison Steele, and then I, aware of a possibly imputable impudence or boldness, lowered my head.

How he had smiled!

How far we are, I thought, from the cocktail parties, the restaurants, the shores of Earth. I was now on Gor, a property, tunicked, marked, and collared.

How he had smiled!

He had always held me in contempt, even on Earth. He had known me better than I had known myself. He had seen how small, vain, pretentious, shallow, superficial, petty, and worthless I was. How he had despised me for my little plots and exploitations. How he had scorned me for the mercenary use of my body, implicitly bartering its promises for favors and acquisitions, hinting at much, reaping gains, and bestowing nothing, a body which was now no longer my own, but the possession of another. No longer could women such as I, brought to Gor, sell our bodies for personal gain; rather, now, it is we who are sold, for the gain of others, our masters. How stupid were the men of Earth, how easily deluded and outwitted. How clever and successful I had been. Then I had found myself in a collar, on Gor, at the feet of men such as I had not known could exist.

How he had smiled!

Did he truly hate me so? Was it not enough for him that I was now rightless and helpless, a branded, collared slave? Was this not vengeance enough for him? Did he not know that I helplessly and hopelessly loved him, that I longed for his chains? Did he not know that it was he before whom I wished to kneel, placing my lips upon his feet? Did he not know that it was his whip I longed to lick and kiss, that it was he to whose feet I wished to crawl, bringing him his switch, held between my teeth?

I did not think I could forget that smile.

Did it not bespeak his triumph and victory? Did it not remind me, by contrast, of my fathomless reduction and absolute subjugation, of my total meaninglessness, that I was now less than the dust beneath a free man's sandals, that I was now a slave?

How he had smiled!

He knew I could not dance. Indeed, he must have known that many *kajirae*, far more beautiful and talented than I, even lesser dancers, must have been whipped from the floor, from time to time, given the moods and demands of masters. He was so clever! He had deftly, mercilessly, exploited a situation, to see me ridiculed, shamed, and beaten. He would bring me to the floor early, before the paga was delivered, that I must perform. He had even delayed the dancing of Lais, to disappoint and anger the tables. How they would be impatient with me, and resent me. How clever he was! I tried to hate him, I wanted to hate him, but could not do so.

"You are ready?" said Ho-Tosk to the musicians.

"Yes," said the *czehar* player.

"Play," said Ho-Tosk.

I rose to my feet, lifting my hands over my head, the backs of my hands facing one another.

In even a brief slave training, of the sort to which I was subjected in the House of Anesidemus, one is taught the rudiments of slave dance. Interestingly, at least in so brief an introduction, more emphasis was placed on emotions, and inward attitudes, on knowing one is a slave, on being a slave, and such, than on the various delicious subtleties of motion. One is told to understand, fully, that slave dance is the dance of slaves, and understand that in all that it means. From my Earth conditioning, in my training, I was afraid at first to move as the slave I inwardly knew myself to be. "She, the slave, is there," I was told. "Release her." "I do not understand," I said, though I feared I understood only too well. "Free the slave!" said the instructress. "I cannot!" I wept. Then, I was whipped. "But men are present!" I cried. Then I screamed in pain, again lashed. "Please do not strike me again!" I begged. I saw the whip lifted once more. My belly then, suddenly, understood that it was the belly of a slave. If I was a slave, why should I not be as a slave? Why should the essence of my being be denied, or disguised? Is honesty so fearful? Is truth so terrible? No longer was I ashamed, for I wanted my slavery and loved my slavery. "Excellent, excellent," said the instructress. "*Kajira, kajira!*"

called men, striking their left shoulders with their right hands. "Next," had said the instructress.

I do not well recall what ensued on the dancing floor of the tavern, the Golden Chain, in Port Kar. I supposed I danced, or posed, or manifested some mixture of the two. I know I moved, and moved as a slave. How utterly different is the movement of a slave from that of a free woman, how uninhibited, how free, how profound, how unapologetically, sinuously brazen, how radically and rawly female; the free woman dances her beauty, the slave, in all her beauty, dances her brand and collar. The free woman is lovely; the slave is lovely and patently needful. The free woman, in her freedom, must hold back, for she is free; the slave, in her slavery, need not do so and may not do so. The dance of the free woman states her dignity and worth; the dance of a slave is quite different; it exhibits an incredibly desirable domestic animal, one which may be bought and sold.

I was a few moments into the dance, or behavior, perhaps fifteen or twenty Ihn, when I realized I had not yet felt the lash. I continued, waiting for the stroke of the leather. I was aware of the nearby hanging tharlarion-oil lamp, dangling on its three small chains. It cast shadows behind me. When would the leather speak?

I continued.

The tables were silent. No one yet cried out in fury, demanding that I be driven from the floor. I heard no impatient cries nor sharp, angry strikings of goblets on tables.

I became aware that the music no longer seemed listless, tentative, perfunctory, or skeptical; rather it seemed awakened, participatory, challenging, even encouraging, watchful, and eager. How wild, sensuous, exciting, and provocative are the dancing melodies of Gor! How they swirl and flame!

The lash had not yet fallen.

Men leaned forward, intent. In the lamp light I could see moisture glistening on the foreheads of some. Lips were parted. Eyes were keenly alive.

I saw Addison Steele, his fists clenched.

Had he not done this to me, to shame me, and make me an object of derision and ridicule, wanting me whipped?

But the lash had not yet fallen.

I thrust my body at him, angrily, defiantly, and then, suddenly, fearfully, well aware of my foolishness and jeopardy, that

I, a slave, might be found displeasing to a free man, I danced, or acknowledged, as well as I could, my helplessness, choicelessness, and vulnerability, that I was now in my collar, where I belonged, and wanted to be, and that I now knew myself nothing, only an object, and beast, a worthless slave, but yet, a needful, begging one. What woman can understand this, but one who in reality, or in her thoughts, has been chained at the feet of a master?

Then I not only danced my slavery, but I addressed myself to Addison Steele, as though I might be his slave, one who craved his collar, one who wished to feel the weight of his chains on her limbs.

The music began to swirl to its conclusion.

I sank to the floor, and writhed my need.

Then the music, abruptly, ended.

I went to my belly on the floor.

I could not move.

I heard shouts of approval, even acclaim. There was the sound of palms of hands striking left shoulders. There was the commendatory crack and pounding of goblets on tables.

Wonderingly, amazed, I realized I had not been beaten.

I felt my tunic being drawn away, over my head.

Then, by a hand in my hair, I was pulled to my feet.

"*Lesha!*" snapped Addison Steele, behind me.

Instantly I flung my head up, turning it to the left, and, at the same time straightened my body and flung my hands, together, behind my back. This response is automatic, immediate, and unthinking. I had assumed the position before I had fully realized I had done so. My hands, together, behind me, were snapped into slave bracelets. "Head higher, slave," said Addison Steele. It was then uncomfortably high. Then I felt the leash snapped about my throat. "Kneel, slave," said Addison Steele. I did so. "Back on your heels. Get those knees apart, more so!" he said. I obeyed. He then shortened the leash until his right hand was a few inches from my throat, and then, by the leash, pulled my head up, high, so that I must look at him. How helpless a woman feels, so positioned.

"Do you think you are a dancer?" he asked.

"No, Master," I said.

"You are not," he said, "but your flanks are not without interest. On Earth I thought they might be of interest, and on Gor, I confirmed my conjecture."

"Yes, Master," I said.

"You are nicely curved," he said. "Your body is clearly a slave's body."

"A slave is pleased, if she is found pleasing," I said.

I could not understand what was going on.

How was it that I found myself as I was, kneeling, naked, my hands braceleted behind my back, my knees spread in the manner of a pleasure slave, leashed, my head held up high by the leash so that I had no choice but to look up, into the eyes of Addison Steele? Where was Ho-Tosk, the Vat Master, the taverner's men?

"Now," said Addison Steele, turning and calling toward the portal, "you may bring in the paga."

Ho-Tosk clapped his hands with pleasure, as four men, in line, each wheeling a barrel of paga, entered the tavern, making their way to the paga vat. The Vat Master beamed. There were cries of pleasure from men, and cries of "Paga! Paga!" rang out, and slaves rushed to bring fresh, brimming goblets to the tables.

"I think I will see to Euphrosyne," said Florian, rising.

"I do not think she will be much pleased," said Addison Steele.

"If she shows the least sign of impatience, annoyance, recalcitrance, or displeasure, I will beat her," said Florian.

"Good," said Addison Steele.

At that moment, Miles, of the holding of Bosk of Port Kar, entered, thrusting a cloaked, trim figure before him. I heard a clinking of bangles and a rustle of bells. The cloak was cast aside and I saw belts of shimmering, threaded coins, ropes of necklaces, bright armlets and bracelets, and swirling flutterings and flashes of diaphanous silks.

"Sandra, Sandra!" cried men, delightedly.

"She is one of the possessions of Bosk of Port Kar," said Miles.

"I think she is the finest dancer in Port Kar," said Florian.

"She was undoubtedly expensive," said Addison Steele.

"Doubtless," said Florian.

I was then drawn to my feet by the leash of Addison Steele, and conducted from the dancing floor. In a moment we were approaching the portal of the tavern.

I was in great confusion, even consternation. I did not know what to do. Should I cry out, in alarm, to Ho-Tosk? Surely someone must see me being drawn toward the portal of the tavern. But I feared, too, if I called out to Ho-Tosk, that he might set his men upon Addison Steele. One cannot simply remove a paga girl from a tavern. It is not permitted. It could even be construed as an instance of slave theft. I tried to hold back against the leash and the collar jerked against the back of my neck. Addison Steele turned about, but did not drag me forward, or throw me from my feet and then kick or beat me.

"May I speak, Master!" I said.

"Very well," said Addison Steele.

"You cannot take me from the tavern," I said.

"You are mistaken," he said.

"I am not an Ahn girl!" I said. An Ahn girl is one who may be taken from the tavern and used elsewhere, for an Ahn, or more, or even overnight, or longer. Such arrangements must be made, of course, with the master.

"I trust not," said Addison Steele.

"You place yourself in jeopardy," I said. "You risk much."

"How so, at the moment?" he asked.

"I will scream," I said.

"Why would you do that?" he asked.

"—if only to protect you, to keep you safe," I said.

"I do not understand," he said.

"To keep you from removing a slave from the tavern without authorization," I said, "even to protect you from the possible charge of slave theft."

"You would scream?" he said.

"Yes," I said.

"Do not do so," he said.

He then drew me forward, and I, stumbling, was pulled from the tavern, into the night. I heard the sounds of music from behind me, as the slave, Sandra, danced, and men, jubilant, and content, well satisfied, too, with a free round of paga, failed to note our departure.

We walked a short time, he striding, I hastening to keep up on the leash. Then we stopped beside a canal. I feared for Addison Steele. He showed little concern for his own safety. Even now the taverner's men, armed with clubs and ropes, might be searching for us. Now, certainly, I would not scream. I did not fear for myself, for Gorean men, and men such as Gorean men, are very fond of women. They enjoy, for example, buying and selling us, owning and mastering us. What true man does not want his slave and what true woman does not want her master? I did know that Addison Steele, despite his low opinion of me, his justifiable contempt of me and my worthlessness, who despised me, found me desirable. I did then expect that he, finding some quiet, convenient place, one perhaps he had in mind, would soon put me to his pleasure, would enjoy me, as is the wont of a master, imposing my shame and degradation upon me, reminding me of my mark and collar, subjecting me to imperious slave use, forcing me to endure rhythms, earthquakes, storms, tides and ecstatic abasements a free woman can never know. How in his arms I might leap, writhe, moan, weep, and beg!

When we stopped, I had knelt beside him, my head, lowered, at his thigh. I realized, moments later, I had done this without thought. I had done it naturally, fittingly. How far we were from Earth! I had assumed this posture of submission, appropriately, yes, without thought. It was right for me. I was where I belonged, and how I belonged.

A bit later, Addison Steele hailed a passing canal boat with its pilot.

"You cannot take me away without the permission of my master," I said.

"Do not concern yourself," he said.

"I do not understand," I said.

"I bought you," he said. "I am your master."

CHAPTER FORTY-SEVEN

I Am No Longer in the Golden Chain
I Rejoice that Talena is now Safe in Cos

We paused before a portal, under the light of a small tharlarion-oil lamp.

"There are stairs inside," said Addison Steele. "They lead up to my apartment."

"You are of Earth, are you not?" I asked.

I had wondered if this might not be the case. Certainly I had first encountered him on Earth, and he had seemed at ease on Earth, familiar with its habits and customs, and had spoken English with no trace of an accent. But I had not been sure. I had found him no different from Gorean men. For all I knew he might easily have been natively Gorean.

"Once," he said. "I make no secret of it."

"But I, too, as you know, am of Earth," I said.

"Were of Earth," he said. "You are now of Gor."

"Surely you, once of Earth, are not going to keep me as a slave," I said.

"Certainly," he said, "unless I give you away or sell you."

"How can you, from Earth, keep me as a slave?" I asked.

"Easily," he said, "utterly and legally. You are a slave, by nature, and now by law."

"But I am of, or from, Earth," I said.

"That," he said, "gives me a little fillip, an additional, delightful piquancy in your ownership."

"Should you not free me instantly, console me, rescue me?" I asked.

"I gather you would not find it pleasant to feel the switch, the whip, on your naked body," he said.

"No, I would not," I said.

"Perhaps then," he said, "you should give more thought as to how you might better please your master."

"Surely you understand it is hard for one from Earth to understand many things," I said.

"What things?" he asked.

"Such as this," I said.

"What?" he asked.

"That you, once from Earth, can be with me as you are, standing beside me, unconcerned, giving the matter no thought, that I, a woman once of your world, am unclothed, completely so; that I am totally naked on an open street, in public, beneath a lamp; that I am branded; that my wrists are confined closely behind me, held in steel bracelets; that I am collared, that I am leashed."

"I do not understand," he said. "Animals need not be clothed; and they are often tethered, confined, or restrained, in one way or another, sometimes quite helplessly; brands are useful in keeping track of them; and collars and leashes are quite appropriate for them."

"Then I am an animal?" I said.

"Yes," he said.

"Then you will treat me, and use me, as an animal," I said.

"Of course," he said. "What else?"

It was what I wished to hear. What slave would not wish to hear that? The slave is, and wishes to be, her master's animal.

Let those who are slaves understand. Let others be mystified.

"I love you," I said.

"Beware," he said, "lest you be beaten."

"Forgive me, Master," I said. I did not wish to be beaten.

I was now well satisfied, my small tests done, having come home to myself.

The apartment of Addison Steele was on the Thieves' Way South, not far from the book emporium, with its street stalls, where I had first seen him on this world, so long ago. It was a pleasant apartment, on a second floor, small but light, and bright with color. It had little furniture, as most Gorean domiciles; it contained, for example, a curule chair, for a master, a low table, about which men might sit cross-legged and slaves kneel, some chests, of various sorts, for storage along the walls, some low flat cushions, and a couch, equipped with chains. There were also slave rings here and there to which girls might be fastened. Whereas there was some provision in the apartment for light cooking and cleanliness, elsewhere in the building one might find a public kitchen and general lavatory facilities. Port Kar has nothing of the great baths of Ar, but most Goreans take personal hygiene seriously, and, in the basement, there were several large tubs in which slaves, standing or kneeling in the water, might bathe their masters.

It was now four days since I had been conducted from the Golden Chain.

"There are many things I wish to know, Master," I said.

"I trust they are important," he said.

"How much did you pay for me?" I said.

"That is not important," he said.

"It is to me," I said.

"You are a slave," he said.

"Even so," I said.

"Perhaps a tarsk-bit," he said.

"I suspect it was more," I said. "I was, after all, a Golden-Chain girl."

"Do not concern yourself," he said.

I was extremely pleased that he was annoyed. That meant that he had paid more for me than he wished, and perhaps more than I was worth. To be sure, what is a girl worth? Surely that is up to the buyer. In that sense, prices tend to be unpredictable, and elastic.

"Ho-Tosk," I said, smiling, "has a reputation for shrewd bargaining."

"That is about enough," he said.

"Yes, Master," I said.

I was pleased that Addison Steele was annoyed, but I did not wish for him to become too annoyed. On the wall to my right, on its peg, suspended, was the five-stranded Gorean slave lash. I had already felt it, twice.

"When was I purchased?" I asked.

"After the Skerry of Lars," he said, "and shortly before your collar was changed."

"I did not know," I said.

"What did you think?" he asked.

"I did not know what to think," I said. "I was still at the Golden Chain. I thought it was a new tavern collar. Euphrosyne had been recollared, as well."

"She had been purchased by Florian," said Addison Steele.

"So I learned," I said.

"Do you like her?" he asked.

"Yes," I said.

"What do you think of her?" he asked.

"She belongs in a collar, and, if she is true to it, she will live in joy," I said.

"And you?" he said.

"Perhaps," I said.

"Let us see how you writhe under the whip," he said.

"Let us not," I said.

"You belong in a collar," he said.

"I know," I said.

"That was clear," he said, "even on Earth, long ago."

"I held it as my secret," I said.

"When I looked upon you," he said, "I saw your throat, and envisioned it, precisely, as it would look in a collar, a slave collar."

"It is now on me," I said.

"I think I will sell you," he said.

"It will be done with me as masters please," I said.

"Perhaps I will not sell you," he said.

"It will be done with me as you please," I said, "for you are my master."

"Crawl here," he said.

"Yes, Master," I said.

"Please, please, please, Master, permit me!" I begged.

"Are you a proud woman of Earth?" he asked.

"No, no," I said. "Let me, let me, I beg it!"

"What are you?" he asked.

"A slave girl," I cried, "a slave girl!"

"What else?" he asked.

"Nothing else," I said. "Only that!"

"Whose slave are you?" he asked.

"Your slave," I wept. "Your slave! Please, please!"

"Very well," he said.

I cried out, beside myself, in ecstasy, gratitude, rapture, and relief. Seldom, happily, did he so hold me hostage; seldom, happily, did he make me so wait.

Yet he could do with me as he pleased.

"You were very noisy," he said.

"Forgive me, Master," I said.

"I effect nothing critical," he said. "It is pleasant for a master to see what he has done to his slave, what he has brought about in his slave. It is pleasant to have her helplessly moan, weep, and beg in his arms. This is not Earth where a woman may pride herself on her sexual inertness, live a life of sexual nothingness, and compete with her sisters on her superiority to sex."

Slaves, of course, are not permitted to hold back. Their responses are expected to be those of the natural woman, that of a slave in the arms of her master.

"Do you know," he asked, "that there are women of Earth who are sexually unresponsive, who even endeavor to be so, who are frigid, or wish to be so, or try to be so?"

"It is hard to be frigid," I said, "when one is naked in a collar."

"In your training," he said, "I expect that you learned about your slave fires."

"They required very little kindling," I said.

"Now," said he, "they rage."

"I, as others, am now their helpless prisoner," I said.

"Good," he said.

"The masters give us no choice," I said. "They do what they wish with us. Our slave fires now rise within us, periodically, uncontrollably."

"Excellent," said Addison Steele. "Now perhaps we shall have some wine, and, if you kneel nicely and serve well, I may consider caressing you again."

I rose quickly to my feet, and went to the side, to a chest with four tiers, and two shelves, to fetch goblets and a decanter.

I would do my best to be pleasing.

I wanted to be caressed again. I hoped to be caressed again.

It would be decided by my master.

If he dallied, I would tie the bondage knot in my hair.

Surely he must note it.

It would not do for me to call it to his attention.

I wanted to be owned. I was owned. I loved being owned.

"Master," I said.

"Yes?"

"In the tavern," I said, "you had great confidence in me, to have me put on the dancing floor, I, a mere barbarian. That is very flattering. You knew I would be satisfactory. You knew I would escape punishment. You knew, somehow, I would not be whipped. For my part, on the other hand, I fully anticipated that I would be whipped from the floor."

"So did I," he said.

"Oh," I said.

"I gather," I said, "that Adraste, the slave, was actually the former Talena, once the traitress Ubara of Ar, she who was sought by so many with so relentless a fervor."

"Yes," he said.

"I had thought that she was safely housed in Cos, as the guest of her former ally, the Ubar of Cos, Lurius, of Jad."

"We generated that rumor, to slow or stop the search for her, to dismay and discourage hundreds of bounty hunters and gangs of bounty hunters, to keep her safer and to divert the search from the continent. Similarly, others had concealed her for a time at the World's End, where Bosk of Port Kar acquired her, and returned her to the continent."

"There is some relationship between Captain Bosk and Adraste," I said.

"Formerly," said Addison Steele. "She was once his Free Companion, but that was long ago, and the companionship is dissolved if not renewed annually. Too, slavery dissolves such a relationship. One cannot be both a Free Companion and a slave."

"Does Bosk still care for her?" I asked.

"I do not know," said Addison Steele. "She was cruel, arrogant, and an arch villainess. I am sure, however, that he does not wish her apprehended by bounty hunters and taken to Ar, to be subjected to lengthy tortures and the eventual impalement of what might then be left of her living body."

"I knew her only as a slave," I said, "a haughty, unpleasant slave."

"She was a slave, and is still is a slave, unless she has been freed," said Addison Steele.

"How strange," I said, "to think of a Ubara, become a slave."

"It is not unprecedented," said Addison Steele. "Wars are frequent. Thus it is occasionally the case that a defeated Ubara finds herself naked and chained, branded and collared, at the feet of her conqueror. She is often, at first, exhibited as a trophy of victory, in triumphs, civil celebrations, court occasions, and such, but later may be simply put with other female slaves of the victor."

"It still seems surprising to me," I said.

"Bosk did not free her," said Addison Steele. "Rather, he realized that she would be safest as a slave. Who would expect the former Ubara of Ar to be in a tunic and collar? Surely most would search for an elusive free woman, hidden somewhere, one of wealth and power. Too, as a slave, she could best be watched, guarded, and protected."

"But, as a tavern girl?" I asked.

"That, I think," said Addison Steele, "was most brilliant. Bosk had her sold from a low market in Brundisium, purchased by an agent, and brought routinely to Port Kar, with others, such as you, as a common slave."

"But people could see her in the tavern," I said.

"Yes," said Addison Steele, "but who would recognize she whom they saw as the former Talena of Ar? Such an identification would be incredible. So obviously displayed, she was best hidden. You must remember that Port Kar is far from Ar, and that few, given facial veiling, hooding, and the robes of concealment, had, even in Ar, looked upon the features of the Ubara. It is not as though her features were publicized in newspapers, magazines, television, and such, not here, not on this world."

"Here, I suppose," I said, "Captain Bosk could keep her under surveillance."

"Certainly," said Addison Steele, "and he did, often with personal attention, until drawn from Port Kar by depredations perpetrated in his name."

"Perhaps done to lure him from the city?" I asked.

"Quite possibly," said Addison Steele.

"Why would he not have kept her in his holding, as other slaves?" I asked.

"One calculates the odds of the cast stones as best as one can," said Addison Steele. "It was thought that keeping her in the holding, either openly, incognito, or, worse, secretly, given the former matter of the companionship, would be likely, sooner or later, to provoke suspicion. Where else would one look for her?"

"Too," I said, shuddering, "being so imprisoned would be frightful. Better the tavern, the fresh air and wind, the freedom of the city."

"Perhaps such considerations," said Addison Steele, "entered into the calculations of Bosk. I do not know."

"But she was taken to the holding," I said.

"When it seemed clear she had been recognized," said Addison Steele.

"She, Adraste, or Talena, might have been acquired by Pa-Kur, of the Assassins," I said, "had you, and others, not seized on the stratagem of disguising yourselves as cohorts amongst the intruders, by means of red scarves."

"Few stratagems were available," said Addison Steele.

"Why did you not seal off the parapet, to prevent the withdrawal of Pa-Kur's forces?" I asked.

"Given the number of his men, we would have been unable to hold it, nor, soon, the holding itself," he said. "Rather we wished to sow uncertainty, confusion, and panic amongst the intruders, and then, while they were disconcerted and fearful, provide them with an inviting, undefended exit from the holding, a beckoning escape route."

"I see," I said.

"It is a common ruse of war," he said. "Strew the road from one's country with pearls."

"Long I thought you a duplicitous mercenary, pretending to serve two competitors, Seremides, whom I then knew as Bruno of Torcadino, and Pa-Kur," I said. "Yet you were a spy for the house of Bosk."

"Stakes were high, perils were real," he said.

"Even a slave may undergo perils," I said.

"Doubtless," said he.

"When I was on the errand which would bring me to the apartment of Dorna, where I was to be interrogated, my life was threatened. I was fired upon. I could have been killed. A quarrel struck a wall not a foot from my head, scattering bits of stone, some stinging me," I said.

"You were in no danger," he said. "It was fired from the bow of Pa-Kur, a superb marksman, to unsettle you, to induce alarm, to make you more readily intimidated, more vulnerable, more receptive, in your imminent interrogation."

"In the marshes," I said, "caught in quick sand, unable to free myself, the tide rising, I might have drowned."

"I gather," he said, "that you were not drowned."

"I managed to seize a piece of drifting wreckage, from Pa-Kur's canal boat," I said, "and utilized it to free myself."

"Fortunate that it drifted by so opportunely," said Addison Steele.

"To be sure," I said.

"I feared," said Addison Steele, "that you would be too stupid to get your hands on it, and that I would have to reveal myself in saving you."

"I do not understand," I said.

"I followed you, easily done through the broken rence, anticipating that you might be caught in the sand, floating the debris in front of me, and then guided it so that it drifted against your back."

"I see," I said.

"Your flanks are not without interest," he said.

"I am not stupid," I said.

"I hope not," said Addison Steele, "else there would be little point in putting you in a collar. Stupidity is acceptable in a free woman, but not in a female slave. Intelligence, as is well known, raises a girl's price."

"But we are sold, nonetheless," I said.

"Of course," he said, "and more profitably."

"I gather that my Gorean is quite good," I said.

"It is excellent," he said, "and that, too, raises your price."

"I am told my accent is that of Brundisium," I said.

"More broadly," said Addison Steele, "it is a coastal accent."

"I learned most of my early Gorean in Brundisium," I said.

"Its nature then," said Addison Steele, "is not surprising."

"Many girls," I said, "think that I am natively Gorean."

"I have been meaning to talk to you about that," he said.

"Master?" I said.

"I gather from Florian," he said, "that you permitted certain sister slaves to labor under that misapprehension."

"Perhaps," I said, "if they did not ask me."

"Slave girls may not lie," he said.

"I did not lie," I said.

"But you must have realized their mistaken assumption, and did not hasten to disabuse them of their error."

"Perhaps not," I said.

"Is that not tangential to lying?" he asked.

"Surely not," I said, forcing myself not to look at the whip on its peg.

"You are under no general obligation to frequently and publicly announce your faults and drawbacks, or your lowly and embarrassing origins," said Addison Steele, "but, in the interests of honesty, you should make no secret of the fact that you are a barbarian. Indeed, as you are quite likely to betray yourself sooner or later by some slip, linguistic or otherwise, it would be wise not to permit any doubt about the matter, lest you be subjected to some appropriate chastisement. Do you understand?"

"Yes, Master," I said.

"Too," he said, "being a barbarian makes you interesting and special. It gives you a certain flavor, so to speak. Everyone knows, for example, how sexually helpless barbarians are in their collars."

"No more so than native Gorean girls," I said. "We are all women, helpless, in our collars."

"True," he said.

"If Gorean girls know I am a barbarian," I said, "they may beat me."

"Not all, surely," he said.

"No, not all," I said.

"It is a risk you must take," he said.

"I see," I said.

"Do not be too zealous to conceal your barbarian origins," he said, "if only as a favor to me."

"Yes, Master," I said.

"Or you will be lashed," he said. "Do you understand?"

"Yes, Master," I said.

"Is that not the bondage knot in your hair?" he asked.

"Yes, Master," I said.

"Come to my arms," he said.

"Yes, Master," I said.

"I wonder," said Addison Steele, "what became of the rogue, Decius of Venna."

"Escaping in the confusion at the Skerry of Lars," I said, "I suspect he returned to Venna."

"Perhaps not," said Addison Steele. "It is rumored a warrant for his arrest awaits him there."

"He was originally allied with Seremides, whom I knew as Bruno of Torcadino," I said.

"Do you think he knew the true identity of Adraste?" asked Addison Steele.

"I do not think so," I said. "I think he only conjectured later that she must have some considerable value, from which feature he hoped to profit."

"I would not expect to see him again," said Addison Steele.

"I would not think so," I said.

"'Decius' is a not uncommon name in the vicinity of Ar and Venna," said Addison Steele.

"I would not know," I said.

"There is, for example, Decius Albus, the trade advisor to the Ubar of Ar, Marlenus," said Addison Steele.

"I have not heard of him," I said.

"From what I have heard of him," said Addison Steele, "that is just as well."

"I did fall into the power of Decius of Venna, briefly, in Brundisium," I said, "when slaves were being removed from the House of Anesidemus, lest they perish in the spreading of a great dock fire."

"Your covering sheet," he said, "was replaced with that of Adraste," he said.

"Yes," I said.

"That was done to protect Adraste," he said.

"I later gathered that," I said. "I could have been killed."

"You were in no danger," said Addison Steele. "You are well curved and nicely collared. There are better things to do with a female slave than kill her. That would be a waste of slave. Who discards coins?"

"Were you in Brundisium?" I asked.

"No," he said. "But Florian and Miles were, both there recruited as agents on behalf of Bosk of Port Kar. Florian arranged for the purchase of Adraste, and Miles was stationed in the house of Anesidemus itself, to protect her."

"It was Miles," I said, suddenly, "who changed the sheet!"

"Yes," said Addison Steele.

"In Port Kar," I said, "I thought he seemed somehow familiar."

"It comes back to you now," said Addison Steele.

"It was dark in the corridor," I said. "We were on all fours. I caught only a brief glimpse of him, switching the sheets."

"It was he," said Addison Steele.

I placed two of Addison Steele's tunics, washed, ironed, and folded, in a chest at the side of the room.

I paused before closing the lid.

"I am still curious," I said, "as to how much you paid for me."

"Curiosity," he said, "is not becoming in a *kajira*."

"Even so," I said.

"Why are you smiling, sleek, possibly-looking-for-a-switching, well-curved she-tarsk?" he asked.

"This morning, on the street," I said, "I encountered my former master, the noble Ho-Tosk. I knelt before him and pleasantly passed the time of day. He inquired after you."

"That was thoughtful," said Addison Steele. "How is the noble Ho-Tosk?"

"He seems quite well," I said.

"Good," said Addison Steele.

"I also asked him what you paid for me," I said. "I was told four silver tarsks."

"Ho-Tosk," said Addison Steele, "has a tendency to gloat over such things."

"I conjecture," I said, "that is at least twice what I am worth."

"The vanity of *kajirae* is astounding," he said. "I would conjecture it was some four times what you are worth."

"You must have wanted me very much," I said. "I doubt that you could get that much for me, for selling me."

"Florian paid more for Euphrosyne," he said.

"More?" I said.

"She is, after all, Gorean," he said.

"Of course," I said, not pleased.

I then closed the lid of the clothing chest.

"Four tarsks, of silver," I mused.

"I plan to get several times that value out of your hide," he said.

"I have work to do," I said.

"It can wait," he said.

"May I speak?" I asked.

"No," he said.

"Much transpires of which you know little," he said.

I lay at his feet, content.

"Pa-Kur," he said, "is a dangerous enemy to Bosk of Port Kar, and seeks large resources."

"Large resources?" I asked.

"Enormous resources," he said.

"For what purposes?" I asked.

"I do not know," he said.

"There is bad blood between them?" I asked.

"From long ago," said Addison Steele, "even from before the war between Ar and the mighty island Ubarates, Cos and Tyros."

I had heard that Pa-Kur had once led a coalition of forces against Ar, winnowed from cities subservient to, and jealous of, Ar. The city had been effectively overcome, but had somehow rallied and turned out the invader. In the songs, a hero named Tarl of Bristol had supposedly been somehow instrumental in this reversal of fortunes.

"The attempt on the holding of Bosk of Port Kar, led by Pa-Kur," I said, "failed."

"It was ostensibly his attempt to seize the slave, Adraste," said Addison Steele.

"Talena," I said, "once Ubara of Ar."

"Traitress, betrayer of her Home Stone, looter of her city, opener of gates to the enemy, sham ruler, puppet of Lurius of Jad, Ubar of Cos, and Chenbar, of Kasra, Ubar of Tyros."

"I knew her from the Golden Chain," I said, "as no more than a collared slave."

"The bounty on her head, the reward for her capture," said Addison Steele, "set by the vengeful Ubar of Ar, Marlenus, is ten thousand tarns of gold, tarn disks of double weight."

"That is much, a very great deal, I gather," I said.

"With such wealth," said Addison Steele, "you could buy cities, hire armies, build fleets."

"Perhaps Pa-Kur and his minions perished in the delta, withdrawing from Port Kar," I said.

"Perhaps," said Addison Steele.

Surely the delta was dangerous, with beasts, with Rencers, with treacherous, trackless marshes.

"There was a monster in the delta, seemingly of supple metal, powerful and vast, consorting with Pa-Kur," I said.

"I saw it," said Addison Steele. "I am not clear on what intelligence informs that beast, or machine. But the technology is surely not Gorean. I suspect that more is involved here than riches, and the fate of cities. I suspect, at times, that the fate of worlds may somehow be involved."

"Surely not," I said.

"Let us hope not," he said.

"Are you in fee, from the house of Bosk?" I asked.

"From the house of Samos, First Slaver of Port Kar, High Captain in the Council of Captains," said Addison Steele.

"But those two houses are allied?" I said.

"Occasionally they share interests," he said.

"Captain Bosk is still at sea," I said.

"In fury," he said, "investigating piracy wrought in his name."

"Then he would know nothing of the discovery of the identity of Adraste, the raid on his holding, her removal from the holding by Seremides, and her departure for Cos."

"Nothing," said Addison Steele.

"At least," I said, "Adraste, or Talena, will now be safe."

"Do you think so?" he said.

"Certainly," I said. "Now secure, now honored, now cherished by her ally, Lurius of Jad, she need no longer fear recognition and seizure, the relentless pursuit of bounty hunters, the chains of guardsmen, the justice of Ar, the wrath of Marlenus, tortures and impalement."

"Ten thousand tarns of gold, tarn disks of double weight," said Addison Steele, "is a considerable sum."

"I do not understand," I said.

"Do you believe that Seremides is her friend, and has her best interests at heart?"

"It seems so," I said.

"Do you not think he would like to rid his own head of the price upon it?" asked Addison Steele.

"Undoubtedly," I said. I had learned that he, too, was wanted in Ar. He, the leader of the palace guard, the Taurentian guard, had been a confederate of Talena.

"How might that be done?" he asked.

"I do not know," I said.

"It would be extremely dangerous, would it not," asked Addison Steele, "for a single person, or a small group, to convey so rich a prize as the apprehended Talena to Ar?"

"I would suppose so," I said.

"Might not Lurius of Jad have much to fear from a risen, potent Ar, from a restored, irate Ubar, such as Marlenus?" asked Addison Steele.

"He might well be uneasy," I said.

"How might he both curry favor with a fearful enemy, and obtain riches for himself and his Ubarate?" asked Addison Steele.

"He was her friend and ally," I said.

"When she comes within the compass of his power," said Addison Steele, "she will be alone, vulnerable, helpless, and defenseless."

"Surely he would not betray her," I said.

"Is Seremides, famed as a killer, and traitor, not his agent?" asked Addison Steele.

"To rescue her," I said.

"To bring her to Cos," said Addison Steele.

"Surely she will be safe in Cos," I said.

"Let us hope so," said Addison Steele.

"Surely the Ubar of Cos, the noble Lurius of Jad, her friend and ally, will care for her and shelter her, will honor her and protect her," I said.

"Let us hope so," said Addison Steele.

"I am afraid," I said.

"I, too," he said.

"What will happen?" I asked.

"We must wait and see," he said.